FÜR

Steven Duff
JAN 2015

HUNTER OF DREAMS

A STORY OF THE UNDERGROUND RAILROAD

BY STEVEN DUFF

A MISHIPASHOO EDITION © 2002
IN ASSOCIATION WITH

TRAFFORD

National Library of Canada Cataloguing in Publication

Duff, Steven
    Hunter of dreams : a story of the underground railroad / Steven Duff.

ISBN 1-55369-311-6

    1. Underground railroad—Fiction. 2. Ross, Alexander Milton, 1832-1897—Fiction. 3. Abolitionists—Fiction. I. Title.

PS8557.U285H85 2002   C813'.54   C2002-901229-5
PR9199.3.D834H85 2002

TRAFFORD

This book was published *on-demand* in cooperation with Trafford Publishing.
On-demand publishing is a unique process and service of making a book available for retail sale to the public taking advantage of on-demand manufacturing and Internet marketing.
On-demand publishing includes promotions, retail sales, manufacturing, order fulfilment, accounting and collecting royalties on behalf of the author.

Suite 6E, 2333 Government St., Victoria, B.C. V8T 4P4, CANADA
Phone   250-383-6864   Toll-free   1-888-232-4444 (Canada & US)
Fax   250-383-6804   E-mail   sales@trafford.com
Web site   www.trafford.com   TRAFFORD PUBLISHING IS A DIVISION OF TRAFFORD HOLDINGS LTD.
Trafford Catalogue #02-0124   www.trafford.com/robots/02-0124.html

10   9   8   7   6   5   4   3   2   1

FOR DEIRDRE AND BILL -

TWO OF THE SHINIEST COINS IN THE FOUNTAIN

ACKNOWLEDGEMENTS

I want to thank the following friends, both old and new, for their help, advice, and general moral and practical support in the writing of *Hunter of Dreams.* Their association with this undertaking has been helpful beyond calculation and has lightened the task in so many ways. I hope I have incorporated their contributions with wisdom, as the final responsibility for *Hunter of Dreams* rests with me.

First and foremost, editor Olive Koyama, for her formidably thorough editing. Not only were deficiencies in English cleaned up, but she also caught some potentially embarrassing historical errors. Bless you a thousand times, Olive!

Donald Carty, of the Ontario Black History Society, who supported the project at its beginning in 1986, for providing a black persepctive to a white writer, and making certain that I did not offend anyone's racial sensibilities, for it was my intention to learn more of the history of our black community. Thanks also to Don's delightful wife Doris for her friendly hospitality and for all the litres of tea drunk at the Carty kitchen table.

Andrew G. Brown, retired Principal, Scarborough Board of Education, for many years of friendship and his interest in my work. A resemblance between Andy and the character of Alexander Ross as portrayed in this book is not exactly a coincidence.

Wayne Hemington, Scarborough Board of Education, for initiating me into the world of computers, a miraculous machine for the writer.

Eva Slezak, Librarian-in-Charge of the Maryland Collection, Enoch Pratt Free Library, Baltimore, Maryland, for putting me in touch with material not available in Canada and for helping me to locate suitable illustrations.

Herbert Harwood, former curator of the Baltimore and Ohio Museum, Baltimore, Maryland, and James A. Brown, retired Director of Commuter Operations for GO Transit, Toronto, for their information on railway practices of the mid-nineteenth century.

Leona Hendry, Corby Library, Belleville, Ontario, for locating a picture of the elusive and notoriously camera-shy Alexander Ross.

Chris Scott, novelist, Senior Tutor at the Writing School, Ottawa, and Adjunct Professor of English at Lake Superior State University, Sault Ste. Marie, Michigan, for his numerous and detailed suggestions about my writing and for his memorable curry.

Brenda Newell, retired from David and Mary Thomson Collegiate Institute and a fellow toiler in the vineyards of history, for loaning me much valuable reference material.

Nancy Hatcher and Sue Baker, Harpers Ferry National Park, Harpers Ferry, West Virginia, for their location of illustrations and for their hospitality.

Averil Kadis, retired Director of Public Relations, Enoch Pratt Free Library, Baltimore, for researching and granting of rights of reproduction of pictures in the Pratt Collection.

ACKNOWLEDGEMENTS Continued...

Dr. Paul Thistle, former student and bassoonist *extraordinaire,* for his advice on medical matters.

Gerald Boyce and Dr. D.T. Brearley, Hastings County Historical Society, and Prof. Peter Swisher, University of Virginia Law School, for their general interest, advice, and help on matters of local colour.

Frances Garber Pepper, Cincinnati, Ohio, a dear and lifelong friend, for all her support, encouragement, and fine-tooth proof-reading.

All these kind people provided essential support to one who is not a professional historian but rather an enthusiast who sees history as a great and all-encompassing form of theatre.

On the production end, Sarah Campbell of Trafford Publishing and Chris Pettinger of Cutting Edge Graphics. I consider them to be the "midwives" of the operation in bringing *Hunter of Dreams* into print.

Finally, the most profound thanks to my wife Debra, who is so accommodating of the *angst* of having a writer in the house and who bailed me out on the numerous occasions that my learning curve on the computer turned into a granny knot.

We are almost ready to begin our (true) tale, but first...

FOREWORD

Except for the narrator James Ramsay, his family, and certain peripheral characters, all personnel in *Hunter of Dreams* actually existed, as did the major events in the story. Central to the drama is Alexander Milton Ross, whose memoirs provided so much historical information and accounts of dealings with the likes of John Brown and Abraham Lincoln. Wherever practical, conversations, correspondences, and newspaper articles have been quoted directly.

Likewise, dates and times have been adhered to as accurately as possible, although some small adjustments had to be made to allow for certain irregularities and inconsistencies in Ross's own accounts.

Ross's career was an extraordinary one; he led a multiple life as an abolitionist, a medical doctor, a naturalist, and writer, and despite great distinction in all these fields, his name is known only to a few today. It is my hope that *Hunter of Dreams* will, in whatever way it can, set the record straight.

Ross is presented in the role of hero, which he undoubtedly was. But equally heroic were the slaves brave, determined, and hardy enough to make the journey from the Deep South to Canada on foot under the cover of night and under the constant threat of capture. Additionally, there were natural threats from weather, wild animals, and so forth. Yet these folks, eventually to become a valued part of the Canadian patchwork, carried onward. Imagine, if you will, attempting a similar journey today, perhaps wearing an orange prison jumpsuit, and you will have some sense of what the escapees, many of whose names we will never know, went through in the quest for freedom. Their story is one that can only excite admiration.

S.D.
"Strathdee"
Parry Sound, Ontario
July 2002

Alexander Milton Ross- an illustration in
Canadian Illustrated News, issue of October 3, 1874.
Courtesy of Corby Library, Belleville , Ontario.

CHAPTER ONE

Nothing excites public interest as much as a struggle. Above the shudders and creaks of the train, I could overhear bets being placed as to whether the locomotive or gravity would be the winner, whether determination or inertia would prevail. I am not a betting man, but if I were, my money would have been on the engine, and with justification, for a few minutes later, the train won its battle with the grade westward out of Hamilton and set course for Windsor.

This was not just another train ride, common as they may be nowadays. The date was January 7, 1854, and this was the maiden run of the new through service of the Great Western Railway across the southern part of Canada now called Ontario. It was a sign of things to come for our infant land and it was on this day that I decided to be part of them.

Evidently so did many others. All seats had been taken and a dozen or so unfortunates in my coach had been compelled to stand or walk unsteadily about. The railway company had issued invitations rather liberally for the occasion, not expecting so many would accept. My father, a judge in Belleville, was on the guest list, was unable to come, and had sent me in his place; had he not, my life would ultimately have gone in a completely different direction. In retrospect, I know I would have had it no other way, though there would be much to endure physically, spiritually, morally, and intellectually. I cannot truthfully say that I would like doing what I was to do, but in the long run, I was more than glad to have done it.

So many guests appeared that the railway had to marshal all its rolling stock available in Hamilton and operate the train in two sections. I was moderately disappointed to be on the second section, but then for a free ride, it would have been churlish to complain.

My seat companion had nodded off to sleep on boarding the train at seven in the morning. His slumbering face now glowed intermittently in the blood-red glare of the rising sun, a spectacle that engaged my attention as much as the progress of the train itself. Of its actual progress, I had what might be called a vested interest in that I had on my bedroom wall a freshly minted degree in civil engineering from the University of Glasgow and was, as were my fellows, looking for a career. Trains, for me, offered a heady attraction, a drama that went far beyond mere machinery. It was not for nothing that folk called locomotives iron horses.

And the possibilities continue to be staggering. As I write this, there is talk of building a line right across the continent, all the way to British Columbia. The railway remains a great and wonderful dream and with this winter day came the final decision that I should be part of it. A railway man I would be, although some of my activities in that field were to be anything but orthodox.

Aside from my luridly glowing neighbour, it was certainly a varied collection of humanity aboard the cars this day, mainly men come as representatives of various North American railways, other men important in business (and therefore potentially valuable clients), men important in governmental and municipal affairs, men of the cloth, men of the law. Many of these pillars of society, I might remark, looked rather the worse from the previous evening's socializing.

My companion's head slid over to rest on the window, his gentle snores changing to a gurgle. The window was by now thoroughly frosted from the cold without and the sweaty moisture from within. The contact with it shocked him awake with the curious remark, "Well, shut mah mouth." He looked around with crusty eyes.

"Good morning," I said pleasantly.

"Migawd. Oh, mah head...reckon Ah'll be all right awhile. Not very courteous of me to doze like that." He extended his hand. "Major Will Ramsay, Columbus, Mississippi. Ah'm here on behalf of the Mobile and Ohio Railroad."

I had to grin. "I'm a Ramsay too. James is the name, from Belleville, Canada West. I'm here in the stead of my father, Mr. Justice Alan Ramsay."

"Well, shut mah mouth," repeated my namesake. "Doesn't that beat all? Wonder if we're related somehow. Mah part of the family came from Scotland in, what the hell was it, 1764."

"Sounds as if you beat us across the water. We came here just before I was born; in fact, you could say I made the crossing under my mother's close supervision..."

The Major bellowed with laughter. "Well, Ah'm truly pleased to meet yew, Jim." I winced; I am a James, not a Jim. In my mind there is a subtle difference. However, I chose not to labour the matter.

Continued the Major, "Ah hope yew'll accept me as yore American cousin, distant as Ah may be."

"Pleased to have a Yankee cousin, Major..."

"Oh, no, not Yankee, Ah'd rather not be called that."

Being confined on the train was a boon to further acquaintance, as was luncheon in the station at London shortly before noon. I learned that my newly-discovered cousin was a cotton planter of considerable means and had merited the courtesy trip all the way to Canada by virtue of being one of the leading shippers on the Mobile and Ohio Railroad. He lamented our winter, remarking that it was cold enough to "kill yew daid". I, an ardent nationalist, was not about to admit to wishing for something more temperate myself, but merely said that I found it far more invigorating than the tropic torpor of Mississippi. The fact that I had never even been in Mississippi somehow never entered into the conversation.

"One day," said the Major, "we'll have a whole network of railroads all over the continent and y'all can travel down to see me. But, hell's bells, Jim, your tracks are wider'n ours. Don't make sense. Can't connect anywheres."

"So-called Colonial gauge, Major. It enables..."

"Make it Will, Jim. Ah'm your cousin."

"Will it shall be, then. Cousin Major sounds a bit silly anyway. To answer your comment, Colonial gauge takes advantage of the generous clearances on this continent and allows for a generally greater carrying capacity, you know, cubic volume aboard your train."

"Yew seem to know what y'all're talking about. Yew a railroad man?"

"Thinking about it for a career. Just graduated in engineering."

"Congratulations. But Ah still think it's damn foolishness. Now, if y'all were sensible, yew'd rebuild up here to standard gauge, and then, yew know what?"

"What?"

"When y'all are real big in the railroad business, yew can have a private coach and come all the way down to Mississippi and visit mah plantation. A mighty fine plantation it is, tew."

"You can count on it when the Mobile and Ohio re-lays to broad gauge."

"Ha-ha-ha! Never happen. Yew'll end up standard. Yew mark mah words."

I marked his words and he was indeed right on that matter, but on certain other ones, he would be as wrong as is possible to be. For the moment, though, he seemed a good-natured sort, relaxed and unhurried in the best southern style; he had thinning, sandy hair, wore spectacles, and was dressed in a cream-coloured suit more fitting to a steaming Mississippi noontide than to the bitter Canadian afternoon.

We talked at some length until Chatham was gained somewhere around four o'clock, and there the train was greeted, as at the previous stops, by throngs of well wishers. The station, so now as to be unpa was still a brave sight, festooned with Union Jacks and, as a gesture will, a few Stars and Stripes. The local cornet band whoozed valiantly freezing wind.

"Folks here in Canada sure love the railroad," drawled the Major. "Good thang, tew. It's a sign of the times, oh, migawd, would yew look at that! It better not be a sign of the times!"

"What is it?"

"Nigras! Loose! Must be six, seven of the buggers..."

My fingers and toes curled involuntarily. Suddenly, having an American cousin lost its charm; he was looking out the window in genuine horror at what for him was a spectacle beyond comprehension.

It took me many months to forgive myself my social cowardice in not discreetly opening the subject of negroes earlier and easing myself into it, for with a southerner it was bound to arise. Now I felt as though I had fallen into a freezing pond. It was not as if I were completely unaware of the matter of "nigras". I was an avid reader of the Toronto *Globe*, whose proprietor, George Brown, had much to say on the ownership of one human being by another and kept his readership up to date on the fairly steady migration of escaped slaves to our part of the world. Up to this moment, I had never even seen a black person, but although the sight was at least mildly startling, it did not fill me with any feeling of unease or agitation. There were indeed seven black youths sheltering from the wind in the lee of the station. While they did not mingle with the rest of the crowd, certainly nobody was making anything of it except, of course, the Major.

"Uh, er," I fumbled weakly, "I guess you don't see them like that very often..."

"No damn way, not at all...folks up here aren't likely to understand our situation, as Ah'm sure yew don't. Let me just tell yew a few facts. In Mississippi, we grow cotton, a *lot* of cotton...Mississippi can get damn' hot, which is why cotton grows so well there, and we need nigras to do the picking because they are constitutionally equipped to work in heat such as we have."

"I can understand that part," I said cautiously, "but about actually owning a person..."

I had been anticipated. "Jim, yew just have to understand that nigras aren't as independent as yew and Ah are. They were in a pretty rude state when first discovered in Africa, just hunting, barely subsisting, no great civilizations, no Christian values, totally underdeveloped...they are far better off with us.

"Now, Ah'm not telling yew Ah'd like to be a slave, no, that would not be honest. But Ah can tell yew this: Ah'd rather be a slave than muddling around in the African bush, trying to shoot mah next meal. A slave gets a little house given to him, gets to depend on someone...hasn't the responsibilities and decisions we whites have."

The Major's well-drilled monologue ceased momentarily for breath as we quit Chatham and the train ambled across the flatlands of the county of Essex on its final lap to Windsor. The excitement of the train journey now forgotten, I waited for more, and it came.

"Jim, Ah would wager that English capital is behind the train we're riding."

"English capital is behind virtually every commercial venture in this country."

"Well, now, Jim, have yew anythang against English capital?"

"No, uh, I don't. Why do you ask?" I was growing more uncomfortable and irritated at every second by a vague and absurd feeling of accountability.

"We planters are a lot like English capitalists in many ways. We are in business. We are responsible for a great many people. We both appropriate human resources, but there the parallel ends. Planters house, clothe, and feed their so-called slaves. That is part of what yew call owning them. Now, a worker in England, he's free, but does anyone do a damn' thang for him? Ah should say not! And Ah know because Ah have been there and Ah've seen it. All these free people in Lancashire - saw some of mah cotton being spun there - oh, they were free, and, Lord, the squalor...so, if y'all aren't comfortable about this, think of it this way: slaves are like being in a family and we just practice a sort of variation on English capitalism. Some rule and others are ruled, so if yew are going to be ruled, why not be spared all kinds of thangs to worry about?

"Ah like to think we're more honest and, well, overt about our position. Besides, we're more friendly. We mingle from time to time with our nigras, visit around and so on, but yew can bet yew'll never see an English capitalist darkening the doors of any of those little Lancashire hovels. No, Jim, our way works for everyone. Afore yew judge us, yew really should come and visit us and see for yoreself. We're not ogres..."

"I hope I didn't say anything to suggest you were."

The Major laughed mirthlessly. "Yew didn't say anythang, but with the press we get in the North and prob'ly up here, folks tend to think the worst of us. Somehow it doesn't bother them in the meantime to be wearing clothes made from good old southern cotton. Let's stay in touch now, Jim. Can't have yew thinking ugly thoughts about mah home state. Look, there's the Detroit River...mah, look at all that ice. Sure would chill a lot of mint julep."

Neither ice nor mint julep seemed terribly relevant for the moment. Ownership of people did, and now made so very bothersome by what seemed such a logical case made for its legitimacy.

A good many restless nights were to march past because of the Major's dissertation, but soon more immediate matters came to hand; I had my engineering degree, the Grand Trunk Railway needed a civil engineer, and my career in "railroading", such as it was, was about to begin.

Chapter Two

Belleville in August was climatically almost identical to Mississippi. In the acid glare of the afternoon sun, a listless, sweat-drenched railway construction crew laboured on the banks of the Moira River a short distance west of where Belleville station was to stand. My particular specialty was foundations and their bearing on rock and soil and on that account I was in charge of preparing the ground on either side of the river for the footings of a bridge. Because of the profusion of limestone, some blasting was necessary and we were preparing to set off a charge.

The river level was low because of the advanced state of the season, making our job easier than it might otherwise have been. But the heat was nothing short of stultifying, and flies buzzed all around us, perching on our heads, lodging in our nostrils, tiny in their tyranny, inevitably when there was no hand free to do unto them before they did unto us.

The crew worked away, drilling holes for the charges. One man was taken ill from drinking too much river water and had to be sent back to the construction camp. Between the heat and the absence of one of our members, progress was slow and the sun was well into the western sky before we were ready to set off our charges.

The fuse was lit and we ran for shelter behind some nearby bushes. I poked my head up to see that the fuse was burning properly, and standing there watching the damned thing was a man, seemingly materialized from nowhere and dressed in a suit as though for business. He was contemplating the burning fuse as if it had no more import than the grasshoppers that were snapping and buzzing nearby.

"Hey!" I exploded. "Run! For God's sake..."

"Blood pudding," muttered one of the workmen. "Just beautiful..."

Our mysterious visitor, bearded, ginger-haired, and somewhat stocky, looked my way, by my estimation about thirty seconds from oblivion. Even if this were to be the only time I would ever see him, I could never forget that face, a face of infinite and ancient wisdom dwelling in a young moon. He looked straight into my eyes and then, with insolent deliberation, stepped on the fuse and ground out the flare with his heel.

"Jesus Christ!" I screeched, leaping over the bush and running towards him, ready to do bodily harm. "You bloody idiot! You've just loused up a good part of an afternoon's work, aside from damned near leaving one God-awful mess for us to clean up!" My crew applauded raucously. "Now get to hell out of here!"

"I will not," he said so quietly that I had to strain to hear him, "get out of here. I will also not be subject to any of your profanity. If you must swear like that, it would indicate to me that you have an insufficient command of the English language to express yourself. I did what I did, in case you were wondering, because what you are doing is an abomination."

"Is that a fact? Do you even have any idea of what we are doing?"

"Whatever it is, it is an abomination."

"Look, mister..."

"Doctor."

"Indeed. I really don't have time for your abstractions. I have a schedule to meet and you're doing your level best to make a shambles out of it without even knowing what we're about."

"What you are doing is creating a shambles."

"Je..."

"You say that name like that again and I'll break your head."

"Look, mister, doctor, whoever you are, you are trespassing on the property of the Grand Trunk Railway. If you don't leave right now, as many of us as necessary will have to remove you."

"Go ahead, then, and remove me." Mister Doctor sat down cross-legged on the ground.

"Just leave 'im there to get blasted, Mr. Ramsay," said Wiggins, our explosives expert. "I'll run a fuse from over there..."

"Never mind, Wiggins, but thanks anyway. I'll handle this." I had no idea how, but it sounded good. I took the deep breath of one who is not fully in command of a situation.

"Let's, ah, be reasonable, sir. We are putting up a railway bridge here. If you're worried about what it will look like, there's no need. We will do our best to make it blend in with the natural landscape."

"What is your name, son?"

Son! My blood pressure rose; he could not have been more than three or four years my senior, but I did manage to behave myself, despite a snicker from one of the workmen.

"James Ramsay. Perhaps you would do us the courtesy of telling us yours."

"I am Alexander Milton Ross." The delivery was such as to elicit the comment "Fancy, eh" from one of my crew. "I am not," he explained, "against your bridge on solely aesthetic grounds. I am not against your bridge for its own sake. I am against this entire railway business. Its potential effect on nature is unacceptable to me and should be to all of you as well. Migratory paths and trails will be disrupted, smoke and filth all over the place..."

"Well, who gives a tinker's damn?" said Wiggins crossly, wanting to get on with things.

"You should, my good fellow. How would you like *your* freedom of movement from place to place hindered and disrupted?"

"I wouldn't," said Wiggins, "but there's..."

"Mr. Ross, I mean Dr. Ross," I interrupted, "the railway will enhance humanity's freedom of movement. Certainly some things of nature *will* be disrupted...in fact, I'm honestly not sure if anyone thought about it. But people will be able to travel in a fraction of the time they do now, anywhere on the continent, the mail will take only days instead of weeks, goods will..."

"You ought to do advertising, Mr. Ramsay," complimented Wiggins.

"He already has," said Dr. Ross abruptly. "Good afternoon." He turned away and started eastwards toward the town.

I let my breath out through my teeth. "Gad, that was strange," said someone.

"That was pretty good, Mr. Ramsay," said Wiggins, who had, I think, regarded me as a bit of a dandy because of my university degree.

"Why, thanks, Wiggins. Nice to know I'm good for something. Let's get back to work here...what the hell do you think he meant about my advertising?"

"Who knows?"

I came to know a few hours later. I was sitting on the front veranda at home, pouring lemonade into myself, for although it was growing dark, the heat continued unabated. Silent lightning flickered to the south; by its faint light, I thought I saw someone on the front walk, looking tentatively at the house.

"Who's there?" I called, fighting a tremor in my voice, feeling about for something to throw if it were a burglar.

"James, is that you?"

"Who is it?" I called loudly.

"It's Alexander Ross. I see I found the right house. May I come up?"

"Oh, certainly. Sorry. Couldn't see who you were. Come along in, Dr. Ross."

"If you wouldn't mind, I'd rather sit out here and talk in private. And I'd prefer to be called Alex."

"Agreed, then. I'll try to forget being called 'son' this afternoon."

"I apologize for that. I was angry."

"At what, me?"

"Nothing personal. No, I was angry at the whole sorry world." Alex sat down on a glider and swayed gently back and forth, as though the motion soothed him. A moment of silence. "James, I have finally given in to a growing conviction that humanity is just...well, base is the word. Jesus tried to bring us out of the depths and now we're sinking again, have been for some time. We're raping the earth, pillaging it for whatever we can get out of it, ruining its beauty with industry and railways, fouling the air, making noise so dreadful as to scramble the brains..."

This was enough. "If this is a religious monologue, I'm really not interested," I responded. "Every Saturday, we get these people with their tracts..."

"This is nothing like that. Just hear me out. Do you think of yourself as a Christian?"

"Is that really any of your business?"

"James, I'm not trying to be nosy. Please don't misunderstand me. Now, let me try that again. Do you think of yourself as a Christian? Do you attend a church?"

"Sometimes. I suppose you could say I'm a Christian with a small 'c'".

"You're probably the most reliable kind. Now, to return to what I was saying, the worst thing about humanity is what it does to other human beings. I have just spent a week in St. Catharines..."

"Do they abuse each other in St. Catharines?"

Alex ignored my remark, which, in light of what I was to learn, was of no merit anyway. "There are," he explained, "some people in St. Catharines who have been *horribly* abused...have you ever heard of a lady named Harriet Tubman?"

"Harriet Tubman," I repeated. "I think so...isn't she an escaped slave? I think I read about her in the *Globe* a while back."

"You did, may the Lord bless and keep George Brown. I met her in St. Catharines. She is regarded by many as a modern Moses and the tales she told were enough to make one weep. I literally haven't been the same since. But she is not simply an escaped slave. She has returned several times to the United States to help others escape, and I hardly need to enumerate the risks involved.

"I met some of those she had helped from bondage into a life among free men, and, God above, James, you would not comprehend some of the things I saw, what their so-called masters have done to those poor people; scars of the lash, burn marks, missing teeth, and even broken limbs that never mended properly. *Livestock* are treated better.

"So that is why I behaved so badly this afternoon. I returned from St. Catharines yesterday and was still so upset today that I had to take a walk in the country, and then I found the country being mistreated and it was simply too much to deal with. You ended up as an unwitting target. I'm sorry."

"Well, you did point out that it wasn't anything personal," I assured him, "so as far as I am concerned, that particular matter is closed. But I think you'll be interested to hear a story of my own. Some lemonade?"

"Please."

As the gas-man came around to turn on the street lamps, I told Alex of my conversation with Major Ramsay on the train over a year before. "The worst part," I said, "was how right he thought he was, how right he thought the whole matter of owning slaves was."

"Oh, they have what they call Biblical evidence in support of slavery," snorted Alex. "I hope someday that I may personally pay this Major Ramsay a visit and walk off with a few of his slaves and bring them to freedom. Now, James, to take another tack, so to speak, there was something you said that made me back away from my crusade against the bridge."

"What was that?"

"About the freedom of movement for humanity. I don't know why it didn't occur to me earlier, but railways could be most useful in the transportation of escaped slaves."

"Slaves on trains?"

"It would be a big improvement over how they get here now. It's a long walk from Alabama."

"But I don't understand something. I thought slave-owning was illegal in the northern states. Aren't they safe once they get there? Why are they coming all the way to Canada?"

"There is a piece of political skulduggery in America called the Fugitive Slave Law; it came in, oh, five or so years ago, and under it, escaped slaves are considered to be stolen property, even though in essence they stole themselves, and they have to be returned to their owners if caught. And it applies to *all* the United States, not just the ones with slavery. I might add that a reward is generally involved..."

"Good God! Like bounty hunters!"

"Exactly. I think your revulsion is starting to match mine. James, do you like your job?"

"Yes."

"Would you be interested in expanding on your job for the betterment of humanity?"

"I thought it already *was* for the betterment of humanity."

"How long have you been with the Grand Trunk?"

"Just a year and a bit."

"So naturally your relationship with your employer is based on caution, just doing as you are asked, regular hours, no risks beyond the routine, that sort of thing."

My initial discomfort was returning. I had the feeling that I was being called on to defend my career and how I was to practice it. "Just what are you getting at, Dr. Ross?" The accumulated fatigue of the day put an edge of irritation on my voice.

"Very well, I'll come to the point."

"Good."

"I am a doctor, just got my medical degree, in fact..."

"Congratulations."

"Thank you...a doctor, and yet I spent all that time in St. Catharines without checking a single pulse or looking down a single throat. I was dealing with another kind of sickness. Large segments of society are sick in spirit, James, and I see myself as someone who can help by whatever means are available. Oh, yes, I could make a comfortable living in family practice right here in Belleville, secure in the knowledge that I was indeed helping people. But I heard a fair bit about slavery when I was young, living in New York...I'll tell you about that sometime...but what really did me in was a reading of *Uncle Tom's Cabin*. Do you know of it at all?"

"Heard of it, but haven't read it."

"I'm going to lend it to you, then, and see if it does to you what it did to me. To me, it was a command, a conviction that it was my duty to assist the oppressed to freedom. I have made the acquaintance of Harriet Tubman and Josiah Henson, another liberated slave...they are surely two people bound for immortality. They make it their business to inform slaves of the haven here in Canada, they and a fair number of others, and in the process, certain well-defined escape routes have taken shape and acquired the unofficial title of the Underground Railroad."

"Do I detect a certain implication in your emphasis on the word 'railroad'?"

"You do. You are certainly nobody's fool, my friend. Your remark about freedom of movement shocked me, you could say, into the realization of railways as a whole new means of moving slaves quickly and in large numbers, and what our movement needs is someone who knows the railway business.

"James, I want you to join us as an advisor on railway transportation. I would like you to travel with me in the southern states; as a railway man, your presence could be so easily explained and you could freely gather information on routes and train movements with ease.

"As for my own presence, well, I am a naturalist as well as a doctor, and would need to roam all over the place, collecting samples of wildlife, particularly birds. I would need slaves as guides and could probably sell them...what a terrible choice of words, but you know what I mean...sell them on the idea of a little trip to Canada, if what Josiah Henson tells me is so, and since he is a minister, I don't see any reason for doubt."

"But my job. How could I leave it? How would I make a living?" I saw a mad adventure in the making and wanted no part of it.

Continued Alex relentlessly, "Keep the job for a while; I'll have to deal with some preliminaries for a year or so anyway before needing you. Then you would have to be prepared for a hand-to-mouth existence for as long as necessary. You would have to be prepared for discomfort, for hardship, perhaps even for actual physical danger. You would have to be like Prometheus in his suffering for the betterment of mankind."

"Oh, wonderful," I said sarcastically. Alex took no notice, plunging heedlessly onward.

"Read Shelley's poem about Prometheus. Read Herder's too; I have a translation at home I'll lend you."

"Along with *Uncle Tom*."

"Along with *Uncle Tom*," echoed Alex. "You might in fact, James, have to prepare to live as Our Lord..."

"I hope longer."

"...to live as Our Lord, rejected and despised of men, certainly in the Deep South. But this will be what it will take. You have knowledge and connections that could be vital to the cause of the abolition of slavery. Now, I'm sure you'll want some time to think this over, that is if you haven't flatly rejected it already. I didn't paint a very jolly picture of the situation..."

"Well, it's not a very jolly situation, so I appreciate your candour. No, I haven't rejected it...there's a sort of dreadful fascination...I think I might like to help, but I want to live too. Let me just think about it."

"Good! I'll come by in the morning!"

"Come now, Alex! You're asking me to turn my life upside down. No, I need more than just a night to think this one over. I'll want to talk to my parents, for a start, and they are out for the evening. There are certain practicalities to be considered..."

"Now, don't go getting mired in practicalities, my friend. Our Lord could have done very well in the carpentry trade and lived to be seventy in perfect safety and obscurity. Practicality can be a stumbling block to true humanity, a refuge, an excuse not to step outside the bounds of normality."

"What is wrong with normality? I rather like it."

"I don't. It's not productive, it's limiting, and it bores me." Alex spoke with a calm assurance that not only frightened me but made my own life seem more irrelevant by the minute. I was wishing that none of this were happening, and yet the seed of the gruesome interest planted by Major Ramsay just refused to die. My world was of rails and roadbed, signals and couplings, things that did not abuse unless mishandled, things, things, things. And Alex was ideas, ideas, ideas. I felt guilty, I felt barren, I felt inferior for liking the security of my world of things. But these same things could serve something far greater than they were on their own.

Here I had my life nicely in order, the same sort of comfortable order mirrored by the horse and carriage clip-clopping up the street, its lantern flickering yellow in the summer night, a shout of laughter from across the way, the creaking of the glider. In the heavy shadows, I could not really see Alex. But I knew he was There.

I arose, waving my arms in agitation. "Oh, hell!" I said helplessly.

"I don't like swearing," said Alex flatly.

"I beg your pardon. You really have got me thinking, but I don't know if I'm cut out for something like this. You'll need to give me time. I need time..."

GERRIT SMITH.
COURTESY OF HARPERS FERRY HISTORICAL ASSOCIATION,
HARPERS FERRY, WV

CHAPTER THREE

I had more time to meditate over Alex's proposal than anticipated. A fortnight after our first encounter, he came over to the house to say good-bye to me and my parents, whom he had met in the intervening time.

"Good-bye?" I said in astonishment.

"More like *au revoir*. And in saying '*au revoir*', you must say hello to Surgeon-Lieutenant Alexander Milton Ross."

"The Service, Dr. Ross?" said Father. Father had a great reverence for the Service.

"Not just any service, sir. We are speaking of the Nicaraguan Army."

"The what?"

"The Nicaraguan Army. It's just a year's commission and it'll give me a chance to observe some tropical birds. Always wanted to see a toucan. Besides, I'll have nothing to spend my salary on, so I can save for my days of penury working on the Underground Railroad. That, James, gives you a reprieve for a while." I was relieved. Perhaps in a year's time, slavery would be illegal and the job of abolition would have been done for us.

"Now, James," continued Surgeon-Lieutenant Ross, "and for that matter, Judge and Mrs. Ramsay, there is something I hope you will do while I am away."

"What would that be?"

"You should drink at least eight glasses of water a day."

"Eight glasses! We'll drown!"

"It'll keep your innards flushed out," said Alex.

My parents were not yet accustomed to Alex, I think feeling of him as I had when he had called me "son", and they nodded politely with tight little smiles. I suspect Alex sensed this, for he added quickly, "Being a doctor for me is more than a job, it's a way of life. I just have to look after everybody. Well, Dr. Ross has spoken. Onward, now, to Nicaragua!"

In a sense, it was only an incomplete departure. The gravity of the slave situation grew as time passed, and the mere fact of Alex's existence nagged at me day and night. Of course, I must help the poor slaves, but I also had a career that now looked most promising and I hated to throw it all away.

To tell the truth, I was terrified of the whole Underground Railroad business and the more I read and learned, the worse my feelings became. The risks could be horrifying in a far-off, hostile land where the wrong ideas on one's part could see one hanging from the nearest live-oak tree, a land where the local perception of justice, at least in connection with negroes, tended to be carried out without duly appointed judge or jury.

It was this extra time to think things over and deal with feelings that simply wouldn't go away that was eventually my undoing. Three clearly discernible forces gradually and insidiously converged on me to force my hand: firstly, the nature of my work with the Grand Trunk would change radically in the autumn of 1856, for then the line to Montreal would be completed and, unless I were to completely re-locate, my work thereafter would be more of a maintenance than a creative nature, save for the occasional addition of passing loops or sidings. The prospect somehow did not thrill me.

Secondly, my father, Mr. Justice Alan Ramsay, Chief Magistrate for the County of Hastings, was, I think, rather taken with the idea of his son as a soldier in the continual struggle for human rights. I was an only child and I have blessed the Good Lord time and time again that my parents were not disposed to thrust upon me every hope they had ever had for themselves, but were prepared to be happy for me as long as I was happy in whatever I was doing. Father was subtle, however, and made one remark that, intentionally or not, preyed on me: "James, if you are thinking of working with Alex, I will go every inch for you in support of humanity. If you need money, for example, you shall have it. Justice, son, is my business, and in this case, I am not prepared to be confined by certain laws that may be legal in Alabama or Mississippi, but immoral throughout the rest of the world. Anyone who tries to defend slavery is attempting defence of the indefensible." So much, then, for the necessity of making a living.

And I trusted Father absolutely. He was one of only a handful of men I have ever known in whose hands I could place my very existence. He was very dark of hair and bushy of eyebrow, long and serious of face, but fans of laugh lines from his eyes betrayed his true nature. His face could be immobile; it was the laugh lines that were to be watched.

Likewise Adele Ramsay, my good mother, also tall, with a round, cheerful face sitting on a stack of chins. Like Father's laugh lines, Mother's chins were a barometer known only to a few. The more chins, the happier Mother was.

Finally, when a well-tanned and less Falstaffian Alex returned from Nicaragua (with samples, many revolting, of virtually all its bird- and plant-life), he wasted no time in introducing me to an American friend of his, a certain Gerrit Smith from Peterborough (in upstate New York and not to be confused with the real Peterborough here in Ontario); Gerrit Smith, in turn, wasted no time in voicing his despair at such an aberration as slavery existing within his beloved America.

Mr. Smith's one and only lapse from his fervent nationalism, at least that I could discern, was his great liking for Canadian ale. Although Alex despised drink on both moral and health grounds (cleaving to his eight glasses of water daily), he did ensure that his icebox was well-stocked with Sleeman's for his distinguished visitor. Gerrit Smith was a former member of the United States Congress for his riding (or I should say Congressional District) in New York state.

Gerrit Smith was striking in both speech and appearance. He was not particularly tall, but his bearing, strong features, and patrician manner made him a singularly dominating figure to whom people were likely to listen.

"James, my friend," he said, "my poor, guilty country cannot be saved as long as the black man is exploited and persecuted. Our nation will be lost to us should such an institution be permitted to continue and flourish. It is the basest of wickedness, and wickedness must die of itself...in our quest for abolition of slavery, God must surely be with us. These are people...they can speak and think and reason and feel. They have their Tubmans and their Hensons, but they cannot be expected to deal with all of this on their own, and they need our help. It is up to us, therefore, to help them deliver themselves from their bondage. On a more prosaic note, Alex, all this talking makes me dry. May I petition for another Sleeman's?"

"Rejoin the Empire and you can have all the Sleeman's you want, right at home," I teased. "And since slavery was outlawed here back in '33, why, we simply extend the law to our new southern colonies and Bob's your uncle."

"Bob's my uncle?"

"A country expression from these parts," explained Alex. "James likes to be rustic from time to time."

"James should be in politics," complimented Gerrit. "There is a certain logic to what he said, although it represents a serious violation of the Spirit of '76. How on Earth did the two of you meet, anyway? I cannot see any such thing happening casually."

Alex and I each gave an account of that first meeting by the bridge, each account so totally different that Gerrit burst out laughing and remarked on the potency of historical bias.

"Well, now, one of you tell me," said I, "how a doctor from Belleville ever became associated with a congressman from New York. An objective account, you understand."

"Oh, Gerrit and I go back quite a few years," pronounced Alex, sounding quite the veteran, although only twenty-seven years old; Gerrit, I would estimate, was about twice that. "I lost my father when I was eleven and my family had no money, so I went to New York City and worked as a compositor on the *Evening Post.* You may have heard of the editor, William Cullen Bryant..."

"Oh, the poet, isn't he?"

"Right you are," said Gerrit more or less simultaneously with Alex, who went on to declaim,

The calm shade of this once-mighty oak
did bring a kindred calm, and the sweet
breeze that made its green leaves dance,
did waft a balm to my weary heart.

"*Thy* weary heart," corrected Gerrit offhandedly.

"I know. My weary heart."

Gerrit sighed, looking meaningfully in my direction. "The word, Alex, is 'thy'."

"'Thy weary heart' it will be, Congressman, which reminds me, I wonder how many mighty oaks have been toppled in the building of this railway of yours, James. A balm to anyone's weary heart a locomotive is not..."

"It is conceivable that locomotives could pull a great number of slaves to freedom, my dear doctor, thereby being a balm to countless weary hearts."

"Bravo!" applauded Gerrit. "I like the way you think. You would certainly be a great asset to the Movement."

"We have digressed from this chapter of my life," said Alex with a touch of firmness in his voice. "Mr. Bryant was the one who aroused my interest in the abolition of slavery. He was absolutely wonderful to me, gave me extra pocket money, almost acted like a surrogate father. He introduced me to Gerrit, which I guess, James, answers your original question.

"New York was really interesting. Another acquaintance that came my way was General Garibaldi..."*

I threw up my hands in mock despair. "You don't need me at all. I'm too prosaic. When you rub shoulders with a poet, a congressman, and an Italian general, you don't need a civil engineer."

"But we *do*, James. Your time is nearly at hand."

The *coup de grace*, as it were, was delivered during a trip to St. Catharines to meet Josiah Henson, the noted beneficiary of the Underground Railroad turned benefactor. I was, at the time, in a state of what might be described as tepid acceptance, if not outright commitment, in the matter of helping slaves, and it was Alex's idea that I should meet an escaped slave in person and hear some of his experiences first-hand. It was by no accident that Alex and I made the journey by train (myself on an employee's pass), and my opening remark on boarding was, "I just don't know how to behave or what to say or anything. It's rather like meeting the Queen. I need direction."

"Just talk to Rev. Henson as you would anyone else. It's not as though you were trying to talk to someone dying of consumption. The only hard part is to avoid going overboard to be nice. Don't make it all seem like an act or that he's some sort of personal project. If you did, it might look as if you thought badly of negroes, as some people unfortunately do, and are just trying to conceal it, or are trying to look liberal or something."

"I did a great deal of reading while you were down in Nicaragua and I'm wondering how much favour we would be doing the negroes by having them here. I gathered quite a few people *do* think badly of them."

---

* Guiseppe Garibaldi was an Italian patriot and military leader in the movement to unify Italy.

"Those people are generally ignorant and immature. But there is no question that the negroes are still better off here in Canada under the protection of the lion's paw, so to speak."

"I like that."

"I do too, actually. Canada is not perfect, but it's an enormous improvement on the slaves' present lot. As to public feeling about the negroes in Canada, well, much as I dislike saying it, there is antipathy, though not in any uniform or systematic pattern. In some places, blacks are considered assets to the community, in others not. The fundamental difference between here and America, of course, is that they are free.

"Now, they may not be equal for some time to come as far as economic opportunities or public attitudes are concerned, but they are certainly equal before the law. Has your father ever tried a case involving a negro?"

"No, not yet, but you and I will be the first to know."

"The time may come, especially if we do our work as well as I hope we will...that was a very general 'we', please understand. I wasn't trying to put pressure on you."

"Of course not, ha, ha."

"Ahem...er...if we were to map the black population of Canada West at this moment, we would find most of them living near the border, partly because they're tired of running and, well, I think some may want to return to America when all slaves are freed by law, whenever that's going to be."

"Why should we," I ventured, "and that's a general 'we'...why should we, then, go to all this trouble and hazard if at the end of it all they are just going to go back?"

"Aside from the fact that America is their home, you have to look at it like this. We're not trying to just do our bit for Canada, we're trying to do it for the human race."

"You don't think on a small scale, do you, Alex?"

"No, I don't. Never could. You know, James, some sort of toilet on this train would be a great amenity. I hope we have time between trains in Toronto."

"It's the eight glasses of water doing you in."

"Impertinent young pup. I'm in pain. Besides, I'm only at number four. How many glasses have *you* had today?"

"Just had a cupful. It formed the foundation of my tea..."

"Oh, dear God. This conversation is ceasing to be intelligent. To return, now, to the subject of prejudice, you see it in some of the unlikeliest places, and what really embitters me is that some of those places are churches."

"Are you serious?"

"Sadly, I am. What Jesus would think I cannot imagine, but perhaps He is concentrating His ire at the moment on certain churches in the Deep South. Most ingenious they are down there. They have twisted and subverted the scriptures to justify slavery, whereas here the negro is simply banished to a gallery in the back of the church vulgarly known as 'nigger heaven', which, Lord knows, is bad enough. I wonder how many have walked all the way from Alabama just to be faced with that."

"This is sickening," I sighed. "I had no idea prejudice was that bad here...this is really a disappointing revelation. To get back to this Henson, now, to deal with the immediate. Tell me a bit more about him so I will know what to say and all that. I want to seem intelligent."

"He's been in Canada quite a long time, twenty years or thereabouts. He's been heavily involved in the foundation of a, what should I call it, a sort of Negro colony called Dawn. It's a training situation, actually, to help blacks to adjust to life in a white society, rather than living apart from it or trying to change it. It's all based on Protestant middle-class thinking in which the Holy Trinity among social values is living cleanly, working hard, and getting an education. Dawn tries to do all of these, though what sort of success it has at the moment I don't know. They've had financial problems and disagreements among themselves..."

"A pity. Sounds like a good idea."

"It does," said Alex, "but it's a bit like reading Plato's *Republic*, you know, the business about how wonderful democracy is, and then he turns right around and shows you everything that is wrong with it and leaves you completely befuddled."

I nodded wisely, although I had never read Plato. Was there no limit to the scope of Alex's interests and knowledge? It verged on the sickening. And he wasn't finished, either!

"Nothing is perfect except nature. With people, you just do the best you can with what you have. And in the rudest contrast to nature, here are the unlovely environs of Toronto. Time to change to the...uh..."

"The Great Western." There! I was good for something after all.

My meeting with the Rev. Josiah Henson was both my first conversation with a black person and my first visible evidence of what some white masters had done to their slaves. I now truly understood why Alex had been so upset on that day we had first made acquaintance; Rev. Henson moved about in a peculiarly hunched-over way, the result of a long-ago beating that had left both shoulders broken. I know that had I been through a similar experience, my bitterness toward the white man would have been without limits. And there were ex-slaves that I met since that time whose bitterness was extended toward my own white brethren right here in Canada, whose help and support was actually refused. Understandable, perhaps, but lamentable nonetheless.

Not so, though, with Josiah Henson. He had a patience and wisdom about him that was enormously appealing, an attitude of "forgive them, Father, for they know not what they do."

"We must be realistic," he said in a gently lilting accent, hardly blunted by twenty-odd years in Canada. "No matter what we do, we ourselves cannot abolish slavery. We cannot abolish it through mere removal and, ah, migration. Some slaves do not even want to escape, because they fear the unknown of Canada and the journey thereto. Some will not be healthy and some will be just plain too ignorant. Slavery is all they know and they don't even want to try anything else. What we *can* do is to force the issue and, through the Underground Railroad, bring the situation to the attention of the general public. They will learn the truth and force the United States government to enact abolition."

"The problem is," commented Alex, "there are too many sympathizers to slavery in the American government at the moment. They have to be relieved of office first. Good, decent American citizens from New England and other unlikely places. They are the ones to be worked on."

It seemed this day that every hour brought a new surprise. "I thought New England was the bastion of the American democratic ideal," I remarked.

"It was," said Alex flatly.

"But if these are non-slave-owning states, how could they support slavery?" I pursued.

"Oh, business reasons," explained Alex. "And there are politicians who rely heavily on the Southern vote in Congress, particularly in the Democratic Party."

"Some democracy!" I snorted.

"Some democracy," echoed Rev. Henson sadly. He drew breath to say something else, to be interrupted by a knock at the door. "Come in!" he called.

Two young blacks, I think in their late teens, entered. Said Josiah, "Gentlemen, let me present two of my brethren, Amos Rogers and Emmanuel Campbell. Boys, meet Dr. Ross and Mr. Ramsay."

"Massa," said the two youths deferentially.

"Now, what did Ah tell you?" said Josiah gently.

"Oh, yes, sorry. A hard habit to break. How do you do?" We shook hands.

"And how did *you* do?" asked Josiah.

"Oh, we done real good, Mr. Henson. Amos got a job as porter at the Empire Hotel, and Mr. Quinn the barber, he goan train me."

"That's wonderful! Good for you both," beamed Alex. "We should have some tea and celebrate."

"Thank you, mas..ah, Dr. Ross."

Through what I had read and pictures I had seen, I had somehow built up a mental image of negroes as a downtrodden, dolorous lot who wept a great deal and sang sad songs about Jesus. Downtrodden they may have been in the South, but these lads had spunk, and of that, Rev. Henson remarked a short while later, "Those two is a credit to mah race, the kind who truly benefit from our organization. Amos was a coachman in New Orleans and Emmanuel was a horse-groom in, let me see, Alabama someplace, Birmingham, Ah think it was. They had the kind of initiative that got them that kind of work in the fust place." He sighed. "Some of the othahs, though, Lordy, you'll wonder why you bothahed. Some lean on the Lord too much, saying He will provide and something will happen sometime...just be patient and wait, and then they end up waiting all their lives. But those two, now..."

"Very impressive," said Alex. "If they are treated fairly and without prejudice here in Canada, although it's a pretty big 'if' at the moment, we could end up holding the torch of liberty and truly deserving it. It was our white forefathers who begat the situation in the first place and now it's up to us to correct it."

Alex looked at me speculatively. "Thinking hard, James?"

"You is needed moah than you could evah know," added Rev. Henson almost pleadingly.

I had read *Uncle Tom's Cabin*. I had read pertinent literature by Wilberforce and Brougham, by William Lloyd Garrison and Theodore Parker, all supplied by Alex, complete with margin notes and underlining of salient points. I had read George Brown's editorials in the *Globe* and saved many of them. A Bible had been thrust on me, passages circled (and there were many) that decried the evils of slavery. I had met Gerrit Smith. And now I was in contact with three escaped slaves, whose own courage and that of the abolitionists had joined forces to give them a chance at a new life. I could stay away no longer.

I rose, my kneecaps fluttering disagreeably. "Count me in. I am with you."

Alex's eyes crinkled with pleasure, Josiah Henson's puddled up, and all three of us clasped hands.

CHAPTER FOUR

My career with the Grand Trunk Railway was officially placed in limbo on October 27, 1856, the day of the first through run from Toronto to Montreal. I had to ride it, of course, and Alex came along, partly out of friendship and partly to observe the milieu of train travel as it might be applied to the Underground Railroad.

As the train surged eastwards through the waning autumn colours, Alex remarked, "It's a pity our trains aren't divided up into compartments as in Britain. In that sort of situation, slaves travelling in disguise might be a possibility, but unless you have other ideas, I see no alternative to crating the slaves and sending them as freight."

"Leading," I remarked facetiously, "to some exceptionally interesting freight manifests. One mummy (female), one daddy (male), two children(assorted), this side up, do not drop..."

Alex gave one of the profound sighs he had taken to affecting when my sense of whimsy got the better of me. "Very funny, James. No, I think we would have to agree on some sort of code and ship the men as ironmongers' supplies and the women as, oh, maybe dry goods or textiles..."

"And," I inserted, "children can be toys or pet stock."

A week or so later, Alex was off to Peterborough (the one in New York) to join Gerrit Smith, and from there, the two of them carried onward to Boston, New York, and Philadelphia to acquaint themselves with the various abolitionist organizations in those cities, as well as the various Underground Railroad routes either evolving or already established. Even in the northern states, where slavery had not been practised for years, our associates were officially operating outside the law because of the existence of the Fugitive Slave Law. That ludicrous political anomaly had no morality behind it, but had been drawn up only to avert voter antagonism in the South. Therefore, all activity, even in the very land where the original colonists had fought for their own liberty, had to be conducted with the utmost discretion.

I, in the meantime, was preparing my own groundwork. Through the good offices of Father, I made an arrangement with the Grand Trunk whereby I would be retained on standby employment at a salary of one

REV. JOSIAH HENSON, COURTESY OF ENOCH PRATT FREE LIBRARY, BALTIMORE, MD

dollar a year. I was issued a very comprehensive letter of introduction, stating that I was on an inspection tour of U.S. railroads to gather information on locomotives, rolling stock, signals, train movements, scheduling, operational procedures, and routes both existing and contemplated. The letter concluded that the Grand Trunk, though being laid to Colonial gauge, was equipped for efficient trans-shipment and looked forward to doing interchange business with American railways. Moreover, the company appreciated any courtesies extended to me and would be prepared to reciprocate. The end result was that I was able to use a pass over virtually all the lines I would be travelling.

And for daily living, hotels, and meals, Father provided the necessary funds: "What you are about to do, James, transcends the grubby business of making a living. You will have many worries and concerns and I do not intend that money should be one of them."

By March, 1857, all was in readiness, but for a brief romantic interlude. Alex returned from his exploratory travels on March 12, which happened to be my birthday, and came over to our house, bringing a lady.

"May I present Miss Hester Herrington," announced Alex on arriving, and then at dinner, "Hester has honoured me by consenting to become my wife."

"Wonderful!" boomed Father, a fan of laugh lines blossoming forth. Mother, going right to her limit of five chins, wiped the obligatory tear of happiness from her eye. "We're so happy for you. When is the wedding to be?"

"The twenty-fifth."

"Of March?"

"Of March."

"1857?"

"1857."

"But that's less than a fortnight off!"

"Yes," said Alex casually. A pause.

Said Hester, "Alex proposed by letter just last week. He is going away again very soon, so we just decided to go ahead and get married."

"Well, er, our congratulations."

"James, I would like you to be my best man, if you would," said Alex. "You're a dear and valued friend that I have come to trust as no-one else."

"I'd be honoured, Alex."

"And, Judge Ramsay, since I have no father– I hope this doesn't sound maudlin – but could you stand in for the day?"

"I too would be honoured," said Father.

Hester's home was in Sophiasburg, a village in Prince Edward county just across the Bay of Quinte from Belleville. The wedding was held in her family's church in nearby Picton on a March day so balmy and springlike that many remarked that it must be a good omen for those who Hester's slightly tipsy cousin called the "New Wedlies." But there were comments as well from people who knew Alex, speculating as to whether a marriage could survive with a gadfly such as he. Hester showed no such reservation, however, beaming happily through both the service and the reception afterwards. I think she was somewhat younger than Alex, but certainly shared his seemingly insatiable curiosity, a gift that was to stand her in good stead through the lonely years that were to follow. Loneliness, though, was far from her thoughts this day, and I envied Alex his good fortune; a delightful young woman was Hester, freckled of nose (an outdoor touch unusual in Victorian womanhood) and with the most wonderfully inviting almond-shaped brown eyes. It is perhaps improper to write thus of my friend's wife, but to deny that I admired her would be far short of the truth.

Alex left for Philadelphia after only two nights with his bride. I followed him on March 29th by train. If I could digress for a moment, that is truly a marvellous trip, especially between Albany and New York, where the train runs right along the east bank of the Hudson River. The passenger fortunate enough to sit on the right-hand side of the coach has an unbroken view of the river for most of the distance, passing through a district known as the Highlands, where great mountains rise right out of the water.

Having savoured the beauties of the Hudson River, I changed stations at New York for the final lap of my odyssey, over the New York and Philadelphia Railroad, to meet Alex in Philadelphia.

"Welcome to the city of brotherly love," he grinned as he met me in the drafty, smoky train shed of Broad Street Station. "A wonderful idea, isn't it? Let us see what sort of success we have putting it into practice."

For inspiration, we visited the Liberty Bell and on the following evening, we had our first meeting with blacks, a gathering arranged by a negro minister named Harold Thompson. There were about a dozen blacks present, only two of whom were actually escaped slaves; two others had purchased their own freedom and the remainder were the children of escaped slaves, the oldest being about sixteen or seventeen years of age.

With the prevailing indiscriminate application of the Fugitive Slave Law, none were guaranteed indefinite freedom, although none of this lot had been challenged or threatened in any way. However, there was no question that they would have been better off in Canada, not only for the sake of their personal security, but for the economic opportunities, for modest though they were, they were an improvement over what obtained in Philadelphia. The most elevated work that any of these youths had was as a bootblack at Broad Street Station. All the others drifted from menial job to menial job, barely subsisting and living in slum conditions. The alarming thought persisted that they would probably be better off as slaves.

All these things (except the last) were remarked on by Alex, who spoke to the gathering with an ease that suggested he had done this all his life, but at the end of his discourse, the blacks simply shrugged and looked at the floor. A thick silence hovered in the room, broken only by a thin drizzle of rain down the filthy windows.

"Well? What do you lads think of this?" said Alex brightly.

"Dis heah Canada be too far," mumbled one.

"I just came from there," I said, my first words to our potential clients. "It took me just two days by train from where I actually crossed the border. For you, travelling on the Underground Railroad by foot, perhaps a month, which sounds like a lot until you compare it to walking up from Louisiana or some such place."

The clients remained, sad to say, only potential. There were more shrugs, excuses, and rationalizations not to make the trip. I felt rage building in me. For such people, such sloth, I had thrown away my career and uprooted my life? If Amos Rogers and Emmanuel Campbell had had the initiative and courage to traverse the Underground Railroad for all its length, then surely this lot was at the opposite end of the spectrum. What could we expect to be more typical?

"Well, thank you for coming," said Alex, not so brightly this time. The potential clients swayed and shuffled out, all but immobilized by their quagmire of hopelessness.

Rev. Thompson was mortified. Alex put a hand on his shoulder. "Reverend, you did what you could and we did what we could. This is nobody's fault."

"Such a human tragedy,"said Rev. Thompson quietly. "Defeat has been bred into these poor creatures. They are immune to their great Biblical examples: Joshua, Moses, Jesus Himself. They are immune from ever being led to the Promised Land...no Exodus for them."

"Stuck with the Pharaoh," I remarked gloomily.

"The problem is that they aren't desperate enough," said Alex. "I'm truly sorry, James. I thought this would be a good initial experience for us. I was wrong. So we go south immediately. We will go where they will *live* for an Exodus."

CHAPTER FIVE

A sunny April morning saw us across the Potomac River to pick up the Richmond and Fredericksburg Railroad to Richmond. Our self-ordained mission was to see what success, if any, we could have there in actually attracting some escapees. I had clearance to ride the locomotive, a high-stepping American type, all the way to Richmond, leaving Alex to languish on the cars among the common folk. The experience in Philadelphia had left me with an almost unbearable sense of futility, and on that account, the possibility of vindication elevated my spirits to great heights, a condition certainly enhanced by being on the footplate.

Virginia in April was lovely. Forsythia and dogwood were much in evidence and many trees were already in leaf or well on the way at a time when in Belleville there was probably still snow lying about. The train's route passed through hill country just in from the coast, stopping to set down passengers, parcels, and the United States Mail at Alexandria, Fredericksburg, Bowling Green, and Hanover.

Virginia was our first state where slavery was actually legal. Whenever circumstances permitted, I made some casual enquiries of the engine crew with respect to slavery in general and their feelings on the matter in particular. They, as it turned out, simply accepted it as a way of life in their state (both were native Virginians) and subscribed to the idea of "nigras" as being helpless and ignorant without the care and protection of the benevolent white man. I could not be angry with them, to my own personal exasperation, for they were so pleasant and hospitable and totally honest in their beliefs, so completely conditioned into a state of almost innocent amorality.

A situation like this would not be solved for even a generation and now that I was travelling straight to the heart of it, I had the feeling of being on a treadmill; the more I was to learn, the more I would know that I had to learn, and so forth. And I would somehow have to come to terms with the fact of delightful, friendly people fully believing in the right to own other human beings. At least the engine crew lacked the debonair malevolence of my "cousin" Major Ramsay.

I did not wish to arouse suspicion by asking an inordinate number of questions about slavery, so I involved myself completely in the operation of the train. After all, I had to justify my free passage, and it was good therapy anyway after my ethical musings.

The fireman, whose name was Howard, helped matters by an almost continual commentary as he hurled logs into the inferno: "These are good engines, Jim, but the durn fewl boiler's too small. Watch this, now, George [the engine driver] and Ah deal with this real good...there's a hill comin' up now...George'll work her hard...coupla wood bits in the old stove...now, watch that pressure drop. Wouldn't happen with a bigger boiler, but it don't make no never mind. Top of the hill comin' up now and pressure's so low it damn' near quits, but George just coasts down the other side while Ah throw wood like crazy, get steam back up again...sorta like mortgaging the boiler, yew could say..."

I made myself useful, collecting orders from the various stations along the way, setting the points for a passing loop, did some heaving of firewood, helped Howard with the standpipe at a water stop, and generally earned my passage with clear conscience, except, of course, for the true purpose of my journey.

By the time we gained Richmond in late afternoon, my clothes were impregnated with the wood-smoke that forever billowed in at the cab window, and my shoes were waterlogged from a miscalculation during a water stop. Alex laughed at my appearance and then waxed all stern and mother-hennish, forbidding me to do anything until I had taken a bath at our hotel and sent my clothes to a neighbouring laundry.

"Look at this," invited Alex as I downed glasses of water five and six for the day. "In case we get into difficulty," he added.

He opened a flat case. In it was a revolver, gleaming black with just a hint of Prussian blue. I went cold. Somehow the thought of guns had not crossed my mind. That sort of thing was for the western frontier.

"Where did you get that?" I quavered. Good God, I had never even *seen* a gun!

"In Boston. Charles Sumner gave it to me. He's the senior senator from Massachusetts and he has an unimpeachable record in his opposition to slavery. He owned this thing for years and told me he wanted something of himself along in our operation. I have no wish to alarm you, James, but I think I'd feel better for your safety if you had one of these as well."

"Why wasn't I told about this earlier?" I demanded, feeling ridiculous making demands while clad in a dressing gown.

"In case you became alarmed and withdrew your services. I couldn't take the chance."

I was still too unnerved to take issue with what was plainly manipulation on Alex's part. Instead, I blurted, "But, Alex, if we were *caught* with this bloody thing..."

"This is America. All manner of people have guns. The United States Constitution guarantees all citizens the right to bear arms and I can assure you that it is one clause of the Constitution that is taken very seriously indeed."

"But we're not American citizens."

"When in America, behave as the Americans. Except, of course, for owning slaves."

In Richmond we were put in touch with another Negro preacher, the Reverend Uriah McLeod. "Sure, Dr. Ross," said the Reverend, "Ah think we may have some interested folk. Ah minister to several plantations nearby and we has several escaped slaves sheltering heah in town, some with a heavy price on their heads. Yes, suh, it may well be that you'll have some new citizens for your fine country."

Rev. McLeod was both true to his word and enormously efficient. Two nights later, to our astonishment, no fewer that forty-two blacks appeared, such an aggregation that Alex and I were genuinely alarmed that unwanted attention would be attracted.

"Jest a prayer meetin'," reassured the Reverend. "Sure, it ain't Sunday, but, well, mebbe someone's kinfolk is ailin'. Sure, someone's kinfolk is ailin', hurtin' inside. Oh, we got plenty of valid reasons..."

We shook hands with and were introduced to our visitors, all of whom were male; they sat, stood, or sprawled where space could be found in Rev. McLeod's modest chapel, and the "prayer meeting" began. Alex explained the route of escape, traversing from Richmond in a north-westerly direction through Pennsylvania to the port city of Erie, where the escapees would be met by a sailing schooner and taken across Lake Erie to Canada.

It was certainly a more alert group than the one in Philadelphia, listening with total absorption and in absolute silence. Every few minutes, to allay the suspicions of any curious neighbours or passers-by,proceedings were interrupted for the singing of hymns. To that end, musicianship was sacrificed in favour of sheer volume, convincing in itself, although we became a bit uncomfortable over repeated references to Moses. The symbolism surely could not escape a discerning listener.

At the meeting's close, Rev. McLeod instructed his flock to talk things over with their families and to assure any of their fellows they could that they were welcome to join the Exodus. And all those intent on escape to Canada should attend another meeting two evenings hence, fully prepared both physically and emotionally to begin their journey that very night.

Alex and I spent a couple of days that truly had us tied in knots with anxiety. How many of these lads would actually undertake such a venture? Their journey would be long; just a look at the route on a map was intimidating. Movement could be made only under cover of darkness, the best distance to be hoped for between twelve and sixteen miles per night. At the intervals of a night's journey were places of refuge, the "stations" on the Underground Railroad, which for the most part were the private homes and farms of those remarkable humanitarians, the Quakers, who had a proud record of anti-slavery work dating all the way back to 1688. If there were any delay and a "station" could not be reached before daybreak, one had to do what he could, taking sanctuary in the woods or in caves or wherever. Under no condition was travel to be attempted anywhere near towns, railways, or roads, for while there were a good many sympathizers along the way, there were also those who would profit as provided by the Fugitive Slave Law. Then there would be storms, problems of finding water, chances of injury or illness. In sum, the prospect would be daunting to all but the stoutest of hearts.

It was certainly daunting to me, and I didn't even have to do it. Were we mad? Could we truly accomplish something and make someone's life better?

We strolled the streets, sat in restaurants, and visited libraries and museums to pass the time. Alex bought some supplies to start the blacks on their way, but without any idea of how much of anything he should purchase. "A picnic for forty-two...impossible...I hope not all forty-two go at once anyway. A mob like that surging through the countryside would be a bit difficult to conceal. On the other hand, it would be devastating if *nobody* went..."

In the final event seven, a manageable number, came to Rev. McLeod's chapel at the appointed time. Their journey just that far was fraught with hazard, as they were travelling with false papers attesting to them having purchased their freedom, papers that would not stand close examination. Two of the men were married and had taken the difficult but courageous step of leaving their young families behind, to be retrieved at a later date.

"Oh, Dr. Ross, Mr. Ramsay, that surely do make me powerful oneasy," said Rev. McLeod sombrely. "Those families left heah may be subject to retribution..."

"Can they be looked after here in case of an emergency?"

"Ah reckon so. Ah will make the arrangements, but Ah don't mind tellin' you, Ah'm powerful oneasy..."

Alex's provisions were ample for seven men and consisted primarily of bread and some sort of dried meat. Each man was provided with a knife, and the designated group leader, the only one who was at all literate, was given a compass and a school atlas, the route inked in by Alex. Tucked into it was a list of families along the way who belonged to the Underground Railroad organization.

"Now, one more thing," instructed Alex. "If, and we hope this won't happen, but if you get into difficulty, the first thing you do is get rid of this list and I don't care how, burn it, tear it up, eat it...even if you only *think* there's going to be trouble, destroy the list. That will be one time you must think beyond yourselves and consider those following you to Canada. Do you all understand?"

"Yes, suh, we do."

"Good man. A lot of people are counting on you, so be careful, even if it adds some time to your journey. Now, finally, here is some money..."

"Money? What's dat?"

"...which some of you have probably never handled before. Now, I don't intend that you should darken the doorway, er, go into any stores. Too risky. You may need this for other things. Do any of you know what a bribe is?"

"No, suh."

"It is a lamentable invention of the white man. If, God forbid, you were threatened with capture, you may be able to pay your captors to let you go."

"Lordy."

"There are, I am sorry to say, some lower orders who would accept your money and *still* not let you go."

"Lordy, *Lordy.*"

"That is the kind of thing that makes me not too proud to be white."

"You can be proud, Dr. Ross, Mr. Ramsay," said the group's leader in a faltering voice, eyes glistening. "You two be a couple of angels, first white folks that really cared about what was happenin' to us. We, well, just don't know how to thank you."

"There's no need, my friend. Just be careful, take your time, and don't try anything foolish. We'll see you in Canada. Just come outside a moment, would you?"

The leader went out the back door of the chapel with Alex, whom I could clearly hear explaining, "See that star, just over the chimney? It's called the North Star. If you get lost or confused, just follow it. It will lead you right to Canada." He poked his head back into the door. "It's time now. Away you go. God be with you."

As each man went out the door, we shook hands with him before he was swallowed up in the soft spring night. As the last one disappeared, I turned to Alex to say, "I've never felt so worthwhile in my life." I felt a curious tightness in my throat.

"Well, James, you've done your part and I've done mine, and Rev. McLeod, bless him, has done his. Between us, we may be able to do something about this unspeakable evil."

"Amen," concluded Rev. McLeod. "It surely has been quite an evening, hasn't it? Befoah you retire for the night, would you gentlemen care for the refreshment of a little bourbon whiskey?"

Alex and I were a bit startled by his offer. Alex, being a teetotaller, settled for a cup of tea, and so I accepted some bourbon in the interests of courtesy. A substance more horrible was almost beyond imagining, and Alex's tea, I was told later, was not much of an improvement; Rev. McLeod, like most Americans, didn't even scald the pot.

A year or so hence, I would have the pleasure of seeing all our escaped friends once again, friends that we never had a chance to know, but friends all the same. The two who had left their families were reunited with them and were living in Chatham, that notable haven of the black man. So this phase of my account had a happy ending. Now it was time to move onward before we were linked in any way with the escape of seven slaves.

"Pack your things, James," said Alex briskly as we tiptoed up the stairs of our slumbering hotel. "Up bright and early in the morning. We're bound for Nashville, rolling on to Nashville."

Chapter Six

For our destination at Nashville, we had been given the address of one identified only as a "Quaker lady", a tactic certainly suggestive of our penetrating more sensitive territory. We proceeded to this mysterious address by cab from the Nashville station, to stand upon the front porch, knocking at the door, and feeling more than a little foolish at not knowing how to address our hostess.

"Ah, good evening," flustered the usually imperturbable Alex. "Are you the, er, Quaker lady?"

"I am. And who may thee be?"

"The bird-watcher and the engineer."

"Please enter." The door closed behind us. "Welcome to my home. My actual name is Ruth Gardiner. Thee will be staying here, in the guest room. It's just to thy right, at the top of the stairs, and if thee would like to take thy bags up, I'll get thee something to eat. I expect thee are a bit weary of railroad food."

For my own part, I never could have wearied of Mrs. Gardiner's food. Her husband had been "taken by our Merciful Lord" something over a year before, and she seemed pleased to have someone to look after once again. She was of particular help to Alex at this time. With some mental respite at hand on the train, he had been thinking of Hester and had grown quite depressed through an unpleasant alloy of guilt and quite simply missing her. The situation was not helped by having to send her letters unsigned in the interest of security ("your friend" conveyed little meaning as far as Alex was concerned); to compound his misery, she could not reply at all because of his constant travelling.

The circumstances were at once reassuring and disturbing. It was reassuring to see that Alex was, after all, human, but disturbing in that, without his knowledge, contacts, and general self-assurance, I would be worse than lost. Nashville was not exactly a stone's throw from Canada West.

Alex wrote another arid letter to Hester from Nashville and in the few moments we were not engaged on Underground Railroad business, he and Mrs. Gardiner had lengthy and considerable dialogue on the condition of loneliness. Mrs. Gardiner reminded me in a curious way of my father, whose mere presence could make a bad situation at least bearable. But Alex continued to be so withdrawn and distracted that I had to speak up.

"You still have me," I said brightly.

"James, as attached as I have grown to you, there are still certain needs which it would be unreasonable to expect you to fulfil..."

We were introduced to a remarkable old negro named Wilfred Smith, who had been able to buy his freedom, a rare circumstance in the state of Tennessee. Mr. Smith was, by his own reckoning, about eighty years old, but had the energy, bearing, and clarity of thought of one a quarter century younger. In fact, I am embarrassed to say, his clarity of thought often eclipsed my own, although I theoretically had youth on my side. I often mention this matter in conversation with those still-numerous people who will try to tell you that blacks have no intelligence or cannot evolve or any of the rest of that sort of nonsense.

As with the other black community leaders we had met, Wilfred Smith was a preacher and, although ancient by the calendar, still practised his profession on a part-time basis, and so had numerous contacts and acquaintances in both Nashville and its environs. It was not difficult for him to procure thirteen men for a "prayer meeting" at Mrs. Gardiner's house on the following evening, a Thursday. These fellows ranged from eighteen to thirty years of age; to my surprise, not all were totally black; at least a third of them were about the colour of coffee with cream, and one lad hardly looked black at all, except for the characteristically woolly hair.

Mrs. Gardiner's neighbourhood was even less secure than Rev. McLeod's in Richmond; as well, a negro prayer meeting would be less easy to explain in a white lady's private residence. So while Alex discoursed on the escape route and the opportunities for negroes in Canada, Mrs. Gardiner and I sat in a couple of rocking chairs on her front porch, watching for any impending trouble. What we would have done in an actual emergency could be no more than chasing everyone out the back door. It was not uncommon for white households to have black labour if not actual slaves on the property during the day, but this was evening in a relatively modest neighbourhood and there would have been some very awkward questions from the law, such as it was, on the subject of slavery.

As Mrs. Gardiner and I sat and rocked in a state of synthetic well-being, I remarked on the varied complexion of our visitors.

"Oh, that," said Mrs. Gardiner rather off-handedly. "That is the result of some rather irregular goings-on. What I mean is that some slave-owners treat their more attractive slave women as, how shall I put it, their private whores."

I shot upright with such force that I had to grab my chair to prevent a capsize. "You jest!"

"I do not jest, James, and if thee thinks there is depravity around here, thee should see it further to the south."

"I suppose the slave owners who do this sort of thing are single."

My bland innocence was too much for Mrs. Gardiner, who sat for a moment ticking with suppressed laughter. Hot embarrassment rushed to my face.

"Bless my soul James, thee are so wholesome! Thee has much to learn. The majority of these ne'er-do-wells are married and have families, but are completely without principle in their, er, lust for variety. For that matter, completely without principle, period...I have heard of plantation owners justifying themselves by saying that they were trying to combine in one being the docility and perseverance of the negro with the intelligence and initiative of the white."

"Great God, like breeding stock."

"Precisely. There are some plantations that verge on being baby farms, improper as it may sound, but that is the way of it. The late Mr. Gardiner knew a man named, oh, Jackman or Jacklin, something like that, down Smyrna way. He used to boast how he had five of his slave girls with child at once and he was *very* married. Oh, he was a randy, that one..."

Two hours went by. Nothing untoward was happening, but the prolonged unease finally got the better of me and I went inside to see what was taking Alex so long.

"It's now Thursday," he was saying. Perhaps things were winding up at last. "I need to hear from whoever is going by Saturday morning. Rev. Smith will be around to ask you. That doesn't leave you much time to make a decision and I'm sorry about it, but I have to know what to get in way of supplies. We saw a group out of Richmond the other evening and we didn't know whether two or forty-two people would be going and our arrangements were a bit untidy.

"I will stay in Nashville through Sunday night. Starting at nine o'clock in the evening..."

"Massa, how do we know when it's nine o'clock?"

"Oh, well, ah, isn't there a church up at the corner? Just keep an eye on the clock and the first of you comes when the short hand is at nine and the long one straight up..."

"That clock has Roman numerals," said Mrs. Gardiner over my shoulder.

"Oh, bother," said Alex primly. "Well, the first of you comes at dark, then; the next of you counts slowly to six hundred...can you do that?"

"Yes, massa."

"No, massa."

"Then those who can count do it for those who can't and then follow them. Can you make that work?"

"Sho 'nuff can, massa."

Alex smiled. "I'm not your massa, and after Sunday, neither will be anyone else. 'Dr. Ross' is just fine. Now, where was I...you will come one at a time to the back door and *scratch* on it, don't knock, all right? We have to be as quiet as possible. We'll be listening for you and we'll try and have you supplied and away between ten and eleven. Any questions?"

"Doan think so, suh, yu've been very thorough. Thunk of ever'thing."

"Good, then. If we're *all* thorough and careful, this will work, but never forget we'll still need the Lord to help us." The Lord's prayer was mumbled and then our visitors left in pairs through the back door.

By Saturday, thanks to some judicious queries by Wilfred Smith, seven men were known to be committed to the flight to Canada. "Seven out of thirteen, James. A far better percentage than seven out of forty-two. Does that suggest anything to you?"

"As an engineer," I said importantly, "I have a unique grasp of the interpretation of statistics, and my interpretation is that more slaves here want to get out. I have spoken."

"And well at that, my friend. The more desperate the people are, the higher the rate of success we will have. I hope you are in the mood now for some shopping."

I am never in the mood for shopping, but it had to be done and discreetly at that. To bring provisions in such quantity to Mrs. Gardiner's house without causing conjecture among the neighbours was no mean feat. However, a high board fence alongside the house provided some concealment and I was able to deposit my booty in a lean-to woodshed.

Since all departing slaves had come to the meeting unshod (unlike their more urban colleagues in Richmond and Philadelphia), Alex was concerned that their feet would not endure the trip, not to mention scent being left on the ground for the inevitable tracker dogs. Naturally, nobody had any idea of foot size, but Alex was determined that all should have shoes, and so he peeled several bills from his roll of money donated by abolitionists from all over the United States and Canada, and gave them to me for purchase of seven pairs of boots in my size in the hope they would be adequate. To buy seven pairs of boots in one store, obviously, would have chewed holes in our subterfuge, which was tenuous at best. So I had the tiresome chore of visiting seven bootmakers. Between that and buying groceries, I came to know Nashville rather well, all seven hills of it as in Rome, and fine exercise it was.

Alex, in the meantime, bought three guns from different sources. He was both gratified for his own purpose and alarmed for American society generally, for buying a gun in Nashville was almost easier than buying a pair of shoes. The only size that mattered was the calibre of the ammunition.

At a few minutes to nine on Sunday evening, Alex, Rev. Smith, myself, and Mrs. Gardiner took up station in the latter's kitchen to listen for our first scratch at the door. It came within a couple of minutes of schedule, and at ten-minute intervals, each negro was shown the use of a gun, issued a pocket compass, food, and twenty dollars for bribes, and fitted with boots. Only one had bigger feet than I and I sawed off the toes of the boots to ensure fit; those with smaller feet simply padded them out with extra stockings. Once prepared, each man waited in the living room for departure, just as in a railway station. After all, this was the Underground Railroad.

By 10:20, our "passengers" were ready. To make sure the coast was clear, I went outside on the pretext of posting a letter. All was quiet in Nashville's streets, but the lack of evident suspicion made me uneasy and departure was delayed for a full hour. The group then left with Rev. Smith escorting them to the edge of town to make any necessary explanations to policemen on their rounds.

A half-hour or so later, Alex and I went for a walk of our own to dissipate the feelings of restlessness and the fear for our charges that plagued us. We walked down a side-street where gas lights had not yet been installed, a street where all the houses were dark and the dome of the heavens vaulted overhead, black, eternal, and limitless, thousands of stars etched in glittering perfection.

"There's the North Star," said Alex in a far-away voice. "I told the boys to follow it, that it would lead them to Canada. They'll understand that a lot better than maps or compasses. They read a map the way I read humanity. James, I am so confused. America is the birthplace of modern democracy, potentially the greatest country in the world, and look what has been done to it.

"And in the Bible, we are supposed to have the perfect guide, and yet it has been so subverted, exploited, distorted...we are given this wonderful book and presumably the brains to interpret it intelligently, and what happens but evil people twist it and mould it to their own ends. Those plantation-owners think they are doing the right thing and *we* think *we* are doing the right thing. Something is terribly wrong. I feel very small right now."

"A grand total of fourteen people are on their way to freedom at this very moment because of you," I reminded him.

"Because of *us*, James. Your role hasn't been exactly passive."

"Then there's Mrs. Gardiner and thousands of others. Fourteen slaves on their way to a new life...how many left to go?"

CHAPTER SEVEN

On the assumption that the United States Mail would move more quickly than fugitive slaves creeping fearfully through the night, Alex was up and about early, writing to an associate in Evansville, Indiana, to Levi Coffin, our Underground Railroad "agent" in Cincinnati, and to someone else in Cleveland, advising them of the impending delivery of seven "parcels of hardware" from Nashville. We took the letters to the local post office for mailing at mid-morning and as Alex was buying stamps, I studied the gallery of wanted criminals displayed on a bulletin board.

"Oh, shit," I said through my teeth. There, glowering at me, seemingly about sixteen feet tall, was a poster advertising our seven escapees from Richmond, a price of one thousand dollars on each of their heads. It was further noted that their escape was likely with the collusion of local abolitionists and I feared for the safety of the gentle Reverend McLeod. And it was an ugly surprise to find an event so far away so prominently advertised.

I showed the notice to Alex, who glanced at it briefly and then steered me away. "Aren't you going to read it?" I said querulously.

"Quiet," he hissed. "If we take an unusual interest in that poster without being local, someone may get curious. We don't want that. This is the price of fame, my boy. Our work is done here and we can do nothing further until the dust settles. Let us see which railway runs to Memphis..."

The prospect of another rail journey brightened my perspective on the world, chilled as it had been by the notice in the post office. "I will polish up my letter of introduction..."

"I think not this time,"cautioned Alex. "If you become noted to be where escapes are happening..."

"Ah, yes, how unspeakably silly of me."

So I rode aboard the cars of the Memphis and Ohio Railroad, with which we connected at Clarksville after a desperate dash from Nashville by stagecoach. It was high summer in Tennessee now, far earlier than at home, and gusts of acrid heat blew in at the windows. It was still much more pleasant than it would have been on the footplate, as the coach was furnished with rattan seats and had a cooler of iced water by the back door, a pleasant amenity that I noted down as a possible idea for the Grand Trunk. A stop was made for refreshments late in the afternoon at Paris; Alex went into the station restaurant while I strolled forward to admire the engine, not so sleek as on the train to Richmond, for our steed had smaller driving wheels, the better to cope with the great hills of Tennessee. I exchanged pleasantries with the engine crew, savoured the smell and sounds, absorbed the details of steamy water dripping onto the track bed, the caked grease and assorted slime on the drive-rod assemblies, soot streaked across the top of the boiler, the polished brass number plate...ah, trains! Practical for the betterment of humanity, yet pleasing to the eyes, the ears, the nostrils, an art-form for all the senses.

"All aboard!" cried the distant voice of the conductor. I scrabbled back aboard to be confronted by a grim-faced Alex.

"Look at this." He passed me a copy of the local newspaper. "SEVEN SLAVES ESCAPE NASHVILLE", blared a headline on the second page.

"God Almighty, how did *that* get here so fast?" I trumpeted involuntarily.

"*Ssh!* Telegraph, probably. Bloody news travels faster than we do. Now, read this. Quietly."

Escape, said the paper, was "with the aid of two abolitionists seen prowling about the city for several days previous. They were seen spending time at the residence of Ruth Gardiner of Walnut St.; Mrs. Gardiner, a widow, admitted in a statement to the police to involuntary complicity in the crime, for the abolitionists, masquerading as friends of her late husband, were armed and made threats upon her life if she failed to cooperate. She expressed belief that the two abolitionists were from New York and that they were bound in that direction.

"Because of her failure to report the matter to the police, Mrs. Gardiner was charged with obstruction of justice, but because of the duress she has been under for the last several days, the charge has been withdrawn and she has instead been given a judicial warning."

The names of the slaves were listed, a bounty of $300 attached to each. For each of the shadowy, sinister, and dangerous abolitionists, the reward was $1200. Alex had to know why I laughed.

"You and me dangerous! This is preposterous!"

"James, for the love of God, try to temper your exuberance. You are like a puppy sometimes. This is serious. Much as I dislike trains, I'd rather stay on this one and not end up in some local dungeon. Isn't this ridiculous, being worth four times as much as a black man! Look, these descriptions are a bit too good for my sense of comfort. We cannot be seen together. At the next station, I want you to pretend to get off and as judiciously as you can, get on another coach. Here's some money in case you have to get another ticket. When we get to Memphis, go to the Hotel Peabody and I'll contact you there."

I did as bidden and was miserable indeed for the balance of the journey. My brief mirth at being thought dangerous gave way to a silent desperation; should Mrs. Gardiner have gone to jail, we would have felt a moral responsibility, yet without the power to help, unless we were willing to jeopardize future operations. To help one person at the expense of countless others? Unthinkable!

I commented on my thoughts a couple of days later and the all-wise Alex, never at a loss to clarify matters, said to me, " James, these are the times to follow the teachings of a great English thinker, Jeremy Bentham. He was an economist and his formula for a successful society was based on what he called 'Utilitarianism', or the idea of the greatest good for the greatest number of people. So it follows that a few must suffer for the advancement of many, and all I can do is thank God things did not go any worse for Mrs. Gardiner. I too would have felt dreadful in the extreme if something had happened to her, but I know she would have born it. I detected something of the Promethean in her..."

At journey's end, we went our separate ways at Memphis Central Station without so much as a nod to each other, myself to the hotel and Alex to the home of John Jordan, the local Underground Railroad "ticket agent". I had a wretchedly bad sleep, all efforts thwarted by a combination of agitation, the hot, stuffy night, and the shrieks and hollers of the local chivalry exiting from the hotel bar until all hours. I finally dozed into a stupor, to be awakened much later when the sun was embarrassingly high and my window curtains were softly billowing in a torrid summer breeze.

Something had awakened me - I could not be certain - but there it was again, a quiet tap on the door. "James!" hissed a voice. "Open up!"

I let Alex in. "We have to leave," he said abruptly. "Those newspaper stories are all over the place and someone has done sketches of us, based on descriptions by Mrs. Gardiner's neighbours. I had a *feeling* that the whole thing just went too smoothly. The sketch of you is pretty awful. In fact, knowing you, you'll probably laugh. But the one of me, dear God, it's like looking in a mirror. Really eerie...we have to change our appearances as much as we can and stay apart. I'm going back to John Jordan's to shave off my beard..."

"So what do I do? I have no beard."

"Then grow one, oh, dash it all, James, use your imagination. Do something, anything. One thing is for sure, we can't stay here. I've looked at the steamer schedule and there's one sailing for St. Louis at 9:00 tonight. I want you to check out of the hotel as unobtrusively as you can and leave your bag at a Wells Fargo office or some place...look for me at the steamer wharf about 8:30. Our ship will be the *General Jackson.* By the by, how is your money supply?"

"Terrible."

"Have more. This will do you for a bit. Sorry if I got a bit snappish. This whole thing is starting to pile in on me. I'm not used to being a hunted man. See you at 8:30...look for a denuded Alex."

I checked out of the hotel as soon as I was dressed and, after leaving my bag for the day at a Wells Fargo agency, I repaired to a restaurant for a late breakfast. Curious to see what we looked like in a newspaper, I bought a copy of the Memphis *Commercial Appeal* and immediately wished I hadn't. I had felt some amusement earlier, but the reality of seeing our graven images on the front page almost made me lose my appetite. Commercially appealing the spectacle was not.

As Alex had remarked, my likeness was indeed approximate, and to make it more so, I immediately removed my spectacles. As a result, my judgement of depth and distance was completely distorted and my poor effort at disguise probably attracted more attention through the mess I made at the table. I had long since given up on American tea and had substituted coffee, which required inordinate amounts of sugar to make it drinkable, and most of the sugar ended up on the table-top. And my ham likewise refused to cooperate. I finished my slovenly repast at about eleven o'clock and left the restaurant to begin my long, fearful vigil in Memphis.

I went to the station for a while to watch the trains, a frustrating business without my glasses. I looked for a museum, but could find none. I did find quite a fine little art gallery out at Overton Park and browsed through a travelling exhibit of new American art. One work that I particularly liked was a canvas by one George Caleb Bingham of fur traders on the Missouri River and I squinted at it wistfully, envying the traders what I imagined to be a tranquil existence, although the reality was likely pretty brutal.

I then retreated to the cool sanctuary of the public library and tried, with only moderate success without my glasses, to read the previous six issues of *Harper's Weekly*. But the presence of the local papers made me so uncomfortable that every time someone went to the desk to check out a book, I was certain I was being reported.

I left the library and on an impulse visited a barber to further alter my outward appearance. He was extremely chatty, as barbers generally are. I was forced to agree with him about the disgraceful number of nigras being helped to escape from their rightful lot. Yes, sir, it was downright scandalous. Them abolitionists were nothing more than thieves and oughta be horse-whipped.

I strolled the streets and looked in every shop window. Though I had no appetite, I felt it must be close on to dinner time, but I could not be sure, since my watch had developed problems over the last couple of days. To my disgust, the clock on a nearby Methodist church said only 2:25. Oh, no, it *had* to be later, but the Presbyterian church across the street verified the hour.

I ate anyway for something to do and immediately wished I hadn't, for growing fear, boredom, and food combined very badly indeed. Striving to suppress my indigestion, I belched my way back to Overton Park where, thank the Lord, there was to be a concert by the cornet band of the United States Army Corps of Engineers, Memphis District. My sundry noises were blotted out by brassy renditions of several marches, *Listen to the Mocking Bird,* some of the haunting airs of Stephen Collins Foster, and a rousing finale which the audience knew well and sang lustily. The tune was called *Dixie.*

Now it was 4:30, four hours until I should meet Alex. I returned to the station to see what was happening, which was not much. I took a walk by the Mississippi, whose waterfront, locally known as Mud Island, was a busy place indeed. No fewer than four steamers were passing through, three up-bound with bales of cotton stacked on their lower decks, and one down-bound, carrying a doleful contingent of slaves in chains and leg-irons. Whereas I had for hours been wandering about in a state bordering on self-pity, thinking fondly of Belleville and perhaps a decent cup of tea made for me by my mother (how I wanted someone to take care of me!), I now felt my entire system tighten with fury.

Where were they bound? Louisiana? Mississippi? There they were, but yards from where I stood, the river's current eddying between the steamer and the wharf, and I could do nothing, nothing at all. I turned and walked away, trying not to let my helpless rage register too obviously. I had to be mindful of my visage having gazed all day upon the general public from the front page of the Memphis *Commercial Appeal.*

I walked back into town, spent some time at a bookseller's, and then went for a legitimate dinner, or was about to, when I recalled that my bag must be collected before six o'clock or it would be lost and gone forever. I ransomed it from a singularly surly clerk whose main ambition in life seemed to be to close up and go home.

Then I went for a truly pyrotechnic dinner of fried pig with Louisiana hot sauce. My system fulminated once more and I had to retire to a nearby park to let it boil off in flares and surges of hot flushes. For a few minutes, I felt almost too faint and feverish to care any more, and the thought crossed my mind that I had been recognized and poisoned for my complicity in rending the fabric of the American way of life. But gradually the discomfort passed as I watched some little birds pecking away at the ground by a statue of Davy Crockett.

I decided to stroll back down to the steamer wharf, which would not cut down the time I had to wait, but the surroundings would certainly be a diversion from the constant, sick fear of being caught. I doubted how much more of this I could sustain and had never been so anxious to be elsewhere. It was a pity, as Memphis is quite nice and I hope to see it again under more relaxed circumstances.

On my walk back to the river, I meditated on steamers as being a form of floating locomotive and therefore something meriting close attention, but the idea of any revellings in mechanical things vanished before the sight awaiting me. A wagon had just pulled into the loading area, bearing half-a-dozen slaves in shackles, singing about the River Jordan with an eloquence that brought a lump to my throat.

A man in a cream-coloured suit strode back and forth nearby in propri-etary fashion. A man alone as I was is a man of suspicious intent, so, on an impulse, I wandered over to him and remarked, "They don't seem too happy, do they?"

"No, sir, they don't, though all this Jesus music'll make a good impression on their new owners. Sold 'em to a coupla planters down Vicksburg way...yes, sir, Ah allus say religion's a valliable thang in a nigra."

"I'd drink to that if I had anything to drink," I said amiably. "Sustains them through difficult times, I guess." Oh, Lord, cut out my tongue!

The man's eyes narrowed speculatively. "Where yew from, stranger?"

My mind seized like a dry bearing; I had no lie at the ready, so all I could do was blurt the truth: "Canada." The spectre of being doomed to spend the rest of my life in some dismal Memphis dungeon loomed before me.

"That a fact, huh? What do yew folks in Canada think of slavery?" It was not so much a question as a challenge, but in my relief at being spared the local *gendarmerie*, at least for the time being, I was ready for it.

"We don't have any now...outlawed in '33. Fact is, some of your slaves have escaped and come up our way, and not too welcome, 'spite of what you read in the papers. Only good nigger" (I almost choked on the word) "is one you own, you know, like you would a horse...on a farm, you know...treat them right and they'll do the work."

My new acquaintance was extremely red of face and smelled of bourbon. He appeared to have a tumour in the left side of his jaw, a tumour that I hoped might be the sort that would kill him.

"Glad to hear y'all say that, fella," was his response. "We've had jest a few too many of these here now busybodies from the North..."

"Like that business in Nashville a day or so ago," I said helpfully. "Did you hear about it?"

"A disgrace, an absolute disgrace..."

"If I lived here," I pursued, "I'd probably own slaves too. What the hell, they never evolved or built any sort of great civilization. So we get them to work for us and it's all perfectly humane if we go about it the right way." I shrugged with expert nonchalance. "Keep them happy enough to work for you, but not give them all sorts of expectations. What I mean is, if they have no expectations to be violated, there's no harm done. Besides, God created a divine order" (if only Alex were around at that moment!). "Some rule, others are ruled...to everything there is a season..."

The man's tumour migrated to the other side of his mouth and he spat a gob of brown muck onto the ground. It shivered gelatinously in the dust. "Way-all, yew are sure enough a man of clear thought, migawd, them hymns are gettin' to be a bit much! Oh, way-all, Ah'll be shut of this lot soon enough. Ain't nothin' anyway compared to the clamour they'll set up at Vicksburg."

"Why's that?"

"Sold half the family to one plantation and half to another. They don't know it yet, neither. Slaves can be powerful queer cattle when it comes to family. Tried to sell 'em in one lot, but most folks don't need six new slaves all at once. So one gets Dad and two kids and t'other gets Mom an' t'other two kids. Here comes the boat now. Nice talkin' to y'all."

At once sickened by my masquerade and hardly able to credit still being at large, I watched the incoming steamer come wallowing ponderously up to the landing with much threshing and surging of paddle wheels. The lines were secured, the gangway swung ashore from a hoist at the bow, and the hapless slave family was marched aboard, shackles clanking. They passed right by me, almost close enough to touch, and I could not help but notice that the ankles of one of the children, a girl, were chafed raw by the leg irons, the injury lividly pink against her black skin. She seemed too miserable to care and shuffled past, eyes to the ground, a portrait of apathy and debasement. I felt literally sick at what I had said to the slave-owner on the wharf, necessary as it may have been for deception. What made me feel even worse was the fleeting thrill I had felt at my powers of invention.

A short time later, Alex came through the thickening crowd at the landing. He was, at least to me, completely recognizable even without the beard, and in that connection, he would have been wiser to leave it on. The sun had darkened him; where the beard had been was dead white, making him look like a poorly made-up minstrel.

He had a negro with him. This was not in the plan. I opened my mouth to ask what was going on. Without looking at me, Alex hissed through his teeth, "Stay away from me. I'll explain later."

Puzzled, but relieved as well that Alex too was still at large, I wandered over to the water's edge and watched the sun sinking low over the Mississippi River downstream of Mud Island, streaking its sullen surface with gold and copper and silhouetting a couple of fishermen in a small boat.

An eruption of conversation behind me filled me with sudden panic - had somebody recognized Alex? I turned to see what was happening, my poor, overcharged heart working up to a furious pace. I nearly groaned aloud with relief, for we were still anonymous; what had created the furor was the arrival of a telegram from Germantown, the next landing down the river, to say that the *General Jackson* was two hours off schedule and would not be at Memphis until eleven in the evening. There were assorted moans and protests from passengers waiting to embark and cotton dealers and freight agents waiting to accept their cargo. And for me and Alex, it meant two additional hours, drawing the whole Memphis experience out to a cruel fineness, although the onset of dusk was putting into recession the likelihood of the Memphis *Commercial Appeal* bearing fruit for any bounty hunters. My dominant emotion was now curiosity over Alex's companion. Surprise I did not feel, for Alex's surprises had become too commonplace for that.

Finally, *finally*, we were aboard the *General Jackson* and quit of Memphis, its lights fading in the undulating paddle wash astern. As the passengers sorted themselves out, Alex came to me with an account of his own activities and of the presence of his mysterious black friend.

"Thank the Lord *that's* over," he said with a trace of breathlessness. "A bit hard on the nerves, wouldn't you say? Well, now to get caught up. After

I saw you at the hotel, I went back to John Jordan's...pity you didn't have a chance to meet him...right in the middle of shaving, I overheard crying and weeping, and I knew immediately it was a negro, something, well, *dark* about the voice, if that makes sense. I finished off my beard - and isn't it a sight? - and went downstairs forthwith to see what was happening.

"Mrs. Jordan was talking to one of John's, uh, clients, a mulatto lady of thirty-five or so, begging to be allowed to go to Canada with us. She was in tears because Mrs. Jordan had told her we were wanted men and could not be exposed to any more danger, but the woman still begged. Besides, she was pretty."

"Aha!"

"Young swine. But, good God, James, you should have seen her back, all gashed and gouged from numerous whippings, the sort of treatment we have been hearing about, and I knew I had to bring her along. I am not a violent man, which you must know, but I wouldn't have minded a session with her erstwhile owner...kick him so high he'd be picking the Milky Way out of his ears." Alex looked momentarily astonished at what he had said.

"Many of the scars are so bad they'll never heal properly. And as if the tales weren't bad enough to start with, her husband had escaped to Canada two years ago and her owner tried to get her to marry another slave."

"But she wasn't widowed or divorced!" I nearly quacked with indignation.

"Sh! But, James, this is a free country. You have the freedom to do with your slaves whatever you want. You know, I almost want to weep when I hear the *Star-Spangled Banner*. So majestic, so expressive of all that is fine in man, and the practice of slavery makes a total mockery of it. God Almighty, the hypocrisy of this place!"

"Alex, you're getting too loud."

"I beg your pardon. Not very intelligent of me. Well, there I was, my picture in the newspaper, you heaven knew where...how was *your* day, by the way?"

"Pretty hideous. I'll save it for later."

"As you wish. And now I had a half-hysterical escaped slave on my hands as well. She too was wanted, therefore I had no choice but to bring her along. So, in summation, that is who my companion is."

"Forgive me for sounding stupid, Alex, but I thought it was a man."

"She is being represented as my valet under the name of Sam. Look, I'm all done in. That's all I can tell you until I get some sleep. I'm sorry, but there just isn't enough money for a cabin. We're going to have to shift for ourselves and find some nice comfortable cotton bales to sleep on. I'd even settle for some boll weevils to keep us company. Let's get horizontal for a bit; I feel like the walking dead."

Chapter Eight

After all the time we had spent in the South and after all we had experienced, it was reassuring beyond words, despite the distance that lay ahead of us, to be bound north. Although our route would soon take us out of slave-owning territory, there was still the Fugitive Slave Law to be considered, so for the entire voyage, Alex and I stayed apart and Sam remained in her dubious disguise, occasional *rendezvous* taking place only in the dining room, where it was quite normal for strangers to share a table.

Northward the *General Jackson* plodded, her paddle-wheels flailing the river with a rhythmic concussive thud. Although it may not be particularly germane to my account, I have to take a few lines to describe this remarkable vessel, for she was unlike anything we are accustomed to in Canada. Besides, steamships to me had become almost as fascinating as trains, so perhaps I may be forgiven my indulgence.

The *General Jackson*, like her sisters plying the Mississippi, looked from a distance like a floating steam-tram. Her hull was extremely low, far too low for, say, Lake Ontario, but quite ample for river service, and above it towered three additional decks, the uppermost of which was called the Texas deck. The wheelhouse was a riot of carving and other decoration, looking much like a garden gazebo.

And the current mania for baroque decoration extended even to such utilitarian fitments as the funnels, placed side by each ahead of the wheelhouse; their tops were so ornate as to remind one of tulips opening in the morning. Aft on the Texas deck were two more funnels, actually no more than thin tubes, called the 'scape pipes to exhaust steam from the engine. To complete this fascinating jumble was a veritable forest of upright posts (spars in the vernacular) and cables, whose tension could be adjusted if the vessel's flexible wooden hull started to sag, a process something like tuning a huge cello.

I had ample time to absorb and study all these details, for the trip was of four nights' and three days' duration. The distance, as far as I can determine, was about three hundred and fifty miles, with calls at Carruthersville, New Madrid, Cairo, Cape Girardeau, Chelsea, and Festus. At the smaller communities, there was no formal wharf and the ship was simply grounded and held in place either by lines to shoreside trees or by the paddles running slow ahead, while business was conducted via the outsize gangway that had to be slung ashore by a crane.

The nights on board were a misery. Even though it was now summer, the nights remained so cold and dank on the river that we awoke each morning, if indeed we could sleep, feeling rheumatic and mildewed. It was a pity, in a way, as if the nights had been more temperate, it would have been quite pleasant lying there, savouring the slightly fishy tang of the river and feeling the cotton bales gently pulsating with the *General Jackson*'s great steamy heartbeat. To compound the discomfort, sleep was oftentimes interrupted during a nocturnal stop when the bales of cotton that made our bed were to be unloaded.

So the three of us were a jolly crew when we disembarked at St. Louis. From there, we took the Chicago, Alton, and St. Louis Railroad to Chicago, with myself in the locomotive cab, now a matter of fiscal necessity; and after a couple of days of rest in the comparative sanctuary of Chicago, we carried onward to Detroit.

Alex's network of friends, acquaintances, colleagues, and accomplices continued to astound me. At Detroit, or I should say in the nearby village of Dearborn, we stayed with an old friend of Alex's, John Pilkington. He was a bit older than ourselves, I would say late forties or early fifties, completely bald and with an almost white moustache. And he was one of those rare but reassuring people that on instinct you know that you can trust absolutely with any situation. I cannot recall what he did for a living, but he was quite well-to-do and able to indulge an evident taste for books and works of art.

With all these comforts, he did not have, on the surface, the crusading fire of the abolitionist, but he wasted no time in saying to me and Sam, "Life has been very good to me, very good indeed, and abolition is my way of doing something in return."

On hearing of our flight from the law and the news coverage thereof, John laughed and said (with Sam temporarily out of earshot), "I would wager those newspapers were just having journalistic ecstasies over what you did! We need to celebrate. I have some cognac here" (I recall it as being 1818) "to fit the occasion.

"Now, Sam" (who was back in earshot), "we need to talk about the final stage of your journey to freedom. I don't want to alarm you, but this will be the hardest part of all. The whole district along the Detroit River is full of government agents enforcing the Fugitive Slave Law, all trying to outdo each other, and the Byzantine intrigue that goes on is unbelievable. They have boats on the river, too, and they'll think nothing of nabbing you, even when you're officially and beyond a doubt across the international boundary. You're not truly safe until you have actually landed on the Canadian side. We had a case just two weeks ago, an entire family that had walked all the way from Louisiana...they could practically see into the kitchen windows over in Windsor and in the twinkling of an eye it was all over."

Sam began to weep and John patted her arm. "I'm sorry, my dear, I didn't mean to frighten you, but these are the realities to be faced. Naturally, all crossings of the river are at night, and one problem we have had is that traffic got so heavy that our own boats were banging into each other and getting confused. It has been less than fun. So we have had to work out a rotation and our turn will be Thursday night. We have had a boat built especially for this, never been caught, and she's manned by four lads who are the very best. We call them the Four Oarsmen of the Apocalypse."

So on Thursday night at about two in the morning, we made our way to the Detroit River with Sam and two other escaped slaves being aided by John's organization. The Four Oarsmen were on hand, sweeps at the ready, the boat's stern to the shore for a quick getaway. Out in the murk, someone would be watching for us.

"In you go, now,""whispered John. "God go with you. Good luck."

I had wondered how the Four Oarsmen would manage the requisite speed with such a load. I need not have worried. "Give way," whispered the First Oarsman, and with a mighty heave that toppled two of the blacks off their seat, the boat scraped free of the foreshore and began her desperate dash across the river, a few scattered lights revealing the slumbering community of Windsor. Canada! Home!

A lantern flickered in the blackness almost dead ahead. "Who goes there?" barked a voice. "Show yourself!"

"Shit!" I muttered, going stone cold.

"Sweet Baby Jesus," lamented one of the negroes.

"Evening, Harry!" hailed our coxswain without breaking stroke.

"I am an agent of the United States Government! I order you to stop!"

"Can't, Harry. We be in one big hurry, right, boys?"

"*Right!*" chorused the other Three Oarsmen.

"Now, PULL!"

I too was nearly toppled from my seat by the acceleration as the Four Oarsmen gave the vessel everything they had, which was considerable. The boat rocketed forward, leaving the unfortunate Harry and his crew wallowing in helpless confusion.

We quite literally hit Canada's shore; Sam and her compatriots were helped to the pebbly beach and up to high water mark, where they fell to their knees, running their hands over the earth and giving thanks for their deliverance. I recall few moments of my life quite as emotional as that one and I have no difficulty admitting, even in our reticent Victorian Age, when it is considered unmanly to cry, that I did just that. It would indeed have been a cold heart who couldn't.

A shadow emerged from the nearby grove of trees. "Welcome, welcome! I miscalculated where the current would put you."

"Blame Harry. He made us change course," explained one of the Oarsmen.

"Where are our escapees? Oh, there you are. Not to be flippant, but I couldn't see you in the dark. Is there a Sam among you?"

"Me, massa."

"Sam, there are no massas here. You can forget the word entirely. I am happy to tell you we have located your husband. He has a job in a barbershop in London. If you can stay awake and get used to travelling in daylight, we can have you back together by tomorrow."

"Praise de Lawd! Hallelujah!"

"And a big welcome to the other...two, is it?...of you. We're not perfect here, but you won't have to live looking over your shoulders now. Big change for you, eh?"

I had always thought the expression "eh?" a bit uncouth, but now it was a sweet sound, the sound of home. All I could think of now was home, of Belleville, of my family, of our garden, of afternoon tea on the front veranda. But the next few seconds would change everything.

"Is there an Alexander Ross here?" inquired our "agent".

"That would be me."

"I have been holding some money for you. And a telegram. It was sent to Belleville and your wife forwarded it." A lantern was lit and Alex crouched down to read the message:

URGENT I MEET YOU EAGLE HOTEL
CLEVELAND FRIDAY SEPTEMBER 2 END MESSAGE
/S/ JOHN BROWN

"John Brown, eh?" said our one-man welcoming committee. "I think I'm going to be impressed

I could almost smell what was coming, but as a formality I asked, "Who is this John Brown?"

"If anybody is going to get some abolishing done, it'll be this fellow," explained Alex. "Well, back I go. James, I'll need you to come too."

"What about Hester?", a self-serving question if ever was. I had been away for five months and I wanted to go home! "Besides," I tried, "I had counted on seeing my family. I do have one."

"But so many people need us and you need to be doing this. I could hear you a few moments ago in the dark, so don't try to fool me. John Brown may be the greatest of all...come with me to Cleveland and meet him, just that much, James, *then* we can go home. I wonder why he wants to see me. Look, James, you *must* come! This is a man who is going to leave his mark on humanity."

JOHN BROWN, AT ABOUT THE TIME OF MEETING
WITH JAMES RANSAY AND ALEXANDER ROSS

Chapter Nine

"Reason has been to no avail," pronounced John Brown. "The situation is as dark as the night you see out there, a tumour on the face of humanity. And what do you do with a tumour? Why, you remove it and you do it with a knife. Much as the means may offend us, I think that is what we are going to have to do."

"Is this a war you are suggesting, Mr. Brown?" I asked quietly. "It was my understanding that violence was not on the agenda of the Abolitionist organization."

"Well, yes and no, young man." (Alex was "Dr. Ross" and I, but three years his junior, was "young man" and it galled me). "It is true that this, ah, *action* would be against other Americans, but you must remember that this is not an issue between America and a foreign enemy, but between right and wrong. If it takes some form of civil war to do what we must, then so be it." He turned towards us, away from the black hotel window, an almost Biblical sorrow in his face.

"We cannot turn our backs to the matter of slavery. We must deal with it totally, no matter what it takes. As a military officer with the rank of captain, even if not officially commissioned as such in the eyes of the law, I have examined the situation and concluded that our best, perhaps only, chance is to incite a negro insurrection in a slave state. Virginia might be a likely choice because of its proximity to Washington, make it seem immediate to the government, make them more disposed to abolish the laws, such as they are, pertaining to slavery."

"Hold the country to ransom, in other words," I said with an abruptness that startled me. It startled Alex as well.

"In effect, yes, if you want to put it that way. Granted, young man, it may be a, well, *evil* way of going about it, but I think it is justified in light of the far greater evil we are fighting. What I have in mind is a variation of guerrilla warfare, like what General Garibaldi has been practising in Italy." At the mention of his hero, Alex sat bolt upright.

"I know, Dr. Ross, that you have had personal acquaintance with the General. We need someone like that here in America, to put a stop to this monstrosity once and for all. It could be me, maybe somebody else, but I don't know of anyone else prepared to take the initiative."

There was such a quality of unreality to this conversation that I could not feel fear, exactly; rather, my feeling was one of Monumental Discomfort, the same as before an oral examination at university, a "please, God, let me out of here" feeling. Evidently it did not register on the good soldier, who plunged onward:

"...fought by small groups of people who depend on the element of surprise and vanish as suddenly as they appeared, more of a harassment or intimidation tactic than anything.

"The pressing issue at the moment is to arm and train negroes to make the first strike, to teach their masters that they are a force to be reckoned with and not merely human cattle. Operations will be carried out by such small and mobile groups that it will be almost impossible for the authorities to anticipate what will happen and when, and likely raw fear will have the desired effect on the general populace before long.

"But without money, gentlemen, we are nowhere. We have to be properly equipped before anything is done. I have just been to the eastern states trying to collect funds, and, frankly, it has been most disappointing. With a few exceptions, the general attitude has been, 'We'll give you money when we start seeing results.' Well, God above, any fool knows we cannot get results until we have some money. All I can say is a lot of folks have a very muddled concept of cause and effect. But it is at least partly our own fault. There have been too many abolitionists in name only who are all talk and no action, many of whom have never even ventured south of the Mason-Dixon Line. Better that they should keep their mouths shut and let us...well, we are the professionals, aren't we?...let us get on with it."

"Professional, hmm?" mused Alex. "You flatter us, Captain Brown."

"Let me show you something, Dr. Ross, young man..." John Brown dug into a small black bag he had brought to our hotel room and pulled out a gun identical to Alex's. "Look familiar?"

"Very. Same source?"

"Charles Sumner. He thinks very highly of you, which is how your name came to my attention. Why, you're the most humanitarian of all of us. This isn't even happening in your country, you don't have to be here, but you have the greater vision of this being a conflict within the family of Man. Your motives are nothing short of Godly. And although I didn't know of you before tonight, young man, I suspect the same could be said of you." I nodded mutely under the glacial stare of this improbable and majestically slovenly Messiah.

"There are others besides ourselves from Canada," said Alex. "We're not the only ones. A former governor of ours, Sir Peregrine Maitland, actually created a township for escaped slaves, Oro, it's called, and, well, whatever I have done would have been far more difficult without James here." Alex patted my forearm in avuncular fashion.

"There is no question that the young man is vital to our work," said John Brown. "Good, very good to have you with us. Now, I am familiar with Dr. Ross's background, but what is yours, young man?"

"I am a civil engineer on leave of absence from the Grand Trunk Railway."

"James is our expert on rail transportation," explained Alex. Mercifully no mention was made of my work with explosives, but the mercy was short-lived.

"Ah, most useful. We contemplate making great use of the railroads, and if we were to get this insurrection under way, young man, perhaps you could command a sabotage team. Being an engineer, you would know what to blow up and how to do it..."

My Monumental Discomfort turned to stark fear. "Not on your life!" I exclaimed in a voice that verged on a squeal.

"Just an idea. Have to explore them all, you know." To my almost hysterical relief, John Brown veered back to the subject of money, thanks to Alex, who produced the envelope he had carried from Windsor.

"I don't know how much is in here," he said, "but maybe it will be of some help." He handed it to John Brown, who opened it, spreading out the bills on a bedside table.

"Most encouraging," said the Captain. "In one envelope is almost as much as what it took me a month to collect. This brightens matters considerably."

"I hope I don't dampen things, then," I said, "if I go on record to say I don't want to get mixed up in a war. I have my limitations. But what I *can* tell you is that I am prepared to render all aid short of actual warfare, and I think you can thank Dr. Ross for that. He has shown me there is much more to sympathy for the slaves than merely feeling sorry for them or using sympathy as a salve for your own conscience."

Captain Brown returned to the window, leaning his elbow on the top of the lower sash. He looked out into the night, speaking with his back to us. "This is how it is with most people, and it's a real human tragedy, a state of paralysis, an inability to translate feelings into action. In the so-called Northern states, oh, yes, slavery is outlawed and there is a sympathy of sorts toward the slaves in the South, a pulpy sort of sympathy, if you see my meaning. The general public perceives blacks as a degraded race, but with an immortal soul that God will take care of in the afterlife, so it really doesn't matter what happens here on Earth. There's some kind of Roman Catholic...pardon me, I hope I didn't tread on anyone's religious sensibilities. It's like a poem I read not long ago, how life is merely a series of preludes to a great and eternal afterlife..."

"Alphonse de Lamartine. *Les Préludes*," said Alex with lazy self-assurance. Was there anything the man did not know, any perfectly-timed remark he could not make?

"Right you are," commended John Brown. "I admire your taste. Well, that's all very wonderful, I suppose, but the Lord did give us life and we owe it to Him to make everything we can of it, both for ourselves and others. It certainly doesn't extend to exploiting others to make our own lives easier. Our Northern whites just keep their distance; they wouldn't want blacks abused, yet don't want anything to do with them directly, but they continue to call this country a democracy. Democracy is not just about freedom, it is about responsibility as well.

"When you come right down to it, the only *true* democrats are the children. If children, in all their innocence and lack of cynicism, were running the country, we probably wouldn't have this situation. Mind you, children can do some pretty awful things too, and I know...have twenty of them in various shapes and sizes..."

"Did you really say *twenty*?"

"Yes, sir, and I love 'em all, the beggars. Well, lost one, but I don't want to talk about it. When children are awful, there's a certain honesty about it that's a lot easier to stomach than cloaking one's self in scriptural self-righteousness. The Bible, and I make no secret of my reverence for that book, carry it with me night and day...the Bible teaches love above all else, and yet so many folks don't recognize from it our duty to love negroes as much as anyone else and on the same terms."

"To what extent?" I challenged. Alex looked taken aback at my apparent brazenness.

"Well, young man, I would venture to say that to treat them...just what did you have in mind?"

"God did intend some sort of difference, or we would all be the same colour."

"Adaptation to their natural habitat." The encyclopaedic part of Alex was on the boil. "The black is from melanin in the skin to protect it from damage in a tropical climate. They don't get fried in the sun as we do. And now they are no longer in the natural habitat, courtesy of the white race. But we can't very well send them all back to Africa, although that has been suggested at home."

"Here as well," said John Brown. "Carry on, young man."

"There must be some harmonious way to live with negroes, although I don't have enough experience to make any really valid comment," I said. "But I really think there would be a limitation where marriage is concerned. There is a question of whether a black-and-white baby would belong to both races or neither."

"Those mixed-race people in Nashville were considered black," reminded Alex.

"I suppose in that light *any* black is all black," observed John Brown. "Your mention of Africa, Dr. Ross, has inspired a most interesting hypothesis. Have you read *Uncle Tom*?"

"Who, by this time, hasn't? I think I know what you have in mind, that part about Africa awakening and pointing the way for other civilizations. I think that was how it went."

I too was awakening. Although only a meagre historian, I observed, "When you consider all the previous great civilizations and how they collapsed because of internal decadence, you can see the seeds already planted for us. Slavery has to be the greatest decadence of all."

"Bravo, young man," applauded Captain Brown. "It *has* to be eliminated if America is to prosper, indeed survive. Of course, the current great civilization is your British Empire, which seems to be doing very well despite certain excesses..."

"Like buying Southern cotton,"I interjected. I was becoming almost as good at that as Alex.

"...a certain sign of decadence, but then there are always blemishes in any great enterprise, and none of them are anywhere nearly as depraved as slavery. At least in the British Empire, slavery is no longer legal, although there is still far more human exploitation than I can live with. But we really cannot clean up the whole world, can we?"

"Sounds as if you're trying a really respectable start at it," said Alex.

"Kind of you, Dr. Ross, most kind. I would like to think that we can return America to her rightful place as a haven for the oppressed, that perhaps, while this century is Britain's, the next may be America's, a new age free of exploitation of any kind. But it will not happen unless our job is done quickly, done completely, and done now."

Captain Brown sat down for the first time that evening, and it had been a long one, for it was now approaching three in the morning. Despite the charged atmosphere, we had to speak quietly to avoid disturbing the slumbers of the other guests, especially any that in retribution might feel bound to invoke the Fugitive Slave Law.

Although a self-designated military officer in command of the shadowy United States Provisional Army, John Brown looked more like a farmer or a western homesteader: wiry, leathery, wrinkles fanning outward from his eyes from squinting at the far horizons of the western plains. The eyes themselves were deep-set and so filled with compassion that I was reminded of that great Biblical description of Jesus as "a man of sorrows and acquainted with grief", a grief that he had come by honestly, for already in fighting for our cause in far-away Kansas, he had lost a son, the child he could not talk about. And to complete his scriptural bearing, this extraordinary face, which I shall never forget, was couched in a bushy white beard.

Despite the difficulties John Brown had endured with shortage of money and a general lack of public support, it was plain to us that he would never let go of his idea, even in the face of the odds against him. To touch off an uprising, before the cause was thoroughly appreciated by the public, seemed too reckless and ill-conceived, especially since at this time Brown had at his disposal only a tiny force, a couple of dozen who were at the moment still in Kansas.

"Gentlemen, it's late and I must be on my way. I am sorry to have kept you up until such an hour,' apologized Brown, picking up his boots. "I will maintain contact with you, although it may be some time before you hear from me."

"That's fine, no need to rush," said Alex and I sincerely and more or less in unison. Personally, I hoped never to see the man again.

As the door closed, Alex and I stared at each other for a moment, and then Alex said tightly, "I don't like this, not one bit. I'm sorry to have dragged you here, James. I think it was a mistake."

"Don't worry about that, Alex; how could you have known? I don't like it either. The man terrifies me. But the awful part is that he may have the answer. I wonder if there is indeed any other way to wipe out slavery."

"By evolutionary means rather than revolutionary. Takes longer, but it works better in the long run. Doing what we are doing, we are just giving evolution some gentle persuasion...look, James, evolution is the secret of the success of the British Empire. Look at the French for contrast. Since their own revolution, the place has been a mess, the Reign of Terror, Napoleon, another Empire, just one crisis after another."

"How about America? It too was born in revolution."

"And with the carbuncle of slavery on its face, it's a mess too, but apparently doesn't realize it, except for people like Gerrit Smith. I'd be very interested to know what *he* thinks about John Brown's crazy idea. The best way to handle this, you know, would be to annex the United States and run it as a British colony with British laws and you and me in charge."

"You can run it. I'll be Minister of Transport. Oh, to get my hands on all those trains..."

"You should also be Minister of Racial Relations."

"What? I never heard of such a thing."

"As Governor, I would create a new portfolio. Let's get to sleep. And, James."

"Eh?"

"God be with you."

"Oh, er, you too, Alex. See you in the morning."

CHAPTER TEN

My repeatedly frustrated goal of getting home to Belleville was finally realised as the autumn of 1857 settled in a warm golden haze over the hills and woodlands of Canada West and the mornings crystallized the landscape in frosty confection. After a spring and summer of continual activity, I was finally able to step back and have a good objective look at the Abolitionist movement. To my pleased surprise, public awareness of it had increased sharply over the intervening months; it was, in some aspect or another, in the newspapers constantly. Cutting out the pertinent articles became a daily ritual, usually with Father in attendance, and these I have saved; I have them by me as I write, though they are now yellow and fragile as the late leaves of autumn.

We Abolitionists were, according to a large number of reports, a regularly-organized group, and I can recall Alex remarking "Would that we were," for in reality we were individual groups grown out of our collective conscience (Alex had given me mine) and initiative (Alex had given me that as well). Any sort of concerted action was largely due to chance.

In the journals emanating from the Southern states, all manner of unsettling editorials passed our way; one that I quote now, from the *Mercury* in Charleston, South Carolina (and I have more to say about the *Mercury* later in my tale), urged large monetary rewards for the apprehension of "those accursed thieves". Furthermore, thundered the *Mercury*, a severe public example should be made of those who were caught. The learned editor was not specific about the actual nature of the proposed punishment, but the vitriolic character of his writing did not invite further curiosity.

After our episode with John Brown in Cleveland, Alex and I decided mutually to suspend activities for a time, reorganize ourselves, and try to raise some money. While we took what we called our sabbatical, operations continued reasonably well in such states as Kentucky and Tennessee, where a certain cohesion was developing among John Jordan, Ruth Gardiner, and others of their ilk. But the greatest challenge still lay in the Deep South, the cotton states, where our liaisons were still extremely limited and any travelling abolitionists were almost completely alone in a country where ownership of slaves was a right comparable to having fresh air and clean water.

To better apprise himself of current developments, Alex made a short visit (despite vehement protests from Hester) to Philadelphia to consult with Gerrit Smith and five other associates of John Brown, an aggregation later to be known collectively as the Secret Six. Through casual inquiries of cotton dealers and shipping agents, they had been able to compile some valuable demography of the slave population in the cotton-growing states, enabling us to do the work more systematically when the time should come. Of this region, John Brown had remarked, "Why nibble at the edges when you can go for the heart?"

Alex, of course, wanted me to go with him. I said a flat "no", electing instead to spend some time with my family and, not incidentally, to raise some funds, of which we were ludicrously short. My father subscribed a generous sum, as did some of his associates in the legal field, and I was asked to speak at three different church services, where special collections were taken. The 1857 harvest, as it happened, was a particularly good one, so our farming population was able to make quite a significant endowment to the abolitionist movement.

I had never fancied myself as a public speaker, but somehow I did manage to muster sufficient intelligence in the telling, in abridged form, of my tale to date. It was all a great success, even to the extent of some folk wiping tears from their eyes when I told of the slaves boarding the steamer at Memphis and of the negro families about to be sundered.

The local senior school as well had me as guest speaker at a special assembly programme and from that I went clanking happily homeward with a jam jar full of silver. Belleville, in short, truly rose to the occasion. Further to the west in Canada, however, the glory of humanity was not flourishing so greatly. Judging from what I was reading in the newspapers, I sometimes wondered what sort of favour we were really doing for escaped slaves by bringing them to our country.

George Brown's fine paper, the *Globe*, furnished much reading on the subject, since Brown himself had shown a very active interest in Abolitionism since the journal's inception back in 1854. It was his intention, stated Brown in an editorial, to provide fellow sympathizers with a "forum for the sacred animosity towards slavery". The *Globe* as well frequently attacked the Fugitive Slave Law, that pathetic and desperate legislative compromise designed to keep the American Union intact. We as Canadians, wrote George Brown, should join him in condemning it "out of a duty of preserving the honour of the continent against slavery".

And what awaited escaped slaves here made truly disturbing reading. Another favourite editorial target of the *Globe* was prejudice against blacks in our own land, specifically in the south-western part of Canada West, which since Confederation has been called Ontario. There were, by way of example, attempts to institutionalize discrimination by the establishment of separate schools for black children. The emerging picture of antipathy towards the negroes was anything but uplifting and, I have to say, damaging to my own national pride. I had thought we could do things better here and there seemed to be forces at work trying to dictate otherwise. What had looked so beautiful and noble from the distant vantage point of Memphis was not so wonderful when viewed close up.

Some of the prejudice, to put it bluntly, was imported; immigrant Americans had not deposited their attitudes at the border, there were Irish immigrants vying with blacks for jobs, and a number of former West Indian planters were not helping matters either.

Then we had our indigenous discrimination, a good part of which emanated from that all-pervasive group we generally call the Lower Orders, a group that can be conveniently (and often justifiably) blamed for society's ills. If this betrays a prejudice on my own part, well, I own up to it with no quarrel. Prejudice is a stain from which few of us are free, but I think in this case it could be excused by some of the ignorances that have poured forth from the Lower Orders and are a matter of public record.

"Nigger wimmen is a bunch of hoors..."

"Dresden? Whaddya mean, 'Dawn'? Folks hereabouts calls it the Nigger Hole."

"Christ, our chicken houses and clotheslines gotta be guarded day and night with them niggers about."

Black crime received far more publicity than that committed by whites; a typical Lower Order verbal editorial was usually something like "Those bloody niggers're bein' let off too light...damn' bleedin'-heart courts...just bein' too sympathetic to their condition and, mark my words, boy, they're takin' advantage, oh, yes, sir, them's a cunning bunch of buggers."

In the town of Colchester, blacks had been called "thievish and immoral" as long ago as 1827.

The middle classes also had to bear some responsibility for public sentiment. The Lower Orders could possibly be excused on the grounds of abysmal ignorance, immaturity, and natural stupidity. But what can you say about city directories, presumably compiled by reasonably educated people, that specify which businesses are run by whites or blacks? Or of newspapers (but never the *Globe*!) that publish racial jokes?

The *Montreal Gazette*'s editorial page said that all blacks should be sent to Sierra Leone. In Windsor, in 1855, a property auctioneer had refused bids from negroes, saying that they should stay together as a group. And two years prior to that, the Elora Debating Society had embarked on the topic "Has the Indian or the Negro suffered more from the aggression of the White Man?" The debate had degenerated into a general condemnation of all negroes as thieves.

The social landscape, then, did not seem to be much of an improvement on what prevailed south of the border. I had to comfort myself with constant reminders that at least the blacks were free in Canada, that at least they had equal protection under the law, that at least we had some foundation to build upon for a more just society. At least, at least, at least...to my unease, I began to appreciate John Brown's discontent with the least.

And I patiently waited for word from Alex on his "short" trip to Philadelphia, word that came towards the end of November with a predictability that was at once exasperating and gratifying:

> Philadelphia, Pennsylvania
> 13 November, 1857
>
> Dear James,
> This is just a quick missive before I depart with Gerrit Smith and a friend of his, Richard Adamson, to the steamer that will take us to----New Orleans! I am not looking forward to this voyage, for the weather has been so violent that rain blows through the cracks around my hotel window. However, I am told that things become gentler as we progress southward - climatically at any rate.
> Here is our strategy. [My stomach tightened]. Would you be good enough to go to my home and help Hester assemble all my bird-watching equipment (list attached) and bring it with you? Yes, to New Orleans. [Oh, no!] I fear any inconvenience to you, but it is necessary, for functioning as an ornithologist is the only way I can explain my presence in the Deep South, which I intend to penetrate right to the marrow. It will also enable me to get in touch with slaves as they are actually at work.
> And you, my staunch friend, will please renew your letter of introduction from the Grand Trunk. We will continue to use our own names for as long as possible to avoid the inconven-

ience and undoubted hazards of false passports and other
documents. Just how long we can carry on thus I cannot say,
but we can't do any better than our best, can we?
I would like you to meet us in New Orleans, timing your arrival
as close to February 28 (1858 already!) as you can. I don't
know at the moment where we will be staying, but I will telegraph the information as soon as we get there.
Now I must convey the glad tidings to my poor wife. This is not
going to be fun. Look after her for me, would you?

Yours faithfully,

A.M.R.

P.S. On your journey, you will likely be seeing more shipments of
slaves, as you did in Memphis. As piteous as the spectacle may
be, you must show *no* emotion. In God's name, be careful!

As Alex's duty to inform Hester of his latest adventure was not fun,
neither was my visit to her to fetch his bird paraphernalia. I had already
visited her once or twice during my stay at home, but not long enough for
any particular conversation beyond a brief survey of our travels. I went now
with my list of requirements and before we had been at our task for long,
Hester blurted out, "James, why does he do this? Why does he do it?"

"He hates people owning other people...no, that's an over-simplifica-
tion. Between that and what he discerns as the physical deterioration of the
Earth, his is a crusade to clean the whole world up. I don't think it's ever
going to stop. Once the matter of slavery is concluded, he'll be after indus-
trialists for contamination of water and air, and then after that there'll be
something else..."

"The whole world."

"I know," I sighed. "He'll settle for nothing less."

"I thought I mattered to him."

"You do, Hester, more than you could ever know. But you know how
guarded he has to be when he writes."

"With his own wife? If he were here like a normal husband, he
wouldn't *have* to write!"

She started to say something else and then choked. I looked up sharply
from my rummaging in a cupboard. "Please, Hester, don't cry," I almost
begged. It was not for Hester that I did not want her to cry. It was for me. I
was terrified of not knowing what to do. I should hold her, perhaps, but she
was both my friend's wife and unusually attractive.

"He doesn't care about me at all...I'm just a thing sitting at home, a
slave in my own sorry way." She hiccupped miserably, making no effort to
wipe away her tears. "He cares about everyone but me. How in the world

did I ever get into this?"

I tried to reassure her. "Alex was worried you might feel this way. He said what he was doing would make him a more complete and worthy human being for you to love and he married you when he did so that he wouldn't lose you to somebody else." I was desperately improvising now, saying anything that entered my head.

"Like a reserved library book," commented Hester bitterly.

"Hester, try, I know it's hard, but try not to be cynical. I can appreciate how you feel, but you're, well, you're married to greatness, really, and there's always a price..."

"I don't need to be told that. What is this man, anyway, a hunter of dreams?"

"I suppose you could say that. He cares so deeply about so many, perhaps too many things."

Hester was leaning against a chest of drawers, still weeping. I dug for a handkerchief and, finding none, I went to the kitchen to look for a tea-towel. I wiped her cheeks gently, trying not to be disturbed by those wonderful almond-shaped, toffee-coloured eyes, so sad and so beautiful, and then her arms were about my neck. Dear God...

"Hold me, James." I held her, but I hardly need to tell how awkward it was; I could feel the presence of Alex, not Alex as the enraged husband, but Alex in his detached scientific persona taking my pulse, by my own estimation running at eighty-eight to the minute and climbing. There was a faint ladylike scent in Hester's hair, this was no good at all, what am I thinking, it is very good indeed, oh, no...

"Hester, no, please," said a distant voice.

"Why not? Do I not attract you?"

"I like you too much and in the wrong way for this to go further. You're my best friend's wife."

"Wife, you say! Two nights and then, poof!, he's gone, looking after someone else. He'd rather see John Brown than me! And then, praise be to God, months later, I get a week, and then he's gone, for Christmas, yet...alone every night, no-one beside me, James, a woman needs some-one."

"Hester, I'm so sorry, I just can't do anything about it."

"Then kindly take these things and leave!"

Chapter Eleven

On February 21, 1858, my family saw me off at Belleville station in a swirling fog of locomotive steam and a torrent of tears from my mother, who was having her usual difficult time coming to terms with the hazards of my new career as a social crusader. Hester knew I was leaving for New Orleans that day, but there was no sign of her at the station, a sure sign that her anger with me for supporting Alex was undiminished. Yet she was all I could think of as the train puffed off westward with a noisy clang of couplings and the rumble of iron wheel on iron rail.

I was at the time totally naive in the ways of women. My experience had been confined to the usually chaste Victorian courtships in which a gentleman understood that the holding of hands was pretty well the limit until marriage. Yes, I had behaved correctly with Hester, but the jumble of feelings unleashed that day haunted me for many a night.

In my confused misery, I thought surely the start in my odyssey to New Orleans would be the lowest point and the only way to go now was up. I was wrong. After a convoluted rail trip to St. Louis, I boarded one of those superb Mississippi steamers for the remainder of the trip. This had been made possible by an unusually early thaw on the river. It was advantageous in the interests of speed (since passenger trains did not yet travel at night), relatively low cost, and of sheer variety.

But I was to pay dearly for the variety a short while later. The absolute low point of the journey (and one of the worst spectacles of my entire life) occurred at Cairo, Illinois; Cairo, the Pharaoh's capital during the time of the imprisonment of the Hebrews (another abused race), although in Illinois they pronounce it "Care-oh". Cairo is at the junction of the Ohio River as it ends its long journey through Pennsylvania, Ohio, and Kentucky, and merges its waters with the Mississippi. On that account, there is a convergence of steamer routes and consequent connections and interchanges. Herein my tale.

My steamer, the *Daniel Boone*, had a rendezvous at Cairo with the *City of Vicksburg*, just in from Louisville on the Ohio River, with a load of slaves from Kentucky being sold south. Since the *City of Vicksburg* was bound down the Mississippi only as far as her namesake city, the *Daniel Boone* took over the portion of her unwilling passengers headed for points beyond, specifically Natchez, Baton Rouge, and the end of river shipping at New Orleans. There were several slave families being divided. Despite my being emotionally prepared this time around, the sobbing and singing of hymns cut me as surely as a knife as a contingent of unfortunates was marched aboard. Because of the highly charged atmosphere (Cairo was, by a matter of yards, north of the demarcation between slave- and non-slave-owning states), the slaves boarding were in chains and guarded by shotgun-toting toughs stationed about the landing.

A young mother was being taken from her children and literally dragged along by the feet, twisting and stumbling as the other slaves marched up the gangway.

"Shush, now, stop that God-damn' screechin'," admonished one of the gunmen. Bearing in mind Alex's warning, I watched as impassively as I could. The wind blows cold in Cairo, went the old song...the sun refuses to shine. Ice floes slithered past on the pewter-coloured current.

The *Daniel Boone* and the *City of Vicksburg* cast off simultaneously and started steaming in company down the Mississippi, close enough that the slaves could call back and forth to each other. I can only conclude that it was someone's twisted idea of fun. The wailing of mothers and children across the narrow strip of water between the two vessels all but drowned out the threshing of the paddle-wheels and the hiss and swoosh of the 'scape pipes.

Some of the white passengers were upset as well, but for a different reason. "Those nigras!" huffed one old biddy who peered out at the world from under a shawl, her sagging, wrinkly face reminding me of an indignant iguana. "What a hullabaloo! Should put black bags over their heads. Maybe they'd think it was night and be quiet and go to sleep." I nodded agreement, hating myself.

And now the worst was at hand. The poor young slave mother I had seen being put aboard at Cairo was so completely demented with grief, reaching out and crying to her family on the other steamer, that she pulled so hard on her leg iron as to dislocate her ankle, twisting her foot to an impossibly revolting angle. I could take no more.

Approaching one of the escorting gun-men, I said deferentially, "Sir, could that woman be relieved of her leg-irons for a while? She's damaging herself, well, pretty badly."

He was smoking a cigar, as many of his type seemed to do. He leisurely removed it from his mouth, but such was the bond between man and cigar that the revolting thing seemingly remained tethered to his lower lip by a thin brown strand of saliva. He looked at me as if I had three eyes.

"Yew wanna steal her, or what? Hey, yew ain't one of them abo-*lition*-ists, is yew?"

"Oh, no, *God*, no. Just look at her foot. Her new owner won't be too pleased."

"Aw, shit, willya look at that! Aw, shut mah mouth..."

Without so much as acknowledging my concern for the perpetuity of the slave business, he bounded over to the woman and unlocked her fetters.

"Jesus Christ!" he grumbled. "Guess Ah better git a doctor...hey, shit, woman!"

He was still upon his knees on the deck; she was on her feet, dislocated ankle or no, racing in one smooth motion, vaulting over the rail, reaching one last time for her babies, disappearing under the overhang of the deck above the water, then pounded into oblivion by the great thumping, flailing paddle-wheel. A few idiots of the Lower Order cheered. I turned away numbed, sickened, feeling unable to go on.

A SLAVE MARKET, SIMILAR TO THE ONE IN NEW ORLEANS.
COURTESY OF ENOCH PRATT FREE LIBRARY, BALTIMORE, MD

Chapter Twelve

Somehow I did go on, unburdening myself to Alex when I got to New Orleans. "That's the hell of it, and I'm sorry to say that down here, we'll be seeing more than less of this sort of thing," he sympathized. "A slave child is the property of his owner and the parents have no say whatever in his destiny. If we carry on in a spirit of evolution, as we discussed in Cleveland, I fear the effect will be simply to buy more time for the practice of this infamy. I don't wish to alarm you, James, but I am now thinking that what John Brown said, outlandish and frightening as it may seem, actually has a certain merit to it. Gerrit thinks so too and is prepared to back Captain Brown fully."

One could not argue about the infamy, but the revolutionary aspect still bothered me deeply; the result could be nothing less than a blood-bath. The greatest bother to me at this point, however, was what could have happened between me and Hester back in Belleville. I desperately needed to talk to Alex about what was happening to his marriage and had to resort to asking Gerrit if I could have Alex to myself for a few minutes.

"As long as you like, James," obliged Gerrit. "The man has been talking at me continuously since the steamer left New York until I don't know whether I'm actually stunned or merely deafened. I'll just step out for glass of water number seven and a good brisk walk."

"Trying to drown him too, are you, Alex?"

"Have you been drinking *your* eight glasses? The body needs continual flushing to stay healthy."

"Alex, I have to talk to you about Hester. Your marriage is anything *but* healthy." My heart quaked disagreeably.

"What? What is this you're telling me?"

"You get married and two days later you're gone. You come back after a long period, stay a few days, and then you're gone again. Hester does not feel like a wife. Is it..."

"*She* told *you* this?"

"There was nobody else."

"Why...well..."

"Come, now, Alex, this can't be any cause for surprise. She's in a bad way. Oh, I know you told her you'd be away a lot, but I honestly don't know how you can be a full-time abolitionist, a full-time doctor, a full-time naturalist, and a full-time husband all at once. You'll have to let go of something."

"It won't be Hester, I can tell you that. Oh, God, James, what am I going to do?" Astonishingly, there were tears in Alex's eyes.

"I'm no veteran," I said, "but what I suggest is that you write her a really passionate letter, quote poetry and everything, and sign your name."

"You know I can't do that."

"Just sign it 'Alex'. It's not exactly an exotic name. Besides, a signed letter from New Orleans won't excite any suspicion. All manner of people come here on business or to visit. She knows what the danger is and maybe any risk attached to signing will indicate to her how serious you are. I want to work with you on the Underground Railroad, but I'll pack my bags and go home tomorrow if carrying on means being party to your marriage disintegrating. Hester threw me out of your house because I was your accomplice. I tried to explain your position and it wasn't easy..."

"That's the problem with women. They only see the world as it relates directly to them..."

"Get off your high horse, Alex. Write the damned letter, or I'll write it for you. This is not the time to be analysing the behaviour of women anyway. For one thing, neither of us is qualified."

While a chastened Alex wrote his letter (and I could scarcely credit my role as chastener), I rejoined Gerrit, who, having had his water and a walk, was now settled into the hotel bar and enjoying a horrifying southern refreshment called bourbon and branch. "This," he explained, "gives me additional water as well as something to ease its passage. And Bob's your uncle. I too can be rustic."

"Of course, Congressman."

Virtually all photographs I have ever seen of Gerrit Smith show him as a severe patrician with mouth set in a determined pout. And in person, he spoke in a most cultivated manner with vaguely Bostonian overtones. But beyond that, the stern demeanour ended, for Gerrit loved to argue for argument's sake on any subject, no matter how outlandish or indefensible his position. He was a Sophist of the first order and the more tenuous his position became, the harder he would argue, disarming his adversaries with a whimsy uniquely his own.

There was neither Sophistry nor whimsy, however, in Gerrit's arguments on slavery; on that matter, he was all business and fully shared with Alex and me the concern over whether evolution or revolution was the solution.

Over dinner, Gerrit remarked, "There is no easy answer. If there were, we'd have found it long ago. I am prepared to back John Brown, but in the full realization that after it is all over, it isn't really all over until the dust settles. In revolution, by definition, we have a swift, likely violent change, and in its speed it will confound and bewilder all concerned."

"Like the American Revolution," I baited.

"And America never recovered. We are still confounded and bewildered, hence the present situation. Alex, pass the hot sauce, would you? It varnishes my insides. I'll live forever.

"The hard part of what we are doing, gentlemen, is not the triggering of a negro uprising, but easing all, not just Southern, but all American society into a situation where all slaves have been liberated. Consider this: if all slaves were freed at midnight tonight, in the morning we would have thousands of illiterate, uneducated, untrained people - well, trained only for one thing - wandering all over the place, being a drain on society. They'd be pariahs here; they'd have to go north, and, liberal as we like to think we are, how many Northern whites would want to train blacks to take away jobs from other whites?

"And when you consider the monetary investment made by slave owners, should they be compensated in some way? After all, what they have done is technically legal even though repugnant to us. And if they *are* compensated, who takes care of it, the government? Some kind of special tax or levy?"

"Whose side are you on, anyway?" spluttered Alex through a mouthful of beet greens.

"I am on the side of justice. James, you come from a judicial background..."

"Oh, no, you don't..."

"No, I am not trying to put you in the position of being moderator. That is what I should do, being the senior member present. But you will appreciate, I'm sure, how many variables there are in any sort of legal case or any other sort of social manifestation, even between just two people. This is not just a, er, black and white situation. It is of the utmost delicacy. An armed rebellion will certainly start the situation on the road to resolution. What we must avoid is any kind of Hammurabic revenge and take a more moderate view, based in law, in which *both* sides of the matter are taken into account."

"What should happen, then?" queried Alex, beet greens forgotten.

"The *Montreal Gazette* had an editorial last fall, suggesting all the blacks in Canada should be sent to Sierra Leone," I remarked. "I thought it was stupid at the time, but might that be the thing to do here? After all, the blacks came from Africa in the first place."

"Ah," said Gerrit, "but you forget that America is their home now, as well as ours. They have put roots down here, they have buried their dead here, and that reminds me, there's an old negro burial-ground I must show you. The grave markers are distinctively African-looking, all made out of naturally-curved logs. It's a very haunting thing to see. But Africa is in their past..."

"America sowed the crop. Now let it reap the harvest," pronounced Alex, advancing once again upon his beet greens.

"Good God, Alex!" I exclaimed. "John Brown scared both of us. Now you're scaring *me*."

"Look, I don't want a war or violence or any of that, but whatever we think isn't going to matter. I have the feeling that it's just going to happen."

"I agree," said Gerrit. "Personally, I think the whole thing is just going to spill over with a hideous roar, whether from a negro rebellion as conceived by Captain Brown or the cotton states resorting to force if challenged in their right to own slaves, well, I cannot say."

"We could," said Alex, "dither about for years being moderate, and meanwhile more young mothers jump into the river..."

"I wish you hadn't said that, Alex."

"I am sorry, James, but it happens. You saw it and you told us. Men are worked to death like cattle, which reminds me, I saw a notice just out there on the street about a slave auction tomorrow. I think we should go."

"Look," I said, "this whole thing with us is like religion. We all three of us have the same goal, but seem to be diverging in our ideas of how to get there. In spite of what I saw on the steamer, I'm not looking for something that will just fly apart and burn up like fireworks, leaving things as bad or maybe worse than they were before." But of my words, I could not be certain; I was trying to be rational and intellectual and with each passing day, it was a less convincing approach. At least part of me would have been very happy with a great, thundering war.

We did indeed go to the slave auction on the following day. Not unpredictably, the spectacle stirred the dark instincts with which I was having a private battle. The market was milling and surging with activity; not only had another steamer-load of slaves been deposited in New Orleans the previous afternoon, but a leading citizen of the city had departed this life earlier in the month and there was an estate sale of his very considerable stable (the local term, not mine) of slaves.

The slaves were housed in two buildings, segregated according to gender, the children being with the women. Trying to look proprietorial, we strolled through the men's warehouse, along with prospective purchasers examining the merchandise. Once again, I am not responsible for the terminology.

A man in the cream-coloured suit standard in this part of the world strode over to one of the slaves and said abruptly, "Open up, boy."

The slave opened his mouth for inspection of teeth.

"Jump about, now." The slave literally jumped about to demonstrate his strength and agility, smiling eagerly as if trying to please. It was sickening, like watching a performing seal in a circus.

"The slave's trying to find a good owner," explained Alex. "Pathetic, isn't it?"

"Show me your back, boy," commanded Cream-Coloured Suit.

"Yes, massa."

"Hmm, not bad. Who's sellin' yew?"

"Massa Wilson." Massa Wilson was the departed leading citizen.

"Uh-huh. How long were y'all with Mr. Wilson?"

"Three years, suh."

Cream-Coloured Suit made a notation in a little book he was carrying and turned away, saying no more. The slave looked crestfallen.

"Excuse me, sir," said Gerrit in the ripest British accent I have ever heard. "We're from England, from Preston in Lancashire, representing

Ramsay, Ross, and Smith Textiles Limited. Are you in the cotton business perchance?"

"Well, indirectly, Ah suppose. Ah deal with transportation. Hinckley's the name. Har y'all?"

"Very well indeed, thank you." We shook hands.

"What can Ah do for yew? Never met anyone from England before. Used to be the enemy, ha, ha, but with the cotton business as it is, and Ah sure am a beneficiary of it, well, money can make friends, can't it?"

"The very best of friends," said Gerrit smoothly as Alex and I tried not to goggle with astonishment. "What we are doing, Mr. Hinckley, is purchasing some plantations for our company, in which case the three of us would manage them, and of course we would need slaves."

"Goes without sayin'."

"Now, we are complete babes in the woods on the subject of slavery, lost ours back in '33, don't you know, and we'd like to tag along with you for a bit if we could get some idea of what to look for, how the business operates, and so forth."

"Shorely, it'd be a real pleasure. Tell me, now, do yew gentlemen feel at all, well, strange about slavery, bein' it's not part of your society any more?"

"Well, in all honesty," said Gerrit with a twinkle in his eye that was almost a gleam, "the idea does take some getting used to, but, as the saying goes, when in Rome, do as the Romans. If this is the American way, well, it'll be our way too. We feel a keen responsibility to be good business citizens."

"It works well enough here, real well, in fact. And the law reads it all our way, too, and yew can't argue with the law, can yew? The Legal Code of the State of Louisiana lays it right out for yew: 'A slave is adjudged in law, taken and reputed, to be a chattel personal'."

"You know your law, Mr. Hinckley."

"Yew bet. Say, let's just stroll over and look at the gals. This is the part Ah awlways like."

We crossed over to the other shed. In contrast to the quiet resignation of the men's housing, the atmosphere here was one of foreboding, and in seconds one could see why. Some of the younger women were being inspected in an unnecessarily personal way, reminding me of Ruth Gardiner's tale of slaves being used as personal whores. I nearly swooned away at the sight of a truly beautiful and extravagantly endowed slave girl naked to the waist and having her breasts squeezed by some degenerate with a wart on his nose and tufts of hair sprouting from his ears. A terrible mixture of pity and, I may as well admit it, raw desire took hold of me. I wanted to stare, but averted my eyes in deference to the girl's obvious feeling of shame.

"Ain't she somethin'!" exclaimed Mr. Hinckley. "Think Ah'll bid on her just for the hell of it. Looks like some mighty good recreation, although

Ah'll bet Mrs. Hinckley would give me Hail Columbia if Ah were to brang *that* one home..."

Gerrit and Mr. Hinckley strolled onwards while the slave girl did up her clothing with shaking hands.

"Alex, let's buy her," I blurted.

"Oh, you old swine, James."

"No, not that...I mean, not now...but she's so beautiful and so sad. We could send her to Canada with a group..."

"It's out of the question. First, it would mean the name of the purchaser being recorded. We don't want to be in print. Secondly, we are staying in a hotel, we have no local address, and nowhere to put her. Thirdly, we don't have the money and even if we did, we would never have enough to buy every slave, which would really be the fair thing to do. As it is right now, she'll be treated just like all the other slaves."

"Badly."

"Right. Isn't equality wonderful? But I have to say I share your agitation...look, James, I don't know how seriously you took being called a swine just now, but I'm sorry. I seem to be developing a sort of brittle flippancy, a fortification against my feelings about slavery, what to do about it, whether or not to support a rebellion, and then there's Hester on top of it all."

"Or on the bottom...that came out all wrong. I'm talking about how she ranks in your scheme of things."

"I hope the eight-page passionate letter with poetry and signed with my name will do something to mend fences...just look at Gerrit there, taking notes and being so objective and so professional. What a fellow he is! One moment...yes, I think things..."

"You mean 'thangs'."

"Very well, then, 'thangs' are starting to get under way."

Some functionary of the slave business blew a whistle for attention. The mumble of voices in the shed died down and several mothers held their children close in apprehension of being separated. There was a faint sound of praying.

"Y'all listen good, now," orated the functionary. "Y'all gonna be sold today an' yew wanna be in the best circumstances y'all can be. Look good, cooperate, look smart, act smart, an' *be* smart."

"I thought a smart slave was a liability," I whispered.

"I doubt he means smart in the intellectual sense," responded Alex.

Continued the functionary, "Now, y'all be quiet, hush, there, no weepin' or prayin'. Wait right here, now, we start in two or three minutes."

The two of us strolled out into a sheltered area between the two sheds where the auction would take place. Gerrit was already there, still "interviewing" Mr. Hinckley, writing furiously in his notebook. Alex shook his head at the spectacle, not out of disgust, but simply because it was, as we were finding, vintage Gerrit.

The auctioneer was already at work, saying something about "...sold separately or in lots at the purchaser's convenience". It reminded me of the sheep sale at the Belleville Fall Fair. Although the ensuing scene could not compare with that aboard the *Daniel Boone* at Cairo, it was heart-rending enough. We stood alongside Gerrit and Mr. Hinckley, who was fanning himself with a Panama hat; although it was hardly even spring on the calendar, the tropic heat was stultifying this day, which, to be specific, was Saturday, March 6th, 1858.

Ttragedy did not take long to unfold. A slave mother in her early thirties had her twin boys sold as a matched set to a friend of Mr. Hinckley's, who intended them as a birthday present to his wife because it would be so cute to have them as little footmen.

"Doris'll be tickled pink," chuckled Mr. Hinckley as the mother of the cute matched set, who would never see them again, became hysterical and had to be removed.

"Can you live with that?" Several heads turned. Mr. Hinckley's head turned. So did Gerrit's and Alex's. Mine did not, for the question had involuntarily been uttered by me. Alex jabbed me in the ribs. The horror of it all! I wanted to evaporate or reverse the clock, anything to make it not have happened.

Mr. Hinckley's glacial grey eyes narrowed. "Mister, Ah can live with that real good. It's the law here. Maybe yew think we're oppressors. Well, so are yew English and so are the Yankees and so is about three quarters of western civilization. The only difference is that we're honest about it."

"Sorry," I mumbled, making no attempt to sound English. "I'm not accustomed...I wasn't expecting, er...that..."

"It's unfortunate, but it's the way it is. Migawd, if y'all had to worry about keepin' slave families together, it'd be so complicated..."

I endured the remainder of the auction in a ferment of pity for the slaves, disgust at myself, and unease at what Alex and/or Gerrit would have to say. At least I did not have to spend a day wondering, like the errant child who has heard those fateful words, "Just wait until your father gets home." The moment the auction finished, Alex turned to me and said calmly but with iron in his voice, "James, if you do a thing like that again, you *will* be packing your bags for Canada. Need I say more?"

"No".

"End of story, then. Well, that was uplifting, wasn't it? I need to go and see a barber. I'll meet the two of you for lunch. Is the hotel all right, or are you sick of it?"

"The hotel is fine and has nice water. I'm lagging behind," said Gerrit benignly.

We were already at our luncheon table in the Hotel Jean Lafitte when Alex returned from the barber. "You never looked lovelier, Alex," said Gerrit, consulting the menu. "You look at least ten minutes younger."

Normally I would have laughed, but so persistent was my mortification that I could only look at my plate. Neither Alex nor Gerrit made any comment about my state, I assume because it was a matter too serious to be forgiven, and I would simply have to atone by greater self-discipline and objectivity. This was not some cloudy, Romantic deed of valour celebrated in a great poem; it was serious and it was real.

The two of them carried on as though it were business as usual, I myself saying almost nothing. Primarily, conversation was a discourse by Gerrit on the information he had gleaned from Mr. Hinckley. "This fellow should have his privates stuck in a wringer and then the wringer given a half-turn every quarter-hour. So, for that matter, should the rest of those people. He had some really choice things to say just after James had his little, er, *contretemps*." (My face suffused with a hot rush of humiliation). "He told me about a friend of his who had bought a young mother whose children had been sold elsewhere, and the poor soul, the mother, that is, had gone mad. No good for anything, said Mr. H., and his friend had been furious because it had meant a thousand dollars down the drain. What a tragedy for the poor man. He also told me that New Orleans is really nice for slaves..."

"Really nice?"

"Really nice, compared, at any rate, to Mississippi, which is reputed to be just about the worst. Out there, they generally get a maximum of seven years out of a slave before he is done for from overwork. The traders don't mind, though. It's good for their business.

"The cynicism here is unbelievable, just unbe*lie*vable. There are endless intimations to the slaves that they will eventually go free..."

"What?"

"It gives them a hope of sorts; to deny them that would be like screwing down the safety valve on a boiler. Cotton state slave-owners are under no illusion as to the possibilities if slaves were permitted any sort of initiative or opportunity. But the reality is that there is no intention of liberating them, now or ever.

"And religion is cultivated in the slaves as a sort of anaesthetic. Slaves have it drummed into them from infancy that they have access to God and it's done in such a way that faith flourishes at the expense of intellect. And of course, when you keep them illiterate, you can tell them any damned thing. They are just left unable to think for themselves and their primary mental activity is superstition. God, this upsets me, and nothing would make me happier than for the two of you to unconditionally join Captain Brown and the rest of us, although, heaven knows, you are taking enough risks and it isn't even your national problem, your national disgrace.

"In fact, I'm so upset I must have another of these shrimp... they're from the despised state of Mississippi, I believe...sometimes on larger plantations, they have what I suppose you would call the chief slave, and he gets all manner of favours and privileges and often as not is completely alienated from his own people. Look at the progress the world at large has made in the last while: there is talk of a trans-Atlantic telegraph cable; there is, thanks to James and his colleagues, a growing network of steam railways; so many things can be bought now rather than you having to laboriously make them for yourselves. And yet, here we are in the Sunny South and what do we get but this hellish marriage between the Industrial Revolution and the Dark Ages. Serfdom all over again. Every morning I wake up, hoping it's just a bad dream, but it never is.

"It goes on and on and it's so firmly established, both in fact and in the Southern conscience, that only some sort of violent upheaval, a revolution, will change it. Slavery, and you'll like this, James, is like a mountain or some other obstruction sitting where you want to build a railroad. You blow it up to get it out of the way. So slavery will have to be blown up too, and if Captain John Brown is the one to get things started, I am prepared to put money on him, and I'm not speaking metaphorically, either.

"My, that was upsetting today at the slave market, and, James, regrettable though your little peccadillo may have been, it was the natural reaction of a sensitive and compassionate human being. My own masquerade, while a small masterpiece, made me feel as if I had lost some of my own humanity. Oh, this is too much for one day. I must try some of this pecan pie..."

Even church, or I should say, *especially* church offered no sanctuary from the madness. The day following was a Sunday and the three of us attended the morning service at a nearby Episcopal church (Anglican to us Canadians), mainly at Alex's urging. My own church-going is sporadic at best, generally limited to weddings, funerals, and organ recitals. I would rather have gone down to the river and watched the steamers, but after my indiscretion of the previous day, I felt it wise to show some solidarity with my comrades, so off I went.

The weather was continuing warm and humid; I sat wedged between Alex and Gerrit in a more or less soporific state, my senses surfacing to listen to the very fine English-style choir composed of men's and boys' voices. The music filled the three of us with a sense of well-being, a sense of well-being that was abruptly dispelled by the sermon:

"...mah friends, we have the pahr, the heaven-sent pahr, to guide ar own destiny and to...guide the destiny of those who cannot do it for themselves. Ever'one benefits, mah friends, despite...despite this label that has been affixed to ar society, that of 'slavery'...but, mah friends, this label carries with it a certain stigma, a certain connotation of exploitation. This is not, simply not, the situation, for we have under ar guardianship, mah friends, a wise and beneficent institution, devised by God for the especial benefit of the coloured race. We are the Chosen..."

Beams of sunlight slanted and fanned through stained-glass windows, one a portrayal of St. Andrew the fisherman tending his nets. Burnished organ pipes waited to rumble to life with a Bach prelude or some good, sturdy Henry Purcell. The choir boys were angelic in their robes and ruffled collars, the countenance of Our Lord was greatly sorrowful. If justifying slavery had to be the central theme of so very much that was spoken or written these days, well, to paraphrase Mr. Shakespeare, the people they protested too much.

A SOMEWHAT BENIGN VIEW OF WORKERS IN A COTTON FIELD,
THE SORT OF SCENE THAT CONFOUNDED JAMES AND ALEX.
COURTESY OF ENOCH PRATT FREE LIBRARY, BALTIMORE, MD.

CHAPTER THIRTEEN

Some days later, the time came for us to divide our forces. A telegram so guarded as to be almost incomprehensible had come from Gerrit's friend Richard Adamson, who since his own arrival in the South had been engaged in setting up an escape route northward from Gerrit's "despised state of Mississippi". He had evidently encountered some difficulty in Columbus - it turned out later that a chief slave had tried to turn him in to the authorities - and Gerrit went up to help him. Columbus, of course, was also the home of my "cousin", Major Ramsay, and I saw through the situation an opportunity to renew acquaintance. Because of the uncertainty at the time, however, of Richard's situation, I was instructed to wait until things had calmed down.

So Alex and I, with nothing constructive left to do in New Orleans, prepared for a lengthy odyssey through the Cotton States, "looking for birds". Alex rendered our "research" credible by drawing on his studies of wildlife in Canada West. According to our story, we were collecting a complete set of bird specimens for a special exhibition by the Western New York Museum of Natural History in honour of the late John James Audubon.

We sorted and organized the equipment I had brought down from Belleville. We bought cream-coloured suits, not only to merge with the locals, but to be more comfortable in the blazing sun, and embarked by train for our journey.

As it happened, Audubon, the well-known naturalist and wildlife artist, had spent some time at the first plantation we approached. That happy coincidence netted us a letter of introduction to other plantations he had visited and any pangs of conscience for our abuse of Southern hospitality were stilled by thoughts of our cause.

There is no need to relate this phase of our adventures in any detail. We criss-crossed the states of Mississippi, Alabama, Georgia, and South Carolina, sometimes by rail, but more often by that most debased form of transport, the stagecoach.

Although we put on a great show of assimilation, there was no escaping our being aliens in a hostile land, even under the tenuous umbrella of Audubon and ornithology. We visited plantation after plantation, seeing nothing of the coarseness and brutality of the slave market in New Orleans. We knew there was unspeakable suffering out here somewhere, but where in God's name was it? And to complete our demoralization, we were unable to establish a single way station for the Underground Railroad. The only group that could be reliably approached in that connection were the Quakers, and there were none that we could find. In fact, among the whites, the Episcopal Church reigned supreme in all its misdirected self-righteousness, much as it had only twenty-odd years earlier in Upper Canada under the stewardship of Bishop Strachan.

Everywhere we went, slavery was not only accepted as an economic necessity but encouraged as spiritually desirable. Blacks were not oppressed, we were told time and time again, because they had no expectations in the first place, and therefore their expectations could not be violated. The symbolic bait of freedom espoused by Mr. Hinckley evidently had no currency here.

To be a slave-owner was thought to be a noble calling, caring for God's creatures (never fellow human beings!), feeding and protecting them as one might pets. Almost as if in a conspiracy to confound us, the plantations we visited on our spurious bird-hunting expeditions were perfect models of paternalism. The slaves were well cared for and not only respectful but actually affectionate towards their masters. Henry, the chief slave on the Williamson plantation near Camilla, Georgia, was especially well-versed in local birdlife, and while showing us some of the choicer vantage points for bird-watching, related, "Massa Williamson, he seriously ill coupla years back. We all thowt we'd lowst 'im forevah, be like a fathah to us, yu see...bee-you-tee-full man, he are...we was orful oneasy for weeks, we was, an' we prayed so hard: Lawd, Lawd, look down on Massa Williamson, ovah an' ovah. An', praise be, He did! Widout Massa Williamson, life wouldn't be worth livin', Ah kin tell yu dat."

We though it best not to hide the fact that we were from Canada. There was enough to deal with without being caught in a lie. We simply made our rounds, welcomed by open-hearted hospitality and carefully guided by our hosts from one plantation to the next.

Staying at such places as the Williamson plantation had us in a miserable state of confusion. Aside from bringing a whole new dimension to the word "hospitality", the family put slaves at our disposal, including those that worked in the cotton fields, for virtually everything; and once we became accustomed to their curious dialect, we were to learn that, contrary to all we had heard, they actually felt quite contented with their lot in life. So where had all the tragic figures in leg irons gone? Where were the mothers sundered from their children? Where were the riding crop and the lash? They existed somewhere, but we could see nothing, hear nothing. Whenever we mentioned the Underground Railroad ("Just curious if you had heard anything") to the slaves and asked if anyone had considered escape to Canada, the standard response was "Oh, no, not me, massa. Ever'thing jes' fine right heah."

Before long, we wondered why we were there. Had the abolitionists perhaps painted the picture more darkly than it really was? Had the spectacle of the slaves on the steamer and at the slave market been anomalies? Although I never admitted it to Alex and I feel mortified mentioning it now, I found myself veering towards the idea that there might be something to slavery after all. Slave owners were their brothers' keepers, just as in the Bible, although few would have considered the blacks as their brothers. But the slaves had, apparently, so many benefits without the responsibility of making major decisions, and although the work was unquestionably hard, there was security literally from the cradle to the grave, especially with the cotton trade as prosperous as it was.

The zeal and indignation we had felt in New Orleans was gradually supplanted with a feeling of aimlessness and lassitude. To compound matters, I had not been keen on birds from the first, tolerating what had to be done with them only in the interests of our subterfuge. Alex had shot a great number of the hapless little things, eviscerated them, and mounted them in pans of wax in a great show of being scientific. And now he had to declare, "I have a dreadful feeling I've sacrificed the poor little beasts for nothing. I really wonder if there is any purpose to this."

We still went through the motions, drifting from one well-upholstered plantation to another, south and then westwards. And at each one we whiled away our evenings drinking mint juleps (one of Alex's rare excursions into the world of alcohol) served by smiling black servants. I actually began to think this was the way to live.

But only to a point was this a way to live, for our sense of frustration was putting us on each other's nerves. I had kept silent about a couple of Alex's picky habits: the abominable insistence on eight glasses of water daily and, of late, a ponderously calculated ceremony of buttering his breakfast toast from edge to edge, still at it when I was long finished eating my own. Likewise Alex tolerated what he perceived as my slovenly and unhealthy ways.

And one evening, relations became heated during a game of cribbage; my mind simply was not on the game and Alex kept catching me with cards I could have played. I cannot even recall where the plantation was, since we had stayed at so many that they were all merging together in my mind, but I certainly remember that game:

"You missed a pair of sevens there, dear boy...look, that eight, two, and five would have given you another fifteen for two more points." And on my third resounding foul-up of the evening, Alex actually grabbed the cards out of my hand to see what new stupidity I had committed. I leaped up, shouting, "Dr. Ross, just mind your own bloody business! Why don't you go through my luggage as well while you're about it? Good night!"

Our host of the moment looked up in bemusement, the click of our hostess's knitting needles momentarily ceased the manufacture of little booties for a new slave baby. I stormed upstairs, mumbling epithets about Alex's nosiness, self-righteousness, and general arrogance.

Alex came up immediately to apologize. "I was wrong, James. I should just let you be a...er..."

"Dunce at cribbage."

"Very well, if you want to put it that way. I know your thoughts were distracting you from the game, and that is how it should have been with me. I was just using the game to distract myself from my own thoughts. Look, you and I know enough and have seen enough to reasonably suspect a conspiracy to steer us around to only the best plantations and get us well and thoroughly confused and demoralized. What we have heard cannot be lies and, God knows, what we have *seen* cannot be lies. Let's see if we cannot dig a bit deeper and find the true underbelly of slavery."

We tried to dig and each time we were neatly directed to another beautiful and gracious household. It was uncanny, as if an unseen hand were orchestrating all our movements. We continued to mention Canada in the same context as before to our slave escorts, and again as before, no interest was registered at all. They had heard of Canada through a fairly active jungle telegraph, but, thank yu, massa, not interested...too far, too cold...

Then, at Selma, Alabama, we stayed with the Hudgin family, who had some acquaintance with Major Ramsay in Columbus, Mississippi. That particular circumstance emerged quite by chance in a dinner-time conversation, blurted out by the lady of the house, who I think later regretted her indiscretion.

"His plantation is, well, rougher than ours," said her husband uneasily. "Mind yew, he does load a lot of cotton, but he certainly isn't, uh, thoughtful of his help."

"I'd still enjoy seeing him again, though. I met him four years ago," I beamed, smiling like an over-active lighthouse. "Alex, we need some Mississippi-type birds for the collection. Perhaps the Major could put us up for a few days."

"Well," said our host, now visibly uncomfortable, "we aren't close friends. I would find it awkward to introduce you."

"That doesn't need to deter us. We're related, you see. I'm a Ramsay too. Kinfolk. That's important."

Important it was, for the entire complexion of our mission was now to be changed. And no longer would a polite network of plantation owners be guiding our movements.

CHAPTER FOURTEEN

"James, since this Major Ramsay took you into his confidence once before, there should be little reason why he wouldn't do it again, especially if Mr. Adamson's crisis has had time to blow past," said Alex. "But if we go ahead and get in touch with him, I think we had better represent you as a lone traveller. I think he'd be less inhibited...we could be on to something at last and I wouldn't want to compromise our chances in any way. But how would you feel being on your own at his plantation? I don't want you to be in any sort of situation you didn't feel confident with."

"I've certainly regained what the military people call a sense of mission. Not to go to Columbus would be throwing away what may be our best opportunity," I said. "As long as I knew where to find you, I think I would be all right, although, to be perfectly honest, you would be missed as more than just someone friendly and familiar. What would you do, though, stay in a hotel? Do we even have enough money? We have already financed new construction for half the railroads in the Deep South."

"On both counts, yes, although a hotel may not be necessary. Mr. Hudgin has a friend near Columbus named Spence who is a very keen birder, so my accommodation problem is solved. But you know, I too find the thought of us being apart...that sounds rather queer, doesn't it?...well, you know what I mean. It's a bit nerve-jangling for both of us, but I'll work out a way of being in touch and we'll certainly do some birding together. That'll explain me and some railway matters will explain you. And, James, one other thing."

"Eh?"

"I just have to tell you how badly I feel about dragging you into something so unproductive as this has been, although of course nobody guaranteed instant results. But somewhere I know we are going to find something truly awful in the way of a plantation, the sort we keep hearing about. We know they exist. It's just a matter of finding them. I don't even want to think of how many we have gone right past without knowing it."

"One thing is certain," I said. "We have been steered around by forces unseen. I just wonder if said forces may sound the alarm if we slip out of their web, especially in the age of the telegraph."

"It's a chance we have to take."

"Let us do it, then. The worst has been concealed from us. We're going to find it."

"There is fire in your speech, James. I like it."

We let Mr. Hudgin deal with directing Alex to his friend Mr. Spence, dropped any further reference to Major Ramsay, and with a cheery good-bye, we struck out westwards on the Alabama and Tennessee Railroad to Uniontown at the end of completed trackage. Speed in communicating with Major Ramsay was of the essence and I stewed over the possible lack of telegraph facilities at Uniontown, knowing as I did the intimate relationship between telegraph and rail lines. Instead of taking some much-needed time to enjoy the rail journey, I fussed and fretted as we rolled smokily past illimitable fields of cotton, the fields dotted here and there with groups of stooped slaves plucking bolls of cotton, past woodlots of loblolly pine (called "turpentine" in Alabama), pausing at country way stations to set down the mail and the occasional planter. We were into August now and stultifying heat lay over the countryside in a shimmering blanket which, mixed with the acrid fumes of wood smoke blowing grittily in at the train window, not to mention a goodly helping of tension, made us feel quite ill and out of sorts.

Our stress turned out to be groundless. Although Uniontown was at track's end, the route through to Meridian, Mississippi, had been surveyed and cleared and the telegraph line was up and working already. Hallelujah! Praise Jesus! So I sent my telegram to Major Ramsay and received a response the next morning:

MOBILE & OHIO R.R. COLUMBUS MISS.
AUG 7 1858 10:17 A.M.
WELCOME COUSIN JIM STOP STAY AS LONG AS WANT STOP
BED MADE UP END MESSAGE
/S/ COUSIN WILL

We made do with the temporary stagecoach connection to Meridian and boarded the Mobile and Ohio for Columbus. We didn't merely suspect, we *knew* the gravity of what the next few days would bring, and it was indeed an introspective and somewhat grim journey, made more so by the prospect of having to operate apart from each other. To have so little mutual reassurance when we needed it the most was a bleak prospect; I know myself well enough to confess without shame that the experience that was to follow would be so draining, emotionally, physically, and intellectually, that not only could I not go through it again, but just repeating it on paper is costing a dreadful effort and is happening only because it is a story that must be told. And since I was there, it falls to me to tell it, even though I fear it has left me impaired in terms of courage. I am still so eroded by it all that the least sort of confrontation with anyone now fills me with horror. If I disappoint by not having been made strong, well, I am sincerely sorry; all I can say is it could only be fully understood by someone in a similar circumstance.

At Columbus station, I was met by a carriage under the command of a youngish slave, who, hat in hand, introduced himself: "Massa Ramsay? Ah'm Joe. De Major, he done put me at yo' service."

Joe was so pleasant and courteous that I unthinkingly extended my hand. Joe looked at my proffered hand in puzzlement, back at me, and said sorrowfully, "Sorry, massa, Ah can't. But thank yu anyway."

"I'm sorry too," I mumbled. I tried to converse with Joe on the carriage ride to the plantation, but between the rattle of the vehicle, Joe's dialect, and his voice being so soft as to be almost a whisper, it was a pretty futile exercise, so I lapsed into a weary silence and watched the flat Mississippi countryside slide past in the deepening twilight.

"Jim, boy, good to see yew!" boomed the Major as the carriage drew up in front of the big plantation house. He whistled. A black Labrador dog came shuffling up, head down, tail wagging stiffly. "Not yew, Colonel, yew black bastard. Wrong whistle. Now, git lost." The dog shuffled sorrowfully off.

"Did you say 'Colonel', Major, I mean Will?"

"Only way Ah get to mouth off at a superior officer. Guess if Ah ever make colonel mahself, Ah'll have to promote him too." The Major whistled again. Colonel looked over his shoulder.

"Kee-rist," said the Major in exasperation. He whistled once more, stridently this time. A black child came tearing up, out of breath, eyes glistening with tears. "Ah is real sorry, massa. Ah was in de biffy..."

"Ah whistle fer yew, yew drop ever'thang, y'all unnerstand?"

"Ah did..."

"Now, then, don't yew back-mouth me, boy. Yew know what happens if yew do, don't yew"?

"Yes, massa."

"Ah want to hear yew tell me."

"Ah gets a whuppin', massa."

I felt as if struck myself. The Major, this sorry remnant of humanity, was enjoying himself, almost strutting with the power of dominion over another human being.

"Damn' right, yew get a whuppin'," continued the Major. "Now, this here is Mr. Ramsay, relative of mine." I tried not to wince. "He's all the way from Canada. Yew take his bags real nice, now, and show him to his room."

I was unable to discern at the time whether the Major was putting on a show of power just for my benefit or whether this was his natural disposition, but evidence of the latter emerged quickly indeed. His abrasive demeanour extended not only to his slaves and his dog, but to his wife as well. In absolutely every plantation we had visited, courtesy between husband and wife had been formal to the extent of the usage of "sir" and "madam" in ordinary conversation; while the practice had a definite courtly charm, it also had inspired some private amusement on my part, speculating on the role of such formality in the bed chamber.

But neither courtesy, passion, nor even simple affection existed in the Ramsay household. The Major addressed his wife, a mousy, downtrodden little lady, as "woman" and referred to her in conversation, not by name, but as "she". Evidently she spoke only when spoken to.

There was a son in the family, I was told, but just two days before, he had left for pre-term training exercises at a military college. "Good choice," said the Major with finality. "Never know who yew'll have to fight and when."

And to round out the Ramsay household, there were two elderly aunts who were "feeling poorly" that evening and whose acquaintance would be made later.

"Quiet life here, Jim," said the Major over a post-dinner mint julep. "But we'll do our best to amuse yew, and town's not too far away."

"Well," I began, "fact is, Major..."

"Now, what did Ah tell yew about what kinfolk call each other?"

"Very well, Will." Dear God, I was sounding like Alex! "What I would really like to do, and this relates to our conversation on the train that time, is to see how a plantation works, see the, er, everybody at work and, uh, how it's done, you know, all that sort of thing. After all, there's a big demand for cotton up home and my company may be bringing some of yours in before long."

I held my breath, waiting for something to be said about our stay at the Hudgin plantation, but nothing was forthcoming. Evidently the acquaintance was not close enough to merit contact, unless there was a letter on the way.

I let my breath out and took another sip of mint julep. Damn, but it was a nice drink! My unease about Mr. Hudgin aside, I had said the right thing. "Ah," said the Major (cousin be damned!) "will have Joe guide yew around. He's not a bad sort as nigras go. Sure thang, Jim. We'll pick a nice day for yew and yew can watch ever'thang to your hort's content. Say, how about a game of snooker? Got a new table in June..."

The following day, the cook made me a packet of sandwiches and I was off with Joe in late morning. We trudged along a dirt road that led from the house into the cotton fields, and the faint conversation and snatches of singing of the slaves could be distantly heard, mingled with the chirpings and raspings of the little creatures of high summer. I did not have Alex's gift for spontaneous conversation, though there was so much to be said, and for the first while, Joe and I were partners in unease. But then Joe took the initiative.

"Yu from Canada, massa?"

"Yes, that's right."

"Ah heah Canada be real nice."

"It really is. I like it, except for the winter."

"Plenty cold, Ah heah."

"It gets that way, but we put up with it. We tell ourselves it's all part of being Canadian."

"No slaves in Canada."

"No, none. It's been against the law since, oh, twenty-five years ago..."

"Any black people up in Canada now?"

"Oh, yes, some."

"Where dey from?"

Momentarily my mind locked; somehow, Joe knew that blacks were not indigenous to our part of the world. "Well, er," I stumbled, "many are from down here." Oh, here we go at last! Alex, where are you?

Next question: "How dey get up dere?"

"They walked."

"Lordy! Far, ain't it?"

"From here, about a thousand miles." Joe looked puzzled. With no education, he had no concept of what that sort of distance entailed. I tried again. "If you can walk twelve miles a night, and it must be at night, I would say it would take you eighty to eighty-five days to get you into Canada."

"Sweet Jesus, dat some walk, ain't it?"

"It is, Joe. It's some walk." I took a deep breath. "Do you want to do it?"

Joe, who was marginally ahead of me, spun around. "Oh, massa...oh, God...gentle Jesus...sorry, massa, Ah doan like to cry."

"That's all right. You've kept too much sorrow inside for too long."

"Dat chile yestiddy, whut tooken yo' bags...dat's mah li'l brudder Peter. Peter been whupped real bad...like dis, massa." Joe took off his shirt and showed me his own back. It was slashed with the most grotesque pattern of scars and welts, and on his right shoulder blade were branded the letters "W.R."

"W.R.!" I exclaimed.

"Yes, massa, we is all branded. Dere's me, Peter, an' our beautiful sister Ruth." Joe wept, wiping his eyes on his sleeves. I put a hand on his shoulder. "No, massa, can't do dat. Thank yu, but..."

"Of course. Pardon me."

Joe fought for breath through great, strangling sobs. "We wuz sold down heah from Tennessee."

"Sounds familiar."

"We wuz just little. Our Mammy and Pappy died heah, worked like to death...buried under dem trees dere...so Ah feels responsible for Peter an' Ruth. Like Ah said, Ruth is beautiful, an' you know whut? Dat dere Major, he done made her his...his...Ah can't bring mahself to say it..."

"I think I know what you're saying. His, uh, *mistress*?"

"Worse'n dat, massa. He done made Ruth his...his...*hooer*...done all sorts of strange things wid her. Wish Ah had de guts to kill 'im, but all de udder slave owners'd probly burn me and do orful things to Ruth an' Peter."

"I can arrange for the three of you to get out and come to Canada." The words just tumbled out.

"Three! Oh, massa, a lot more'n dat! *All* of us wanna go. We's twelve of us. An' dat poor dog wanna go too, Ah'll wager. An' mah elder brudder, he slave on a plantation up at Ellerslie, we want him to go too, be all togethah. An' poor Missis Ramsay..."

Oh, this was great! A potential escape of thirteen slaves, possibly a dog, no word from Gerrit or Richard, Alex temporarily *incommunicado*, no knowledge of any way stations on the Underground Railroad, reminding me, "Joe, have you ever heard of a thing called the Underground Railroad?"

Joe looked astounded. "A railroad unda de ground?"

I laughed with no more than a subtle touch of hysteria. "I'm sorry, Joe, I didn't mean to laugh. It's underground in the sense that you can't see it. It's a secret escape route to Canada."

"Guess Ah have, though it weren't called like dat."

"Well, it exists and I'm part of it. That is why I am here. A friend of mine is staying at the Spence plantation and he's part of it too. We'll get something arranged for you."

We had reached the edge of a woodlot at the back, or southern, edge of the plantation and Joe sat down on a log. He leapt back up again as if stung.

"What's the matter?"

"Ah'm so sorry, massa, shouldn'a done dat."

"Done what?"

"Sat down."

"So what's the matter about sitting down? Oh, I see, the slave has to stand when the master is present, right?"

"Dat's right, massa."

"Well, you're not my slave and I'm not your massa. In fact, I hope we'll get to be good friends. Let's sit down and have a bite to eat." I unwrapped my sandwiches, bit into one, and then realized that Joe had none. I held one out to him. His eyes widened. "Have one," I encouraged.

"Oh, massa, Ah can't."

"Joe, tell me honestly, are you hungry?"

"Yes, massa, very."

"Then let's stop fooling around. I can't eat all of this anyway, so you may as well share it with me. This could be history, you know. Could be the first time a slave and a white man have ever had a picnic together." Joe had no idea of what a picnic was and I had to explain it to him.

I returned to the plantation house late in the afternoon, enveloped in a strange calm, just in time to witness a singularly brutal spectacle that demonstrated conclusively that the wraps and shrouds were certainly off *this* plantation. Just behind the main house was an outbuilding called the weighing shed, in which each slave's share of the day's cotton harvest was weighed and recorded. The Major, I learned, had a wager with some of his fellow planters as to which plantation could produce the most cotton; to work his slaves to the maximum, he had resorted to the simple expedient of having the slave who brought in the lowest weight for the day given a good whuppin'.

The verdict this afternoon was delivered against Rebecca, a careworn woman of thirty-five or so; she was stripped to the waist and given several well-aimed blows by the Major himself, although his overseer, a loutish type named Edgar, was plainly anxious to perform the task. Edgar was a true professional in his occupation, one of those rare types who wish to deliver more than the minimum.

"Good-for-nothing black sow," grumbled the Major, coiling up his whip and putting it into its special carrying case. "Now, y'all button up there, woman. Don't leave yer tits hangin' out like that."

"Yes, massa."

"And pick more tomorrow."

"Yes, massa."

And to me, the Major continued, "They get that useless, there ain't much to be done."

"How long has she worked here?"

"Eight years and seven is usually the limit, so Ah guess Ah can't complain. Just hate spending money on new stock, Ah guess."

"What happens to a slave who is, uh, all worn out?"

"Take 'im out an' shoot 'im."

"What?" I exclaimed. Rebecca hung her head sorrowfully.

The Major laughed. "Oh, Jim, no need to git your bowels in an uproar. No, Ah think the time has come for her to have a couple of babies for the stable. Ah'd offer her to yew for the night" (I gulped), "but she's a bit of a pot roast. 'Sides, she's dumb and has no imagination. Now, Ruth, she's a different story altogether. Ever' now and then, the wife goes to see her ma down in Hattiesburg, so Ruth an' me, we have some fun together. Why don't y'all have her while you're here? Yew'd be powerful welcome to indulge."

Lord, have mercy! Had I not enough on my mind already? For this I was not prepared. I had seen Ruth, although without knowing who she really was, but she certainly was a woman to be noticed. Not only that; in practical terms, she could be a useful conduit of information with the slaves, giving me some leeway in my possible motivations. I professed enthusiasm with the most revolting utterance of my entire life: "That sounds like great fun, Will. Come to think of it, I'm really in the mood for some nice dark meat!"

The Major looked delighted. "Never had a nigra, huh?"

"Never in my life." Never had anyone else either, but that was beside the point.

" 'Bout time yew did,then. Ah'll send Edgar over to her cabin, tell 'er to warsh real good an' be in yore room for nine o'clock. Don't want her smellin' funny for yew."

"One thing, though."

"What's that, now?"

"If she were to get pregnant, well..."

"Shucks, it don't make no never mind if she dew. Another addition to the stable, ha, ha! An' a little biddy black cousin for me!" Oh, wonderful, James. The father of a slave child!

The elderly aunts, Jane and Isabel, were present for dinner that evening, a distillation of elderly Southern womanhood in microcosm. In appearance, they were almost exact opposites. Aunt Jane was painfully thin, almost emaciated, with a thin, reedy voice, and Aunt Isabel , in contrast, hovered on the brink of obesity, her voice was deep and husky, and little black hairs grew from her chin. There was something endearingly repulsive about them, like a bulldog with loose skin.

The two of them wasted no time whatever telling of their life's tragedy and it was quite plain that their needs were such as to impose a drain upon those about them. Whereas, so far in my visit, the Major had abused to various degrees all those within sight or sound, he positively fawned over these two. I suspected, though never knew for certain, that there was some sort of inheritance at stake.

"Beet greens, Auntie? Some vinegar, my dear?" No such consideration was extended to poor old She. Be funny if she took the Underground Railroad too. The first white escapee...

The saga of Jane and Isabel was told at great length and in much detail. As young women, they had both demonstrated quite a formidable musical ability, Jane as a pianist and Isabel as a contralto singer. They had been sent up to Baltimore, to the Peabody Conservatory, with the ultimate objective of appearing in joint recitals as the Ramsay Sisters. And then Jane had taken a spill from a horse, damaging her right hand. Rather than seeking medical attention in the despised North, she had opted for a lifetime as a semi-invalid. And Isabel had opted for a lifetime of perpetual care for her sister. They never performed again, simply staying at the family plantation and living the life of a couple of drones.

I listened to this tale of woe, of Aunt Jane and Aunt Isabel falling upon the thorns of life and bleeding, with courtesy and a great deal of attention, considering that in the space of a day I had made contact with slaves (who themselves had a certain intimacy with the thorns of life) desperate for escape to Canada and one of whom was evidently destined to be the first woman I was to have. At this point, it was difficult to discern which consideration loomed larger.

I spent the entire evening, then, absorbing the old aunts' prattle, and at the hour of nine, as ordained by the Major, I excused myself and retired to my bedroom in a state of the highest anxiety, a white virgin about to be deflowered by a reputedly expert slave girl. Somehow it was all very exciting, uplifting, and degrading all at once, and on my way up the stairs, in a moment of timidity, I somehow hoped that for some reason Ruth might not be in my room.

But there she was, demurely sitting on my bed, wearing a simple white night gown. Her first words to me were "Good evenin', massa."

"Good evening, Ruth." I bowed formally, my face engulfed in hot foolishness. Ruth cast her eyes downward. I sat down next to her, reassured by the feeling that she was as uncomfortable as I.

"Has Joe told you about me?" I asked.

"Yes, massa. Please. We must whisper."

"Of course. I beg your pardon."

"Joe say yu a very kind man."

"Well, you may as well know Joe is someone I admire. Look, Ruth, I want you to understand this wasn't my idea, you and me...I hope that didn't sound insulting."

"No, massa." Her eyes lost a bit of their frightened roundness; probably her experience had taught her that all white men were beasts of the worst order. I wanted to change that.

"When you're with Major Ramsay like this, do you have to call him 'massa'?"

"Yes, massa, Ah do...an' Ah lets him do whatevah he wants."

"I'm not going to do that. And there's no need to call me 'massa'. Try 'James'."

"Ah...can't..., massa."

"Ruth, I'm far more interested in being your friend. I just never could be comfortable with this 'massa' business, so I want you to try again. What's my name, now?"

"Massa Ramsay."

"No, no, the other one. My first name."

"J...", she spluttered as if learning to speak all over again.

I couldn't help but smile. "Try again."

"J...uh, James."

"See? You did it! Was it so hard?"

"Yes, mas..."

I shushed her with my finger tips. "It'll get easier. Just practise it a bit." I had no idea what to say next or any idea of anything at all. It was appalling. I felt like a locomotive whose valve gear was locked at dead centre.

To stall for time, I pulled off my shoes as slowly as I could. Now, what to do? Give her a good-night kiss? Too soon in my Anglo-Protestant Upper-Canadian Victorian estimation. Shake her hand? Ridiculous in anyone's estimation. So I took the coward's way out, simply said, "Good night," and settled into the armchair, leaving Ruth sitting primly on the bed. A moment of the thickest silence I have ever heard.

"Massa...James, rather...yu ain't spendin' de night in dat ar chair, is yu?"

"Oh, I'll be fine. Don't worry about me."

"Yu won't be fine an' Ah'll worry mah head off. Ah'd go back to mah cabin, only de Major'd whup me an' mebbe rape me, an' ah knows, on account of he done dat to me twice already. Nevah saw a man go so wild. Yu kin come in wid me an' if'n yu wanna do me, well, dat's what Ah'm heah for."

Sensing the ruination I would feel if I spent the night in the chair, I relented and climbed into bed with Ruth, clothes and all. In the battle between desire and fear, fear was gaining the upper hand.

We lay side by each like a couple of Egyptian mummies; I studied the patterns made by the cracks in the ceiling. Somewhere a door slapped shut and the Major's voice could be heard admonishing the hapless Colonel. Ruth sighed a sigh that spoke volumes.

In the depths of my cowardice, I dozed off, cosily tucked in with a woman whom any man, Victorian gentleman or no, would have killed to be with. It was a situation beyond sorrow.

I awoke in the night to find Ruth, in all her wondrous convexity, pressed against me, and for a flash I thought My Time Had Come. But there was some sense that told me, and rightly, as I was to learn, that she was pressed against me for security rather than desire. Our hands touched and then entwined. It was all the intimacy either of us needed.

As the new day broke, Ruth was propped up on one elbow, all bed-warm, looking down at me, a smile in her eyes. "Good morning," said I intelligently.

"Mornin', massa, Ah means James." God, she was lovely! "Ah was just thinkin', Joe tole me about de sandwich. Said yu was a real gentleman, an' aftah las' night, Ah see what he meant. Ah was real scared yu'd do strange things like de Major."

"Well," I blustered, "it just didn't seem right to take advantage...I'd like to get to know you first."

"Ah like de way yu done hol' mah hand in de night. Nobody evah done dat but my mammy an' she done daid now."

"It wasn't done in quite the same way as your mammy, or at least that wasn't quite what I intended..."

Ruth laughed softly, a wonderfully silken laugh. "Ah knows. Ah wants to come to yu again tonight. And Ah wants yu to tell me all about dis heah place Canada."

Can a mother forget her suckling child?

The tender mercies of the wicked are cruel.

SCENES ON A PLANTATION, A SCENARIO
CLOSER TO THE REALITIES OF THE DEEP SOUTH.
ILLUSTRATION FROM *THE LIFE AND ADVENTURES OF HENRY BIBB,* 1850.
COURTESY OF THE ENOCH PRATT FREE LIBRARY, BALTIMORE, MD

CHAPTER FIFTEEN

"How was she, Jim?" asked the Major with much nudging and winking as we went into breakfast.

"Breathtaking!" I said sincerely and with at least a modicum of truth.

"She's yores any time, then. Take her again tonight if yew want."

"I took the liberty of making some, er, arrangements. Hope you don't mind."

"Mind? Aw, hell, no. Not only are we both Ramsays, we're men, and real men at that. Say, Jim, Ah got a real good 'un fer yew. How long does a Real Man take to fill up an awl lamp?"

"A which?"

"An awl lamp. Yew know, yew fill the thang with awl..."

"Oh, oil. I see."

"Well, how long does he take?"

"Uh, well, he first has to unscrew..."

"Hah! Gotcha! It doesn't take him any time at all."

"It doesn't?"

"No! A Real Man doesn't fill it at all. He isn't afraid of the dark!"

"Silly Willy!" scolded Aunt Isabel lovingly in her contralto-turned-baritone voice. "What stories yew tell!"

Aunt Jane and She completed the quartet for breakfast, this one raising the curtain on Saturday, August the 10th. I am not particularly a collector of dates, but this one has stayed with me all these years, for it saw an especially singular combination of breakfast diners. When we were about half-way through a plate of ham and grits, the plantation's major-domo, whose name transliterated as something like "Jerge", announced a visitor.

"A visitor?" said the Major in surprise. "Brang 'im in here...hello, stranger." But a stranger it was not. It was Alex. I tried not to look too interested; Alex, of course, was supremely imperturbable.

"Very kind of you to invite me in," he said smoothly. "I hope I am not imposing."

"No, no, not at all. Have some coffee?"

"Yes, please, if it's not too much bother. My name is Alexander Ross, of Buffalo, New York. I wonder if I could ask a favour."

"We'll dew what we can. What have yew in mind?"

"I'm a naturalist with the Western New York Museum of Natural History and we're in the process of assembling the most comprehensive collection of North American birds to be found anywhere."

"Live birds?" I said quickly to establish an apparent disassociation with Alex.

"No, young man. The birds are shot, dissected, and preserved." He turned back to the Major, leaving me to plot revenge for the "young man" reference. That stupid joke about Real Men might actually be useful.

"I have been lodging with your distant neighbour Mr. Spence," resumed Alex. "We are both admirers of J.J. Audubon's publication *Birds of America*. You may know of it."

"Can't say Ah dew."

"A pity. I am devoted to the study of wildlife and have found admirers of Mr. Audobon's work *most* helpful. You, sir, I take it, are Major Ramsay."

"Right yew are, stranger, only you're not a stranger any more. Allow me to present mah wife...mah aunt, Miss Jane Ramsay...mah other aunt, Miss Isabel Ramsay...and mah kinsman, Mr. James Ramsay, all the way from Canada."

"Canada, eh?" Damn it, Alex, Americans don't say "eh"! They say "huh?"

"Why, that's just across the water from us," said Alex. "In fact, I can see Canada from the back corner of my garden." Oh, careful, careful! In America, you have a "yard", not a "garden". Alex turned to me. "When will you people see the light and join our union?"

"Never!" I said stoutly. "Friends, yes, family, no. We're part of the British Empire and not a little proud of it too. Living under the lion's paw, so to say."

"Ah, the British Empire," said Alex, sitting down by Aunt Jane, who was gazing at him adoringly. "May I have the cream, madam? Thank you so much. How anyone can have a conscience and an empire at the same time is quite beyond me." Could this really be Alex? It sounded more like something Gerrit Smith would have said.

"Why, an empire,"I pronounced grandly, "is a family of nations, of diverse peoples united under the Crown..."

"Under the lion's paw," crooned Aunt Isabel, the pitch of her voice dropping a minor third so that she sounded to be at the bottom of a well.

"A ruling position inherited by parasites," said Alex impassively. What he had in mind was uncertain, but I was becoming alarmed at the direction the conversation was taking. Any controversial reference to slavery that might emerge was the last thing we needed, so I steered the exchange onto a different course.

"Look at it this way," I expounded. "The Crown provides continuity, while presidents and prime ministers are in and out, in and out. The Monarchy furnishes stability, which is why the Empire is as it is, embodying evolution rather than revolution, bringing order to disorderly masses..."

"Empire is oppression," stated Alex flatly. Oh, no, there he went again! "Oppression," he repeated, "sanctioned by all manner of bizarre and irrelevant ceremony, those dreadful agony bags..."

Since Alex had a perennial love affair with the pipes and drums, I threw back at him his own words on the subject. "Why, the pipes, well, Mr. Ross, they are not merely ceremonial. They symbolize the very essence of human existence...the three drones are a constant chorus, a Holy Trinity of sound, and their sound is as the eternal motion of the universe..." My memory of Alex's response fails me here, but I had done what I needed to.

The Major laughed. "Looks as if yew two boys are going to get along just fine. So, Mr. Ross, y'all're looking for birds."

"I am, specifically for Mississippi kites, Bachman's warbler, and purple gallinules. And wood ibis; they tend to live in marshland and since you have the only swamp in the area, so Mr. Spence tells me, down back of your woodlot, it seemed a likely place to look, given your permission."

"Aw, shucks, y'all're most welcome. Don't know much about birds mahself," said the Major, "exceptin' crows. They're allus picking at the cotton seeds at planting time and Ah've shot off more rounds account of them than all other varmints combined, the black bas...er, so-and-soes. Say, Jim, yew've been around the property a bit. Maybe yew could be Mr. Ross's guide."

"I have quite a lot of equipment," put in Alex. "Any chance a slave could be spared to carry it?"

One of the Major's sandy eyebrows rose. "A Northern gentleman using a slave?"

Alex shrugged. "When in Rome, well, you know the saying. I've never been one to violate local custom."

While all this was being said, my mind was racing in circles; we needed to talk to a slave or slaves, but what I had discovered since the day before was that any slave missing work for such reasons as escorting guests had to make up the weight of cotton he would have picked during that time, and I hated to see any slave put in that sort of position. That is not to say it was the practice on all plantations, but it certainly was on this one, ruled as it was by the arbitrary and despotic Major Ramsay.

"Glad yew see it as yew do, Mr. Ross," said the voice of the despot. "Ah get mighty tired sometimes hearing about these Northern busybodies who know nothing of why we do as we do but are so quick, yes, sir, to damn...excuse me, dear aunts...to judge and condemn us. Without slavery, those folks'd have no cotton and 'd be going naked in the world.

"But yew can't be too careful. Had a Northern fella nosing through here coupla months back, sayin' the wrong thangs to the wrong people, all kinds of poppycock about slaves gettin' away. Got away on us, or we'd have tarred and feathered him." The Major could only have been speaking of Richard Adamson.

"Look, Ah'll give yew Joe, Jim here knows him a bit, and he'll tote yore stuff wherever yew want it. Me, Ah must be off to town to arrange a couple of freight cars for next week's shipment on the good ole Mobile and Ohio. Some railroad activity, huh, Jim? Yew bet."

"Thank you for the coffee, Major," said Alex, who hated coffee, rising and shaking hands. "And for everything else. This is more helpful than you could ever imagine."

"A pleasure, Mr. Ross. Good huntin', now, y'all hear?"

Joe was already out in the fields and was not only surprised to be taken from his usual labours for the second day in succession, but possibly perturbed at once again having to catch up on his quota of cotton. The Major could have chosen someone else; the unpleasant thought occurred that he may have been trying to run Joe ragged.

I remarked on this, adding, "We'll only keep you an hour or so, Joe. I know how Himself operates."

"Doan worry, Massa Ramsay, Ah doan care. Mebbe better if'n Ah picks de least cotton today an' git a whuppin' 'stead of poor Rebecca. She been gittin' a lot lately, can't take no moah."

"Whatever happens, somebody gets whipped, right?"

"Sho' thing. An' if'n two people shares last spot, dey *both* gits a whuppin'."

"Jesus Christ," I murmured involuntarily.

"James, how many times," began Alex primly as if on cue.

"Said in supplication, not agitation. There's a difference. Joe, this is Dr. Ross, the man from Canada I told you about."

"Oh, massa, massa," said Joe pleadingly, "help us deliver ourselves, for Jesus' sake."

"We will, Joe. Believe it. I have two guns with me and they are both for you. There are four knives and some bread and cheese in a bag too, enough to keep you going for four or five days.

"James, I have heard from Gerrit; if Joe and anyone who goes with him can get to the Snider farm near Booneville, they can be directed to the next two stations from there. Beyond that, I'm not certain, but Gerrit did indicate that he and Richard have things pretty well in hand now all the way up the line. This will be the first trip up the new route and it's going to have to be run a bit like a treasure hunt."

We had been walking all the while this was being said and we had reached the edge of the providentially-situated woodlot. "We hide the supplies here," said Alex. "Are there any hollow trees about?"

We searched, the exercise being oddly like children's forest games, but we could find no hollow trees. The supplies had to be well-hidden, yet accessible in the dark, meaning that exactly the right place had to be found and it just was not happening. We carried on with our quest as a breeze breathed upon the Mississippi woodlands, sending down gentle showers of green morning sunlight.

"We're too far in," said Alex. "You'd never find this in the dark." We circled back the way we had come, back to where the woods ended and the cotton fields began, and there we found a highly acceptable substitute for the phantom hollow tree, a great pine uprooted by some bygone tempest. The bag fitted nicely under the overhang of roots and the leaning pine would be easy to find, even in the dark.

Joe brought up the subject of his brother at Ellerslie and kept at it until Alex had to say, "Joe, we don't know how many want to go from here and we need you to find out for us. In any case, we can't run groups from different plantations and try to connect them. And we have to keep the groups to a manageable size, a dozen or so at most. I'll go to Ellerslie and see to things, I promise you that."

"Oh, massa," said Joe forlornly.

"Just trust us. You're going to have to do that. I want to get you moving by Monday night, so there's enough to occupy us here. Now, I guess I'd better do my duty and sacrifice a few of God's creatures for the betterment of mankind."

As Alex strolled off, gun in hand, I said to Joe, "I guess you heard about me and Ruth."

"Ah did, Massa James, an' she said yu was a real gentleman. She said yu very sweet man, very gentle and thowtful. 'Bout time somebody treated her right."

"Well, she's someone special. I would be less than honest if I didn't tell you I have had difficulty thinking of anything else today."

"Oh, doan go lovin' her, Massa James, please. Black an' white ain't goan mix. Yu has eddication, we don't...can't even tell de time."

"You can learn. In fact, you're going to *have* to. You are just as smart as anyone. Don't let anyone make you believe otherwise."

But somebody already had. "Oh, Ah doan know..."

Our mission would go on for years beyond physical liberation of the slaves. They would have to be liberated from the attitudes that had been deliberately, methodically, and with malice aforethought cultivated in them for generations, attitudes that in some situations had reached the point where slaves actually preferred the status of the victim on both ethical and religious grounds, for they could go straight to heaven unstained by the guilt of having harmed someone.

Periodically a shot resounded through the countryside as Alex went about his spurious task, and several slaves working nearby looked up in bewilderment. I waved at them by way of reassurance, and to my surprise and pleasure, they waved back.

"Dey knows who yu is, but dey shouldn'a done dat," said Joe in apprehension. "Doan want Edgar thinkin' somethin's gonna happen an' tell de Major."

"You're starting to think the right way, Joe. I shouldn't have done it either. We have to get accustomed to thinking the worst." Rising tension was giving me a headache, the kind that feels like a cord being tightened about the head.

Alex went on his way about noon with a convincing collection of bird bits. "James," he said in parting, "this is the opportunity we have worked towards for so long and I want to make the most of it. If as many people want to leave as Joe says, they will need a leader..."

"Oh, shit."

"...and it would have to be you. I would need to be free to deal with

Ellerslie."

"Alex, don't joke about this. It isn't funny."

"I know it's not, which is why I am not joking. I've heard enough in town to know that once these people clear out and we are connected with them, our lives won't be worth the paper for a death certificate. I think our prospects for effectiveness and ultimately our personal safety depend on us working apart for a while. Everything but the actual number is ready for Monday night. Here is a map and a list of everything I know about the route from here to Canada, which isn't much. I may travel north with the group from Ellerslie, I may carry on getting other groups going, I don't know. God bless you, my friend. See you in Canada."

"You hope."

"I *know*. Hope is not enough."

I retired early that night, truthfully pleading a headache. Not only had the damned thing not gone away, but its intensity had increased, fuelled by thoughts that Alex might be putting himself at such appalling risk that he was afraid of exposing me too and was sending me on my way for my own safety. I lay there in my torment, listening to the curtains rustling in the evening breeze and the tiny denizens of night whirring and twittering into action.

The latch on my door clicked - good God, I had all but forgotten Ruth! Now I needed her desperately, but more in the way of reassurance than passion, not a good feeling at all if I were to function as Fearless Leader.

Ruth slipped into the room and sat down on the edge of the bed. "Massa James, Ah has things to tell yu."

"What things?" I rose on one elbow.

"We *all* wants to go to Canada, exceptin' Edgar. We didn' even bothah askin' *him*."

"All? How many is all?"

"Doan know. Can't count."

I did a quick mental calculation; Joe had thought twelve, but I knew of a baby and a couple of children, putting the real number at fifteen. I must have turned pale in the dusk.

"Massa James, is yu orl right?"

"Oh, I'm fine," I lied smoothly. "It's just, ah, the excitement."

"Yu want me wid yu tonight?"

Doan go lovin' her, Massa James... "Yes, Ruth, I really want you with me tonight." There was no disguising the wobble in my voice. "Ruth, I'm going to have to lead your people to Canada. I'm scared. I'm sorry, I shouldn't have said that to you, but I had to tell somebody."

"Ain't nuthin' to be sorry about. Just remember de Lawd is wid us, no feah of dat. We be crossin' de Ribber Jordan, all togethah. Bet Jesus was scared a lot o' times...thing to do is not to give in to it."

"Remind me of that when things get rough."

"Ah will, Massa James. Now, whatevah yu wants to do wid me is jes' fine."

"I think I'd just like to hold you."

"Well, den, hol' me yu will. Yu some sweet man, Massa James. Yu goan be our saviour."

Ruth snuggled up to me and I put my arms about her. Moments later, I was ready for far more than mere holding. She pressed me to her, breath quickening, not the sound of a woman about to be abused. And her hands roamed me, hands daring to go where no hands had ever gone, exquisite intimacy, gentleness temporarily displacing the mounting fear of this mad adventure, black, white, oh, who could care in the face of this?

It could go on forever, this warm, lazy, timeless cocoon of, what, passion? Too gentle. Love? Probably, despite Joe's injunction. Black and white, it was irrelevant anyway, we were human and we wanted each other...

A door crashed open downstairs and the Major's rage filled the night. "God damn it to hell! That black bastard Joe has buzzed off!"

Chapter Sixteen

I had no time even for a sigh of regret. Almost by reflex, I leapt from the bed, more or less vaulting over Ruth. As I pulled my clothes on, I sent her on her way to tell everyone that plans were suspended until Joe was accounted for and that I would be helping to look for him. A hasty kiss, and then I was on my way downstairs, three steps at a time, to find the Major in the dining room with Edgar the overseer.

"Let me help you look for Joe," I panted, trying not to sound overly virtuous. "I don't want you thinking that my being from north of the border has anything to do with his disappearance."

"Ah know yew don't, Jim, but that fella Ross, Ah just don't know. Moved outa Spence's an' is stayin' in town now. Well, Ah'd shorely appreciate your help. Let's go out back and round up some nigras to help."

"You mean they'd help look for one of their own?"

The Major laughed disagreeably. "It's in their best interests and they know it. They'd have to make up the weight of cotton Joe would miss picking. 'Sides, Sunday is tomorrow and they won't be working anyway, so this'll give 'em a chance to find him before they have to do his work for him. Here, Ah'll lend yew a gun; know how to use it?"

"More or less, but why?"

"Keep the buggers in line. Let's get going."

"At night?"

"Shore, at night! Joe could be miles off by morning. Problem with these bastards is yew can't see 'em at night , but what the hell. Let's get out there and get those nigras and get their black butts moving. Yew too, Colonel, yew black bastard. Rent your space in the world..."

I followed Edgar and the Major out behind the weighing shed, hoping with unparalleled fervour that Ruth would have had a chance to explain my role in the search to the slaves, that I wouldn't be taken as some sort of a Judas. We went to the cabin of the senior slave couple, Jerge, whom I had met, and his wife Gladys. Gladys, realizing our intent, threw her apron over her face in the classic expression of sorrow or consternation. Jerge was instructed to round up the other slave men, getting them out of bed if necessary; his response was a weary, toneless "Yes, Massa."

My poor brain was grappling all the while with a major problem. I knew Joe must have gone up to Ellerslie. The question was this: should we simply go after him and find him since I knew where he was and then leave with him that night? Or should I just feign ignorance, thereby not placing the Ellerslie slaves in any danger if it were necessary, in view of Alex's uncertain status, for them to escape with us? I was of mixed opinion, for I wanted to be of service to more than a few slaves, especially in view of the fruitless four months since New Orleans; but I also did not wish to be in charge of an unmanageably large group.

That was the analytical part of James thinking. The other part of James thinking, if thoughts could be heard, was a great long whine of "Why me?" In any event, I elected not to try and influence events, but to deal with them as they unfolded, as manipulation is not something I am good at or have a taste for.

We could have practically sat on Joe and not known it, so dark was the night once the moon had set. So intense was the darkness, in fact, that I concluded that when our time came for escape, we could simply use the roads, not incidentally avoiding leaving clues in the form of trampled grass and underbrush, and diving for cover in case of an emergency. A plan began to formulate. To return to the present, the futility of doing as we were doing was plain, but the more time we wasted, the safer Joe would be. The cotton fields were arid and dusty from summer's heat and a hot orange ball of sun climbed above the pine trees. Still no Joe. Yet the Major persisted, past breakfast-time, although I felt as if about to digest myself, and past lunch-time as well.

Between the heat, the lack of food, and a tormented feeling of self-doubt, I would not have particularly cared had I dropped dead, a pretty sorry attitude for one who, but hours before, had promised the lovely Ruth to be a saviour to her people.

And the thought of Ruth gave me just the sort of uplift I needed. Regrets for what might have been the previous night were displaced by a sort of serious joy at what might be tonight, and the prospect of not only having my own needs dealt with but being needed in return filled me with an almost overwhelming sense of purpose. So heartened was I, in fact, that I pretended to be having fun in the hunting of the unfortunate Joe, even referring to him as a nigger in the guise of solidarity with the Major. And I successfully feigned disappointment when the search was called off at about four in the afternoon. We returned to the plantation, the Major in the lead, Edgar next, then half a dozen slave men, myself riding shotgun, as they say out west, and Colonel, who had been reviled more times than I could count, poor beast, shuffling along at the rear.

Since Joe was absent from his usual duty as pilot of the carriage, old Jerge was ordered to deputise for him, and, still foodless, the Major and I rattled our delirious way into Columbus. We called at the police office to pick up a constable the Major knew and then made for the hotel. It was only then that the nature of our mission dawned on me , and there was no chance of warning Alex. So all I could hope for was the slim chance that he had left.

We drew up in front of the hotel in a swirling, gritty cloud of dust that sparkled in the low evening sunshine, and strode in through the door. "Landlord!" snapped the Major imperiously.

"Yes, sir. What is it, sir?"

"Do yew have a man named Ross registered here?"

"Why, yes, Major. Yew wish to see him?"

"Ah shore as hell dew."

"One moment, please. Ah think he's in the dining room." So much for Alex having left. The whole thing had gone so awry as to be almost comical, or so I thought in my malnourished state. The landlord disappeared momentarily, returning with Alex, who, as elegant as ever, was patting his mustache with a linen serviette.

"Major Ramsay! What a pleasant surprise! Perhaps you and Mr., umm..."

"That's him! Arrest him!" barked the Major to the constable.

"Why?" said Alex in a tone of innocent wonder.

"Damned abolitionist! Yew stole mah nigra! Ah'll have yore heart's blood for this!"

Several guests and spectators were now gathering. It was like a spontaneous little theatre, complete with a gallery arranged in orderly fashion up the staircase.

"Abolitionist?" said Alex, overlaying his innocent tone with a touch of sorrow that anyone could accuse him of such a thing. "*Me*? You, sir, should think your accusation over very carefully before you proceed further."

"Ah last saw this nigra with yew yesterday afternoon. Then Ah hear last night that yew left Spence's plantation. *Then* the nigra disappears, so what else is a man supposed to think? Constable, handcuff this bloodsucker. Right now, right *now*! What're y'all waiting for?"

Alex made a curious gesture, which he later told me was the Masonic sign of distress. I can explain it no further because of its highly confidential nature, but there was, by the greatest good fortune, a member of the Masons in the crowd, whose voice cut through the growing commotion to say,

"Just one moment, everybody. Ah think this man should be allowed to speak."

Instant silence. Alex, still with serviette in hand, still in total command of the situation, addressed the multitudes: "I have been charged - unofficially, I might say - with violation of your laws. You will be acting the part of cowards if you allow Major Ramsay to stir up hysteria and perhaps incite you to murder, for, as a Northerner, I am under no illusion as to the fate of active abolitionists at the hands of devout slave-owners. I am not in Mississippi for that purpose anyway.

"Or you can act as brave men and grant the only request I have to make, which is to say a fair trial before your magistrates, for I believe that in this country, one is assumed innocent until shown conclusively otherwise." It was Alex at his finest, dressed impeccably with watch chain in graceful swoop across his waistcoat, one hand on hip and the other brandishing the serviette as if it were a banner of truth. He was like a spiritual matador about to fight his accusers, calm and stalwart. I, by comparison, felt as tremulous as an aspen in a windstorm.

"Come along, Mr. Ross," said the constable. "Quietly, now, bein' yew ain't got a licence for public speakin'. Yew'll get yer fair trahl."

"Well, now, Jim," said the Major as Alex was led up the street. "Ah haven't been very hos*pit*able today. Ah just realized we've had no food, so let's the two of us take advantage of the facilities here and have us a real good dinner. Some bourbon and branch to stort with, then a good steak..."

We settled down in the hotel dining room as a waiter cleared away Alex's half-eaten dinner. I had no love for bourbon and branch, as already recorded, but, thirsty to the point of desperation as I was, I drank deeply of the stuff into the emptiest stomach of my entire life. A great T-bone steak followed and our feast was rounded out with red currant pie.

We then returned, tipsy and bloated, to the carriage still attended by poor Jerge, who had yet to have his dinner. Propped up in our seats, the Major and I sang all the way back to the plantation, and I managed to sing all the right things too, including a rendition of *Dixie* that had Aunt Isabel moved to tears as we rolled up the driveway.

"Oh, sweethort," she fussed, helping me up the stairs. "Can Ah get yew anything? Look what that silly Willy has done to yew!"

"Oh, Isabel, dear Isabel!" I carolled recklessly. "I did it all to myself, all on mine own. We do not have bourbon and branch in Canada. It is the nectar of the Gods...send me a bottle for Christmas and I'll love you forever!"

I collapsed into oblivion on my bed, even though it was still broad daylight; I lay in coma for a spell and then awoke to see a silhouette standing by my bed. "Ruth!" I slurred. "My beautiful Ruth! Let me hold you..."

"Ah think not, Massa James. Dere be somethin' orful in yo' bed."

I shot bolt upright, galvanized into a waking state by the somethin' orful, a pool of red currants laced with morsels of T-bone steak marinated in bourbon and branch. It was all over me; I coughed and a currant popped out of my left nostril. My debasement was total and complete.

"De demon drink," said Ruth piously.

My head swirled and swam. I wanted to put it down somewhere, anywhere. "Oh, God, Ruth, I'm sorree, so...urrh...sorree. See, I had nothing to eat all day and it was so hot and the Major..."

Ruth grimaced at both the spectacle and the smell of my misfortune, but said bravely, "Ah unnerstand, Massa James. Lemme get dese heah now linens off'n yu...get yu cleaned up a bit. Massa James, yu is one big baby!"

"I can clean myself up...sorry...oorp...that sounded kind of abrupt. Di'n' mean to. I jus' don't want to burden you."

"Ah've been burdened for two hunnid years. Don't make no difference to me. Anyway, Ah loves yu and wants to help. Ah heah Joe's still out dere. What we goan do, Massa James? Ever'one wanna know."

"We can't do anything until we know where he is. I know you and Peter wouldn't want to go without him, and if we went and you didn't, the Major would probably take it out on you. No, all we can do is wait, hard as it may be." The effort of thinking felt as if stretch marks were forming on my brain.

I drew a laboured, foul breath. "That's not all, Ruth. My friend Alex, who works with me on this, the Major thinks he is responsible for Joe's disappearance and had him put in jail."

"Oh, Lawd a'mercy! Ah done heard tell of de calaboose in Columbus...has bugs, has rats..."

"Well, that's another reason we can't leave. Aside from the fact that I can't just walk off leaving him in jail to face God-knows-what, he can't have had anything to do with Joe taking off anyway. Do *you* know anything? Did Joe tell you what he was up to?"

"Not a word." Ruth began to cry, but shrank from me as I reached for her. This would not do. I shrugged resignedly, thinking of just getting Alex out of jail and then chucking the whole thing and going home. Things were becoming simply more than I could manage.

Chapter Seventeen

While most affairs in Mississippi seemed to progress at the rate of pouring Upper Canada white honey, justice, such as it was, functioned with the utmost despatch. While I was enduring breakfast with the two old aunts the next morning, a Monday, a functionary from Columbus rode up to the great plantation door with the message that Alexander Milton Ross was to be tried for slave-robbery at eleven in the forenoon and that the Major's testimony would be required.

While I had made a full recovery from the excesses of the previous day, the Major was still in rather a bad state, his condition compounded with anxiety as he was still short of the two carloads of cotton he was committed to ship out two days later on the Mobile and Ohio. He was, of course, deprived of the talents of Joe, and going into town meant pressing Jerge into service once again, there just wasn't time for this foolishness, well, sir, the black bastards would just have to make up Joe's daily quota of cotton and that was it. And when he got his hands on Joe, there'd be the greatest whuppin' on record, oh, y'all just wait and see.

At the courthouse, a young white man of visible intellectual shortcomings had just been acquitted of rape, even though his black victim was visibly pregnant with what I learned months later was a mulatto baby. But when justice could function at such speed and economy of motion, surely occasional lapses of accuracy could be tolerated.

The same judge was to officiate at Alex's trial and was sorely vexed with the August heat, not to mention the aggravation of that wretched slave girl stirring up trouble for a good white man who drove the golden spike, why, hell, boy, any nigra bitch should be pleased at that, shouldn't she? Yew bet!

"Brang in the defendant," twanged His Honour in a voice with the timbre of a mill file. Alex was ushered in, now dishevelled and rumpled, but with dignity and bearing intact. If only Hester could see this! A couple of women sighed adoringly. I made a mental note to tell her about it whenever I could, not to make her jealous, but to flatter her that her own husband, difficult though he was, was coveted by other women and yet he remained faithful. Mental composition of a suitable speech was interrupted by the start of the trial.

"Plaintiff, state yore case," commanded the judge, pointedly looking at the clock. Likely he wanted what would take days or weeks in Canada to be done by lunch-time.

The Major took the stand and repeated essentially what he had said to Alex in the hotel lobby. Alex listened, his head cocked to one side, a look of sardonic disbelief on his face. "That is mah case, Your Honour," concluded the Major.

"The defendant has waived legal counsel, I might say against our advice," pronounced the mill-file voice from the bench. "Yew may proceed, defendant, at yore own peril."

"Thank you, Your Lordship, pardon me, Your Honour. This is all very reassuring..."

"Don't get sarcastic with this court, boy, or yew'll get cited for contempt. And what's this 'lordship' stuff? Yew being funny, or what?"

"I'm sorry. I was a witness at a trial in Canada a while ago and that is how they address the judge. I guess I got used to it. As to the present trial, all I can say is that I am innocent. As to solid proof, well, I have none, but let me put it to the court this way: were any of you involved in such an escapade, would you have stayed for dinner in the locale of the crime? Now, I suppose you *could* on the premise..."

There were sudden sounds of scuffle in the hallway outside the courtroom, the door crashed open, and, like the hounds of hell, in raced Joe. This actually happened and is not some sort of literary artifice on my part. It was simply the sort of situation that makes one believe in the play of cosmic forces.

The bailiff gestured toward the bench in helpless apology as Joe ran into the room, sliding on his knees to a stop at the feet of Major Ramsay. "Massa, oh, massa...gasp...had to see mah brudder real bad...jest wuz goan up to Ellerslie Satiddy night an' git back foah Sunday... but...gasp...Ah hurt mah foot, did mah ankle in a groundhog hole. Jes' got back to de plantation an' Ruth tole me about Massa Ross...mah fault, massa, not Massa Ross's...Ruth, she done tole me about Massa Ross's trouble, an' Ah'm heah to tell yu, he didn't have nuthin' to do wid what Ah done..."

"All right, boy, that's enough," said the judge. "On yore feet, now. Well, Major Ramsay, is this explanation satisfactory to yew?"

"Yes, Your Honour, Ah reckon it is."

"Shall Ah withdraw the chorge?"

The Major pondered for a moment, as if trying to find some other way of avenging himself on Alex.

"Major Ramsay, Ah'm waitin'."

The Major sighed in resignation. "Yes, Your Honour, withdraw the chorge. Please."

"Y'all're free to go, Mr. Ross, but Ah recommend yore immediate deporture from this town. Have yew any closing remorks?"

"Only this, Your Honour: that Major Ramsay not punish this man."

"Nigger-lover, huh?"

"Your Honour, I was falsely arrested. People sue for that sort of thing. I'm not going to. Just call it compensation for a very disagreeable night in your jail, which I might say..."

"Awl right, awl right. Gawd. What d'yew think, Major?"

"Ah'll agree," said the Major, venom in his voice. Alex continued to look blandly innocent.

"Case dismissed, then."

Alex, without a backward glance, returned to the cells, presumably to pick up his belongings; the Major, Joe, and I went out to the waiting carriage, from whose heights Jerge beamed with pleasure. "Ever'thin' come up orl right, Joe?"

"It did dat, Jerge."

"Saw yu runnin' in dere like all de devil's demons was after yu."

"Stop jawin'," snapped the Major. "Joe, yew jest get up there with Jerge and keep yore black mouth shut."

"Yes, massa."

Jerge turned the carriage around for the journey back to the plantation. As he did so, I decided, what with Joe's return and on the assumption that Alex would heed the judge's admonition to get out of town , that tonight, as planned, would be the night of Exodus. Now that affairs were resolved, I felt oddly peaceful, even in the face of a thousand-mile journey on foot at night with God knew what sort of hazards and obstacles to be dealt with. I sank into a reverie, envisioning myself as a modern Moses, someone fit to join the ranks of Harriet Tubman and Josiah Henson and all the other heroes of the Underground Railroad, wondering if God Himself might speak to me.

"In here," said the Major suddenly.

"Heah?"said Jerge incredulously.

"Oh, Lawd, massa, no!" pleaded Joe.

"Eh?" I said stupidly, coming out of my fantasy.

"Massa, yu promised no punishment!"

"Shuddup, yew black bastard! This'll teach yew to slip away like that."

"Massa! Yu promised! Ah'll be good, honest..."

"The more yew talk, the bigger a whuppin yew'll get. Now, shut yore black mouth and get down." We had stopped before the door of a premises which bore the legend "Gurney's Whipping House - Punishments for Slaves of All Sizes."

"A *whipping* house?" I said plaintively. This was preposterous, something out of a nightmare.

"Yes, sir," said the Major, "and Phil Gurney is one of the best." Joe was looking about wildly in a manner that suggested to me that he was no stranger to Mr. Gurney's business.

"While we tend to this, Jim, could yew be a good fella and go and get mah mail? Here's mah mailbox key, box 18, and the post office is right over there."

"Oh, yes, I'd be pleased to." I was unable to look either Joe or Jerge in the eye. Relieved to put some distance between myself and Joe's whuppin', I crossed the street to the post office, where I was the lone occupant. I found Box 18 and could see some letters through the little glass window. I unlocked it and out of idle curiosity I riffled through the letters, looking at the postmarks: Hattiesburg (a letter for She), Meridian (an invoice for baling twine), Mobile (an invoice from the Mobile and Ohio Railroad), Selma (a letter from somebody named Hudgin), another one from Meridian, oh, Sweet Jesus, a letter from Hudgin! I almost vomited in horror; in something approaching panic, I stuffed the letter into my pocket, and shakily crossed the street back to the whipping house.

Equally shakily, Joe came stumbling out of the whipping house, ribbons of blood oozing through his shirt, a look of Biblical stoicism about him. I looked at him, almost in veneration; he looked straight back at me with the serenity of one who has suffered for the last and final time. My fears of the last few days, my newly found mysticism, the shock of what I had found at the post-office, all were displaced by a savage glee at what I was about to do. Now all that remained to be done was to convey final instructions to the slaves, and for that Ruth would be needed.

"Joe," I said none too gently, "tell that sister of yours I want her again tonight. At sundown."

Joe could sense what the purpose was, but revealed nothing, looking suitably doleful and meekly saying "Yes, massa" for one of the last times in his life.

I spent some time in the commode that adjoined the house, long enough to read the letter that could have terminated the whole project and put me and Alex into prison until the end of time. I tore it into little pieces and threw it down the hole, so I cannot quote it in full. But it did reveal some unease on Mr. Hudgin's part that Alex and I might not have been what we appeared and after some thought, he was taking pen in hand in the hopes that it was not too late to urge caution lest we were indeed Abolitionists.

I excused myself a bit early from the dinner table that evening and went upstairs to prepare myself for the adventure that lay before me in all its yawning enormity. I could take nothing beyond my money and the clothes on my back, so I had to select the sturdiest and most practical garments.

My bravado of the afternoon, already having been shaken by the letter and then returning in full flood, was fast diminishing again. I kept telling myself that I would feel far better once we were under way and had gone some distance from the plantation. And to keep my mind occupied with other things, I lay down upon my bed and meditated on the possible outcome of the other evening, had Ruth and I not been interrupted.

I was all a-tingle in quaint places when soft steps sounded in the hallway and my door whispered open. I rolled off the bed and took Ruth in my arms and she took me in hers and we stood thus for a good minute before I said, "Tonight. Midnight."

"Truly, Massa James? No foolin' around?"

"No fooling around. Would you go out and tell them now, get the word going?"

"An' den?"

"Then I would like you back here."

"Ah'll be back befoah yu knows it."

"One more thing. I will need to know *exactly* how many want to go. Let's see, if you can't count..."

"*Ever'one* wants to go."

"Including Agnes?" Agnes had a new baby. This I did not need.

"Includin' Agnes. An' de baby. Even babies got to be free."

I sighed. "All right. We'll take the baby. But I want you to make something clear to everybody, and tell it just the way I am telling you. If anyone gets too sick or hurt along the way to continue, I'll... have to shoot them."

"Lordy!" Ruth hissed in horror.

"I don't like it either, but we have to do what is best for the whole group. Now, how is Joe?"

"Hurtin'. But it be mos'ly his pride. Dat's de wust thing about a whuppin'."

"Tell Joe to go to the woods when it is completely dark and get the bag we hid there the other day. Now let me hold you again a moment before you go."

"Massa James."

"Yes?"

"Our brudder an' some of de slaves from Ellerslie comin' too. Dey is lookin' out foah us each night. We gives dem a special whistle so dey knows it's us."

"*They* are coming with *us?*"

"Dat's why Joe run away, tell dem we's goin' to Canada. He done arranged it. So we gotta go by Ellerslie..."

"I *know!* But all these people, it's impossible..."

"So was de Exodus."

"This gives us over twenty people. It's in*sane!*" My whispers had amplified into a hoarse growl.

"They's all countin' on yu, Massa James."

So what could I say? "Very well, we'll do it. I don't know how yet, but we'll do it. Now go. I'll see you later."

To appear sociable to my host, I made myself presentable and went below for some sort of evening festivity, oddly enough feeling a bit hungry, maybe in anticipation of the privation I would feel over the next couple of months. The cook had retired for the night, but Aunt Jane made me some tea and Aunt Isabel prepared some dainty little fingers of bread and butter. We sat and rocked with She and the Major on the great pillared front veranda, listening to the sounds of a late-summer Mississippi evening, a cacophony of crickets, tree-frogs, katydids, all singing, yammering, chirping, a perfect screen for our getaway.

Following our refreshment, I returned to my room, wondering if Ruth would be waiting for me, which she was not as yet. I bathed, brushed my teeth, generally made myself desirable, and climbed into bed with nothing on. I felt daring indeed, the tingling sensations returning; was I really doing this?

A fly buzzed in the window curtains, a crow cawed out on the cotton fields as evening's last glow faded. When day came again, I would not be here, nor would the Major's entire "stable" of slaves.

There was a soft tap at my door. "Come in," I said in a stage whisper, in a brief panic that it might be Aunt Isabel come to tuck me in or some such absurdity. But, no, it was indeed dear Ruth, dressed in what I instantly recognized as a very simple and very removable chemise.

"No, doan get up, Massa James."

"Please stop, once and for all, calling me 'massa', all right, Ruth? If you call me 'massa' again, I have no choice but to call you Mistress Ruth, and then what would people think? Besides, if I were to get up, you might be shocked. I would not look like any massa *you* ever saw."

"Is yu *nekkid*, Ma...uh, James?"

"Well, er, yes, I am...wanted to feel as close to you as possible. Ruth, I've never done this before and, uh, I'm sort of nervous."

"Doan worry about a thing. Ah *have* done it, many times, but it weren't on account of I wanted to. Tonight Ah wants to. So we is startin' out togethah."

"Oh, mercy, you're lovely!" I whispered.

"Yu make me feel lovely, jes' like a real woman."

"If you aren't a real woman, then there's not..."

"Ah um a slave woman, have been all mah life. Take me a long time to get ovah *dat* idea." She lifted the bed covers and lay down beside me. We held each other close, so tightly as to almost strangle one another. Something wet trickled down my shoulder. "What is it, Ruth? Are you all right?"

"Yes, Ma...James. Ah doan know why Ah went like dis. Dere's somethin' about yu, so wonderful, a saviour...so gentle...Ah guess Ah'm so happy Ah'm boilin' ovah like a kettle. Nevah felt dis way..."

I wiped her cheeks with my fingers and held her close, peace coming over me. Alone, I had so little confidence, so little of Alex's self-assurance; never would I have been able to talk my way out of a predicament like Alex's, good heavens, it had happened only that morning!

But with Ruth beside me, I felt almost lion-like, the feeling fuelled by Ruth's voice, now husky and urgent, saying, "Kiss me, James. Yu is goan be mah man now." Ruth rolled over on her back. "Come to me now, James."

It was the most natural thing in the world. We came together in a gentle farewell to an innocence long since gone stale, a farewell from which I have never looked back, and she clasped me to her, murmuring some sort of sensual monologue that I could sense rather than understand.

" James, we is togethah...Ah um your woman now...We is one, now, James, black an' white. Ah loves yu, Massa James."

"I love you too, Mistress Ruth."

She chuckled. "Caught me, din't yu? Guess Ah *is* yo' mistress now."

"Ruth!" I whimpered like a child.

"Oh, Massa James!" gasped Ruth as we whirled together down into a

dark, warm vortex. Our last awareness was the creak of a floorboard outside the bedroom door, and then we fell asleep, entwined as if shielding
each other from the dangers of the darkness outside.

NOTICE TO "STOCKHOLDERS" OF THE UNDERGROUND RAILROAD.
COURTESY OF ENOCH PRATT FREE LIBRARY, BALTIMORE, MD

CHAPTER EIGHTEEN

Abruptly I jerked awake, feeling Ruth wedged against me. A feeling of need welled up, but also of urgency, and I reached for my pocket watch to see if it were yet midnight. I angled it to the pale moonlight, and for a moment of horror thought it said 3:00. I drew breath for a curse, then realized it was only 12:15. The moon would be up for another half-hour, but for all that it was high time to get going.

"Ruth. *Ruth*! Wake up."

She stirred. "Massa James," she purred.

"Ssh! It's after midnight. We have to go. Now, if you..."

"Once moah, James."

"Not now! Look, Ruth, when the others are around, I'm going to have to act distant. It wouldn't be fair for them to think I'm playing favourites, but do not forget for one moment that I love you."

"James..."

"Hurry, now. You leave by the hall and if anyone is up and about, just tell them I wasn't feeling too well and thought it best if you went back to your cabin. I'll follow in two minutes."

"How will yu get out?"

"The window. The back porch roof is right under it. Now go."

Ruth's magnificence gleamed momentarily in the moonlight, was shrouded in the chemise, a quick kiss, and then she was gone. I pulled my clothes on, and in the urgency of the moment, on the brink of the most important and dangerous thing I have ever done, they, like any inanimate thing in times of stress, conspired to fight me. My feet stuck in my trousers, my shirt turned into a horror of *culs-de-sac*.

I rolled up my spare clothes and arranged them in the bed to look like a sleeping body, all the while thinking how dashing and glamorous it would be to write a parting note to the Major telling him exactly what I thought of his treatment of humanity and leaving money to cover the cost of whatever I had eaten. But this was not a novel or a play and I was not the Count of Monte Cristo. It was actually happening, my funds were finite, and I was terrified.

There was a gauze screen over the window to keep out the insects; I undid it, climbed out on the roof, did the screen back up the best way I could. I had no castle wall to scale nor moat to hurdle, but I dislike heights and the ten or so feet to the ground looked daunting enough for me. If I stand around contemplating this, I thought, I'll be here until Doomsday. So, taking a deep breath, I launched myself off and landed with a thud, lurching to my knees

"Woof!" spoke a voice of thunder.

"Colonel!" I whispered. "Shut up! Please."

"Woof!"

I reached out a hand, knuckles upward; Colonel padded over, sniffed, and was satisfied. I scratched around his neck. "*What* a good dog," I whispered.

"Aww...woooo...."

"Ssh, Colonel. Go back to sleep." I stood up and started on my way over to the slaves' cabins, trying to stay in shadow. The moon was behind the house now, but there was still quite a strong patch of light out by the weighing shed, and I prayed that no-one should be watching. Colonel trotted behind. "Colonel, for Christ's sake."

"Nnnnn," he whined, butting up behind my knees. I took off in a sprint through the moonlight, Colonel pattering behind me, past the weighing shed, past the cabin of the odious Edgar, and up to Joe's front step. The door silently opened and in I went to find the place jammed with humanity, all ready to head for the North Star, for Canada, for freedom under the protection of the lion's paw.

"Massa," said Joe, "Ah has de food and de guns. Got 'em a bit ago."

"Good lad. Now, listen carefully. Ruth has told you how we have to do this. Agnes? Where's Agnes?"

"Heah, massa."

"And you have the baby?"

"Yes, massa."

"You will be responsible for keeping it quiet *at all times.* Is it asleep now?"

"No, massa, but she be quiet yet. She be on de tit." Someone snickered nervously.

"Then keep her there. We'll be going in a couple of minutes, just as soon as the moon is down. Ruth will be right behind me with Agnes. The rest of you will follow in a single line. Joe, how are you? Can you walk all right?"

"Massa, for dis Ah walk like de wind."

"You're someone I wouldn't want to be without. You take one gun and give me the other. Are you used to guns?"

"No, suh."

"Well, neither am I, but I do know to carry it pointed at the sky so you don't shoot anyone by accident. I'll put you at the back, oh, no, I'll need you to show the way to Ellerslie. Jerge, you take the gun and get at the end of the line and Joe comes up front with me."

I cracked the cabin door. The moon was now set, leaving a waning glow in the western sky. The time was 1:05. "God bless us all," I said in a low voice. "Follow me, now. Here we go."

The plantation faced north; we skirted the eastern edge of the property, where a line of trees sheltered us in deep black shadow. We managed virtually complete silence, except for a brief whimper from the baby as she was adroitly switched from left to right by Agnes. Dew soaked my shoes and cold soon ate its way up my legs. The crickets and tree frogs still chirped occasionally, I hoped enough to disguise any noises we could not avoid making.

We found the pale ribbon of road as it ran eastward past the plantation and then angled north toward Ellerslie. I was glad of my decision to stick to the roads as much as possible, since at night traffic was unlikely and there would be less chance of losing anyone in the dark.

As we trudged silently past some open fields, it occurred to me that we would be in the direst trouble if some night-riders should come along, for there were such folk who were known to patrol the countryside at random, living off the rewards for escaped slaves. There was always the ugly possibility of the Major himself, God forbid, putting in an appearance, and we had no emergency plan for concealing ourselves. I cursed myself for such lack of foresight. Alex, of course, would have thought of all contingencies beforehand, but it was my habit to learn as I went, a grave deficiency in an engineer and a possible source of deadly peril for an abolitionist.

I stopped the group. "Listen carefully," I said as loudly as I dared. "If we should hear anyone coming along the road, I will say 'go!' You will leave the road, run to the count of ten, and then fall flat wherever you may be, hoping for concealment. In a place like this, I'm not too sure. Now, I'm going to count you off and give each of you a number, just like in a butcher shop...oh, sorry, I guess you wouldn't know...anyway, remember your number. If we scatter, even numbers go to the left, odd numbers to the right..."

"What's an odd numbah?"

"Ah doesn't know left from right."

"Left is here," I explained as patiently as I could, although my nerves were screaming with exasperation, "and right is that way. I'll tell you whether your number is odd or even. I'm number one...I'm odd, ha, ha..." Chuckle, chuckle in the chill darkness. "Joe, you're two - even - Agnes, three - odd - Peter you're four - even - what's this? Oh, say it isn't so..."

"It be de dog, massa. He be black, jes' like us, wanna git away."

"Dear Colonel."

"Do he get a numbah, massa?"

"He's with me. One-A. Now, where was I..."

I finished counting everyone off and then we resumed our walking, past a woodlot and two more fields, one of which fronted another plantation. "Go!" I said on impulse. The group scattered, some of the women twittering in dismay. But they followed instructions well, for within ten seconds none were visible.

I walked back, saying into the darkness in a low voice, "Don't move. This was just for practice, but I wanted to see how well it would work...good...those white aprons will have to be hidden...but I don't think I could spot you unless I knew you were there. All right, back in order, now."

It took a couple of minutes to reorganize and I was most uneasy the whole while because of the proximity of the plantation. Off we went again, my feet crunching noisily on some loose stones. Against my original expectations, all the slaves had shoes but for Joe's brother Peter and another little boy. They would have to be equipped at the earliest opportunity, and I prayed in the meantime that they should last the night's walk; it would be daylight in another four hours or so. Onward we trudged, beckoned by the North Star. Regardless of what happened on the ground, it would be there in the silent, black heavens, guiding the slaves to freedom and myself homeward.

We came to a crossroads west of Ellerslie. Joe put his hand on my arm, saying "Stop heah, massa." The scuffling sound of our progress stopped and a blanket of silence settled about us. Joe whistled like a nightingale and silently from the bushes, like black ghosts, arose another contingent of slaves, almost as large as our own. I was aghast. "Joe, in the name of God."

"They all wants to go to Canada. What could Ah say?"

The combined numbers gave us a group at least twice the size of what was thought advisable, but, to echo Joe, what could I say? What could I do? I now faced the dreadful possibility of being turned away from Underground Railroad "depots" just on the basis of sheer volume. But all I could do was do my best with what I had, and it was not much; there was enough bread and cheese in Joe's bag only for the women and children and only for one night. I shrugged.

"Well," I said, fighting a tightness in my chest. "*Well!*" But before I had a chance to improve on the intelligence of my remark, a scream tore the night and automatically I snapped, "Shut up!" The tightness concentrated itself in the area of my frantically knocking heart. A heart attack! My travails would be over before they had scarcely begun.

"Lordy, what in God's name is that?" said an awed voice. In silhouette, the object of astonishment looked like a man with branches sprouting from the top of his head. Whoever had screamed was now whimpering, muffled by someone else, but so horrifying was the spectacle that the screamer now had my reluctant sympathy.

"Dis be Joshua," explained Philip, the brother of Joe, Ruth, and Peter. "He been done real bad. Tried to escape coupla months back and massa had de blacksmith make dis heah now cage for his head. Got bells on it like a cow, so's he couldn't git away again."

"He can't come with us," I said abruptly. Breath was drawn in the dark for the requisite lamentations.

"No, no, massa," said Philip hastily. "Joshua, he be orl right. We done stuck cotton in de bells. Won't be no noise."

"There had better not be," I said rudely. "All right, let us be on our way."

I kept Philip and his siblings all together towards the front with the venerable but apparently tireless Jerge continuing shotgun duty at the rear.

Daylight was but three hours off now, we had covered only about six miles from the Ramsay plantation, and I wanted to do at least three or four more miles before calling it a night.

After some initial confusion, I had the newcomers numbered and organized, establishing a new and horrifying total of twenty-seven. We resumed our northward march, the unfortunate and top-heavy Joshua wobbling uncertainly along. How long he could proceed thus was a matter of speculation and I was wondering if any of our "station-masters" would be able to remove his terrible encumbrance.

We had been nicely on our way for a half-hour or so when the next crisis struck. A small child from Ellerslie started to cry with an ear-splitting wail and I spun around in the darkness, trying to locate the source of the sound, groping my way back down the line, oh, God, I do not need this, put a bag over its head.

"Shut up, shut *up*!" I snapped. "Who's doing that? You'll get us all killed, for Christ's sake!"

"Ovah heah, massa," said a distraught voice. The poor mother was beside herself - her wretched (or so I thought at the time) child had smashed his bare foot (more shoes to provide now) against a stray rock, was bleeding profusely, and was roaring so continuously that I could not discern whether he was bothering to take a breath. I put my hand over his mouth and was promptly bitten.

"Madam," I said to his mother, "this child is quiet now, *right now*, or you take him right back to the plantation."

"Massa, Ah doan..."

"Look, little fellow, you see all these people?"

He stopped bellowing. "No, massa, it be powerful dark." He took a great draught of air to resume his howls.

I clapped my hand none too gently over his mouth. "There are almost thirty people here," I said through clenched teeth, "and they'll all get whupped real bad if you're not quiet. So, for that matter, will I. In fact, I'll get whupped worst of all. That seriously disturbs me. Shush, now, or *you'll* get whupped. By me."

The child stopped his struggle with a gurgle of terror. I resumed my place in the lead, wondering how deeply I was going to be loved, how revered I would be as a saviour or a Moses or whatever when this whole mad escapade was over with.

Shortly after six o'clock in the morning, the sky started to lighten and birds began to call back and forth. We scattered into a woods, walked well back from the road, and concealed ourselves as best we could. I worked out a system of lookouts, although the value of such a safeguard was dubious, since in the event of an alarm, all that could be done would be to give a warning that would scatter our members in the hope that at least some could get away. And they would be assured of freedom only until the next crisis.

As I pondered, a voice behind me, the deepest voice I have ever heard, rumbled, "Excuse me, massa." I turned around to look straight into the chest of the biggest man I have ever seen. The night must have been dark indeed for me to have missed such incredible bulk; good God, with this chap along, we were as good as armed by half again. His upper arms were almost as large as my thighs, which are by no means negligible.

"Mistah Ramsay," rumbled the voice again, as if from the very bowels of the earth. I tilted back on my heels to get a better look at the face, which surprised me by its genial, almost baby-like countenance, surmounted by a great shock of woolly hair.

"Mistah Ramsay, Ah ain't met yu properly yet. Ah um Precious."

"You are?"

"Ah um indeed. Precious Gormley, to use mah full title. Ah um entirely at yo' service. Joe's an old friend. Ah um from Ellerslie, yu see, know his brudder Philip real good. Joe, he done said some fine things about yu, so whoevah is good enough for Joe is jes' fine for me. He done got high standards. So, when we is marchin' to Canada, Ah would like to be in front wid yu. What numbah do Ah git?"

My mind, so alert a few minutes ago, could not handle a simple concept of numbers. I could not face renumbering everyone, so I just said wearily, "How about One-A for the time being?" Colonel was already One-A, but the fact had momentarily escaped me.

"One-A sound real good. What kin One-A do right now?"

"Get some rest, uh, Precious. I'll be needing your help tonight."

With the coming of light, I was able to more fully comprehend the plight of Joshua. The perverse ingenuity of the oppressor was in full flower here. The poor man looked like a walking chandelier and his chin and neck were worn raw.

Joshua's eyes were inflamed from almost continual weeping because of the pain, the degradation, and from sheer frustration as the horrid apparatus kept catching on tree branches and twisting his neck. For the first time in my life, I hated with the fullest measure of gall and I am sorry to report that I drew a strength from it that was almost exhilarating. Useful it was, to be sure, but it did not reflect too well on my humanity.

"We'll get that God-damned thing off you somehow," I tried to reassure Joshua. "Just give me a few days to figure something out." Joshua peered uncomprehendingly out of his mobile prison with big, glittering eyes. Evidently he was beyond speech and I feared for his sanity.

"Di'n' tell Joe about Joshua," said Philip apologetically. "Di'n't wanna ruin our chances of gittin' away. Sho' took some doin' to choke dem bells. Joshua said jes' to leave 'im, but it was because of what happened to 'im we wanted to git away. Coulda bin any of us. Massa thowt it was so funny, paraded Joshua about like a pet...Joshua ain't talked since. We is powerful oneasy, it ain't natural."

"No, it ain't, er, isn't," I agreed. "But we should have some help in a few days."

I tried to sleep, but could not, and instead prowled around during the day as the heat grew more and more torrid. There were several nerve-jangling scares, as we could hear sounds from the nearby road, but it was never anything more than a passing farm wagon or a planter's carriage, all oblivious to anything more than a few feet to either side.

I had been apprehensive that Colonel might be a problem. He had, from time to time at the plantation, demonstrated a proclivity for chasing horses, but now he stuck by me like a limpet, and whenever I sat down, he came and burrowed his head into my chest. "He yo' dog for sure now, massa. Wondah what de Major thowt - us gone, de dog gone, *yu* gone, oh, Lordy, hallelujah!"

By mid-afternoon, I was too exhausted to care how everybody fared for the next few hours, and I lay down for a sleep. It was horrible - flies and mosquitoes buzzed all around and the woods were fetid and airless. Colonel snapped at the insects with a great clack of his jaws and fidgeted and padded about, but was never further than ten feet away and created no disturbance at all.

I slept for about three hours and awoke all soggy around the front of my neck and with a truly abominable headache. Ruth was sitting on the ground beside me and reached out her hand. "Shouldn't do this," I mumbled, reaching back.

"Shouln't *not* do it, Massa James," she smiled. My headache began to ebb almost immediately and soon I thought it was time to pay some attention to my little colony.

"How is everybody? Any difficulties?"

"Li'l Noah's toe is real bad, massa, all sort of black wid flies buzzin' all around." Noah was the little lad I had had to threaten with a whuppin'.

"Wasn't Noah's toe black to start with?"

"Doan be sarcy, now, James."

Our group was scattered all over the woodlot and it took a bit of doing to find young Noah, who was bearing his pain a great deal more stoically than last night. The affected toe was all scabby and the nail had indeed turned black, giving the toe a curiously sleek, metallic appearance. Evidently Noah remembered how I had spoken to him and he looked at me with more defiance than was usually accorded a massa; and while I was not a slave-owner, by God I was massa of this outfit until we were safely in Canada, and I aimed to keep it that way. I thought a bit of diplomacy was in order, however, and I crouched down to match Noah's three-foot height.

"How's your toe?"

"Hurts, massa."

"Heard about Indians, Noah?"

"Some, massa."

"You're an Indian now, a member of the Blacknail tribe." Noah grinned shyly. He was only five or six years old.

"We may need an Indian guide from time to time," I continued. What inspiration! "The Blacknails were the best - and they *never* cried when they were hurt."

"Ah won't make no mo' noise, massa."

"Good lad. Thirsty?"

"Yes, massa, very."

"We'll find ourselves some water tonight. You can help. The Blacknails always knew where to look."

Besides an appalling shortage of water, the food problem was extreme. The provisions from the bag under the tree had been so inadequate for such a mob as to be a joke. We had to find food and water quickly, or before long we would be too weak to walk. And we could not hunt and blast guns off, for no matter where we were, we were likely to be on or near some-one's plantation or farm property. The Blacknails may have known what to do, but James Ramsay certainly didn't.

ESCAPE ROUTE THROUGH THE STATE OF MISSISSIPPI.

CHAPTER NINETEEN

At the sun's going, the heat gave way to an awful penetrating chill, a reminder that autumn was on its way and we had so very far to go. I got everyone organized and we started on our way an hour or so before midnight. The moon would linger later for each of the coming nights, but it would light our way and, the habits of country folk as they are, it was unlikely anyone would be up and about, except, of course, for ambitious night-riders.

Joshua's cage, besides circumscribing any prospect of real rest for him, was such a burden that he now had to walk with the support of two of his fellows. This clearly could not go on and I hoped fervently that our first Underground Railroad agent would have a file. How the dread thing could be removed, however, without damaging Joshua in the process would have to be left to someone more expert than I.

After a couple of hours of walking, we happened on the town of New Hamilton, a major obstacle since it was entirely out of the question to go trooping down the main street in one big jolly horde. Instead we circumvented it by detouring to the west, at which time I could discern the gnarled shapes of apple trees.

We paused for a harvest, a nerve-wracking business with the lights of a farm-house gleaming not far away, but with dehydration certain and starvation imminent, the chance had to be taken. Working in silence was a virtual impossibility, although some of the tension was relieved when the lights were turned down and blown out for the night.

The women's aprons would have been useful as bags, but being white, they had had to be jettisoned, so some of the men donated their shirts, despite the chill. Whatever apples we could carry individually we ate as we walked along, and all was well now, with something in the way of nourishment (improved blood sugar level, Alex would have said, and where would *he* be now?) and a bit of juice. I was sorely missing the eight daily glasses of water.

We fumbled through some fields for quite some time with no idea of what sort of trail we were leaving. And then, as the moon was about to set, we found the road once more and were able to move along relatively unhindered. I did not even have to look at my compass, for the North Star told me all I needed to know in way of direction.

A couple of hours' walk saw us to Aberdeen, which we skirted and then struck out in a more westerly direction; avoiding roads was just too slow, cumbersome, and revealing with such a large aggregation. Roads themselves offered a faster passage but with the constant risk of ambush or night-riders. To the west, however, was the Mobile and Ohio Railroad, which, if followed, would take us straight to our first "depot" at Booneville.

My knowledge of railroads would bear fruit at last.

We were perhaps a mile past Aberdeen when Gladys suddenly doubled up with a groan. I myself had been feeling a bit crampy, but had thought little of it. Gladys, however, was in a bad way. "Jerge! Get Jerge! Oh, mercy, it's dem apples, Ah knows it. Oh, turn yo' heads...Jerge, help me wid mah knickers, Ah's goan have de trots real bad...ooh, dis be orful onconvenient..."

Gladys's "orful onconvenience" began to spread rapidly to other members of the group and modesty was thrown to the winds with astonishing swiftness. There were two unfortunates who could not get out of their knickers in time for the inevitable, but stood, steaming sheepishly in the darkness. I remember making some heartless remark about enriching the atmosphere, for which I was to pay but moments later.

Those who had messed themselves had, of course, no spare clothes and to continue as they were would have been a cruelty to everyone, so we had to stop for the night; still, we had made surprisingly good mileage, I think nearly eighteen, and it was the adherence to roads that had helped, despite standard Underground Railroad procedure. Just further along, a matter of yards, was a small creek where the two incontinents could rinse out their clothes. We threw away the apples and the people in need wore some of the shirts that had done carrying duty for the night to hide their nakedness. We drank from the creek (upstream, of course, from the laundry site) to replenish lost liquid and hopefully to purge the poison from our systems.

Despite the temporary horror of our condition, we had, as an ensemble, a better day than the one before. There was the reassurance of distance from the two plantations and we were well-hidden from the road by trees that swished in the morning breeze, masking any sound we were making. The forest here was quite lush and extensive, offering good shade as we tried to make day into night. As a matter of fact, it was quite ferny and pleasant and free of insects and I had a relatively good sleep, disturbed only by the faint passage of a wagon on the road.

It was found early on in our impromptu campsite that unusual care had to be taken in avoiding the leavings on the ground from those in whom the diarrhoea persisted. Colonel, out of some dark doggish instinct, rolled in some of the more fragrant excrement and had to be forced to go for a swim until clean, at least as clean as dogs ever are.

There was still the better part of a hundred miles to go before our first resting place on the Underground Railroad. With progress to date, even as respectable as last night had been, the distance seemed almost beyond hope; as for Canada, I literally could not think that far ahead. My own country, my home, had faded in my consciousness to a vague and unattainable dream and so overwhelmed did I become with a feeling of inadequacy and unfulfilled responsibility that a grey curtain of lassitude and inertia descended about me. The worry about Alex did not help my state either, compounded by the fact that I would know nothing of him until I was home.

As twilight deepened, a few desperate souls retrieved some of the fatal apples, only a few, and ate them slowly with great draughts of creek water, mercifully without a single "onconvenience". That was encouraging, but we were a bit worried about the baby, for Agnes, with her disrupted intake of fluid, was not lactating properly and the baby was becoming fretful. To add to the fun, as the sun sank in the west, its rays fanned out from behind a billowing bank of clouds as dark as charcoal, the distant artillery of an impending thunderstorm setting the air a-tremble.

Threatening weather aside, with no moon we could start the moment it was dark and really do some distance this night. "Let's start on our way, my buckoes."

"What, already, massa? It goan storm real bad."

"We can take advantage of it. We will be concealed and can make all the noise we want, except Noah can't cry. He took an oath as an Indian guide. We'll get soaked, but that's just too bad. We have to make miles and it won't be much of a night for night-riders. Let's get up on the road and be on our way."

"Ah doan wanna go in no storm."

"Very well, then, stay here, get caught, get a whuppin'. It's all the same to me. I'm going home, thank you, and whoever wants to come with me is welcome." I started to walk and so did everyone else. The atmosphere among us, previously cordial and cooperative, suddenly was tense. But it was, with just one brief exception, the only time that anyone would be faint-hearted about anything.

The storm was about three hours in coming, at which time our little army had wasted about a quarter of an hour fumbling about. Some of us had become confused in the dark where the road forked and I had had to halt the group and hike back to round up the stragglers in the sullen nocturnal silence. The night creatures had stopped their sundry symphonies and silent lightning flickered in the thick, warm darkness. The feeling of it all I did not like one bit.

We were just coming up to the village of Egypt to pick up the northbound Mobile and Ohio line when the rain slashed down in steaming, thundering fury. Aside from the natural discomfort of being soaked, we were flayed mercilessly by cold needles of rain, and some of the children, Noah included, started to scream with pain and terror.

"Massa, we can't go on..."

"We had this conversation a couple of hours ago. I'm going on. I'm not hanging about in this damned country any longer than I must. I'm going home. You can come or you can stay."

I carried onward and so did the blacks, to a one. The hiss and rumble of the storm made conversation impossible, leaving me to my own thoughts. Here it was only our third night of Exodus and already I was placing my own interests ahead of the company's, certainly not in the Biblical tradition. A saviour, Ruth had called me, but at this moment I certainly didn't feel like one. I just wanted to go home.

Onward we toiled in the hissing, dripping darkness, the sweet rainwater dribbling into our mouths, the smells of late summer hanging rich in the steamy air. The initial lightning and wind squalls passed by, leaving the world black and drenched, so black that we simply carried on right through Okolona without digressing from the railway line, unobserved save by a sad, sodden kitten whom Colonel thoughtlessly chased up a telegraph pole.

Shortly after Okolona, there was a renewed onslaught of the elements, booming flares of lightning and thunder, a roaring wind from which there was no refuge. "Joe," I shouted, "I'm going back along the line to see if everyone is still with us. I should have done it before."

"Orl right, Massa James, jes' do what yu gotta."

"Ah come too, please, Mistah Ramsay," rumbled Precious.

As we walked back, I had an unsettling feeling of regression, of being drawn back to Ellerslie, to Columbus, to the volcanic wrath of the Major. And just feet away, huddled phantom figures passed sightlessly by on their way to freedom. My God, there were a lot of them! End of the line at last, Jerge with the shotgun, oh, dear Jesus, where was Joshua?

"Ain't seen 'im, massa. Thowt 'e was up ahaid."

"Stop!" I bellowed. "Everybody stop! Where is Joshua?" I walked forward again, repeating the question. I could not for the life of me remember Joshua's number.

"Oh, Lordy, massa, he done gone, Ah think," wailed one of his volunteer escorts. "Can't see 'im nowheres. He wuz wid me at dat place a bit ago, di'n't want to be propped up no moah, but now, Ah jes' doan know. Ah's so sorry, massa." The man began to weep.

I put a hand on his shoulder. "Not *your* fault, my friend. Nobody can see anything in this, and of course he never said anything. Maybe we should stop and look a bit. He couldn't be far. What do *you* think, Jerge?"

"Doan like de sound of dis at-tall, James. Yu wanna take a look, we take a look."

"We will, then, but if we can't find him, we'll just have to carry on."

"Lordy."

We got the blacks well away from the rail line in the interests of safety, and then Precious, Jerge, and I started back towards Okolona, battered by lancing needles of steely rain.

"This is hopeless!" I shouted in the wind's roar and whoop after about half a mile.

"Anudder few minutes, massa, please," implored Jerge. "Mebbe he had to pee or somethin'."

We slogged along, toes catching on the wooden sleepers, blinking the water from our eyes. A renewed and sustained blaze of lightning lit up the sky in a greenish glare.

"Look, James, dere he be!"

Joshua was on his knees in a great puddle at the foot of the rail embankment, head cruelly caged, hands held high in supplication for deliverance. And come it did with the next lightning. The entire world was engulfed in a great hissing light and Joshua's head erupted in a towering shower of sparks. Almost simultaneously, a monster concussion sent the three of us sprawling.

"Lordy, Lordy!" cried my companions.

"Oh, shit!" I exploded as I rolled painfully over, picking cinders and bits of rail ballast out of my face. Jerge was on his knees, praying as if his life depended on it, which at this moment it probably did. Leaving him at his frantic devotions, Precious and I slid down the grassy embankment to where Joshua had been, my vision a confusion of swirls and colours. I wondered if I had been blinded, the horror of the possibility eclipsed only by the horror of what I was about to see if I hadn't.

Another lightning flash, now safely away to the east, revealed Joshua, lying face down in the puddle in a haze of vapour that clung to him, even in the wind.

"Sweet Jesus, it's like he got cooked!" exclaimed a horrified Precious. "An' look at dis!" Joshua's cage was half-melted, the iron cleaving to what was left of his face, the dreadful bells silenced forever.

"God!" roared Precious at a sky too busy having a storm to heed any of Man's feeble protests. I put my hand on his huge arm.

Jerge scrabbled down the slope, his prayers abandoned. "What done happened, James? Joshua, he look like de burnin' bush."

"Joshua was struck by lightning," I tried to explain.

"What yu mean, massa?"

"He was, well, struck dead."

"What!" screeched Jerge. "Who done dat?" He looked wildly about. To the negro slave way of thinking, there was always a Someone behind every happening. If it were not a human Someone, there was only one alternative.

"It was God," I improvised. "He took pity on Joshua and put him out of his misery. And now Joshua's spirit is on its way to Canada and will guide us there. Let us be on our way now. The others will be getting worried about us."

Jerge was beside himself with pity, horror, and fear; the huge and usually imperturbable Precious was not faring much better.

"Boys," I said almost pleadingly, "there is nothing we can do for Joshua now. We all did our best, now we have to let him go. We can't endanger the whole group. Come along, now."

"Massa..."

"I'm nobody's massa, Jerge. I wish you folks would stop calling me that. Now, come *on*!"

"Just a minute, please, James," said Precious, withdrawing into the darkness. He reappeared, carrying Joshua.

"Oh, *please*, Precious!" I bleated.

"We give him a propah Christian burial, James."

"Very well," I said meekly. I was not about to trifle with Precious. In fact, a dark corner of my mind speculates to this day about what might have happened if Precious had ever returned to Ellerslie and expressed his feelings to his and Joshua's former massa.

The three, or perhaps I should say the four, of us turned northwards once more, Jerge and myself with our arms about each other's shoulders. The storm stopped with the abruptness of a lamp being blown out and the chill started to diminish as we crunched along the trackbed. So intent was I on getting away from this awful place that my sorrow for Joshua was quite diluted by rueful thoughts of the three or four miles that could have been gained were it not for this.

As we rejoined the main body, I had Precious stay in the background with his pitiful burden. I responded to a blizzard of inquiries about Joshua only with a curt "we found him", and we stepped along until a creamy grey dawn started to silhouette the countryside to the east. I stopped the cavalcade, saying in a low voice, "Just gather around me as best you can. Can you all hear me? I don't dare speak any louder."

"Heah yu jes' fine, Massa James."

"I don't know how to do this gently...now, don't make a sound when I tell you this, but Joshua is dead."

"Daid!" wailed several voices. "Oh, Lordy..."

"Ssh!" I hissed to no effect. "Shut *up*! Shut your mouths, now! Do you want to be heard and get caught and end up picking cotton again for the rest of your *lives*? Probably in *chains*?"

"No, suh." But behind the meek utterance was a look of defiance I did not like, even allowing for the circumstances.

"Don't you look at me like that!" I flared. "You've had enough massas and I have no wish to be another one. But I will if it's what it takes to get us safely to Canada, so you will just bloody well do as you are told. We will bury Joshua now, but in silence, except for me. I will say what needs to be said. No singing or crying. I think there's a farm over there" - a cow mooed to confirm my suspicion and my heart constricted at such a normal, homely sound - "so let's get on a bit and into these woods."

In the strengthening daylight, Joshua's physical condition was hideous beyond description. His head in essence had been cooked and his eyes had literally melted and run down his cheeks; his upper body was actually charred in spots and of his hair there was no sign.

We had, of course, no shovel, but the awesomely powerful Precious managed to twist one of the protrusions from Joshua's cage and use it to dig a grave in the wet soil. It took no little time and it was mid-morning before we were able to lay Joshua to rest in the third day of freedom he had ever known.

If we lost someone every two days, there would be none of us left after two months. Freighted by that unhappy thought, I dozed off for a bit with

Colonel's damp carcass wedged reassuringly against me.

The wet from the night made our rest a complete folly. I felt as if I had been struck in the lower back and on the kneecaps with a piece of timber. Others either shared my particular misery or were sneezing and coughing to the point where I wondered if I were to be faced with the spectre of pneumonia.

Rebecca, the woman whose whuppin' I had witnessed but a few days ago, was in a particularly bad way, but there was nothing to be done for her without warmth. She lay in the fetid woods all day, among dank, tropical-looking ferns, while thick, damp cloud lay all over the countryside. At one point, Rebecca actually turned pale, her skin going an awful chalky colour as she wheezed, coughed, and generally laboured her way through the passage of time. So wet was my gunpowder that I could not have shot her, even out of mercy. I lapsed into a strange, glassy calm of resignation to these things I could not change: fear, horror, hopelessness, irritation at times from my human burden, and now this.

The combined group had sorted itself out, as any group does, into the leaders and those who had to be led. There was, of course, the already-indispensable Precious. And Gladys, Jerge, Joe, and Ruth continued as my closest allies and lieutenants, sacrificing their own rest and comfort for the benefit of others, tending to Rebecca, to Agnes and the baby, to other young mothers. Little Noah, although his foot was still not in very good shape, had been exemplary in his quiet determination and desire to fulfil his destiny as an Indian guide. He had even found a bird's feather, which poked rakishly from his woolly hair as he now slept in his mother's left arm, his cheek sprouting whiskers of leaf mould. His mother, at the brink of her own rest, smiled up at me, saying "God bless yu, Massa James."

"Thank you for that. It makes me feel human again."

"Lotta responsibility, massa, an' so orful about poah Joshua. Ah knows yu is hurtin' like we is, but nuthin' to be did now...gotta sleep now. Good night, or good mornin'...Ah dunno...all topsy-turvy..."

In such a crisis-ridden night, Ruth had vacated my mind, but now she was back and I needed her company, especially as I thought she might have felt frozen out during my nocturnal battle with my demons. I went to seek her out; she was with Agnes and the baby, who was making thin baby noises, restlessly flexing her tiny fingers and rubbing her feet together in jerky, spastic rhythms. She had no father, poor little thing. The Major, on some arbitrary whim, had sold him elsewhere.

"How's the milk situation, Agnes?" I inquired, not feeling the least strange.

"Doin' bettah, massa." Both women smiled up at me. From Ruth's smile I divined that she understood the nature of my conduct of the night before and resented it not at all.

Colonel strolled over and gave the baby a gentle lick on the top of her head. Agnes chuckled. "Dog nevah like dat around de Major. Change of massa done him good."

"Look, I'd really like this massa business to stop, once and for all. I'm nobody's massa, not even Colonel's. I'm just sort of an uncle to him."

"We is free," said Agnes with a certain grandeur, "an' *we* will decide about who's a massa, won't we, Ruth?"

"Sho' 'nuf will, Agnes. Now we ain't slaves, we gets to de-cide a few things. Dey is some people yu respect so yu jes' *gotta* call 'em massa. So, Massa James, dat is what we have de-cided, and dat is dat."

"You're both being very generous," I said, "but you should know I'm doing this because of someone else."

"Who dat?"

"My friend Dr. Ross, the man who left you the food and the guns. He's the one Major Ramsay thought had stolen Joe. He introduced me to some escaped slaves four years ago and, next thing I knew, I was working with him for the abolition of slavery. At first, I didn't want to do it, I'm embarrassed to say. I had a nice job with the railroad and everything was just as I wanted it to be, but Dr. Ross persuaded me to stop thinking only of myself and do something for others."

"Yu is doin' just dat."

"Because Dr. Ross persuaded me that it was the right thing to do. This is just as much his journey as it is ours."

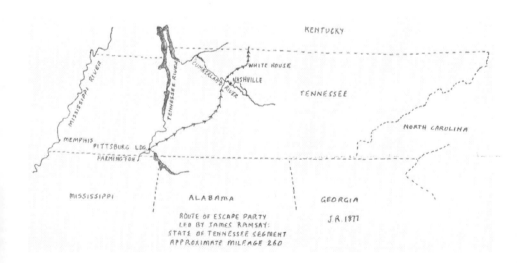

ESCAPE ROUTE THROUGH THE STATE OF TENNESSEE.

Chapter Twenty

Our first "depot" on the Underground Railroad was to be at the farm of a Mr. and Mrs. Snider, just south of Booneville, Mississippi, itself not too far short of the border with Tennessee. I could not be sure of the exact distance from our present encampment, but it looked to be in the region of forty-five miles, certainly in excess of a reasonable two nights' walk. A concrete goal such as this, however, became something of an obsession: a few hours' relief from this dreadful burden of responsibility, the prospect of food, shelter, perhaps even a bed. I discussed the time and distance with my charges, taking note that Rebecca's condition had improved remarkably, and we agreed to try for it, even if it meant carrying the little ones for part of the distance.

If my map was to be believed and if we were where I thought we were, the next station up the railway line was Koonowah, about a two hour walk away. And as far as I could judge, train operations became sparse if not non-existent during the night, at least in this part of the country. So there seemed little risk in setting off before sunset; with no further discussion, we were under way, paying last respects to our fallen comrade Joshua on our departure.

And there was even a sun to set that night, the overcast having moved off to the east just before what would have been dinner-time in a normal environment. My obsession to be under way, though, nearly demolished our endeavour even before we were quit of the state of Mississippi, and it happened like this:

We were but half an hour on our way when a train very suddenly and very "onconveniently" came on the scene from our rear, sweeping around a curve unheard by us because of an evening breeze swishing through the trackside trees. Jerge, bringing up the rear, had the presence of mind to shout "Go!" but we had not had an emergency drill the night before - there had been too many real emergencies to deal with - and there was some confusion as people tried to remember whether to exit stage left or right. *Exeunt*, then, twenty-six fugitive slaves, one Labrador retriever, and one horrified Canadian; enter one clanging, huffing locomotive wearing its smoky plumage like a French empress at the Palace of Versailles and carrying, like veils, the white flags that denoted an extra train movement, striding majestically past, oh, wonderful, with a *passenger* train, curious faces pressed to the windows, faces that could not fail to see us as we sprawled in the trackside grasses, sending a terrified flock of butterflies scrabbling skyward in a fluttering clutter. *Exeunt* the train now, but, hark, there is a rasping sound of brakes being applied. Behold, we have been sighted...

I raised my head. "They've seen us!" I shouted. "I've made a complete mess out of this. I've got to go and talk our way out of it. Stay put unless I wave both arms, and if I do, run like hell and forget about me."

"Massa, we couldn't..."

"We have no choice. Some train crew are coming now, God Almighty, they have guns! Perhaps I can wheedle our way out of this." I realized at the moment the folly of my instruction to scatter if I waved my arms; we were in a shallow cutting fringed by trees, the train effectively boxing us in. I felt in my pocket for the money from the bag Joe had rescued from under the tree at the Major's plantation. It was quite insufficient for a proper bribe; and we weren't even out of Mississippi!

I hurried forward as the train crew came ambling along in languorous confidence. There were two conductors in their waistcoats and flat-topped caps as well as a quartet with guns.

"Hey, boy," said the leader of the quartet, squinting in the last evening sunshine. "Quite a crowd back there, huh?"

"Yes, quite a crowd, and I might add a very desperate one. If you go any closer, there'll be a bloodbath. They have knives and guns and know how to use them. And they are very angry with white people. I'm the only one they trust."

"Yew jokin'?"

"Believe me, I wouldn't joke about a thing like this."

"How do we know that?"

"By listening to me."

"Look, boy, yew watch yore lip."

"I am trying to save you from an ugly situation. These people are armed and there's this one big fellow named Precious..." Precious was nearby and as I called his name, he rose ponderously from his cover.

"Aw, shut mah mouth. This boy's tellin' the truth. Nobody could make up a name like 'Precious' an' nobody could invent...that."

I addressed the two conductors. "Where are you bound for?"

"We're a special for Memphis. Gotta make a connection at Farmington."

"Your management will be very upset if you are late. Who stopped the train?"

"Ah did."

"You'll have some awkward questions from your management unless you get on your way."

"Cain't have loose slaves all over ever'where."

"I wonder if your management would see it that way, at least if it interfered with operations. I know these things because I too am a railroad man. Grand Trunk in Canada. You're Mobile and Ohio, are you not?"

"Yup."

"I'd like to be able to put in a good word for your company with my own. Good for business," I said. "Now, about the present situation. I have a fair sum of money here, which you can have. It will compensate you for temporary blindness. You can tell your passengers that everyone had vanished by the time you stopped the train and had a look. And that's the truth. Look around." Precious had hidden again and there was indeed nought to be seen but the singular spectacle of Colonel hiding behind a sapling, only his eyes concealed from his would-be-pursuers. His black sides protruded bulbously from either side of the little tree. One ear flicked at an insect.

"Cute dawg. He cain't see nothin' neither. All right, fella. Call it a deal. We ore in a hurry."

Numbly, I handed over our entire operating budget, still in the state of Mississippi. "Thanks, boy. Y'all have a nice evenin', now."

The crew ambled with leisurely arrogance back to the train, dividing up their unexpected wealth. My throat was as dry as felt. It had been a costly aversion of catastrophe, but an aversion nonetheless, and we were still on our way, at least on our way once I had recovered from my horrified palsy.

Some time after midnight, yet another train came upon us, tramping up from behind, orange light flaring from the firebox, a livid streamer of steam against the starry sky. Most of the cars were stacked high with tarpaulined bales of cotton. This was our first encounter with a train after dark and I wondered uneasily if night-time operations would be more common as we moved towards the industrial north. The saving grace was that there was far more warning than from night-riders.

The railway line was relatively straight here and once we were into the rhythm of track-walking, we were able to make the best progress yet, some-what in excess of eighteen miles, before dawn forced another stop. We found another little creek and some wild fruit that was indistinguishable between pears and apples. At risk of another "onconvenience", we ate it and it did help, but there was no question that we were now seriously weakened from lack of food. The Snider farm was our only answer.

We pushed onward the following two nights, this time with no incident. And all too soon, the second night ended, the cock crew, and we had a farm to find, and that instanter, to use the local vernacular. There would be no second chance if we were sighted marching through the countryside or if I were to walk into the wrong farm nattering about hardware and dry goods. There would be questions eclipsing any asked by railway management concerning the punctuality of connections to Memphis.

Alex had given me a hand-drawn map (courtesy of Richard Adamson) that showed the immediate surroundings of the Snider farm. A country road crossed the track at an acute angle a couple of miles south of Booneville. This we were to follow to the right past three plantations, now alarmingly visible in the rapidly focussing dawn, then on the left there would be a modest brown farmhouse with an oil lamp hanging on the front porch.

There it was, now; this had to be it. Up the lane came the Lost Tribe of Mississippi, to whom I whispered hollowly, "Get down by those trees over there and stay down until I come for you." I strode up to the old farmhouse door and rapped on it as prescribed: three slow knocks, a pause, and two quicker ones. Immediately the door opened a crack and the Underground Railroad ritual began.

"Who is it?"

"A friend of a friend."

"What is thy business?"

"I have a delivery."

"Of what?"

"Fifteen packages of hardware and eleven of dry goods."

There was a hiss of indrawn breath. "Pray give me those numbers again."

"Fifteen hardware, eleven dry goods. We had an unexpected, ah, addition to the shipment."

"What is thy name?"

"James Ramsay. And yours?"

"Charles Snider. Ah think we are properly identified. But twenty-six! Mercy! Oh, well, we'll just dew ore best. Bring them in before all mah unworthy neighbours get to wondering why Ah have twenty-six black visitors."

"Make it twenty-seven. The dog is black too."

"Dear Gawd."

My brood poured all over the little farmhouse, perching anywhere they could as their beleaguered legs gave out. Mrs. Snider set about preparing breakfast, quite forgetting that our days were totally backwards, but food, any food, was to be embraced with a fervour unparalleled in my experience. Starvation, and that is not too strong a word, had left me queasy and light-headed.

The Sniders, like many of the Underground "agents", were Quakers, and their traditional form of address merged intriguingly with their Mississippi dialect. This led to one of those little breakdowns in communication that affect us all from time to time. "Would thee like porge?" I was asked.

"I beg your pardon?"

"Would thee like porge?"

"Uh..."

"Thee knows, hot cereal."

"Oh, *porridge*! Oh, absolutely. Yes, thank you." So long had I been in the South now that my pronunciation of "you" was beginning to sound more like the dreaded "yew".

So Mr. and Mrs. Snider, the indefatigable Precious assisting, cooked a huge vat of "porge" for twenty-six slaves, myself, and even for Colonel, who virtually inhaled the stuff in a great canine display of smackings and retchings.

The dankness of the night was dispelled in the warm kitchen. Following all the "porge" any human could eat, we retired to the barn to sleep for the day, a movement that had to be handled with the utmost discretion, with Ruth, Precious, Joe, and Jerge in charge, and Mr. and Mrs. Snider and myself acting as lookouts. This was only their third experience with the Underground Railroad and they were taking no chances. Once in the barn, we descended to a cellar beneath, for the premises had already been visited twice by bounty-hunters.

So determined was Colonel to be with us, despite an offer that he should stay in the kitchen, that Precious had to carry him down the ladder, slung over his shoulder like an outsized black baby. And once settled in, we slept the sleep of the blessed. I had gradually ceased to be terribly concerned about Ruth's and my public impression, so I slept with my head cradled on her shoulder. Colonel slept with his head on mine, his quick breaths fluttering in my ear; Jerge was to remark that the three of us made a sweet-looking family.

A cool cellar is not the most comfortable place to sleep, particularly if it mirrors, concentrates, and distils the rankness of twenty-seven unwashed people and one dog. But it did have the virtue of being dry, safe, and undisturbed beneath its artfully concealed trap door. And on that account, my travelling companions slept so soundly that they had to be prodded awake a couple of hours before sundown.

My own sleep had been terminated a bit prematurely, as I had awoke having to relieve myself, a condition aggravated by Colonel, who had shifted his head to rest on my full bladder. Relief, while not impossible in the cellar, would have been at best thoughtless, so all I could do was to shift Colonel's head, grit my teeth, and ride it out.

At the going of the sun and after an outsized dinner, we were ready to move again, gladdened and uplifted by the humanity of Mr. and Mrs. Snider. Their little farm was to be burned flat the following spring by out-raged slave-owners, but not before their home had seen 276 souls on their way to freedom in Canada.

We took to the rails again for the night, toiling ever northward, hop-skip, hop-skip from sleeper to sleeper in a rhythm that had become as regular as any heart-beat. We had a visitation from an oncoming freight train, but with ample warning, both aurally and visually.

We had a bad scare near the village of Rienzi; although it was a Sun-day, some of the local gentry had been out for a late-night toot, perhaps at someone's farm. Being on a railway line should have insulated us from such goings-on, but just north of Rienzi, around a bend in the track we came very abruptly upon a road-crossing. Two wagon-loads of hollering stupidity came tearing out of the darkness right in front of us. We hit the ground where we stood, but it was a poor performance and only the im-paired condition of our passing fellow humans spared us discovery.

That was our last full night in Mississippi. We made our day's encamp-ment, dined on fresh bread from Mrs. Snider's kitchen, and struck out northward again, taking the long way around Farmington; it was a major junction between the Mobile and Ohio and the Memphis and Charleston Railroads, with much consequent coming and going. Much as I love trains,

I had no capacity for more surprises and, of course, no funds for further bribery.

We gained Tennessee by the time the great rose of dawn bloomed forth. Now we were free of Mississippi and the escapees, as one, sank to their knees and sang one of the songs from their vast repertoire about the River Jordan. Although there were no farms or plantations visible, I had no wish to startle any locals with the sound of a full choir outdoors at daybreak. But there was no stopping them, verse after prolific verse. Even in my agitation I could not help admiring the high degree of musical sophistication, spontaneous and untrained though the singers may have been. Aside from the natural beauty of the voices, there was a remarkable usage of harmony, a capacity I have always admired, for in my own singing experience, my voice has always been drawn to the melody like a moth to a candle.

We sheltered for the day on a wooded hillside with a pond at the bottom and ate more of the bread that Mrs. Snider had baked for us. It did us well and after a slightly chilly day of sleep we were able to continue. To avoid being drawn too far westward for a direct journey, we diverged from the railway to head to the north-east, and after a spell of relatively easy going, the old and familiar symptoms of apprehension returned as I realized I had made a mistake. I had not checked our direction carefully enough; the broad and deep Tennessee River lay in our path and had to be crossed by a ferry operated by one Amos Grogan at the village of Pittsburg Landing. My fears were realized when we reached the river about two hours before dawn. Not only was there no sign of any settlement, I had no idea of whether we were too far up- or down-stream. There was nothing to be done for the moment, so, some miles short of where I would have liked us to be, I gave the word for everyone to bed down for the day. Because it was still dark, there was a fair bit of confusion that took no little time to resolve.

I took Precious aside to explain my problem and indicated that I would be away for most of the day to look for Pittsburg Landing.

"Ah'll do it mahself, James. Dere'd be hell to pay if'n yu was to leave yo' people. Dey needs yu."

"I don't want you going alone. Maybe Joe or Jerge could go with you."

"Ah could take Noah. He be our Indian guide and he ain't had a chance to do much."

"For God's sake, Precious! He needs his sleep. He's only little."

"Gittin' so sho' of hisself Ah keeps forgettin' he's little."

"I know what you mean. We're all growing in some way..."

"Ways we nevah dreamed."

"You're a thinking man, Precious. Look, I'll send Joe with you. He has ways of getting around and Jerge should be with Gladys."

So the slender, wiry Joe and the barn-like Precious set off up-stream into the thinning darkness as wispy tendrils of mist slowly uncoiled from the bubble- and weed-mottled river's surface. The river was very pretty and restful and all those good things, but it was also in the way. And I was too fretful to sleep; if Joe and Precious could not find Pittsburg Landing, they would have to try on the following day in the other direction and we would lose an entire night of travel.

With her own brother on this reconnoitring expedition, Ruth could not sleep either. She held my hand, a quite frequent and open occurrence now, since everyone seemed to accept us as A Couple, and we talked all morning about the nature of friendship and whether it was more enduring than love or passion.

Ruth chuckled. "Kin hardly say we made friendship dat last night at de plantation. Ah nevah felt so loved in all mah life." If this were heroic fiction, I would have wanted to do it again, right on this very spot, but this is not heroic fiction. I was scared, I was unspeakably tattered and dirty, and my entire nervous system felt as if it had taken a trip over a cheese-grater.

To our unutterable relief, Joe and Precious returned at mid-afternoon to report finding Pittsburg Landing a three-hour walk distant, which translated as somewhere around nine miles. I could relax again for a short while and I promptly nodded off from exhaustion, as did Ruth and Joe.

But not Precious. As the Lost Tribe slept, he made a weir with some stones at the side of the river and managed to entrap an astonishing quantity of fish for our dinner or breakfast or whatever we should call it. His fish-loving former master had taught Precious this trick and it amused me that such a skill should now be turned to our own use.

I have a certain difficulty with fish; my mother always thought I was just being obstinate over it, and because we were a practising High Anglican family, the dreaded stuff was always on the table for Friday's dinner. It always had an extreme reluctance to go down my gullet and could be persuaded only by great draughts of water. Now it had to be faced again, but now my choice was either revulsion or starvation.

According to Precious, there was no habitation for miles, so we felt it safe to make a fire, our first one, taking care to make it as smokeless as possible. We roasted the fish on sticks, the smoke flavour rendering it less objectionable. But after we got under way just after dark, I found myself feeling more and more peculiar, hot, cold, and sweaty all at the same time, and in the dark I felt a curious sense of disconnection with my feet.

After a couple of miles of winding along the river, my progress was so erratic that Philip asked me in a low voice, "James, is yu orl right?"

"Don't I seem all right?"

"Ah cain't tell time, but Ah would say we is goin' orful slow."

"Well, then, let's step out a bit." Oh, God!

"Yu is still goin' orful slow, James," echoed Precious, moving in along-side. "Is yu orl right?"

"I'm sorry, boys, it's the fish. Fish makes me ill, any fish. I was just too hungry to care."

"Ah'll fix yu up, just as good as new," said Precious gently. Without breaking stride, he moved in behind me, picked me up like a rag doll, and squeezed me about the middle with such strength that I vomited with the force of a firehose. "Whut wuz dat dere noise?" queried a voice in the darkness.

"Precious cleanin' out Massa James," explained Philip offhandedly. "Dat dere be somethin' of a specialty."

Unsavoury as it may seem, Precious' arcane treatment worked extremely quickly ("Allus wanted to do dat to a white man," he remarked) and in a few minutes, I was able to navigate normally, although becoming almost insane with hunger, so thoroughly had Precious purged my system.

Precious diverted me from my discomfort with some truly interesting conversation. All education, literacy, and any skills not related directly to slavery had been withheld from the blacks. Precious, however, knew how to read, not out of concern on anyone else's part, but because his previous owner had a nearly-blind old mother. One of Precious' duties had been to read to her, the principal offering being the Bible.

Interpretation of the Bible offered a revealing insight into the difference between black and white thoughts on religion; where we tend to look for symbolism in the Good Book, the negroes looked at it literally and without question.

"It be de perfect book, simple as dat," Precious explained earnestly. "Funny dat white folks writ de thing, den udder white folks try to pick it apart. It's like tryin' to unscramble a aig. Yu know what Ah thinks, Ah thinks dis, Massa James, an' Ah hopes yu won't take no offence, but Ah thinks we niggers has better access to God than white folks, jes' like de li'l shilrens, on account of we believes so completely.'

I soon found that, to my embarrassment, not only Precious, but most of the other blacks as well had a far better knowledge of the Bible than I did, for so many Biblical stories had been passed orally from one generation to the next with amazingly little distortion. And when conversation on this trip turned to religion, it became definitely lopsided with me, the holder of a degree from the University of Glasgow, as a mute listener. Why could we not talk about trains instead?

Continued Precious relentlessly, "Think of it dis way, James. We puts our faith an' trust in yu because yu knows de best way to make us free. We doesn't try to question yu an' debate wid yu, does we? No, suh! An' so we don't debate wid de Lawd, an' He leads us jes' fine. Fact, Ah reckon he's leadin' us through yu right now. Helps us through de valleys of despair...'

I have never been comfortable with a docile acceptance of religion. In addition to giving us the Bible by whatever means, the Almighty has also given us the capacity to think and analyse and religion is best acquired with some effort on our part if it is to mean anything. But then I have never been a slave. Religion was the one thing they had without all manner of toil and struggle.

I must say that in some ways I envied the blacks their uncluttered intellectual landscape (no pejorative intended) and their complete assurance in the matter of eternity, although in some it verged almost on a martyr complex. But for the most part, my flock had no apparent fear of death, whereas, whenever I faced it, as I had faced those guns a few days back, the mere thought of it tied me in knots. And I thought I was a free man. But I suppose, in our own way, we are all slaves to something.

ESCAPE ROUTE THROUGH THE STATE OF KENTUCKY.

CHAPTER TWENTY-ONE

Thanks to Amos Grogan and his two sons, we crossed the Tennessee River on a sort of flat-bottomed scow that served as a ferry and could take eight or nine people at a time. The three trips thus necessary took most of the night and a pink dawn was brushing the eastern sky by the time we were all across. Amos must have given us all his household provisions, as we now had food for about three days, which in such isolated country we would need.

The remainder of the state of Tennessee was negotiated in thirteen days, rather more slowly than I had planned, but much of it was very hilly and on that account was pretty laborious going. There was the major obstacle as well of the Cumberland River and without a ferry service provided by the local Quakers, as on the Tennessee, it might have been the end of the line for us. Tennessee was, however, far better for the nerves than Mississippi, it being far easier to conceal ourselves in the wooded valleys and ravines. As well, we were now out of plantation country and into a region that was either totally wild or, at most, populated with widely scattered farms.

Several of the Underground Railroad routes, of which ours was one, converged on Cincinnati and, after some days of steering an erratic course dictated by topography, we were now able to move more consistently to the north-east. To further enhance the situation, there were more Quakers and consequently more "depots", and the further east one moved in Tennessee, the fewer people cared for slavery, although whether from personal preference or being too poor to own slaves may be a matter of conjecture.

In any event, we reached another "depot", just before the crossing of the Cumberland River near Nashville. Almost inevitably, it was maintained by a Quaker family, one with the singular name of Lambsbreath, whose speech was so encrusted with "thee" and other archaisms that I felt as if I had retreated in time to the England of Queen Elizabeth.

We were quite a battered and gaunt ensemble by now, having lived off the countryside since our last "depot" on autumn fruit, pig corn taken from farmers' fields, and the like. What Mr. and Mrs. Lambsbreath did for us was nothing short of spectacular. Try to imagine a roast beef dinner for twenty-seven guests, with mashed potatoes and green beans, and with second helpings at that. And apple pie to follow. And cold milk. There is something peculiarly gratifying about food by the trough.

And Colonel was not overlooked. Mrs. Lambsbreath was so touched by the story of how he came to be with us, so touched with pity at his growing emaciation, that she prepared him a great plate of beef scraps "to fatten him up". Anyone who has ever had a dog will know that these worthy beasts quite lose their judgement around food; as with the "porge",

Colonel inhaled the contents of his plate, uttered a cavernous "quack!", and was rushed outdoors to be copiously sick.

We slept in the cattle barn, whose usual tenants were out to pasture for the day. Ruth and I had a stall to ourselves and for the first time since that magical last night at the Major's plantation, we made love. I was going to say "the inevitable happened", but it sounds far too coy for what actually transpired. Out of respect for the others, we had indulged in little more than holding hands. In any event I had been too preoccupied and exhausted to have the will anyway.

Even at this time, I was asleep less than a minute after bedding down, but awoke again almost immediately to find Ruth and myself entwined and the whole world spinning lazily around and around. It was divine. We tried to be quiet, but moments after our release, we could hear one of the married couples in the throes of the same thing. Ruth smiled her wonderful smile in the dusty, sunbeam-dappled shadows of the barn and said something about how we were an inspiration to others. We dozed off, still locked together.

Cold blew the wind in the next two days. September was upon its way now and the odd patch of red or yellow was showing through the foliage. And since our movements were at night and our clothes were disintegrating from both general abuse and actual rot, we were suffering more than just a little, especially the few who had for all this time been without shoes. At our next station, near White House (east of Nashville), we spent two days and a night while our hosts, luckily a large family, visited other members of the Quaker community and of the Underground Railroad organization. They were able to muster enough hand-me-downs to completely re-equip us, including, finally, shoes for everybody.

Onward, then, we pushed, our calloused feet and aching muscles tramping over hills, along river-beds, through the daily heat and nightly chill of advancing autumn. Children had to be carried. We were the walking wounded. Cuts and scrapes occurred daily. There were weals from being slapped in the face with tree branches, still the occasional insect bite. Looking at my ragged map, I could think now in terms of our next state, Kentucky. It was not to be attained, however, before little Noah, our Indian guide, came within a hair's breadth of annihilation and our company was struck with tragedy once again.

The situation was nobody's fault. At dawn on the misty morning after quitting White House, we prepared for sleep (and I was remarking to Joe and Philip how fortunate we had been with the weather), when there was a scream of raw fear from the other side of a low, wooded knoll. We raced around it to see what was happening and in the confusion I didn't think to bring my gun. Of course, this time I truly needed the beggarly thing, for there was poor wee Noah, hanging by his hands from a tree branch, a wolf leaping and snapping at his heels. And this was no ordinary wolf; its eyes were all runny and a yellow mucousy matter spattered from its muzzle.

I had never seen rabies before, but knew enough to recognize the symptoms. I turned to run for my gun to encounter the glorious Colonel racing the other way towards the embattled Noah. He launched himself, jaws wide like a mythical black monster, and sailed through the air to land on Noah's assailant. The gun was rendered superfluous for the moment as the two animals battled to the death in a frenzy of snarling fur and blurred blood.

The wolf, nearly twice the size of Colonel, flopped and flipped all over the place as Colonel heaved it about by the neck. The wolf howled horribly and then went limp. Colonel sat down and contemplated it, looking not bad for the circumstances, his left ear turned inside out. But the wolf's blood all over his muzzle dictated what I must do next and I felt sick at heart beyond words.

Noah sobbed in his mother's arms. She sobbed as well, comforted by Rebecca and Gladys and I wanted to sob too.

"Stay away from Colonel!" I ordered. At the sound of his name, Colonel came towards me as I retreated to where I had left my gun.

"Massa..."

"Stay right where you are." The familiar shuffle-shuffle followed me through the leaves and underbrush. I picked up the awful weapon, turned around, and took aim. Shuffle-shuffle. Colonel's left ear popped back right side out and flickered at something. I squeezed the trigger, the gun roared like a thunderclap, Colonel did a leap and a sort of half-spiral, to collapse lifeless on the ground.

"Massa!" screamed several voices in unison; in the heat of the moment, they were reverting to the habitual form of address established during two centuries of servitude. I was aware of black faces, hands to cheeks, over mouths, over eyes. My knees gave way like two stems of cooked noodles, and I have a vague recollection of half-sitting on the ground, I suppose in some sort of shock, sifting some dry earth through my fingers.

Ruth was staring at me as if I had killed one of her people. It was too much. I, thought to be another Moses to twenty-six escaped slaves, whose duty it was to be strong, silent, and imperturbable, pitched on my face into the dirt, sobbing miserably and without remission. It was the sort of terrible gasping sobbing in which one fights for breath and is yet beyond caring.

My charges gathered round, Precious gingerly removing the shotgun from my grasp. "Why yu do dat, James? He were a real good dawg, he saved Noah. He wuz black, like us, comin' to Canada. Now he daid."

I fought to get the words out. "The wolf had a sickness...called rabies...if he had bitten Noah, Noah would have died...horribly. Colonel bit the wolf and...likely would have got rabies himself. Rabies makes animals go crazy"(pause to choke down a whimper) "and they bite people and give *them* rabies. I couldn't take the chance. It's the hardest thing I've ever had to do. I loved that dog..." I put my hand over my face and wept until I could weep no more.

Someone had covered Colonel with a tattered old shirt. We had no tool to dig a grave, so the men, all of them, scooped up earth, rocks, and any other debris they could into a little burial mound. While the others slept, I kept a vigil all day, the loneliness eased by Ruth, who, understanding the situation (more than some of the others, who had to have it explained to them again and again) stayed with me until she dozed off from sheer fatigue.

At twilight, we formed up in numerical order, and before pushing onward for the land of the North Star, we filed past the pathetic little mound, a corner of blood-stained shirt showing beneath. And then we were gone, leaving the valiant Colonel alone to sleep out eternity in the Tennessee woodlands.

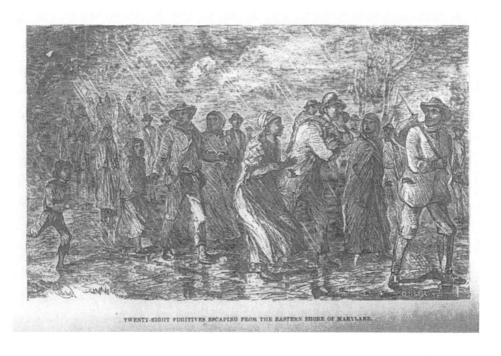

TWENTY-EIGHT FUGITIVES ESCAPING FROM THE EASTERN SHORE OF MARYLAND.

SLAVES ESCAPING FROM MARYLAND IN A STORM SIMILAR
TO THAT ENCOUNTERED BY JAMES RAMSAY'S ESCAPE PARTY.
COURTESY OF ENOCH PRATT FREE LIBRARY, BALTIMORE, MD

CHAPTER TWENTY-TWO

Onward our band trudged, all of us in a curiously numb state of suspension, toiling ahead as much out of sheer instinct as anything. My map had been hand-copied out of a school atlas and was certainly approximate as to scale, so I was able to take heart now having reached the state of Kentucky without having my spirits dampened by the realization that, with all we had been through, we were only about a third of the way to our destination. There was still urgency, though; aside from our still being in slave territory, September was wearing on and that, in concert with the increasing northerly latitude, was starting to make our nights chilly almost beyond endurance.

All in all, however, we had fared rather well, at least in comparison with other groups I was to hear of, for we had been endangered only twice by nature, once by white people, and a small number of times by our own collective health.

Only a day or so after these reflections, nature had another go at us, immobilizing us in a storm for half a night near Bowling Green, Kentucky, peppering us with freezing cold rain and tearing ragged torrents of yellow leaves from the trees. So terrible was the wind, possibly the worst I have ever seen, that I was worried about falling branches and flying twigs, but just as midnight drew nigh, the storm subsided and gave way to clear, though cold, starlight. The North Star beckoned us on our way. Somehow it was looking bigger now than it had in Mississippi.

Further up-country, we lodged at the home of a Mr. Sloane, which, at first glance was a large, prosperous slave-owning dairy farm. In point of fact, Adolphus Sloane maintained the place as a blind for the Underground Railroad; he was what the British would describe as a "gentleman farmer", having retired a short time before as chairman of one of Kentucky's largest coal-mining companies. As the Lost Children of Mississippi dined hugely in what from the outside was a barn, but in reality was a dormitory, Mr. Sloane told me something of his career as an abolitionist.

"Used to own slaves myself. Treated them pretty well, too, but still owned them. I love newspapers, get them sent from all over the country and from Canada too. I did a fair business up there with coal, and let me say, your *Globe* is a hell of a paper. Well, sir, I read quite a few editorials and articles about slavery and it was like standing back and taking a good look at myself. Mrs. Sloane and I talked it over and found that, well, we just didn't feel right about it. We had eight slaves at the time - they were servants and horsemen and the like, so their lot wasn't bad, not like what you saw in Mississippi - and we made an arrangement with them that they could stay in our employ, but were free to leave any time, just giving a fortnight's notice like any other employee.

"They stayed, all of them, and I suppose we would have continued that way, feeling that we were doing our bit for abolition, until the brother of one of our men was sold south to one plantation and his wife sold to another. To be honest, Mrs. Sloane and I had never paid much mind to that sort of thing, never had sold anyone south ourselves, but this was getting too close to home. Made us so doggone angry, we had to do much more to fight slavery than just free our own people.

"Well, out of the coal business I had made more money than a body could ever need, so, when I heard about the Underground Railroad from a fellow named Coffin up Cincinnati way, I retired early and we bought this farm. Pretty, isn' it? We produce just enough cheese and butter to make it look legitimate. All our old slaves help with it, pretending to be real slaves, so the spectacle of a lot of blacks about isn't unusual. Just have to be careful how many are outside at one time.

"We figure on a lot of fugitive slaves passing through the next while." Mr. Sloane laughed. "Just hope they like cheese. Oh, the things one's neighbours don't know. Isn't it shocking!"

Leaving our Underground Railroad "depots" was becoming progressively more and more difficult, much like having to get out of bed on a cold winter morning. It would be so pleasant to stay longer with a roof and a dry place to sleep. So leaving the Sloane farm was not an easy matter, though we left it enhanced by the gifts of some blankets and, mercifully, some money, the need for which was to arise but two days later. I have an economic theory that the moment you have money, relief is guaranteed to be on its way. By this I mean someone will relieve you of your money and this incident merely supports my hypothesis.

We were at this time spending a raw, blustery autumn day encamped near Shelbyville in northern Kentucky, doing our best in the absence of an Underground Railroad station. Agnes, having brought her baby all this distance, had fallen ill again and could not feed the child. She lay shivering and sweating under her blanket, her face of an ominous, chalky cast. The hungry baby fretted and fidgeted in Ruth's arms.

By evening, I had to make a decision. We could not move unless some went ahead and the rest stayed behind with Agnes until she either recovered or died. Or, according to my original operating instructions, I had the option of shooting her, but having suffered over Colonel as I did (with plenty of company, I should say), I could not bring myself to kill again. There would be the additional complications of caring for a motherless baby and of concealing a body so that Shelbyville would not be revealed to lie on an Underground route. Indeed, some routes had to be abandoned because of this sort of situation.

I sat in council with my panel of advisors: Ruth, Joe, Philip, Gladys, Jerge, and Precious. "We has money now," observed Jerge. "How about goin' to dat ar town an' gittin 'us a docta?"

I explained about the Fugitive Slave Law. "A doctor could make far more money from that than from us. He'd probably treat Agnes, take our money, and then run her in."

"Lordy. Look, Massa James, we could diddle aroun' all de night while Agnes gets wuss an' de baby starves," said Precious. "Let's yu an' Ah go inta town an' find us a docta. Look, we'll tell' im Ah um yo' slave an' Agnes is mah wife..."

"How do we explain her being off here in the woods?"

"Ah'll carry her. Tell de docta we's off de train or somethin'. Let's go."

Precious picked up Agnes like a rag doll. "Massa James, yu take de baby. We get dem both fixed up."

"Ah, telling me what to do, are you, Precious?"

"Ooh, Ah um real sorry, massa. Didn't mean it dat way."

"I know, Precious. It's all right. I was just fooling around, but I just realized if anything happened to me, you could take over. You're not afraid to make decisions. Joe?"

"Yes, Massa James?"

"If we're not back by this time tomorrow, you and Jerge take charge. You fellows know what to do too. So much for helpless slaves."

"Lordy."

Shelbyville was on a line of the Louisville and Frankfort Railroad, whose iron ran through a grove of trees just to our left as we faced more or less north. It was by now about nine o'clock of a Saturday evening and as dark as the inside of a hat. We had some initial trouble finding our way until we reached the track, which at this point was on a low embankment. The lights of Shelbyville twinkled in the frigid darkness and an uneasy wind rustled the desiccated grasses by the right-of-way.

The baby wriggled fretfully in my arms. Step, hop...step, hop from sleeper to sleeper as we neared Shelbyville. Soon we could see the station, its windows still glowing a mellow yellow from the oil lamps within. Nearby stood a small shunting engine, apparently unattended, a thin streamer of waste steam blowing from its safety valve.

I went into the station to ask the agent where I could find a doctor. "Dr. Appleby," he drawled around a well-masticated toothpick. "Turn right at the crossing, right again two blocks later, an' he's right at the corner. Got a sign, too. Good huntin', stranger. That there yore baby?"

"Belongs to my, er, slave. Thank you. Much obliged."

Dr. Appleby's house was unlit and deserted. "Bloody shit!" I lamented. "Oh, wait a minute." In the door was a card indicating that in an emergency the doctor could be located at Murphy's Tavern. Armed with that bit of reassurance, we retreated to the main street of Shelbyville, guided unerringly to Murphy's by sounds of alcoholic revelry.

I entered through the traditional swinging doors, leaving Precious outside with the comatose Agnes. The scene in Murphy's was not one to hearten the soul, especially if the soul needed medical assistance. My lingering recollection all this time later is one of semi-conscious humanity propped up at various angles, many with their feet up on the tables and chairs. Nothing resembling a doctor was in sight.

I went to the bartender, Agnes's baby tucked under my arm like a pet. "Kid's under age, stranger!" trumpeted the bartender with a screeching guffaw.

"The mother of the kid in question is very ill. I understand Dr. Appleby is here."

"Dr. Appleby! Way-all, Ah can't rightly say whether he is in a fit state to practise the art and science of medicine, but he's here somewhere." The bartender squinted through the lantern-lit, tobacco smoke-enshrouded gloom.

"Well, where?" I urged.

"Somewhere."

"Can you be more specific?"

"Whuddya need 'im for?"

"I *told* you, you fool. The baby's mother. She's sick."

"Fewl, huh? Look, stranger, Ah don't rightly like people who walk into my place an' call me a fewl."

I could have apologized then and there, but elected somehow to make the situation worse. "I didn't call you one until you acted like one."

Murphy, for it was indeed Murphy, leaned over the counter towards me, his jaw working rapidly on a plug of chewing tobacco. I could hear (and smell) his breath rasping in rhythm with the chewing. "Yew jest giddouda here," he pronounced, "an' take that there li'l black bastard with yew." Suddenly Mississippi seemed not that far away.

"You're Murphy, right?" I was angry and out of control by now.

"Yeah, Ah'm Murphy."

"Well, it's good to know you have another name besides 'arsehole'. Now, for the last and final time, where is Dr. Appleby?"

"Yew smart-mouth son-of-a-bitch!" snarled Murphy, grabbing me by the collar and pulling me halfway over the counter. The baby, an unwilling buffer between me and the bar, screamed. Such an alien sound in a saloon made heads turn, and one man, a bit friendlier than the rest (or less hostile; the distinction was academic) came over to intervene. "What's up, stranger?"

"I need a doctor. Now. And this...this creature..."

"Awlright, awlright. Fred Appleby is right over here. What he can dew in his condition is anyone's guess, but he's the only sawbones in town. Anyway, let's get yew outa here before Murph gets yew with his bull-whip. He don't have a very nice disposition tonight."

Dr. Appleby was dislodged from his seat, his boots removed from the table, and he came lurching out of the saloon in an invisible haze of bourbon from the distilleries of nearby Frankfort, a haze of bourbon undiluted with branch. "Oh, shut mah mouth," he complained.

"Come on, doctor, sober up and do your duty. We need you."

"What the God's hell kind of baby is *this*?"

"Well, what the God's hell does it look like?" Oh, if my good mother could have heard *that* one!

"Er, black."

"Very good, doctor! In tomorrow's lesson, we can learn some other colours. Her mother is the one needing attention. Over here."

The doctor was suitably awed by Precious, gazing up at him as if at a huge black cathedral. "Where yew folks from?"

"Mississippi. Just passing through. These are my slaves."

"Passin' through how?"

"We were on the train. The woman became ill and we had to get off. Now here we are."

"The train, huh? The northbound came through at noon. Ah was at the station to pick up a porcel at fower this afternoon - urrp -to pick up a porcel an' y'all weren't there. Know what Ah think? Yew is on a railroad, all right, but it runs underground, know what Ah mean? Hee, hee, hee!"

"Very well, I won't try to lie to you. That is the situation. But I have more money here than you would get by running these people in. You can have it all. And there's something else. Just a moment."

I ducked back into Murphy's Tavern and went to the bar. Murphy was not pleased to see me. "*Yew* again, huh? Yew wanna be up to yer knees in floor or somethin'?"

"I want a bottle of bourbon. I'll pay double."

"Double, huh? Maybe we can do business. Oh, looky there..."

In my concentration on the business at hand, I had been oblivious to my cultural surroundings, but on "looky there", I could see, in the fog of tobacco smoke, two enormously fat men in a cleared area of the floor. Hands in hip pockets, they charged at each other, stomachs shaking and waggling, colliding with a whoosh of escaping air. "What are they doing?" I said irritably. I had no time for this.

"Somethin' we like to dew here. We call it belly-buckin'. Real good fun. Look at 'em..."

"May I please have my bourbon?"

"Jest a minute. Y'all can have it for regular price if yew buck the winner." The two behemoths flew at each other, impacting with a great "oof!".

"Not on your life," I quavered, my bravado deserting me. "I'll just pay double."

"No deal. Yew gotta buck the winner."

"Do I have to win?"

Murphy laughed disagreeably. "Nah, Ah jest wanna see yew flat on yer sorry ass."

"Oof!" exploded one of the belly-buckers, sent sprawling among some chairs with a splintering crash.

"Awl right, stranger, yer turn," said Murphy maliciously, his chewing of tobacco accelerating with dread anticipation. "Here, Rufus, here's yer next opponent."

"What, him? Hey, Murph, be serious. I don't wanna be had up for murder."

"Ah want him on 'is ass, the smart-mouth whipper snapper."

"Awl right, Murph," said Rufus with almost a sigh, a sigh that implied that what was about to transpire would be far more painful to me than to him. "Hands in yore hip pockets, now, fella. Nothin' personal, yew unnerstand."

"Of course," I croaked. Amid sarcastic applause, I stepped out into the arena, hands in pockets as directed, clenched, nails digging into sweating palms. Rufus contemplated me for a moment and then charged, a monumental jiggling castle of fatty tissue, filling, indeed overflowing, my field of vision. The world darkened, as in an eclipse of the sun, and all I could do was stand there like a hunted deer.

And then Rufus struck. Succumbing to the laws of gross tonnage, I was sent flying, stumbling backwards, hands jammed irretrievably in pockets, slammed to the floor, and slid to a stop under a table.

I had offered so little resistance that Rufus had completely miscalculated and lost control of his very considerable momentum, landing on top of the table that was my shelter, my rock of ages, cleft for me, let me hide myself in thee, and it collapsed with me underneath. I screeched, thinking that my pelvis had been broken.

The raucous merriment stilled. "Jesus H. Christ, Rufus, Ah dew believe yew've kilt him," said a disembodied voice in the far distance. Blood roared through my ears, so I wasn't dead. But my pelvis...

"God's hell," said Rufus plaintively.

"Let's git this poor son-of-a-bitch outa the wreckidge."

"Probly looks like one o' them blood pancakes the Spics like."

"Ah wouldn't know," interrupted Murphy, taking charge. "Quit jawin' an' git that damn' table up. Yew git the bill, Rufus."

"Go screw yerself, Murph, yew put me up to this."

"To hell with the table!" I squealed.

"Gawd, 'e's alive!"

Lightened of the intolerable burden of the table and of Rufus, I left Murphy and his *confreres* to sort things out, got my hard-won bottle from the bar, and crawled out of the saloon.

"What the God's hell happened to yew?" slurred the doctor, grabbing at a hitching post to maintain balance. I was starting to think that "God's hell" was Shelbyville's New Expression and everyone was trying it out. "Somebody buck yew?"

"Yeh. Fella named Rufus." I was slurring too. Nothing was working properly. Perhaps I had brain damage.

"Oh, him," chuckled the doctor. "Lucky yew didn't end up in traction. Yew'll be walkin' fine in about a week. Let's go." He eyed the bottle of bourbon greedily.

We steered him back to his residence without incident, although I was profoundly displeased at his guffaw when I addressed Precious by name. "Yew guys got somethin' funny goin' here? Precious! Jesus, what a label."

Once in his surgery, Dr. Appleby pulled himself together sufficiently to minister to Agnes. "Don't look like pneumonia, not that Ah could dew a God's hell of a lot if it were. Nearest hospital's in Frankfort. Got a fever, though." He probed about with a stethoscope. He frowned.

"What is it?"

"Shit on a shingle. Ah dew believe this lady has dropsy."[1]

"So what does that mean?"" I had always thought dropsy was a disease that made you drop things.

"Tew much fluid...URRRRRH!...Gawd above...around the hort. Got a new pill here, Ah'll give yew a whole piss-pot of 'em, got mercury, quill, and foxglove[2] in 'em. Keep 'er good and warm. Pills'll act like a diuretic, yew see, get the fluid out. She'll be right as rain in a few days, ha, ha, about the time yew'll be walkin' natural again.

"Now, the - urp - baby. Milk's in the icebox. One of yew can heat some up...think the stove's still got some fire in it, feels like it dew. Mah old lady took off coupla years back. Need a woman for this, know what Ah mean?" It was never made clear whether Mrs. Appleby had left the equation because her husband was a drunkard or whether he was a drunkard because she had left. However, there were more immediate considerations.

We fed the baby and tucked Agnes away on a couch while our business was concluded over the bourbon. With a stab, I thought of Alex, how he could have ministered Agnes without these explorations of the netherworld of Shelbyville society. Where was my friend? Was he still free or in some unspeakable calaboose? It would be a long time before I found out.

We all three drank bourbon, Precious and I sipping daintily and trying not to get drunk. The doctor, predictably, drank deeply of the awful stuff, and soon he was in a complete torpor, head on table, where it would stay until we had made some distance out of town. In any event, he would not soon be trying to collect a bounty.

"What a combination we is, Massa James," huffed Precious as he bore Agnes along to where the others were encamped. "Mark mah words, we'll make it to Canada yet. Ah, dere it is."

"What?"

"Dere be de North Star. We be on our way."

---

[1] The contemporary term for dropsy is pulmonary edema.
[2] Foxglove contains digitalis, a form of digoxin.

Yours Truly
Levi Coffin

LEVI COFFIN, POPULARLY REGARDED AS
PRESIDENT OF THE UNDERGROUND RAILROAD.
COURTESY OF ENOCH PRATT FREE LIBRARY, BALTIMORE, MD

CHAPTER TWENTY-THREE

On Tuesday, October 1, after a march of fifty-one days, our ragged band found refuge in a Quaker household at the edge of Florence, Kentucky. It would be our final town on the Underground save for Covington before crossing into Ohio over the river of the same name. And in crossing the Ohio, we would be across the Mason-Dixon line, the division between free and slave-owning states, but by no means would we yet be out of reach of the Fugitive Slave Law's crippling claw.

What faced me now was the most difficult of predictable situations along this particular route of the Underground Railroad. Cincinnati, just across the river, was known to the general public as a focal point for the Underground, and of this, our Quaker host at Florence, Jeremiah Fitzgerald, explained, "Thee can count on the Ohio side of the river to be quite aswarm with bounty-hunters. Fact is, there are some who actually make a living at it, so we can't afford to take any foolish chances.

"One thing thee should know, James, is that thy group is by far the largest I have yet heard of. Our river-man can take only five at a time and that makes an awful heap of trips. Too much could go wrong. I think thee should go on thine own to Cincinnati and see Levi Coffin. He will help you devise some other means of getting across. Thy people will be safe with me and Mrs. Fitzgerald in thy absence."

In my own clothes, I looked by now like the worst kind of tramp, to the degree that I should have attracted adverse attention in even the most squalid of Mississippi towns, let alone among the urbanites of metropolitan Cincinnati. Thus was a problem posed, for Jeremiah, being shorter and stockier than I, could lend me no clothes that would fit. Moreover, he had no idea whom he could trust as a lender of clothes.

"We could go to a haberdasher's," I suggested, "and tell him I'm your poverty-stricken cousin from Canada and you'd like to buy me some clothes for my birthday." I smiled ingratiatingly.

Jeremiah scratched his head in cogitation. "Problem is, James, I'm not known as an extravagant spender. Folks would surely talk...Covington...let's go to Covington, they don't know me there."

"I have no money to cover this."

"I have. Let us be on our way."

I vaguely assumed that my new clothes, which I have kept ever since, were purchased with funds supplied by the Abolitionist Society; I only discovered years later that Jeremiah and Rachel Fitzgerald had chosen to live plainly and save their money for emergencies such as this.

While Jeremiah spent some time in heavy prayer, since the ethics of fabrication, even to a possible enemy, weighed upon him, I had my first proper bath for the better part of two months. We had all had to content ourselves along the way with the odd (and usually frigid) splash in creeks and rivers, less and less as the weather grew cooler, and by the time we reached the Fitzgerald farm, we were a pretty rank group of people, some of us afflicted with sores in onconvenient places.

Jeremiah and a well-scrubbed James drove in his wagon to Covington in a warm, golden, hazy Indian Summer sunshine. There was the sour tang of burning leaves on the air, the smell of Belleville in autumn. Never again would I complain about raking leaves!

We did our business in Covington, had my new clothes altered while I waited (made possible by a substantial bribe for the tailor), and then I was on my way aboard the ferry to Cincinnati. There I was to seek out Levi Coffin, whose reputation was such that he was generally thought of as the president of the Underground Railroad.

"Welcome, Brother James," said he, ushering me into a home of evidently ample means. "What is thy business?"

"Well, now, I deal in both hardware and dry goods." Even though I had been through the ritual many times now, I still had difficulty in taking the sound of it seriously. It seemed too much like a children's game.

"Hardware and dry goods, hmm? Thee are in the right place if thee wants transportation. The size of thy shipment?"

"Fifteen hardware, eleven dry goods."

"Saints above!"

"That's rather like what *I* said!"

"That is by all odds the largest shipment I have heard of. Where is the, uh, shipment right now?"

"Florence."

"Jeremiah Fitzgerald?"

"Right you are."

"Pray come and sit down, Brother James." Levi Coffin was an enormous man, though not enormous in the same sense as Precious. He was very tall and evidently quite muscular, although now, I judged, somewhere in his fifties. There was no sign of grey in his crinkled hair and his face bore few lines, but there was a wisdom there that spoke of age, something of the quality that Alex had.

"Mr. Coffin, before we get down to business, I need to know something. Do you know of one Alexander Ross?"

"Oh, indeed I do. From Canada, isn't he? He is *very* highly thought of in the Movement."

"He and I were together down in Mississippi and we lost touch."

"He was in jail or something down there, was he not?"

"He was. He got out the day before my, er, shipment departed and I know nothing of him since. I wondered if you had heard anything."

"I only know what you do, I'm sorry to say. I'll see, though, if there is anything I can find out here. Meantime, it behooves us to get down to business. Bringing a shipment the size of thine across the river would be too slow and hazardous," opined Mr. Coffin over a cup of proper British tea. "What we can do, and this has been tried and it works, is pack the shipment in crates and bring it across the river by wagon on the ferry. I have some friends in Glendale, not far from here, who have some particularly fine storage facilities. As a matter of fact, if storage is rendered unsafe for, ah, any reason, the cargo can be moved through a tunnel to another facility." He sighed meaningfully. "With so much burglary and crime these days, thee cannot be too careful. The world is just not what it used to be..."

I spent the night at the Coffin residence in a real bed, and in spite of the situation prevailing along the Mason-Dixon line and my continuing unease about Alex, I was so reassured by Levi Coffin's involvement that, for the first time in months, I slept like the proverbial baby.

We had to estimate the size of the crates needed and in the process decided that Precious, Agnes, the baby, and perhaps Noah should travel on foot, represented as my slaves. Precious in a crate would have been unmanageable, the baby and Noah might cry in terror of being in a closed box, the baby would need Agnes, and so on. And with this sort of division, the remaining escapees could be crated in pairs. If they weren't good friends by now, they would be after travelling together in a box.

Levi Coffin was a business-man, a legitimate merchant of dry goods and hardware. He had the necessary connections to procure eleven stout packing crates, and on October the 7th, a Monday, Mr. Coffin and I made our way back to Florence with the crates to find a crisis in progress. In our absence, two other contingents of slaves had come on the scene, one from Mississippi and the other from Louisiana, and my own people were camped out in a woodlot under the joint command of Precious, Joe, and Philip. The Fitzgeralds were almost beside themselves with the comings and goings of the better part of fifty blacks, and although they continued to be most gracious and friendly, I suspect they were relieved to see the end of us.

As a historical footnote, I should relate that when the lamentable War Between the States was to break out a short time later, Jeremiah and Rachel Fitzgerald, not caring for the side they found themselves on geographically, gave up their home and moved across the water to Ohio. Jeremiah, since his Quaker teachings forbade combat, was to serve with distinction as a medical aide for the Ohio Light Infantry.

Mr. Coffin and I set out from Jeremiah's house sometime after midnight in the wagon to pick up the "cargo" from the woodlot, with Jeremiah following on foot. A strong north wind had come up, driving an icy drizzle before it, but despite our discomfort, in the interests of concealment we could not help congratulating ourselves for having chosen such a night.

Crossing Jeremiah's property in the wagon would have been foolhardy on such a night and instead we drove out to the main road and turned right towards a sort of secondary lane that led to the edge of the farm. Scarcely had we turned onto the road than our two horses suddenly whinnied and skittered to a halt. A lantern flared to life. Four horses and four men, all armed, stood in its glare. One of the men took the bridle of our right-hand horse. "Well, well, well, what have we got here?" he drawled. All those miles of travel, the storms, the illnesses, Joshua, Colonel, the belly-bucking business in Shelbyville, the Mason-Dixon line virtually within sight - and now the dreaded bounty-hunters! My mind went numb and refused to function.

"Crates is what we have here," said Mr. Coffin laconically. "We were on our way to Florence to pick up some freight and got lost in the storm. But why am I explaining this to thee? Pray put that gun away..."

"What kind of freight?"

"Nosy, aren't thee? Hardware and dry goods, if it means that much to thee, not that it is any of thy business. But thee are the one with the gun."

"Hardware and dry goods, huh? Goin' where?"

"Cincinnati, if thee must know. Now, just let..."

"Come on, fella! Yew jokin' around, or what? That kinda stuff comes *from* Cincinnati."

Another of our unwelcome guests sprang into the wagon, peeling back the tarpaulin over the crates. "Well, shut mah mouth!" he exclaimed with unconcealed glee. "Why, Ah'll bet that's about the right size for a person. Call it two persons. Black persons. How many boxes? Hey, George, gimme the God-damn' light."

As George came forward with the God-damn' light, there was a smooth, barely perceptible motion in the inky darkness that obtains just outside a circle of light, and George's head tilted back with a squeal of "Hey, shit!" There were two heads visible now, George's and Jeremiah's. To Mr. Coffin's and my stupefied surprise, a gun was wedged against George's nose.

"Drop those guns, or this man is strawberry jam all over the road," pronounced Jeremiah with dread certitude. "Very good. I am glad thee are prepared to be sensible about this. Ah, ah, don't move, now. Two of these boxes are for thee. Thee are taking a trip to Cincinnati in the morning and will be set free after our delivery. And pray do not get any bright ideas about raising a ruckus. I will be standing over these boxes with my shotgun for the whole way and will blast them full of little tiny holes if there is so much as a peep. Now, thee had better turn thy horses loose and answer the call of nature, because it will be the last chance for a while."

Jeremiah prayed in the storm for forgiveness and once his soul was purged, we did the "packing", including our four wet and indignant bounty-hunters, which is why I crossed the Ohio the next morning with an entourage of eight slaves rather than the planned four. We must have been quite convincing, for no-one took notice of me in my guise as a well-heeled landowner in the suit Jeremiah had bought for me, or of my suitably obsequious "slaves". So well did they play their role, in fact, that their only sign of discomfiture, one reasonable in any circumstances, was at the sight of some of their colleagues who had been ensnared by the Fugitive Slave Law.

They were being put (in chains) on the return trip of the ferry for the long journey back to the South and to slavery, that most beneficent of institutions, mah friends.

250 miles ahead of us lay Lake Erie and the port city of Cleveland. There we would embark on the final segment of our odyssey to a freedom which, though flawed, was still a far greater freedom than what any of my charges had yet known.

CHAPTER TWENTY-FOUR

In a handful of months, I had seen more of America than most Americans do in a lifetime. I had met gracious Southern families who treated their slaves with respect, consideration, even affection; by contrast, I had been at a slave-auction and almost within the doors of a whipping-house. There had been the Sniders, the Fitzgeralds, Levi Coffin, and all the other good and decent people who had helped us on our way at such appalling risk; and then there had been the saloon-keeper Murphy, the inebriate Dr. Appleby, and the quartet of brigands in Kentucky. In the shadows, for the moment at least, were Gerrit Smith and the other members of the Secret Six, and their would-be-beneficiary John Brown.

What was America, then, but a huge and unwieldy family tragically at odds with itself, an enormous ship blundering into a tempest with broken rudder and tattered sails? Comparison between America and Canada had become a fact of my existence and I was uncomfortably reminded of our own schism between English and French, but the resolution of these divisions would be reflected by the respective nature of progress in Canada and America. Canada's maturing into a proper country could be likened to the flow of a pastoral, tree-lined creek, just taking its placid and dull but safe time to get to where it wanted to go. America, in contrast, was more like a river at spring break-up, raging and snarling, ice flows ramming and grinding into each other, waters in complete chaos. Canada was unhurried evolution, America was revolution; in Canada, things would happen in the fullness of time and, in America, they would happen yesterday at the latest.

From seeing this perplexing country in intimate detail, I would at long last realize my dream of how railroads could help our cause. Levi Coffin did a large volume of business with the Cleveland, Columbus, and Cincinnati Railroad, such a volume, in fact, that a few more boxes would not attract attention, at least as long as their cargo did not reveal itself. Twenty-two blacks were to be shipped to Cleveland in boxes by freight train, a hideous way to travel, but at an enormous saving of time. And I, posing as an agent of Levi's, was to follow by passenger train, accompanied by my family of "servants" - Precious, Agnes, Noah, and the baby. A ship would be waiting to take us across Lake Erie, to freedom, to Canada, to home. Ah, home!

While the arrangements went forward, I was lodged once again at the Coffin household; the bounty-hunters were freed and the escapees sheltered in the outlying community of Glendale. Cincinnati was as full of bounty-hunters as bad meat is of maggots, and they roamed through squalid and opulent districts alike. All praise to Glendale, there was a strong anti-slavery bias in the community, and some of the residents had gone to great personal expense and inconvenience to adapt their homes, most of them quite large and some downright enormous, to Underground Railroad traffic.

My own group was shared, in a sense, by two homes owned respectively by Thomas Moore and Robert Adderley. The houses in question were connected by a tunnel. Unknown to me at the time, a contingent of bounty-hunters, dressed in business suits and purporting to be government agents, had come to the Moore home to investigate. They had even been equipped with a forged search warrant. With bland innocence, they had been admitted to the Moore residence, but had found nothing, for the slaves had fled through the tunnel over to the Adderleys' house by way of a hatch hidden in the bottom of the coal bin. And of course, when the alleged agents called on Mr. Adderley, the process was reversed.

My short separation from my flock, to be honest, was something of a relief. We had moved through a whole spectrum of feeling in our relationship, from almost blind trust to the episode of defeatism on the part of a few, from a couple of instances of sullen defiance to mutual respect and not a little affection. I would miss these people when the time came for parting.

But I had also been, functionally speaking, a parent to them, although with much help, but the time comes for everyone to have solitude. The time was now mine. With Mr. Coffin in charge of the decisions for the time being, I was able to rest my poor brain, although troubling thoughts were now intruding. What would happen with Ruth once we were in Canada? Could our relationship remain valid under "ordinary" circumstances, or were we just two souls thrown together by chance, seeking haven in the storm? Would Ruth be accepted by my family and friends? What would be the social status of our children? Should black and white even be mixing?

My nights, then, were freighted with much uncertainty and unhappiness. I craved some counsel from Alex, although how reliable he would have been on matters of love, marriage, and family at that time I can only guess. Perhaps my parents could have helped, but this was one situation that you actually had to experience to understand it. And I was the first white man I had ever known to be amorously and sexually involved with a black woman. In fact, I am *still* the only one I know, so the world has been pretty barren of advice.

Mrs. Coffin, although I discussed nothing personal with her, was in her own way a wonderful help. She quite spoiled me. Not only was she a wizard in the kitchen, preferring to do most of the cooking, although the place had a couple of servants; she was a wonderful teller of tales about the Underground Railroad in their enormous variety of the tragic, the absurd, the terrifying, and the wildly comic. Mrs. Coffin was the first person I had been with for months with whom I could just sit down and share a good laugh.

But Mrs. Coffin, kind as she was, was rather like the *scherzo* in one of our more modern symphonies, the brief emotional rest from weightier matters. I loved Ruth more strongly than ever, but in a different way from at the beginning. Desperate, terrified passion had evolved into a warm and indispensable friendship, as if we had both shrunk back from the complexities that passion brings. Opportunities for love-making had been few, and yet there was little frustration, for just her presence was all that I needed. I earnestly hoped she felt the same as I, for although I had seriously considered marriage, I had gradually and sadly come to the conclusion that it was totally out of the question. Intellectually I would wither away with a woman whom I had had to teach to tell the time. And, as suggested earlier, children of such a union might be welcome nowhere, and for that I could not be responsible. I was resigned now to breaking off with Ruth once in Canada and prayed for the strength and sensitivity to do it without hurting her. I had not openly discussed marriage with Ruth, but I wondered if in the wake of what had gone on between us that the expectation might be there. Only time would tell.

The chosen train to Cleveland was to leave the Cincinnati freight depot at four in the morning. The "hardware and dry goods", therefore, were to be loaded into two wagons for transit to the train, and the operation was every bit as nerve-wracking as the night we had left the plantation of Major Ramsay. In a sense, it was even worse, for if someone in the "cargo" were to so much as cough or sneeze in the presence of the wrong ears, it would be all over, escape being totally impossible from a nailed-up crate. Mr. Coffin, from his own pocket, arranged for the rental of two wagons and teams from a German friend of his who operated a livery. The German fellow, whose name was never mentioned, evidently was accustomed to doing business with Mr. Coffin at strange hours. Whether he was actually privy to the Underground Railroad I do not know, but, whatever the situation, he was understanding, cooperative, and asked no questions.

We debated as to the optimum time to crate the escapees. From Glendale to the rail yard was about twelve miles, for which three hours should be allowed. Too close to train time was risky on general principles and too early posed its own hazard in that it would not be long before the crates began to smell as no dry goods or hardware ever did. On that basis, we opted to get the blacks into their little wooden prisons shortly after midnight, which was done without mishap or molestation. The slaves came in pairs to the coach house adjacent to the residence of Levi's friend, Thomas Moore, the place with the tunnel, while two other men prowled the grounds on the look-out for bounty-hunters.

As we got to work, Levi remarked, "Those false agents operate around the clock and can appear at any time. How they *get* the time I do not understand, although some of them collect so much bribe money and rewards from the Fugitive Slave Law that it becomes a full-time job for them. Parasites!" he spat in fury. "I beg thy pardon, Brother James, I think I sprayed thee."

We went about our work in both darkness and silence, no mean feat with crates that were to be nailed shut. For quietude, we wrapped our hammers in cloth, and working thus in the dark is certainly not my idea of fun, especially in light of eleven boxes times about forty nails each. As a souvenir of that night, I still have a distorted joint on my left thumb.

It was decided at the last moment that one wagon would attract less attention than two and be more wieldy anyway, so we loaded accordingly, opened the coach-house doors, and Levi led the horses down the driveway. The night was cold and still, a nearly-full moon shedding its chill benediction upon our progress. In the crystalline silence, every clank, jingle, and rattle known to the Christian world clanked, jingled, and rattled. It felt rather like one of those bad dreams in which you find yourself running down the street without benefit of clothing and absolutely everyone is aware of your presence. But somehow we were able to go unimpeded, surmising that the bounty-hunters had perhaps called it a night.

Onward we clanked through the frosty countryside, past the village of Wyoming, the scattered lights of an outriding suburb of Cincinnati twinkling in the near distance. It must have been about this time that I became conscious of a slight lateral swaying motion in the back end of the wagon. Since nobody remarked on it, I said nothing for a few minutes. But then I could no longer contain myself, for it felt like no wagon I had ever been in. "Mr. Coffin, does this thing feel right to you?"

"No, it does not. I fear we have made a mistake. The load is too heavy and I truly wish we had brought the other wagon. Let us just pray that we can get to the train. After that, the wagon can fall apart for all I care. Just get us to the train..."

Into the gas-lit streets of Cincinnati our spastic conveyance rumbled, clanked, and swayed. In the uncertain yellow glow, we could see the right rear wheel skewing alarmingly, and Levi stopped the team momentarily, that one of his men could get a look at what was happening.

"Bearing's on its last legs, Mr. Coffin," he reported. "Ain't nuthin' we can do until we get back to the stable."

"Pray," said Mr. Coffin tersely. We prayed. We prayed down the streets and around the corners. We prayed our way past stately tree-shrouded homes. We prayed our way into the commercial district, past stores and offices, no-one to be seen except one other wagon and a couple of policemen making their rounds. Evidently they recognized Mr. Coffin and tipped their helmets in greeting.

We prayed our way past the small, grimy houses of the poor and the

THE RAIL JOURNEY FROM CINCINNATI TO CLEVELAND.

near-poor, the acrid smell of wood-smoke now seasoning the night air. Almost, almost, and now we were trundling across a set of railway lines, a right turn into the loading area by the freight depot. We had made it with but twenty minutes to spare. Mr. Coffin leapt from the driving box and with surprising fleetness for so large a man, he raced for the freight office with me in pursuit.

"Well, well, Mr. Coffin," said the clerk, "wondered if you was goin' to make it. You're sharing an L.C.L. with Mr. Hickman. He's got a half load of textiles goin' up to Columbus." L.C.L., I should explain, is railway talk and means "less-than-carload lots".

Continued the clerk, "Train's all made up and your car is number 363. I think it's about the fourteenth one back from the engine. Just bring your wagon along here."

The poor wagon could take no more. As the horses heaved it over the crossing of the nearest track, the afflicted wheel buckled and the whole issue subsided into a diagonal tilt. Muffled sounds of consternation issued from the hardware and dry goods, but the freight clerk, walking alongside, appeared not to hear. Maybe he chose not to.

"Annoyin', ain't it?" he sympathized instead. "Look, couple of our boys are deadheadin' up to Cleveland in your car. I'll get them to help load. Just a minute."

"People riding with this lot we don't need," I said tightly. "They could collect a big enough reward to last them the rest of their natural lives. I think we'd better not do it."

"What else do we do, James? It would look pretty strange if we cancelled the shipment at the last possible minute right on railroad property. Besides, the wagon is too far gone to get them out of here anyway, so we have no choice. This could actually be good. These two fellows will want to ride with the door open for air and it'll be beneficial for our, er, cargo."

The two deadheads, which is to say railway personnel catching a free ride, came to help. Although good-natured, they were plainly members of the Lower Order, given to breaking wind with a sound like ripping canvas and then guffawing raucously. As well, they were none too gentle with the crates, stowing two of them upside down despite the legend "This Side Up" carefully stencilled on the lids. Levi thought it was because they couldn't see; I think it was because they couldn't read. They didn't seem the type. In any event, four of our people had an uncomfortably inverted ride to Cleveland.

An inspector's lantern came bobbing through the gloom as a final check was made that all couplings were secure and all wheels were on the track. A husky six-coupled freight locomotive stood at the head of the train blowing off excess steam, a sight I ordinarily would have savoured but for the possibility of a brigade of bounty-hunters coming charging out of the night. Bloody train, go!

Ultimately it did after much consultation among the train crew and yard personnel, chuffing and clanking its way out of the freight yard, the red eye of a lantern on the rear end slowly being swallowed up in the blackness of the night. The crippled wagon was temporarily deposited in a shed where the railway company kept its own freight wagons, and Levi, his two helpers, and I walked the team of horses back to the German livery.

I had my own train journey to prepare for now. My head ached so badly from the fatigue of being up all night, not to mention the attendant prolonged anxiety, that the pain had actually found its way into my lower jaw, making me feel as if I had some terrible dental disorder. But, as usual, there was no time for self-pity. I shaved, washed up, and dressed in my new suit to commence my role as James Ramsay, Esq. travelling to Canada on a business trip with his negro servants. Like me, my "servants" were dressed in their Sunday best, supplied by one of Mr. Coffin's numerous colleagues; the appearance of Precious, as well as his personal comfort, was somewhat lacking, as fabric and buttons were strained to the limit to contain his vast bulk.

"Massa James, Ah can't wear dis," he said plaintively. "Ah um orful oncomfortable..."

"Precious, you are only a couple of days from freedom now. For that, you can be oncomfortable for a bit."

None of my "servants" had ever been on a train and in their puzzlement at the experience were curiously like cattle in a rainstorm. They had endured so much and yet were completely intimidated by the urban hustle of the station and the industrial noises and smells of the trains. Virtually all of the other passengers were white, as were the station staff, except for the porters. Agnes was extremely cordial to one, as though greeting a cousin she hadn't seen for years, and I had to remind her to act as if this were all normal for her. Thinking for others had become exhausting beyond endurance, and yet I had to endure, please, God, just until journey's end.

Across the flat farmlands of Ohio the train crawled, smoke fumes seeping in around the closed windows, which were soon opened as a strong sun blazed from a cool, clear sky. In order to act appropriately aloof from my "servants", I sat in a seat slightly removed from them. This little Noah could not comprehend after all those weeks of being my Indian guide and so persistent and obnoxious did he become in wanting to sit with me that Agnes smacked him in desperation.

Cries filled the coach and heads turned, mouths pursed in annoyance, and when it was realized that the cries emitted from a nigra, well, you could have knocked folks over with a feather. I stepped over to where they were sitting and said to Noah, very quietly I said, "Noah, you're to stop that right now, and if you do, you can go with me at the next station to go and look at the engine."

Noah snuffed and gulped his way into silence as Agnes asked anxiously, "Massa, yu think othah massas do dat?"

"Dis one do," I said sloppily, too tired to care what I sounded like.

Noah and I took advantage of a mid-morning water stop at Xenia to visit with our iron horse, and so enchanted was he at the spectacle that the performance was repeated successively at Columbus, Delaware, Galion, Shelby, and Grafton; and the final viewing took place at Cleveland, ten hours after leaving Cincinnati and covering a distance that would have taken between fifteen and twenty days on foot.

Levi Coffin had arranged for us to be met by a youngish abolitionist named Elijah Hacker, not surprisingly yet another Quaker. I was so impressed with the Quakers that I was actually toying with the idea of becoming one myself, although I have yet to take the final step. I had steeled myself for the possibility of being greeted by the police, a likely circumstance had the escapees been discovered, but the Lord, or Somebody, was with us, and it was Elijah who stood upon the platform at Cleveland Union Station as our train drifted to a stately stop.

Elijah had brought a carriage and I rode on the driver's box with him as we jogged towards the harbour in the fading light of an October evening. "Thee can expect some fame out of this," said Elijah admiringly. "This is the greatest number of bodies we have had through here at one time yet. Thee will be happy to know they have been aboard the ship for the last hour and everything is ready. We have the *Mayflower* for this trip, good fast schooner. Captain Woolsey sails her, done eight or nine trips for us already, and won't take any money for it either."

"How was the, ahem, cargo when it came off the train?"

Elijah shook his head. "The fortitude of those people is astonishing. Most had wet themselves, some were, um, soiled, and a couple had vomited and all had to lie quietly in their own, er, leavings. No food, no water, not to mention the horror of being shut away in darkness all those hours, unable to move. I think I would have surely gone mad.

"The smell when we opened the packing cases was like to asphyxiate thee, yet there was no peep of complaint."

"The blacks are the ones deserving the fame, not I," I said quietly. "At the beginning, I doubted the determination of some of them, but no more. What a tough and determined group of people they are, may God bless them!"

"For a certainty. Captain Woolsey was all prepared with tubs of water and extra clothes, so they should be more or less normal when thee sees them aboard ship. But as if it all weren't enough, two crates had been stowed upside down and there were a couple of men sitting on one of the others, eating peanuts and passing gas and then wondering why the smell was so bad."

"A blessing in disguise, perhaps."

Elijah said a hasty goodbye on the quayside and I boarded the *Mayflower*. I eyed the hatch-covers all secured for sea, secured to protect our cargo of dry goods and hardware, and nearly laughed aloud at the bizarre undertaking that was now all but accomplished.

I shook the huge paw of Captain Woolsey, a great shaggy eminence from the Lake Erie fishing village of Port Dover, Canada West. He eyed Precious and remarked, "I think this is the first time I've ever met a man bigger that I."

"He's Precious."

"Eh? Is that a fact?"

"It's a fact."

"Funny bloody name, isn't it?"

"That too is a fact. It's drawn some pretty strange looks along the way."

"Is that a fact?"

"It is. Another one."

"Well, Mr. Ramsay, I said I'd get your lot across, so we'd better get ready. There's some stew waiting for you in the galley. Rest all got fed when they came aboard. I've got a tug coming shortly, wind's all wrong for getting out of here under sail."

How good it was to hear the word "out" said properly, instead of the twanging American "aout", which in print looks like the French for August.

A hard breeze was blowing, humming and rattling in the rigging, and in the fading twilight, the waves could be seen surging sullenly at the mouth of the Cuyahoga River. Over the dull violet horizon lay Canada, home for me and a new beginning for twenty-six souls who had known only bondage for all their lives, until the few desperate weeks of making good their escape. Joshua should have been here. And there should have been a shuffle-shuffle of doggy feet on the deck and a black head butting the backs of my knees. The thought made my eyes sting.

The tug came at dusk, took the *Mayflower* in tow, warped her about, and guided her out through the river's mouth and into wind-tossed Lake Erie. I had never been aboard a sailing vessel before, not even to cross the Atlantic to university (I had opted instead for one of Mr. Cunard's splendid mail steamers from Halifax), and I was quite non-plussed, first at the racket the sails made when the crew raised them and then at the way the ship tilted as they filled with wind. There was quite an outcry from down below, but I was forestalled from going below to dispense reassurance just yet, as too much unusual deck activity could still attract unwanted attention. I would have to wait until we were further off-shore, so I tried to ignore muffled fragments of prayer and references to Jesus.

The tug dropped her tow-line and lurched drunkenly as she put about to return to the shelter of Cleveland harbour. Unfettered now, her sails pregnant with wind, the *Mayflower* charged off into the night, bound for Canada, her green starboard light gleaming coldly on the racing carpet of foam surging from the bow. I could begin to like this, I thought in the dementia of having weathered a forty-eight-hour day.

I was let into the hold through an inspection hatch. "Hello, group!" I called into the blackness below.

"Massa James!"

Someone retched. "Ah'm sick, James, real, mizzuble sick!"

"Likely seasick. I was a bad fellow and didn't tell you that might happen. Come along up and get some fresh air, you'll feel better."

Up they came: Jerge, Gladys, and Joe; Philip, Peter, my beautiful Ruth, and all the rest, all together for the last time. Our journey had been an unspeakable trial, barely within the limits of human expression, and yet I felt a curious melancholy that it was nearly over.

Some were excited, some terrified at being on this great inland sea in the middle of the night. "Look your last on America, my friends." Cleveland's lights twinkled astern, already growing diffused.

"Where be Canada? Ah can't see nuthin'."

"You probably won't until morning, but just keep watching the North Star. It's done its work. We're almost there."

Ruth's hand slipped into mine. Responding to the unspoken message, we descended into the hold, hid behind a couple of the empty crates, and held each other. I was emotionally so exhausted, so drained, so tired of being strong, being the leader, making all the decisions, that I became quite unhinged. I know that in this age of Queen Victoria and the growing Empire and all that sort of thing that my condition might have been thought of as unmanly. I would wager that it happens more than people would like to own up to. After all, in the arts, people bare their souls all the time. Shelley fell upon the thorns of life and bled, Hector Berlioz paraded his tormented feelings for the Great Beloved in his *Symphonie Fantastique.* So if art imitates life, there must be something for it to imitate.

In any event, I felt fully entitled to let it all go, and Ruth held me, stroking my hair and murmuring, "Massa James, Massa James" over and over. Could I really do without this woman? I had to and yet couldn't. It was so damnable and only served to deepen my state of torment.

"Massa James," she repeated.

"Not a massa," I kept mumbling ineffectually. I was still in my Sunday best, awkward garb indeed for love-making, but the need was overwhelming, and when I began fumbling for my buttons, Ruth put her fingers to my lips, saying, "James, yu don't have to."

"Ruth," I croaked, "I could have done nothing of this without you. You gave me the strength to carry on and I wanted you to know. And I need you, but what are we going to do after tonight?"

"Tonight is tonight an' tomorrow is tomorrow. Right now we loves each othah." We did.

And as Ruth and I loved each other, passionately and comprehensively, our compatriots up on deck, after weeks of muzzled, fearful silence, began to sing above the roar of wind and sea:

"Swing low, sweet chariot,
Comin' for to carry me home..."

There was some interruption to the music as the lights of another vessel bore down on our own sweet chariot from the west, but she carried on-wards down the lake, leaving the *Mayflower* to pound and buck her lonely way across Lake Erie.

After the divine encounter with Ruth, and I daresay no lover was ever as elegantly dressed as I, I dozed off and when I awoke, a dusty pencil of sunshine was streaming down through the open inspection hatch. We went up the ladder out of the hold and there, smack in front of us, was Canada, specifically the little village of Port Burwell. The wind had died away to nothing and the entire crew were in a small boat, trying to tow our ship.

The negroes watched mutely as we crept along upon a glassy swell, the look of people who could not believe this was actually happening. They probably felt as I did in those last moments before my farewell to innocence with Ruth. I was now openly holding her, feeling like Romeo about to part from Juliet, trying to convince myself that there were limits to black-white compatibility-- and yet we had this special, unparalleled bond that nobody could take away. But there was no escape from the fact that our bond had been imposed by external forces, and once in what for me were ordinary civilized circumstances, which is to say the *milieu* of white society, I would end up as Ruth's teacher in the most commonplace and ordinary matters. I was not certain that I could deal with that on a daily basis, and yet how could I abandon her when she had taught me the eternal mystery of Woman? It was all too much and I decided to spend some time thinking after it was all over and then discuss it later with her. This was no time for any sort of rational or binding decision.

Port Burwell drew slowly nearer. Neither the palaces of Venice nor the towers of Constantinople could look as beautiful to the homecoming wan-derer as did this little Canadian village on a late October morning, the trees almost barren but for stubborn clusters of faded colour here and there. The huddle of houses was nestled by the mouth of a river under a pale blue sky, mirrored languidly by quiet, silvery water.

Joe, Precious, and some of the other men did relief duty at the oars, to the surprise of some of the crew, who thought blacks could do nothing and suffered their presence only out of pity. But row the blacks did, and quite well at that, although they had never done it before.

After an hour or so of heaving and tugging as the sun climbed higher, spreading its fragile autumnal warmth, the *Mayflower* was berthed alongside Port Burwell's town wharf. A fair number of townspeople were on hand to greet us and very cordially applauded us as we walked down the gangplank. Immediately they turned away out of respect for our privacy, as my flock fell to their knees, caressing the soil of Canada, praying and singing.

"This is what makes it worth it," said Captain Woolsey, shaking my hand with much clearing of his throat. "And that's a fact." He seemed notably disinclined to look me in the eye. "Good luck, Mr. Ramsay. I hope we can do some business together again."

"Thanks for all, Captain. Happy sailing." I, last off the ship, swung over the rail to the wharf to find my "buckoes" lined up for the last time in numerical order.

"Yu is one...yu is odd, James," grinned Joe tremulously, eyes glittering.

"Joe, my dear friend...good luck...we'll stay in touch...Philip, all the best...Peter...Rebecca...no more whuppin's, right?...come, now, Precious, you're not going to go and cry on me, are you?"

"No," gulped Precious.

Now it was my turn to gulp.

"There's something I need to say to all of you, now that I can speak up without being heard by someone we'd rather not hear us. That's one of the nice things about Canada." Chuckles of appreciation. "There were some times I wasn't too nice to you and I'd get impatient and say or do some things that I didn't feel too good about, like the times I got all upset when you couldn't remember left from right or tell the time. I had grown up learning all those things, but you had been deliberately kept in the dark."

"In de dark?"

"Just an expression. Means someone makes sure you don't know something. And those first few days, good God, I wondered if some of you even wanted to go anywhere.

"I may as well tell you I was scared too, more scared than I have ever been or want to be again. Yes, you were scared, but, being slaves, you had no idea at all of what you really could do. You had been brought up not believing in yourselves, but now that you have done what only a few people could do, you can look anyone straight in the eye and feel proud of yourselves and your people. You got to be pretty good at reading a map. Wait until you look at a big one of North America and see how far we came. Think of the stories you can tell now..."

"James, 'scuse me, yu is about to fall off'n de dock."

"So I am. That would not be a story I'd want you to tell. So here we are at last. Welcome to the greatest country in the world. A big speech is the last thing you need right now, but I just had to let you know how I felt. God, how I'm going to miss you!"

My leave-taking continued. "Agnes, look after the wee one for me, would you? Jerge, Gladys, thanks so much, you were just wonderful...Noah, my man..."

And now what I truly dreaded was at hand. Ruth was at the end of the line. "Ruth," I said with mock severity, feeling as if I would burst, "I thought you were number seven."

"Ah um free now, James, thanks to yu an' de Lawd. Ah kin be any numbah Ah wants."

"You'll always be number one with me. God bless you, my love."

CHAPTER TWENTY-FIVE

February 25, 1858

Dear James,
I wish there were some way of your receiving this before your
return from the U.S., whenever that may be. What you must
think of me hardly bears imagining, both for my rudeness and
for my indiscretion, which was averted only by your gentlemanly good conduct. Please come and see me when you get
back. Hopefully you will be bringing my husband with you.
H.H.R.

Bringing Alex back, of course, I was in no position to do; he was still at
large when I arrived home in Belleville, but to my boundless relief, contact
had been re-established a month previously and Hester had taken care to
inform my parents.

As to Hester herself, I felt a visit with her to be of the utmost priority,
partly to clear the air over last February's episode and partly because I
needed a woman to talk to about Ruth. That situation I was not, rightly or
wrongly, ready to share with my mother.

As soon as I was reasonably well-organized at home, I walked the short
distance to the Ross residence, noting the subtle changes along the way,
and, I must say, quite in awe of what I had done and seen since the last time
I had traversed the route. The feeling was so enormous that I can only
describe it as cosmic. The house was locked and of Hester there was no
sign. With a mixture of disappointment and relief, I turned about for home,
but then along she came with a shopping basket on her way home from
market. I escorted her into the house and helped her to put away her groceries in an atmosphere absurdly like playing house, an atmosphere sustained by all manner of unnecessarily formal conversation revolving around
Alex's recent communication. At least we knew at this stage that he was all
right and that he was somewhere in Georgia.

"Thank you for your help, James," said Hester primly. "Would you like
some tea?"

"Hester, I would almost kill for a cup of tea. Where I have just come
from, they are absolute barbarians when it comes to tea. Some are absolute
barbarians, period. They don't even scald the pot."

"That is definitely barbarian."

As Hester filled the kettle, I took the plunge into what was yet unsaid.
"Hester, responding to your note was the first thing I wanted to do. My
father had saved it for me and it was actually going yellow with age. We
both needed a friend and..."

"I have to say this quickly, James," interrupted Hester. "I do not have the instincts of an adulteress. I have just been alone so much that my judgement was impaired..."

"There's no need for explanation. I understood then and I understand so much more now." Recollections of Ruth were burning holes in my heart. "Why don't we consider it a closed matter?"

"I wish it were that simple. My husband wasn't here and you were. Here we are eight months later and my husband *still* isn't here. But you are. I have made my commitment to Alex and I will stand by it, but in all truth, you are unusually attractive. That fact and Alex's perpetual absence conspire to make me pretty susceptible. This is completely *entre nous*, but I have had some pretty impure fantasies about you; however, it is my intention to keep them just that way, as fantasies."

"So why did you tell me about them? Now that I know, I cannot help being intrigued. But you're right. They must remain as fantasies, otherwise I could never look Alex in the eye again, couldn't work with him or anything."

"Damn the man anyway." Hester's hand flew to her mouth, her eyes widening in horror.

I had to laugh. "Hester, it's all right. I understand. After what I have witnessed, good Victorian manners and conventions don't seem particularly relevant. Pray continue...just listen to me, you can tell I have been around Quakers."

"Damn the man," repeated Hester with just a hint of relish. "He's never here, yet always here...would you have any idea when he is coming back?"

"I know even less than you. My last word with him was in the form of an instruction to escort a group of slaves up from Mississippi."

Hester's wonderful toffee-coloured eyes widened. "You mean you..."

"Yes, ma'am, twenty-seven slaves...well, one got killed by lightning...on a hike of nearly a thousand miles...I guess it will always sound like fantasy. The experience has left me so wasted that I could never contemplate doing it again. The kettle is boiling."

Over tea I recounted my adventures, which took no little time, especially when it came to the matter of Ruth, although certain crucial details were omitted in the initial telling. "I miss her so badly, Hester. I have spent every waking hour wondering if we could have a future, even though I really knew from the start that a permanent union would be impossible, but I just couldn't face up to it. Our backgrounds are as different as black from white, ah, in a manner of speaking. I had to teach her how to tell time and right from left and I would have ended up more like a father than a husband. And if she lived here in Belleville, she would probably be sort of a curiosity. I wouldn't want that for her."

"If not worse," said Hester. "There's no knowing what other townsfolk might do or say. There is a lot of talk about how you and Alex are being Christians and taking up the white man's duty..."

"...which is to undo the damage the white man did in the first place."

"But somehow I don't think it extends to marriage to a black woman," said Hester. "I'm certain Belleville wouldn't be ready for it, enlightened though its citizens may be. Besides, I have to say I would find the idea a bit peculiar myself. If the Almighty had intended us to mix and marry, why did He make us different colours?"

"So we free them but keep them away from us." I could feel tension clawing at my guts.

"It doesn't have to be that extreme, although I have heard about a lot of folks who would subscribe to exactly that idea," observed Hester. "But there is little question, I think, that any offspring would be pariahs to the races of both parents. It would be a social impossibility."

"That is my own sad and reluctant conclusion," I agreed. "There are certain realities I can't change and that is one of them. But any intellectual-izing of the situation is so badly clouded by Ruth being my first real love."

Hot colour surged to my face and Hester's left eyebrow rose slightly. "Were you..."

"Intimate? Oh, yes, indeed. You have no idea..."

Hands flew to mouth once again. "Oh, forgive me, that was so nosy of me, oh, how I wish what I just said was written in disappearing ink..."

"Why, Hester, I do believe you are getting flustered. Actually, not only do I not mind telling you, but I actually want to. I *need* to talk to someone about it and I think the idea is just too revolutionary for my parents."

"It may be a bit revolutionary for me too, but do continue," said Hester, looking at me with something suspiciously like veneration.

I told about Ruth being loaned to me by the Major, our gradually weakening discretion in the course of the Exodus, of our last desperate act of passion in the hold of the *Mayflower*. As I spun my tale, Hester became all breathless and blushy, nervously caressing the base of her neck with trembling fingers. Oh, Alex, when you get home...

While I had been at least able to find sexual company, even under circumstances that verged on the impossible, Hester had had to be content with sporadic letters from Alex, although I must say that for a while he had improved his frequency of verbal intimacy, especially in the wake of my coaching in New Orleans. There had been a long and disturbing silence following our departure from Columbus, Mississippi, and then the new communication, in which Alex initially appeared to have regressed to simply reporting the most arcane information.

He had written from Dublin, Georgia, and the letter in part read: "The intensity of religious fervour in this part of the world, especially in the country, is quite beyond belief, a fervour whose intensity is unparalleled anywhere in my experience, for we are dealing here with a most fundamen-tal kind of practice. Yesterday, not having been to church for some time and feeling the need, I sought out what was available and was treated to a most extraordinary service. The preacher, as a minister is called here, was almost hysterical in his delivery, playing liberally and freely on the locals' fear of the consequences of sin.

"There were people falling all over the place, crying 'Hallelujah!' and 'Praise Jesus' and that sort of thing, much more vocal than we are accustomed to. There was a kind of earnest exuberance to the whole thing.

"One woman fainted dead away and, thinking she were having some sort of a fit, I rushed to her assistance, to be admonished by the command 'Leave 'er there where Jesus flang 'er.' Well, I left her there where Jesus flang her (if James ever heard that expression, he'd never let go of it - have you heard anything from him?) and about a quarter of an hour later, she emerged from her trance, apparently none the worse for her experience."

I turned the page. Aha! Alex had evolved after all...

"James, you can't see that."

"Why not?"

"It's...intimate."

"I told you everything. Let's be fair. I want to be as thrilled as you were."

Hester turned the most divine shade of crimson. "James, be a gentleman."

"Very well." But I had already caught a glimpse of the closing sentence: "You are the Empress of my very existence and the thought of you sustains me through each day." I can quote it with such accuracy because it had been on the list of suggestions I had made for Alex back in New Orleans.

"Whenever he does come back, I can predict what it will be like," sighed Hester. "He'll be all repentant, there'll be the same shyness as on our wedding night...I should bite my tongue. Ladies do not talk like this and I have already said too much this afternoon."

"Few ladies are in your circumstances."

"Few ladies are foolish enough to be. I don't even know if in talking about Alex whether I am talking of love any more."

"What?" I sat up with a jerk, rattling my teacup.

"I don't know whether to even try to love him or simply worship him and take what crumbs I can. But I can tell you this. I simply cannot do without him."

Marietta, Georgia
December 14, 1858

Dear James,
Word has just reached me of your recent business success. I want you to know that many others join me in congratulating you for a job well done and we trust it portends well for the future of commerce between the U.S.A. and Canada. I am happy to report considerable success here as well. This will not reach you in time for Christmas, but perhaps I can still extend

best wishes to you and your family for a happy and prosperous 1859.
Yours,
A.M.R.

Alex's letter reached me on the last day of 1858, but did little to ease the situation that had by that time evolved. I had become quite ill and depressed since my return from the South, a circumstance made bearable only by the opportunity to be ill and depressed at home rather than in some place like Shelbyville under the suspect care of Dr. Appleby. Part of me was restless now to resume activities on behalf of the Underground Railroad; part of me was far from ready, a condition that did nothing to improve my outlook.

I had pouted and sulked my way through the Christmas service at church, though young, fundamentally in good health, and free. On the way home, I had complained to my parents, "I am supposed to be of good cheer and trolling the ancient Yuletide carol and all the rest and I just feel so, well, empty." I had still not been able to bring myself to talk about Ruth, but my parents still had a pretty accurate perception of the causes of my *malaise*.

"Pretty hard to feel the Christmas spirit, knowing what you know," commented Father as we swished along through some freshly-fallen snow.

"And for weeks you had no rest that was worth anything," added Mother. "You were borrowing rest from the future, which happens to be now. Your health was functioning only by sheer willpower, just like your father so much of the time. Then you got home, relaxed, and fell prey to every germ and every gloomy thought. I felt the same way after I had you..."

"Thank you, dear Mother."

"...though not for long. I think you're at loose ends. Maybe you should see how your people are getting on now."

A short time later, I heard that Joe, Ruth, and Philip were all working at a hotel in London (the one in Canada West, not England) with young Peter assisting as a sometime messenger. On an ill-advised impulse, I went out to London to see them in mid-January, 1859, and while they were happy to see me, I knew immediately that there was really no hope for me and Ruth and it made me sad.

They reported that things had gone well for them since arriving in Canada, but for one incident in which Peter had been taunted by a group of boys who had called him a blackamoor and stolen his jacket. The closeness between me and Ruth had gone of its own accord, as it had with the others, for the circumstances were different now and we were all moving along with our lives. It was one of those melancholy inevitabilities like the letting-go between parents and children or graduation from university, the leaving of something that meant a lot but whose time had passed.

On conclusion of my visit, there was but a quick hug and a chaste kiss from Ruth, and then I never saw her again. Many years later, I heard that she and Joe had moved back to America, to work in the American Hotel in Boston. As far as I know, Ruth never married and I wonder if I could have been the only and true love of her life.

Mother was right about the loose ends. I had to do something and being busy would help to dispel the gloom. Without Alex there was little impetus to spend the days reading newspapers and collecting data on the negro situation, so I went back to working on the Grand Trunk. My old job was not available, but I did get another one as Inspector of Permanent Way, Kingston Sub-division, meaning that I could be back with my beloved trains and working on a railroad that wasn't underground. As an added convenience, my place of work was primarily an office in Belleville station, and so I was able to live at home.

I was now approaching twenty-eight years of age, rather too old to still be making my home with my parents, but it enabled me to save a considerable amount of money. The fundamental truth was that I was not prepared for the irritations of running my own establishment and certainly welcomed their company, as being on my own was still too hazardous for my sensibilities.

During this time, I had one card from Alex (Hester was faring far better) postmarked Raleigh, North Carolina, a cryptic little number that read, "Prosperity beckons. May need help. More later.

A.M.R."

And on April 6, a telegram:

URGENT YOU ATTEND BUSINESS CONVENTION PHILADELPHIA STOP CONTACT ME SOONEST LIBERTY HOTEL END MESSAGE A.M.R.

I showed Hester the telegram. She had not seen Alex for over a year, had never had Christmas with him, and I feared an explosion. Instead she simply shrugged; I said I thought she could do better and showed her how to throw her apron over her head slave-style.

On requesting another leave of absence from the Grand Trunk after only two months in my position, I was fired and told not to come back, ever again. No letters of introduction would be issued. Obviously I had no commitment to the railway, was just taking advantage, and so on and so on. I was stunned. I had not anticipated being summarily cut off like this.

"Well," said Father, polishing his spectacles with the air of someone with momentous thoughts. "So here you are at the age of twenty-eight, a university degree, and no means of supporting yourself. Well."

"I didn't think I'd be let go," I whined.

"They want people they can count on, James."

"I can understand that, but..."

"But what?"

"But...I can't think of anything to say."

"There are, though, numerous others who *do* need you." The polishing of spectacles continued. "You know who I mean. No parents could be prouder of their son than your mother and I are of you for what you have done. Even if you never again did what you have done, I would be proud of you until the last breath left my body, not only as my son but as a fellow human being.

"Your friend Alex awakened something in you and now it is time for you to answer its call once again. You have some money saved and beyond it, I will see to it that money will to be of no concern, save that it should be spent sparingly. Go to Philadelphia."

Since my ties with the Grand Trunk were now officially sundered, it would be a bit harder to explain my travels in America, where casual strangers were far more likely to strike up a spontaneous conversation than in Canada. So to ease that possible predicament, Father gave me as a parting gift a set of calling cards that advertised me as "James Ramsay - Consulting Civil Engineer - Railways a Speciality".

I had no idea what to expect at the "business convention"; I simply went to Philadelphia and hardly was I in the door of the Liberty Hotel but there was Gerrit Smith.

"James, my dear boy! I am impressed, *impressed* beyond words with what you have done. You have quite put the rest of us in the shade. When are you doing it again?"

"Again?"

"But of course! When you have such a success, wouldn't it be worth repeating? You're a celebrity now. Don't rest on your laurels."

"I suppose I *should* do it again, but I don't know if my nerves would take it."

"Ah, you're of strong stuff, sturdy British stock and all that. Your lot did very well, you know, especially compared to a contingent that showed up today in Evansville, Indiana. We got this telegram, oh, two hours ago. Let me show you."

HARDWARE IN POOR CONDITION STOP
CAN ANYONE ASSIST END MESSAGE NO SENDER INDICATED.

"Good Lord, I wonder what happened." There but for the grace of God...

"I suppose we're about to find out. I last saw Alex upstairs. He's really excited about seeing you again, and he has some tales to tell too. Let's see where the dear boy is."

In point of fact, Alex was too distracted to be particularly effusive about seeing me. "James, I'd prefer not to do this to you, but don't bother unpacking. We don't know the nature of the situation in Evansville, but I am assuming it to be medical. They must be desperate or they wouldn't have sent the telegram. Do you still have your Grand Trunk pass?"

"It's been withdrawn. They fired me."

"They *fired* you?"

"They preferred that I should serve commerce rather than humanity."

"Fie on them," said Gerrit genially.

"I need you with me," continued Alex, "and you need money."

"Don't worry, I have piles."

"How uncomfortable," sympathized Gerrit.

"Of money, Mr. Smith," I retorted. I would have to re-acclimatize myself to Gerrit.

"James, could you do me a favour," said Alex, "and run down to the front desk and see if they have a railway schedule for Pittsburgh?" Alex was becoming Americanized; he had said "skedjool" instead of our Canadian "shedjewel" and it jarred me.

"Did you say Pittsburgh?"

"Indeed. We take the train there and then get one of your beloved steamers down the Ohio River."

I was able to unpack after all, at least to the extent of my nightshirt, since the next train for Pittsburgh was not until the next morning. But it was far from a restful night, as Alex wanted to hear my saga in every detail. I included, omitting little, the story of Ruth and its aftermath, and of it, Alex said, "I can't say I'm comfortable about it, in fact, I wish it hadn't happened. The whole business is complicated enough without sexual involvement, but I certainly can't judge you for it. I wasn't there and you were and you were scared and lonely and needed someone."

"It probably wouldn't have happened at all if the good Major hadn't...imposed is hardly the word..."

"I know what you mean. The good Major will have a lot to answer for on Judgement Day and I'd love to be there for it, but in the meantime, I have to know, how is Hester? Honestly."

"Honestly. She wonders if she should even bother loving you and just be content to worship you. Those were her words to me. Going home once in a while might help."

"I keep trying to and then something interferes. It's horrible, as if I were losing control of my life. So many times I need her, but I can't look after her under these circumstances."

"I would say you weren't looking after her at all, oh, Lord, Alex, that didn't come out the way I intended..."

Alex looked at me bleakly. "Whether or not you actually meant it, you are dead right. If I stopped this before the issue of slavery was finally and completely resolved, it would be as though part of my soul were amputated. I have to be able to stand before my wife and before God and say, 'I believed in the evil of slavery, I fought against it, and I won'."

"She called you a hunter of dreams once."

"I suppose I am, but let me tell you, I am becoming awfully impatient for results, even if it means a violent upheaval, even if it means John Brown being the wild card in the deck. I just want to get my work done and go home and be with my wife."

"Tell her that."

"I already did."

Alex's own account was saved for the train journey on the Pennsylvania Railroad, a journey on a rainy day, but by no means a depressing rainy day, for under it, the Pennsylvania countryside was blooming once again after winter's dormancy.

The ride from Philadelphia to Pittsburgh was delightful. The rails struck westward to the state capital of Harrisburg, crossed the Susquehanna River on a splendid stone viaduct, and then carried onwards parallel to the Juniata River into a range of great hills. As our coach rocked, clicked, lurched, and shuddered along, Alex recounted his own doings since our curious and irregular parting in Columbus.

"It was a certainty that Joe would jump ship after my so-called trial, and when he did, of course, I would be blamed as well as you. So the moment I was out of the calaboose, and what a hell-hole *that* was, I took a stage coach up to a little village called Iuka and put on a great production of buying a through train ticket to New York as a decoy. It cost me a fortune, too, and, Lord, all those little coupons. It looked as if you had to ride fifty different lines to get to New York, but it worked beautifully. The station agent was so excited about selling a ticket all the way to New York that he invited all the bench-warmers and hangers-on that you get at country stations to come and admire it. So my spurious departure to New York was well-advertised indeed.

"My actual and real destination was Huntsville, Alabama. I was there for about a month, doing my usual things with some success, though fretting about you at every waking moment. It was like having your cat out in a thunderstorm. I got two fair-sized groups of slaves going out of that area, since I was now visiting the sorts of plantations the we had been so carefully steered away from.

"Then there was Augusta, Georgia, and it was a difficult place indeed. There had been Abolitionists about already and so there was constant and close supervision over the slaves. I was under suspicion because of not being a Southerner and there was no way I could masquerade as one. But in spite of being spied on, I was able to get, oh, I forget the exact number, but it must have been a couple of dozen slaves on their way north. But that, plus the lot out of Huntsville, represents two months' work and can be no more than an annoyance in comparison with the major disruption that we seek.

"Southern communication is, by and large, ridiculously poor, but astonishingly fast when it comes to escaped slaves! I went up to Charleston, South Carolina, to find that the news from Augusta had reached there before I did. So Charleston was not the place to be, although it truly is a delightful town, very friendly and gracious and I'm sure pleasant to visit under different circumstances. I got out of town and I, well, James, I was a bit panicked now, and I found myself headed blindly north with no clear idea of where to go or what to do next. The experience in Columbus had really put me face-to-face with the possible consequences."

"Your performance in Columbus was the most mind-boggling one I have ever seen," I assured him. "It had everything - calm, presence of mind, definite panache. You're a hero in Belleville. I made sure of it."

Alex smiled wearily. "Bless you, that's nice to know, very nice, actually. Anyway, once I had pulled myself back together again, I settled in at Raleigh, North Carolina to see what I could do. It wasn't much. There I was at breakfast doctoring my morning tea, and what should I hear but a conversation between four businessmen about the escape from Augusta and how some 'Englishman' was suspected and hadn't been seen since the slaves had disappeared. And there I was at the next table, tea and all.

"But Englishman indeed! I guess if you're from more than a couple of hundred miles north of the Mason-Dixon Line, they think you sound English. I can only speculate. But being thought of as English got my dander up. We are Canadians and it is Canadians doing this thing, reaching out and giving a new home to people who quite literally have nothing but their health, and in so many cases, not even that.

"And English morals are a bit clouded at the moment anyway because of the perceived need for cotton. Funny, isn't it? The English took the lead in abolishing slavery in 1833* and yet in the interests of business cheerfully overlook it in one of their major trading partners. So I don't really want any part of being an Englishman. My sense of Empire has been severely eroded. All the signs point to Canada becoming a proper country, a self-governing dominion, and I hope our little railroad may become part of its heritage. If more of our countrymen can come to their senses, Canada could be the ultimate haven for *all* oppressed people."

"A lot of our countrymen will *have* to come to their senses," I said. "There's more rubbish than ever in the newspapers, you know, the same tired old shit - pardon - about how negroes are lazy, have no morals, just sit around playing the banjo and eating watermelon."

"Anyone who is willing to walk from Mississippi or Georgia or wherever is not lazy. Anyone who can do that has more guts and determination than ordinary mortals can comprehend. Prejudice is not a subject I can deal with right now anyway.

"I'm getting sleepy, but before I nod off, I just have to tell you what I did. I put on another of my theatricals, went English with a vengeance, accent and all, don't you know, and went to the hotel office, pretending to be an English cotton agent. I made some inquiries regarding one of the

---

*Interestingly, anti-slave legislation had been enacted in Upper Canada as long before as 1793. Although slaves would remain slaves for life, no new slaves would be admitted to the colony. Additionally, the children of slaves would attain freedom at the age of 25.

biggest local cotton shippers, can't remember his name at the moment, but he was known to be fanatically pro-slavery, had written all sorts of pamphlets and treatises, dreadful stuff, all of it. I hung about long enough that my face should be remembered, and then I was off to Washington."

"You do get about, don't you?"

"It's a way of life now. I can't seem to help myself." Alex's impending doziness had evaporated. "I went to see our friend and ally, Senator Charles Sumner, fine fellow, and he had some news that truly disturbed me. Well, it's not really news, but do you remember that time in St. Catharines we were talking to Josiah Henson?"

"Clearly."

"Remember what was said about the Democratic Party?"

"They tacitly endorse slavery, if memory serves me."

"Right you are, and what Senator Sumner said was that the Democratic support of slavery is so entrenched now that it would take something unusual, impeachment or something, to get rid of the people responsible. And it's all political, all for the sake of getting Southern votes. The tail really wags the dog in this country. Not only that..."

"It's not enough, is it?"

"Oh, Lord, no. Our job has to be made as hideously difficult as possible. The new south-western territories, Kansas and places like that, are all aiming for statehood and the Democrats want to get themselves ensconced in the new state governments with a pro-slavery agenda. That is why John Brown was so active out there for a while, trying to stop what these people want to do. The Mason-Dixon Line confines slavery to the South, but there is nothing to prevent its spread to the west, oh, and hear this one. Out in Oklahoma, there are some *Indians* who own slaves!"

"Indians?"

"Indians. Unbelievable, isn't it? But the unbelievable is becoming commonplace and it scares me. These Democrats are a nasty bit of business."

"Gawd strike 'em daid an' leave 'em there where Jesus flang 'em," I said in my best and broadest Mississippi accent.

Alex's eyes became as saucers. "Where did you ever hear that?"

"Oh, I heard a wise old man say it once. Can't remember where. Look, the train's slowing. It must be the lunch stop at Altoona."

We descended from our coach at Altoona in the April drizzle and hopped our way between the puddles on the station platform to the restaurant, or to be generic, I should say "lunchroom". Of course, the lunchroom was jammed and we had to wolf our meal lest we miss the train.

The idea of our country as a place of refuge was never far from our consciousness, and it re-entered the conversation as the train steamed away from Altoona. Fuelled with Pennsylvania Railroad meat pies rinsed down with sarsaparilla, we debated whether or not we should become politically involved and perhaps push for immigration to Canada being completely open and uncluttered with the current restrictive regulations on the basis that it was the Christian thing to do.

"It is that self-same Christianity that is used to justify slavery," said Alex. "But, yes, if we were to pick the right text. There's a good line somewhere in Isaiah, goes like this:

'Hide the outcast, betray not him that wandereth.

Let my outcasts dwell with thee. Be thou a convert to them

from the face of the spoiler.' What literature that book is!"

"No question," I said, "although I'm not nearly as avid a reader of it as you are."

"You would be if it had a chapter on trains."

"Oh, spare me the sarcasm, Dr. Ross! But here we are doing what is beyond question Godly work, and what do we get at home but all this discrimination against those we are helping. It's appalling, so much sympathy until you get blacks right on your doorstep."

"Consider this, though," said Alex. "The most resistance to blacks is in urban and industrial districts. Canada at the moment has a much greater rural population, proportionally speaking, than the U.S. and so much country to be opened up. Negroes might make good settlers, and if you're homesteading out in the back of beyond, there's no threat of losing your job to a negro because he is willing to work for less. If people can be trained now to be more tolerant in the future, if they can attain the necessary *maturity* and can see beyond skin colour, then maybe absorption of the oppressed can happen spontaneously and naturally." He sighed. "At least I keep telling myself that, but even though it has sanction straight from the Bible, it still sounds so hopelessly naive."

CHAPTER TWENTY-SIX

Alex's medical powers were put to very good use indeed in Evansville. The "merchandise" was in truly sorry condition, having had to take to riverbeds and swamps to avoid almost continual harassment by bounty-hunters and their tracker-dogs, something my troops had been spared entirely. The escaped slaves had all manner of foot fungus and unhealed sores that had degenerated to putrefaction and there were even a couple of cases of suspected pneumonia.

This was my first time seeing Alex practising medicine; there is an expression growing in currency, "bedside manner", which attribute was Alex's particular strength. It was truly impressive. I am certain he made each of his patients feel as if he or she were the only one in his life in maybe a minute or two of treatment: "There, there, old fellow, you'll be as right as rain in a day or so...now, my dear, tell me just where you hurt...I see...I can fix you right up, although it'll take a while. Don't be frightened, little one, I'm just going to check for fever, and then you know what I'll do? I'll fix it!"

Through all this, I acted as a nurse, feeling a little strange at first, as this was considered women's work, thanks to the sterling work by Miss Nightingale in the recent conflict in the Crimea. In the face of what had to be done, however, such reservations quickly lost relevance.

After a fortnight of medical care, the blacks were adjudged well enough to continue onward to Dearborn, Michigan, and into the care of John Pilkington and the Four Oarsmen of the Apocalypse for the final dash to freedom. Alex and I returned to Philadelphia, having in the emergency missed the "business convention" completely. But waiting for us was a message from a vanished Gerrit Smith.

April 22, 1859

A.M.R. and J.R.,

Our agents looking for new sources of cotton. Vital you proceed to Boston soonest and enlist more dealers. The market is booming!

Your friend,
G.S.

"Boston!" I exclaimed. "This means we get to try the New Haven line..."

"You're insatiable and incorrigible, James. Machines and more machines..."

Up to a point, there is no need to dwell on this particular journey, save to mention that by this time Alex was roundly sick of trains and, in his growing fatigue and deepening guilt about leaving Hester for so long, went into remission as far as caring for my company was concerned. While I eagerly watched out the window for passing trains and locomotives shunting in freight yards, Alex read the Bible or *Harper's Weekly*, or dozed with his eyes half open, looking like a sleepy oyster. He wasn't at all companionable, so I left him there "where Jesus flang him".

But it all changed at Springfield, Massachusetts, a dinner stop, and since our coach halted directly opposite the door of the "lunchroom", we were seated at a table before many of our fellow travellers were even off the train. This time we had New York and New Haven meat pies washed down with sarsaparilla, and hardly was the first fateful bite taken when a solitary man at the next table abruptly picked up his dinner tray and brought it over to where we were sitting.

"Mind if I join you?" he said. "I'd like that family over there to have a table together."

Without awaiting our consent, the man sat himself down, took up his utensils, and said rather off-handedly, "How's the hardware business?"

It was John Brown, looking even more Scriptural than he had in Cleveland. And his mission was unchanged, indeed, his mission to abolish slavery was stronger and more stubborn than ever. And Alex and I, at the end of patience for significant results to our efforts, were only too ready to listen.

"I am staying in Springfield tonight," said Brown around a mouthful of ham. "I'd like it if the two of you could join me for a talk. I think we have a lot to talk about."

Since the Springfield-Boston segment of our tickets had not yet been collected, an impromptu night in Springfield was easy of arrangement, and so, pending dessert, I removed Alex's and my belongings from the train and we put up for the night at the Hotel Shamrock. The three of us shared a room in the interests of economy.

All of us had something to report. "Let James go first," said Alex generously. "What he has done will inspire and encourage the rest of us."

"Oh, come, now, Alex..."

"Speak!"

So James spoke as we lay on our beds like three Egyptian mummies in the flickering glow of a single gas light. My story, of course, took some time, even with the part about Ruth edited out.

"Young man," said John Brown when I had finished, "you are no less than a white Moses. Because of you, over two dozen human beings have been given another chance. God was assuredly with you, guiding and protecting you, for He too believes in what we are doing. And if He is with us, casting out His enemies, and there are so many, all things are possible. Dr. Ross, tell us *your* tale now."

I snoozed a bit through the start of Alex's tale, but let me assure that my conduct was from fatigue rather than boredom. I have talked at length about my own activities through many pages, but what Alex had done was even more extraordinary. He had sent more people to freedom than I had, although not in one outsized instalment, but at the same time had kept himself at constant hazard without any rest time at home. While Alex talked, I slipped in and out of consciousness several times, vaguely aware of a soft rain pattering against the window, of the muffled clop and jingle of a horse and wagon in the dark street below.

At my final surfacing, Alex was sitting on the edge of his bed and John Brown was pacing the floor. Alex had just described his being jailed in Columbus and Brown was positively choleric. He grabbed Alex by the wrists in a grand gesture, exclaiming, "God alone brought you out of that hell!" Perhaps some ingenuity and even some luck in the fortuitous reappearance of Joe had had some bearing on the outcome as well, but neither of us were disposed to debate the point.

Continued Capt. Brown, "Those wrists have been bound and you have been cast into prison for doing your sacred duty. I vow that henceforth I will not rest in my labour until I have discharged my whole duty towards God and my brothers in bondage!"

He released the wrists of Alex, who was looking quite discomfited at his vehemence, and sprawled into an armchair in the corner, the crags of his face sharply etched by the gas light. He was silent for a moment, and then said so slowly and so deliberately that it seemed as though the words were being wrung from him, "The Lord has permitted you to do a work that falls to the lot of but a few."

He took a small Bible from his pocket. "The Good Book says" - and he quoted without even opening it -"'Whatsoever ye would do that men should do unto you, do ye even so to them'. That one little sentence, gentlemen, is to me a summation of everything that is human. I have devoted the last twenty years of my life to prepare for the work in humanity's service which I believe God has given me to do.

"What I am doing at this moment is this. I have under training twenty-two men who have been with me in Kansas, twenty-two of my own people who know me well and whom I know well. Trusty lads, all of them. They will be the backbone of a force to start an insurrection of slaves in Virginia, the prospect of which, I hope, does not make you uncomfortable. Let me just remind you that there is much Biblical precedent. These boys could be modern-day Maccabees, if you like, besides which I myself, remember, am a soldier, I have a certain talent for soldiering which the good Lord gave me, and this, I think, is the noblest direction for my talent.

"I am, in a short while, going to be calling on your noble country for additional manpower and money. I have arms and ammunition stored away for two hundred and I have commissioned the manufacture of pikes to arm an additional two hundred, all negroes. It costs less that way, you see, and requires much less training. Should be enough to raise some hell among the ungodly." He gave a dry chuckle.

"Have you any particular time in mind, Captain, for this, er, uprising?" asked Alex in a way that betrayed our growing interest.

"Next autumn. Not much time, so much to be done."

I was so tired that I ended up sleeping in my clothes, moving Alex to remark the next morning that I looked like someone's old laundry. John Brown took care of whatever business he had in Springfield before breakfast and we caught the 8:45 mail train for a fairly quick run to Boston through the pleasantly rolling hills of Massachusetts, the greenery of spring now firmly established.

"Nice spring this year," remarked John Brown pensively. "May the good Lord grant that I could *enjoy* spring one of these years. Too much to worry about in the meantime."

"What is your most immediate worry?"

Brown sighed. "Money, always money. I need to find a thousand dollars."

"A thousand dollars! That's no casual sum."

"I need it to pay for the pikes. I have everything else, except that I still will need money to transport my force from their training ground in Iowa. That is why I am bound for Boston."

Alex pondered for a moment as the train galloped along, the telegraph wires rhythmically rising and falling by the track-side. "Captain Brown," he said tentatively, "I have to be truthful with you. I too am out of patience and I don't know if I speak for James as well as myself, but I still find out-right violence a questionable means of settling matters of history. However, our objective is identical, and that being the case, I will do all I can to help you as long as it does not compel *me* to violence."

"Me too," I committed myself.

Continued Alex, "As far as the financial situation is concerned, I think Boston is the right place to be. Although I regret America breaking away from the Empire, and I venture to say this situation would not be permitted under the Empire, I think Boston, because of its role in American history, would have a unique sensitivity towards any struggle for freedom."

"Was that all one sentence?"

"Don't be flippant, James. To start another sentence, the American Revolution was fought only some eighty-odd years ago..."

"And," said John Brown, "we are about to fight the greatest violation of what the revolution stood for, so it stands to reason that in Boston we should get as good financial, practical, and moral support as anywhere."

Sad to report, it was not to be. We contacted Gerrit on our arrival in Boston and began our task of visiting about and soliciting funds, our zeal fuelled by outings made at Alex's urging to places that had played key parts in the American Revolution: Concord Bridge, the scene of the famous Tea Party at the harbour, Old North Church, and Faneuil Hall. The last-named gave us some difficulty, as we gave it a vaguely French pronunciation so that it sounded something like "Fanooey" Hall, and nobody knew what we were talking about. Only later did we discover the local pronunciation to be "Funnel" Hall.

Our tangible, which is to say financial, results were meagre indeed. John Brown actually generated about five hundred dollars on his own and Alex and I grossed about two hundred between us, but we were still far short of immediate requirements. It was sadly evident that the cradle of the Revolution was pretty complacent these days; nobody here, except for a few ordained Abolitionists, was directly involved. Most of those actually sympathetic to the slaves would have been content to confine slavery to its present territory and have the Fugitive Slave Law revoked. They had no desire at all to finance a war that would cleave America in twain.

All three of us became totally despondent, as did Gerrit, who had expected far better things of Boston, and one rainy afternoon, the four of us stood aimlessly on a bridge over the Charles River, watching an equally disconsolate Harvard College rowing crew at practice. Their crimson shirts were the only relief from the misty gloom.

"These people are so...so *flaccid* in their thinking," lamented Gerrit. "Not those university lads, just everyone in general. I abhor war, but, by God, when all else fails, I would support it in every way possible. I don't mean to suggest life is cheap, but if you look at the cosmic tapestry and weigh the loss of a few lives for a short time against the gain of freedom for many for all eternity, well, the choice becomes pretty plain."

"Amen to that," said Capt. Brown, "and war will come and I will start it. Nobody likes surgery either, but if you are sick and may die, there *is* no choice. Dr. Ross, Young Man, I am going to need you when the time comes."

Alex and I glanced at each other, moving Brown to reassure us, "No, I would not ask you to imperil your lives or kill anyone. You have done enough and been in enough danger already. What I *will* need is someone I can trust absolutely, someone who, if our operation is a success, will travel among the slaves and alert them to our purpose. And that will be dangerous enough."

With thirty percent of the required funds still not secured, I had a personal doubt that the "operation" would actually happen. I looked at Alex as he stared at the receding Harvard crew. "That crimson,""he murmured, barely audible above the tinkling rain, "there'll be so much of it. But, yes, Capt. Brown, you can certainly count on...both of us?"

"Oh, certainly, count me in too," I said, rather too casually in view of how the year 1859 was to conclude.

A POPULAR PERCEPTION OF JOHN BROWN IN HIS CRUSADING MODE.
COURTESY OF HARPERS FERRY HISTORICAL ASSOCIATION,
HARPERS FERRY, WV

CHAPTER TWENTY-SEVEN

Chatham, Canada West
May 5, 1859

Dear Friend,

I have called a quiet convention in this place of true friends
of freedom. Your attendance is earnestly requested on the 10th
inst.

Your friend,
John Brown

"And here it is the thirteenth!" snorted Alex. "I don't know whether the
Royal Mail or that railway of yours is responsible, James, but this is certainly
less than sterling service. I would have liked to have been there."

"I'm just as happy you were here," purred Hester, ruffling his hair. Had
Hester been ruffling *my* hair, I would have forgotten slaves, the U.S.A., the
entire world. But Alex was all but oblivious to this simple but eloquent
gesture as he sat slumped in his favourite armchair, a great bulbous maroon
fortress with things like doilies over the armrests.

"I should have been there, *we* should have been there," he said
abruptly. "It is the position...I'm sorry, my dear." He was suddenly aware
of the ruffling of hair and took Hester's hand in both of his. "We have
laboured so long, and for myself, the lack of a final outcome has been
eating at me. I am becoming so unreasonable and snappish..."

"Because of you, directly or indirectly, over one hundred people are
now free," pointed out Hester. I still felt good about my twenty-six, but
even over one hundred was not nearly enough for Alex.

"But there are so many more," he sighed. "Let me put it to you like
this: if you had an awful disease, say, cancer, wouldn't you want your
surgeon to remove all of it? I guess part of my problem is seeing only the
beginning and the end of the escape process. The feeling for you, James, at
Port Burwell after that long ordeal must have been beyond description."

"That it was." The mere mention of Port Burwell unleashed a fresh
flood of reveries and recollections of Ruth. Seven months past now and I
was still haunted by her. When would she let me go?

"About this letter," said Alex. "The good Captain is not being very
discreet. If the wrong eyes ever saw this, it could mean serious difficulty.
He even signed it in full and my name is on the envelope, why, the potential for disaster is absolutely appalling. With that kind of carelessness, I
cannot see this rebellion or whatever succeeding, and I'm afraid it's the only
hope left."

"Alex, calm down."

"I can't! I am sick and tired of the whole business, the complacency, the stupidity, and now such carelessness by our leading ally. Some days I feel like chucking the whole thing and going into seclusion like Matthias Grunewald after the Peasants' Rebellion." I had no idea what that was all about, but let it by.

"This is Canada," reminded Hester. "There won't be people spying on the mail."

"I wouldn't wager on it. Oh, God, I don't trust anyone any more. I don't know what is becoming of me."

"For one thing, you're exhausted," reminded Hester. "Look after *yourself* for a change. You have done enough..."

"No, I have not! The only 'enough' that I understand is freedom and equality for everyone. Dr. Alexander Ross, the great healer, has to take on the entire human race." He buried his face in his hands. This was not like Alex at all.

"So did Jesus," said Hester. "You are more than you think, my husband. I just hope your life expectancy is greater than Jesus'. I would like to see something of you in this life."

"And I have neglected you so badly," said Alex, a terrible heaviness in his voice.

I felt by this time like an intruder. "Shall I step out for a bit?"

"If you wouldn't mind, James. Very thoughtful of you. Come along back for tea in a couple of hours."

Alex's *malaise* was of mercifully short duration and we spent the balance of the spring and early summer, sometimes together, sometimes separately, doing church and school speaking tours around the counties of Hastings and Prince Edward and as far east as Kingston. We realized some modest revenue, augmented by Father through his numerous contacts in the legal profession, and sent a portion of it to Gerrit Smith and the so-called "Secret Six"* in the aid of John Brown's cause. It was enough to equip forty slaves with pikes and I still have a strange feeling when I think about it.

Alex, on a trip to Toronto, managed to pick up some intelligence as to the content of the "quiet convention" in Chatham. He had a chance meeting with Stewart Taylor, a young man from the near-by country village of Uxbridge and an accomplice of John Brown, who revealed the basic plan for the insurrection.

---

*The Secret Six, it may be recalled, was the group backing John Brown in his proposed insurrection. Besides Gerrit Smith, it included G.L. Stearns, a Massachusetts industrialist; Franklin Sanborn, an educator; Rev. Theodore Parker of the Boston Unitarian Church; Dr. Samuel G. Howe, a Boston teacher and clergyman; and Rev. T.W. Higginson, who openly advocated the abolition of slavery through a bloodbath.

As Alex reported to me, "They are going to strike somewhere along the border between Maryland and Virginia and the surrounding mountains will be an escape-hatch if things go badly. Brown is arranging a base of operations as I tell you this.

"Our friend Brown does not do things by halves. This convention - there were over thirty blacks in attendance, by the way, but Stewart didn't know if they were actually going into the rebellion - this convention endorsed a plan that was, well, unusual in that an additional government would be formed for the United States."

"Additional?" I said in surprise. "I never heard of such a thing except when there were two Popes, and that isn't quite the same thing."

Alex nodded approvingly at my growing mastery of trivia for the right moment. "I hadn't either. They call it the Provisional Government of the United States, and its primary, indeed only, mandate is to enforce the prohibition of slavery. And it has its own army, with Brown as Commander-in-Chief, so the title 'captain' gains some legitimacy. I suppose the idea is to leave the mundane things like the postal service and the roads to the government already in office.

"I hope this Taylor chap knows what he is in for. He's a nice enough lad, early twenties, I think, but so baby-faced they probably won't allow him the vote until he's seventy. He's the only Canadian going in and I think he sees himself as one with the knights of the Crusades. Pretty naïve. But you know what, James, even though it's completely crazy, there's a magnificence to it too."

To reassure ourselves that we had done some good, when not engaged in fund-raising, we went to visit with escaped slaves. There was no question that we had done an extraordinary amount between us, but the accompanying disillusionments bothered us, even though they were by no means unexpected. As in the Northern states, there was general commiseration towards escaped slaves, thanks in good part to the Toronto *Globe*, which wasted no opportunity to enumerate their sufferings and ordeals that propelled them onto the Underground Railroad in the first place.

But there was also a general discomfort at what amounted in the public mind to the spectre of negroes as neighbours, negroes nodding a greeting in the street, negro women saying good morning over the back fence as the laundry was hung out, negroes all over the place. Having been in a black *milieu* as I had been, I could not see what all the fuss was about, but then, of course, I had had the advantage of black company and my earliest odd feeling at seeing the group of blacks at Chatham station the day I met the Major was now all but forgotten.

In counter to George Brown's *Globe*, there were other publications, generally those that catered to the Lower Orders, that had no scruples about the publication of unkind caricatures of blacks, almost invariably with a banjo or a slice of watermelon in hand. I am ashamed to tell this, but one day I actually joined the Lower Orders by laughing at one of these unenlightened portrayals. It looked so funny that I could not help myself.

In short, then, when abstract ideals became practical reality, there was a change of public attitude, though, for the most part, antipathy in Canada was far more subtle and polite than in America. One seldom heard of "blackamoors" or "niggers" here. But there were references, sometimes frequently, to "the coloured element" or "those of, er, darker persuasion."

The greatest concentration of blacks continued to be in the southwestern part of Canada West, where they tended, understandably, to live in close proximity to each other. It was this very clannishness, unfortunately, that invited prejudice, and it seemed to occur to nobody that if the roles were reversed, we whites would likely have behaved in the same way. There was a well-founded fear among the blacks, for instance, of being kidnapped right here in Canada and being carried off by slave-traders or persons wishing to cash in on the Fugitive Slave Law. A variation on this had already happened to the daughter of a black hotel-owner named James Mink; she had married a white man from Virginia, moved there, and been sold into slavery. Her rescue by her father makes an epic tale of its own.

A sense of community and safety in numbers, then, were very much to the point. Keeping a balanced viewpoint in relating all of this is extremely difficult. But I must point out certain situations in which blacks isolated themselves, segregating themselves into all-black churches, mainly black communities like Oro or Colborne, and such organizations as the Negro Order of Odd fellows and the Sons of Uriah, shutting out whites just as whites were shutting *them* out.

I will not attempt to judge, since I was not in the middle of the situation. It is cause, though, for much sadness when such a sorry situation can create a mirror-image of itself. But whatever else was happening, we needed to keep a sense of proportion by reminding ourselves that negroes - at least the men - could vote and now there were trials of law in which black jurors played a part. Under the law, at least, they were treated equally to us.

A good many of our fellow Canadians, mainly those without direct contact with negroes, were either unaware of local prejudice towards our new citizens, or just chose to ignore it. At various gatherings and meetings, Alex and I were told time and time again how "British" we were being and how Canada's "acceptance" of blacks was part of a glorious tradition (if a span of twenty-six years can be called a tradition) and a demonstration of our moral superiority over the United States. But this self-same wonderful and humanitarian "acceptance" was, to be perfectly blunt, based on a rapidly-growing and somewhat hysterical anti-American sentiment.

The United States at this time had its eye on some real-estate to add to its own dominion, specifically Canada. Members of the Legislative Assembly of Canada West (and I talked to a few who were acquaintances of Father) looked with a kind eye upon our status as the northern terminus of the Underground Railroad, for if we had a large black (and free) population, voters in the Southern states would be less likely to support what many Americans regarded as their Manifest Destiny, which is to say the domination of the North American continent. The blacks, therefore, were considered a useful deterrent to our absorption into the American union.

Politically, the black presence was seen as a virtue. To certain others, it was a threat to the Anglo-Saxon purity of this part of the Empire if black immigration were to continue unchecked. "These people", it was said over and over, should wait to enter Canada legally and in controlled numbers to ensure a harmonious assimilation. This sort of idiocy, thank God, never came to be; I cannot comprehend what it would be like to walk all the way from Mississippi in constant peril to be stopped by some bureaucrat at the border telling you to wait your turn. Harmonious assimilation would be preferred, of course, but in times other than those of total human desperation. All I can say is that anyone prepared to complain about the "black hordes" should direct their displeasure towards our ancestors who introduced slavery in the first place.

As summer waned, Alex and I were desperate for money of our own, Underground Railroad or no Underground Railroad. Alex had a wife to support and a house to maintain and I was ridden with guilt at continuing to depend on my parents. So Alex did some part-time work relieving other doctors at the local hospital and I, the nature of my previous departure from the Grand Trunk evidently forgotten, stood in for the night-time agent at Belleville station, who was away ill.

It was not a great job, but it was still a job and it was income. The hours took some getting used to - midnight to eight in the morning - but even with such an eccentrically-timed work day, I found it rather pleasant in the empty station, keeping track of the various nocturnal train movements over the telegraph and writing up orders as necessary. And when September came, it was an exceptionally fine one, summer's left-over perfumes wafting in at the open windows and the little creatures of nature chirping and whirring far into the night.

The regular agent returned to work at the end of the month, but I was not to be idle for long. One afternoon I was raking up the first leaves of autumn, the frigid blasts of a northerly wind making a shambles of my progress.

"James, my boy!" cried the voice I now knew so well. "Look at this! The fat is surely in the fire now."

Chambersburg, Pennsylvania
October 6, 1859

Dear Friends,
I shall move about the last of the month. Can you help in the way promised? Kindly address your reply in care of Isaac Smith, P.O. Box 54, Chambersburg, Pa.
Your friend,
J.B.

"Good Christ!" I exclaimed with sufficient awe that Alex did not take issue. "He's going to do it!"

"Could there have been any doubt? Well, old friend , we have committed ourselves, well and truly. We were involved before, now we are committed."

"What's the difference?"

"Contemplate your breakfast bacon and eggs. The hen that laid the eggs was involved. But the pig, James, was committed!"

"What! We're going to be killed!"

"No, we're not, but we are in well and truly deeply. There is no turning back. This time I leave my bird things behind and take my medical kit, just as I did to Evansville, not to mention that odd little expedition to Nicaragua. This is going to be like the opening of a great social carbuncle."

"A beautiful simile, Alex, just beautiful."

"Well, they will need a doctor, won't they? I don't know about you, but I have just been rotting away..."

"Rotting away! You have continued an unremitting stream of good works, practising medicine..."

"There are many others qualified to practice medicine. But you and I, on the other hand...oh, good afternoon, Judge Ramsay."

"Alex, good to see you. What's the blow?" Father's use of slang usually made Alex laugh, but this time, he did not, his initial exuberance displaced.

"Here's the blow, Judge. Look at this."

"Well," said Father in his Voice of Portent. "Well...*well*..I'll see Mr. Childs at the Dominion Bank first thing in the morning. No, I have a trial at ten...I'll go to his house right now and ask him to get five hundred dollars ready for you and a letter of credit if you need more."

"Five hundred dollars!"

"Is that not enough? I could arrange..."

"No, no, this is, well, wonderful."

"Well, spend it wisely and avoid the highwaymen. James, tell your mother where I have gone. And why."

It took us but a day to make our arrangements, although Alex had a bit of difficulty cutting loose. He was enjoying his home life and being a husband, and some of his friends were not helping matters by trying to talk him out of what they perceived as a mad adventure that involved him too deeply in American politics and social issues.

"They're probably right in a way," said Alex. "But you know me. I took this on as a human rather than a political thing. And we did make a promise to John Brown. Didn't we?"

CHAPTER TWENTY-EIGHT

The first tangible intelligence of Captain John Brown's unleashing of the Apocalypse came to us on October 17, a dull and overcast Monday. Alex and I were spending the afternoon in the parlour of the Columbian Hotel in Richmond, standing by for instructions from John Brown and waiting for a sign, any sign, that something was afoot. We were just debating whether it would be indiscreet to do some espionage at one of the local newspaper offices when Alex grabbed my arm. "James, listen."

An agitated conversation had suddenly erupted by the hotel desk and someone was saying, "My God, my God" over and over again. Someone else mentioned Harpers Ferry.

"Stewart Taylor said something about Harpers Ferry. Let me look into this." Alex joined the knot of people by the desk and then rejoined me.

"It just came in on the telegraph and it's a bit muddled," he said tensely. "The first report had a band of robbers capturing Harpers Ferry, but it was almost immediately revised to a force of abolitionists led by someone named Smith. I have no idea where *that* name came from."*

"Unless Isaac Smith is in on it."

"Isaac Smith?"

"The chap from Chambersburg, you know, where Capt. Brown's letter came from."

"Oh, of course. I wonder. This army or whatever is said to be murdering local inhabitants and abducting slaves; dear God, this is just tying me in knots. I think at this point we can check the newspaper offices without showing undue interest. *Everyone* will be interested by now. This word-of-mouth business has probably inflated the thing beyond its real dimensions anyway."

We went our separate ways in the rising wind and spitting, icy rain, Alex to the offices of the Richmond *Times-Despatch* and myself to the *Examiner*. Both premises were in an uproar with a press deadline of five o'clock, both trying to bring their information up to date as it chattered over the telegraph. And both places attracted a crowd which pressed and surged, trying to read the blackboard in the window.

Alex, over at the *Times-Despatch*, fell into conversation with an old negro, who had bought his freedom and whose sons had escaped to Canada. He was unable to read and so asked Alex to tell him what was on the blackboard.

---

*Smith was the name assumed by Brown in the rental of a local farm for his military headquarters.

"A small force of abolitionists," read Alex, "under one Andrews or Anderson,* has taken over the Federal buildings in Harpers Ferry. Several casualties have been reported. There has been no contact as yet with the leader, but it is assumed that this incident is part of a plot to stir the Negro population to revolt..."

"Can dey do it, massa?" said the old man. "Can dey truly do it? Lawd, look down on dem..."

By the time the paper went on sale the following morning, there was an addendum on the front page: "The leader of yesterday's raid on Harpers Ferry is now in custody and has been identified as John 'Ossawatomie' Brown." Hardly had Brown's dream of a negro uprising begun than it was all over. Both Alex and I abhorred violence, but nonetheless it had been a dream, if a fleeting one, and we could not even be demonstrative of our despair as the people of Richmond rejoiced over the Captain's capture in a fashion that verged on the demonic. There were no blacks among the celebrants. But to all who believed in human dignity, Harpers Ferry from that day forward would be a shrine, a Culloden, a Jerusalem.

All America learned about the little village in a matter of hours, about how it occupied a promontory overlooking the confluence of the Shenandoah and Potomac Rivers, the latter forming the border between Virginia and Maryland. The surrounding Blue Ridge Mountains that Brown had chosen as an emergency shelter were already famous, for the district had been a favourite of Thomas Jefferson and he had gone so far as to write that the view from his private rock above the town would be worth a trip over from Europe.

The village of Harpers Ferry itself is a huddle of buildings strung out along the main line of the Baltimore and Ohio Railroad, many on the grounds of the United States Armoury. And connecting the village with the Maryland side of the Potomac River was a covered bridge about three hundred yards in length and shared by the railway and a road.

On Sunday night, October 16, William Williams was on watch duty on the bridge and was particularly anxious about the lamps, for they could be temperamental critters on a blustery night such as this, blowing out, smoking up their chimneys, or running out of oil unreasonably soon. The bridge may have been covered, but a south-westerly wind would come funnelling straight through, as it did this night.

Shortly after 10:30 p.m., with an hour and a half of penance left, Will was up a ladder, cleaning a lamp chimney, when a voice hissed through the darkness. "Stand still, friend, put the ladder down real slow, don't turn around, and you won't get hurt. Hey, I said, *don't turn around!*"

"Who the blazes are you? What are you doing?"

"You will find out in due course. Just cooperate. Come with us."

"Who is that, God damn it?"

---

*There was, in fact, a Jeremiah Anderson in Brown's force.

"Ssh," said someone in the dark.

"Look," said Will, trying to keep a wobble from his voice, "I don't know what you guys are up to, but I have work to do. This ain't funny."

"We know. We too have work to do, as you shall see. And it isn't funny either."

"Wires are out, Captain," reported a new voice.

"Cut 'em again on the other end of the bridge. Come along, now, watchman."

William Williams' counterpart in the Armoury grounds was his friend Daniel Whelan, at the moment sheltering from the weather in the fire station, and when he heard the wagon rumbling to a stop, he mumbled an expletive and went outside to see what was going on. No shipments were scheduled, oh, sweet Jesus, there were guns pointed at him!

"Open up!" cried a voice. This was definitely not a regulation delivery. It was a profound annoyance that moved Daniel Whelan to draw on his Irish ancestry.

"The hell I will!" he retorted angrily. "This is U.S. Government property." He edged back towards the fire station to raise the alarm. There was a screech of sundered metal, the gate opened, in came the unauthorized wagon, and Daniel was overpowered in as much time as it takes to tell. He was more angry than scared, however, and, once again invoking his Irish background, gave vent to a full broadside of obscenities.

"That's enough!" snapped a voice with more authority than the others. "You are our prisoner now, along with your colleague here. We have come here from Kansas. This is a slave state. I am going to free all the negroes here..."

"You serious?"

"Never more." It was John Brown, looking frighteningly Old Testament in the guttering light of a lantern. "I have possession now of the United States Armoury and if any citizens interfere with me, I must only burn the town and have blood."

"Christ."

"Let me just reassure you that no harm will be done to you personally, unless you choose to do something heroic." He turned to the trembling Will. "We would just like the use of your bridge for the evening."

It was not to be the only bridge under consideration. Three blocks away to the south was the bridge over the Shenandoah, and sent hither to take control of it was Brown's son Oliver and a couple of others. The main body of personnel, in the meantime, took over the rifle works.

The entire operation was progressing so quietly, with the exception of Daniel Whelan's brief hullabaloo, that Harpers Ferry slumbered in sweet oblivion to the events that would earn its place in history forever. The five churches scattered about near the rail junction struck midnight in an untidy clangour, the citizens of Harpers Ferry turned over in bed.

There was considerable coming and going now in Harpers Ferry.

Among the going was a contingent headed by Brown's lieutenant, John E. Cook, who had lived in the district for a year as he gathered information, had taught school there, and had married a local girl. Cook and his force disappeared into the night on "borrowed" horses, riding south straight into the rising wind. There were gaps in the overcast and a cold sliver of moon played tag with the rags of clouds.

Cook and his men dismounted at an estate called Bellair, the home of Colonel Lewis Washington, with whom Cook had become acquainted while educating the young of Harpers Ferry. Cook appropriated Colonel Washington's collection of historical weapons, an interest that had brought the two of them together in the first place, and arrested the Colonel in the name of the United States Provisional Army for ownership of human beings. A farm wagon was requisitioned and loaded with Colonel Washington, his confused and befuddled slaves, and his weapons collection. As well, the Colonel's neighbour, a Mr. Alstadt, his sixteen-year-old son, and seven slaves were taken into custody.

Custody meant confinement to the Armoury and another unwilling guest there was a badly-shaken Luther Simpson, a member of the crew of the Wheeling-to-Baltimore mail train. The train had appeared right on schedule at 1:25 a.m. and had stopped just short of the west end of the bridge because of a "reported obstruction" on the track. The driver and baggage-master had climbed down to investigate and run straight into a party of Brown's raiders.

An altercation broke out, attracting the attention of Hayward Shepherd, the night baggage agent at the station. Out he came to investigate and, on being challenged by a raider, turned and fled back for the station. One of the raiders shot him and, mortally wounded, Shepherd stumbled through the waiting room door and collapsed. The first casualty of the raid, he was ironically not only a black man but a free one as well. It was noised about that he had been shot for refusing to join the insurrectionists.

Luther Simpson was taken under escort to the Armoury to negotiate for the train's release, a somewhat academic exercise in that the raiders had no idea what to do with it anyway. Simpson talked to John Brown and was held captive for an hour or so, observing, as he reported in an interview with *Harper's Weekly* (the October 29, 1859, issue), "five or six hundred negroes, all having arms; there were two or three hundred white men with them..." How Mr. Simpson arrived at such figures is a mystery and Alex and I could only conclude that the darkness, confusion, and anxiety augmented his sense of numbers.

Permission for the train to proceed was denied. Aside from that, there seemed no point in detaining Simpson further, so he was released. On his way back to the train, he turned aside to Chambers' Tavern, seeing it lit up and apparently fortified. The shots directed at Hayward Shepherd had jolted some of the townspeople awake, a few of whom had fled, but there were about thirty here in the tavern, fuelled by Mr. Chambers' potions and ready to do battle with any damn Yanks who dared to come fooling with them. Not wishing to be in the middle of a bloodbath, Mr. Simpson had a quick draft to calm his shattered nerves and then returned to the train.

Hayward Shepherd expired as grey dawn began to seep across the eastern sky, despite the best efforts of the local physician, Dr. John Starry. Despite being up most of the night, the doctor then went into action to warn the superintendent of the Armoury and the inhabitants of nearby Virginius Island, and to organize some sort of resistance force. Additionally, he despatched one of his neighbours to ride to Charles Town, eight or nine miles to the south, to alert the Jefferson Guards, the local militia company.

The train, in the meantime, had been allowed to resume its journey; the raiders, after pondering the situation, had adjudged it to be an encumbrance, a matter which I will not attempt to editorialize. It had huffed off in indignant plumes and wreaths of steam, past the impotently dangling telegraph wires, and onward to its customary though tardy stop at Monocacy Junction, Maryland. The station agent, who had been beside himself trying to find the durned fewl train for the last five hours, was instructed by conductor A.J. Phelps to send a telegram, and that instanter, to the personal attention of B. and O. president John Garrett:

BALTIMORE AND OHIO R.R.
MONOCACY JCT., MD.
OCT. 17/59
7:05 A.M.

WHEELING-BALTIMORE MAIL TRAIN EASTBOUND UNDER MY CHARGE STOPPED THIS MORNING AT HARPERS FERRY BY ARMED ABOLITIONISTS STOP THEY HAVE POSSESSION OF THE BRIDGE AND OF THE ARMS AND ARMOURY OF THE UNITED STATES STOP BAGGAGE AGENT FIRED AT STOP THEY SAY THEY HAVE COME TO FREE THE SLAVES AND INTEND TO DO SO AT ALL HAZARDS STOP THE LEADERS OF THOSE MEN REQUESTED ME TO SAY TO YOU THIS IS THE LAST TRAIN THAT SHALL PASS THE BRIDGE EAST OR WEST STOP IF IT IS ATTEMPTED IT WILL BE AT THE PERIL OF THOSE IN CHARGE STOP IT HAS BEEN SUGGESTED YOU HAD BETTER NOTIFY THE SECRETARY OF WAR AT ONCE STOP THE TELEGRAPH LINES ARE CUT EAST AND WEST OF HARPERS FERRY AND THIS IS THE FIRST STATION I COULD SEND A MESSAGE FROM END   /S/ A.J. PHELPS

John Garrett was totally astounded, all but choking on his morning coffee at the start of what he later described as a "damned interesting day". He alerted the commanding officer of the Maryland Regiment, Governor Henry A. Wise of Virginia, and the current occupant of the White House, James Buchanan, to inform them that a white-assisted slave revolt was in progress at Harpers Ferry. Governor Wise was uncomfortably reminded of the Nat Turner rebellion in his own state back in '31, a disturbance that had taken a toll of nearly fifty lives.

At about the time all this traffic was humming over the wires of Western Union, a band of Harpers Ferry inhabitants, desperately looking for some means of defence, found some arms stored in a building the raiders had overlooked, and now were in a position to defend themselves. By mid-morning, the invaders were cornered. But John Brown insisted on staying put against the advice of raider John Kagi, who pointed out that help for the town was probably *en route* by that time and the insurrectionists should withdraw into the Blue Ridge Mountains while they could still get out. But John Brown ignored him and by noon was in a hopeless position, for the Jefferson Guards and an assortment of volunteers from Charles Town were counter-attacking in two groups. One forded the Potomac a mile or so upstream and entered the town from the north-east across the B. and O. bridge; the other approached from the south over the Charles Town Turn-pike.

It was in the action on the B. and O. bridge that the first of the raiders was killed: Dangerfield Newby, a black man, whose only wish in life was to free his wife and children. He was felled by a six-inch spike fired from a musket.

Belatedly, Brown acknowledged the nature of his situation and resorted to the negotiation of a truce. But the first emissary he sent, William Thompson, was promptly taken prisoner and threatened with lynching by a hysterical mob of the burghers of Harpers Ferry.

Another essay was made at bargaining, this time at the cost of another life. Aaron Stevens and Brown's son Watson went forward under a very obvious flag of truce, but so aroused were the locals by now that the two unfortunates were both struck by gunfire, Watson Brown so severely that he expired a short time later.

This account, I should explain, was compiled from newspaper and magazine reports read in the wake of the raid, for while it was actually happening, news reached us disjointedly at best. Nonetheless, we absorbed all we could, for we were a part of it and yet completely helpless, watching it all unravel in a strange, twilit sense of unreality.

In recounting this part of my tale, I would venture to say that John Brown's raid, if not turning out differently, would likely have been pro-longed were it not for the presence of the Baltimore and Ohio Railroad. A train was hastily assembled in Baltimore to transport the personnel and weaponry of six military companies to what was now being referred to as "the front". It steamed out of Camden Station shortly after four in the after-noon, with what we railroaders call a "highball" all the way to Harpers Ferry. Unless I am mistaken, this must be the first time anywhere in North America that trains have been put to military use.

In addition to the train, the B. and O. contributed a number of its own employees, who stormed the Armoury with such fury that John Brown and his surviving henchmen were driven from there and into the little fire engine-house.

The casualty list continued to mount. Raider William Leeman, deciding that he had had enough, sprinted for the Potomac with a view to swimming across to Maryland. Caught in the current, he was swept against an off-shore boulder. Under a hail of gunfire, he pulled himself up onto it, only to be killed moments later. His body lay on its rock all afternoon, being shot at by people when they ran out of anything better to do.

In mid-afternoon, a local planter, George Turner, died from a raider's bullet, and shortly after, the mayor of Harpers Ferry, Fontaine Beckham, was killed by raider Edwin Coppoc. In the return fire from enraged locals, Brown's other son, Oliver, was mortally wounded.

The original emissary of truce, William Thompson, who had been incarcerated in the Wager House Hotel, was seized by a mob of townspeople, marched out onto the Potomac River bridge, shot, and his body dumped in the river.

Dr. Starry, who was having the busiest day in an otherwise uneventful life, was instrumental in driving three raiders - John Kagi, Lewis Leary, and John Copeland - from the rifle works. In their attempted escape across the Shenandoah, Kagi and Leary never made it, and Copeland, who was black, was caught and threatened with lynching. Dr. Starry intervened and the terrified Copeland was put into protective custody in the village jail.

At the sun's setting, Harpers Ferry was one big military encampment. A desperate Brown, backed into his corner, tried again to negotiate - he would surrender upon giving up his hostages if he would be allowed to escape into Maryland under his own guarantee of good conduct. The authorities laughed and the fighting continued.

And into the fray at various times during the evening flowed yet more military units: three artillery companies from Old Point Comfort, Virginia, and a company of United States Marines from Washington, all under the overall command of Colonel Robert E. Lee.

As Monday darkened in its inexorable journey towards Tuesday, Colonel Lee's men were formed up by the Armoury and, peculiar as it may sound, spectators had to be cleared out of the way. In the thick silence that generally precedes catastrophe, a young lieutenant, J.E.B. Stuart, took a message to the insurrectionists that they could go quietly and be turned over to the appropriate legal authorities with complete guarantee of safety. Otherwise they would simply be seized by the waiting soldiers and marines.

Brown's response, a not particularly rational one, was that he would surrender only if he and his men were allowed to escape with a reasonable head start. "For God's sake!" exploded Lieutenant Stuart. "Y'all have to be declared dead before you'll quit. Have it your way, then, Mr. Brown. It's your funeral." Stuart waved his cap, the signal for attack.

A raiding party of U.S. Marines stove in the doors of the fire station, using a ladder as a battering ram. "How Greek," murmured Alex as he read the news account.

Lieutenant Israel Green beat Brown senseless with the hilt of his dress sword and when he came to, John Brown of Ossawatomie was under arrest.

As the exhausted and despondent raiders were brought out of the firehouse, the watching crowd broke into a rhythmic chant of "Shoot them, shoot them!"

"There, now, there, none o' that," snapped Jeb Stuart. "Due process of law...none o' that, Ah said, y'all hear? Watch yourselves...stand back, please..."

In thirty-six hours, John Brown's great dream, of which Alex and I were now reduced to the role of trustees, had ended up in ashes. Ten of his men were dead, including his sons Watson and Oliver, and the baby-faced Stewart Taylor from Uxbridge, Canada West. Five were taken prisoner along with Brown; the remainder had escaped, but of that number only a few would remain at large.

An invisible haze of unreality hung over the little town. Nobody yet was considering the notoriety; for the moment, a numbed populace was trying to come to terms with the horror of such violence from right within America, a nice fella like John Cook mixed up in it, citizen against citizen.

The hero/villain of what was to become an American passion play was led away under heavy security to be held in Charles Town jail for intensive questioning, questioning that would be fuelled by evidence against him that lay in almost contemptuous profusion about his lodgings, a nearby farm rented from a Dr. Kennedy: two wagon-loads of arms, including the pikes we had partially financed, ammunition, assorted other military supplies, documents relating to other abolitionist activities, letters (including one initialled by Alex and myself), money, and a bank draft in the amount of one hundred dollars with Gerrit Smith's full signature.

The Lion of Judah fought the fight, says the Book of John. Now America had her own Lion of Judah, whose fight, though brief, would eventually have an impact that would match the dreams of the Lion Himself.

JOHN BROWN'S LAST STAND AT THE FIRE STATION. COURTESY OF HARPERS FERRY HISTORICAL ASSOCIATION, HARPERS FERRY, WV

CHAPTER TWENTY-NINE

"We can do nothing further here," said Alex over breakfast on Wednesday morning, the *Richmond Examiner* spread out over half the table, "not that we have done anything anyway but sit around being helpless. I feel so, well, empty, a sort of dreadful tranquillity."

"The tranquillity of futility," I remarked. "I know what you mean."

"Poetically put, James, but I can't help thinking that the futility will not be permanent. Whatever happens to John Brown, I think things are now in motion that cannot be stopped." Ringing words they were, but Alex was not buttering his toast completely from edge to edge this morning; could this have been a sign of shaken faith? When Alex was firmly in the saddle, as he liked to put it, and he was most of the time, he could still be buttering his toast when mine was long gone, as though buttering toast was something that could not be hurried, like fine wine.

"What should we do, then, Alex?"

"I think our next step should be to go up to Washington and see the temper of the government. That should guide us in our next decision. We are behind the scenes at the moment, so let's be totally vigilant about what we say. How are we doing for money?"

"Not very well."

"Perhaps some can be pried loose from Gerrit. I'll telegraph him from Washington. When is this damnable rain going to stop? Things are bad enough without nature herself weeping all over us."

The clearing weather in Harpers Ferry certainly hadn't come near Richmond. Nature wept all day upon the glistening roadbed of the Richmond and Potomac Railroad as it took us north to the American capital. It was not a trip on which I could absorb the atmosphere of "railroading", that wonderful American verb now so firmly rooted in my own vocabulary. Instead, we circulated casually but systematically through the cars, well-patronized this day by slave-owners and their political and commercial sympathizers, going to Washington to agitate for John Brown's execution. We had to exercise our discretion to the limit as we heard him denounced variously as a God-damned traitor, a despoiler of the American way of life, trampling on people's independence (plainly slaves did not count as people), and that sort of thing. There was a gruesome kind of conviviality as our fellow travellers tried to outdo each other in their invective and virulence. It was like being in the middle of an emotional cattle stampede, so inexorably were the sentiments of the people headed in one direction.

Our stay in Washington would not be one to uplift the spirits of those dedicated to life, liberty, and the pursuit of happiness. "This place is a moral slaughterhouse!" stormed Alex during a chilly walk by the Potomac River, a belated afternoon sun glittering icily on the water. "Slavery has not been practised in the Northern states for years, but you'd think these fools were *afraid* of the bloody South. They all but wring their hands and apologize for Brown's attitude and for the raid. These Northern senators and congressmen remind me of dogs going after scraps of meat. They'll do anything for Southern support, even in violation of their own consciences, if indeed they have any."*

"Why this fetish for Southern support anyway? We've read about it before, but I'm getting a bit muddled here. Refresh me."

"Ah, these senators and so forth are all armchair Presidents," explained Alex. "They want to be ready for the Southern vote ten, twenty years from now if they run for office. They resort to evil in the pursuit of power, just as Machiavelli wrote all those years ago. It would be a joke if it weren't so disgusting. James, are you all right? You don't look very well."

"I, uh, I'm all right, Alex, thank you. Just a bit tired and on edge."

"I don't think you speak the truth."

"Is there no escape?"

"No, James, there is not." I generally like my name, but it does have an unfortunate way of lending itself to disapproval and reproach.

"Look," I protested, "there's no *time* to be sick. There's enough..."

"Back to the hotel and into bed with you. I can recommend a very good doctor who, even though six hundred miles from home, is totally equipped."

While Alex haunted the corridors of the United States Capitol building and the offices of the *Washington Post,* I stayed in bed, laying there where Jesus flang me, incandescent with fever, aching even in my toes, moving only to visit the commode. I cannot abide chamber pots.

"Alex, I'm so damned sorry," I moaned during one of his periodic inquiries after my welfare. "So much to do and I'm too sick to even care."

"Better here than in the hills of Kentucky with twenty-six fugitive slaves. Try this, now; I brought you some chicken soup. One of the chefs here claims it to be the ultimate remedy."

Whatever it was, my condition worsened. In a couple of hours, despite the chicken soup, I was insensible, immune to all cares and miseries but my own, tormented by the strange, fragmentary dreams that fever invariably brings. Alex tells me that I lay thus for fully twenty-four hours and when I regained my senses, there he was at bedside, dressed as for business and exuding the chill one does when just in out of the cold.

---

*Reinforcing the division between the free and slave-owning states was the Missouri Compromise of 1820. In that year, Maine was admitted to the Union as a free state and Missouri entered as the only free state in the erstwhile Louisiana Territory north of parallel 36 degrees 30 minutes to be allowed slavery. Thus the American Union was symmetrical in the sense of having twelve each of free and slave states, but Thomas Jefferson accurately predicted the "knell of the Union" because of geographic delineation.

"How are you feeling? You've had me worried."

"Oh, God," I whimpered. "Alex, would you brush my teeth for me? They itch."

"Uh, well, a doctor I am but a mother I'm not. We've already had to deal with the chamber pot..."

"I don't remember any chamber pot."

"Well, I do. I had to help you aim. It was not a success."

"I want my mother."

"James, I'm going to need you to pull yourself together for a bit. We have a visitor and we need a place to talk where we cannot be seen or heard. This, I'm afraid, is it."

"Oh, God," I repeated. "All right, I'll patch myself up. Just as long as I don't have to move."

My head still swimming, legs of rubber, I cleaned up and dressed while Alex made my bed and aired the fetid smell of plague out of the room, bustling about with his usual implacable efficiency. I, in contrast, was completely spent with ten minutes of sustained activity and propped myself up in an armchair to await our guest. I dozed off, wanting no more than to be left alone, not only because I still felt so dizzy and nauseated, but a certain vanity makes me dislike being seen thus.

"James. James? Wake up, old man."

I opened my eyes. Our guest was a young woman, or maybe an old girl, uncompromisingly plain, with round, shadowed eyes like a frightened racoon.

"James, may I present Miss Annie Brown."

"A pleasure, Miss Brown. I'm sorry, I cannot get up. I have just been very ill, so I'm not at my best. Please forgive me."

"Mr. Ramsay, there is nothing to forgive. Dr. Ross has explained your situation. I should ask *you* to forgive *me*."

"Again, there is nothing to forgive," interrupted Alex quickly. "James, Annie is John Brown's daughter."

"His daughter!" I exclaimed, wanting to rise gallantly but unable to. "I never even *knew* he had a daughter!"

"With so many brothers, a daughter tends to get overshadowed, besides which I was in what theatre people call a supporting role in this disaster." She shrugged in a gesture of self-explanation. "I've never visited with gentlemen in a hotel room before."

"You've never had a celebrated father in prison either," I countered, suddenly lucid. "Have you been able to see him?"

"They won't let me. It's all such a nightmare. I guess you know about my two brothers..."

"Watson and Oliver. We're so sorry..."

"And Frederick was killed at Ossawatomie in Kansas, oh, it's all too much. And now my father needs me and I need him too and I just don't know how to go on." Her composure disintegrated and she began to sob.

"You're not alone, my dear," soothed Alex. "You have us for a start, and, believe me, there are many friends out there in the night who will help when the time, er, when they are needed."

"I don't know what to do," wept Annie. "Neither my mother nor I can see him, so I came to Washington to see if there were anyone with common sense and there isn't..."

"National capitals seldom abound with it," said Alex. "Now, we'll see what we can do. You could begin by telling us what you knew of your father's plans, anything you can think of, you know, things he said, any thoughts he confided, whatever."

"I know my father so very little, I was surprised he asked me to help in this. Most of his inner thoughts he saved for my brothers...girls are not supposed to understand...now I've lost two of them and another in Kansas, and I just know I'm going to lose Father as well. These people are out for his head." A freshet of tears spilled down her cheeks. Wordlessly, Alex passed her his handkerchief.

Annie hiccupped two or three times, struggling to begin her narrative. "I'm sorry... all right. My sister-in-law Martha, she was Oliver's wife, she and I were engaged to do the housekeeping at the farm Father rented in Maryland. We moved down from our home in North Elba, New York, on, what was it, July the third. At first, it was fun, especially in the evenings. I would sit on the porch, watching and listening to the katydids and the whip-poor-wills. There were the fireflies and the shadows on all the old trees, and the mountain ridges on fine moonlit nights. I could have spent the rest of my days there...I knew what Father was up to, but on evenings like that, it just seemed very far away."

"The rest of your days? How old are you, anyway?" I heard myself ask.

"I am seventeen, Mr. Ramsay. I suppose that leaves me a great many days, but they don't seem worth much now. Anyway, things started to change in September. Fifteen boxes of what Father called 'tools' were brought down from Chambersburg; what was really in them were two hundred Sharps rifles and nearly a thousand of those awful poles with knives on the ends. The pastoral life was over, but the feeling now, it was like a Crusade or something."

"Which is essentially what it was," said Alex. "Something Romanesque about it..."

"Martha and I did lookout duty, warning the men if any visitor approached." Annie laughed wistfully. "One time a farm implement salesman came at dinner-time, and here we were with twenty-three men at the dinner table. Martha and I talked to him on the front porch and by the time he got into the house, only Father and my brothers were there. All the others had disappeared, taking their dinner, the tablecloth, everything with them."

Interesting as the anecdotes were, Alex needed to be informed. "This incident aside, Annie, what was the general routine of the place once the, ah, tools had been delivered?"

"The boys spent their time servicing the rifles and making things like, oh, pistol holsters, that sort of thing. Aaron Stevens, he was sort of a military advisor, he trained the boys in military tactics, but it was all done indoors, you see, twenty-three men chasing each other all over the farm and shooting at things would have looked a bit odd to the neighbours.

"When they weren't making preparations for the raid, the boys played a lot of checkers. Father subscribed to the *Baltimore Sun*, and that and an old copy of Paine's *The Age of Reason* were the only reading matter available. Between twenty-three men and two women, that does not go very far. It got to the point where any of us could recite the horses-for-sale advertisements for the previous three weeks." Annie was still taking her time setting the stage, as it were, as though postponing reference to the present situation. Certainly no-one could blame her.

"When we first moved to the farm, I knew Father even less than I do now, you know, from all the time he had spent away travelling and having battles...it's so curious, it all seemed normal at the time, but it was lonesome too, especially when I found out that the fathers of what few friends I could make all did sane and orthodox things, not likely to change or influence anything, but certainly good and safe. But Father spent a lot of time with me at the farm, as if trying to shoe-horn seventeen years into a couple of months, and you should have heard how he spoke of the two of you: 'Dr. Ross and the Young Man'. Could never remember your name, Mr. ...oh, now it has happened to me too. I'm sorry..."

"Just call me Young Man."

"Oh, I couldn't!"

"James will be fine."

"And call me Alex. Seventeen for us was not that long ago."

"That makes it so much easier," said Annie. "When I heard you were in Washington, I came expecting to find a couple of Gods..."

"And found a pudding-shaped small-town doctor and a fevered, unemployed civil engineer!" I croaked gleefully, breaking up into a fit of coughing.

"Medical services withheld," said Alex expressionlessly. "You're recovering too quickly for your own good. Please continue, Annie, and just ignore him. Pudding-shaped, indeed!" By way of reply, I barked wetly a couple of times and blew my nose.

"I feel so helpless with all these lies written in the newspapers," continued Annie plaintively. "I have no idea where to start putting them right, that is if anyone will listen. Who is going to listen to a seventeen-year-old girl anyway, especially if her position isn't exactly objective?"

"*We* are listening," I encouraged.

"But we are not United States citizens," reminded Alex bluntly. "We are just a couple of meddling colonials. I'm sorry, Annie, you didn't need to hear that, and, James, I guess I sounded a bit rude. My apologies. We do know many people, well-placed people, so please try to relax and carry on."

Annie sighed deeply. "To begin with, the newspapers don't even understand Father's plan correctly. The idea was not just to make a fast raid and then disappear into the mountains. That was to happen *only* if things went wrong, and didn't they just? He wanted to hold Harpers Ferry for a short time, maybe a fortnight, and terrorize - no, that's not a good word to use, is it? - well, coerce the local slave-owners and send agents into the plantations to rally the slaves. Then, with additional forces drawn from the sympathizers he thought would flock to the cause, he would gradually penetrate further south, right down to Alabama.

"Father has a friend, a Mr. Forbes, he's an English silk-dealer in New York, this Mr. Forbes has experience with that sort of thing. He fought in Italy with Garibaldi" (Alex's face lit up at the mention of his hero), "I guess about ten years ago. I heard Father telling Mr. Forbes that he figured on getting two to five hundred negro supporters just on the first night of the raid. It didn't happen that way, and that poor man from the railroad station...it has all gone so wrong." Her chin trembled.

Annie took a couple of deep breaths and carried on. "Never in my life, short as it may have been, could I believe anyone could be so single-minded. Father's entire being has been directed toward freeing the slaves and now it has cost me three of my brothers. Until the Harpers Ferry raid, there were so many different schemes...he was going to turn the President out of the White House..."

"Oh?"

"Oh, yes. I know how it must sound. He also talked about simply getting bands of slaves together and equipping them for defending themselves as best they could. Tell me, did Father ever mention a Reverend Higginson to you?"

"Gerrit Smith has talked about him," I wheezed.

"Isn't he that nasty bit of business that sounds like something from the Reign of Terror?" queried Alex.

"That's him," said Annie. "He told Father he favoured a civil war over everything else. Father originally picked Baton Rouge in Louisiana for the raid on the supposition that the slaves would be so militant..."

I snorted.

"Excuse me?"

"Pardon me, Annie. I escorted twenty-six slaves from Mississippi to Canada last year and got to know them rather well. But on first meeting, there was no way they could be called militant. Alex and I visited plantations throughout the South and most of the slaves we met were so conditioned to their lot that inertia rather than militancy would have been the primary adjective. Unless things were totally different in Louisiana, your father would have been very disappointed. He would not have gotten results as immediately as he would have needed. But don't misunderstand me here; once my group of slaves had some distance between themselves and the plantations, they showed determination and courage and a capacity for learning that made me proud to have been associated with them.

"The point here, Annie, is that so much abolitionist literature, well-meaning though it may be, paints a false picture of the average captive black, and I stress average. There have been at least four violent negro uprisings I can think of and there are others I cannot remember at the moment.* But those, of course, were not average situations, although they did get a generous, I might say *overly*-generous amount of exposure in the Abolitionist press. But the majority of slaves are not ferocious by nature or eager to take the initiative and rebel on their own. It's not a racial attitude, but a cultural one, because of how they have been manipulated by the white man. I think your father may have been deceived by what he has read." All through my brief monologue, Alex had been smiling like a proud father. It was what I called his "there's hope for James yet" look.

"That could be," said Annie sadly. "In any event, Father finally settled on Harpers Ferry, mainly because of the Armoury, but he said nothing until all the boys were assembled at the farm. They had thought he was just going to try an expanded version of a raid he did in Missouri last year, and when he told them what he had in mind at Harpers Ferry, well, Lord above. My own brothers, even, said it couldn't work, too few ways to escape, the Army to be dealt with. But John Cook, who knew the geography of the town better that anyone, thought it would work, and so did Aaron Stevens, who would say 'yes' to anything crazy or dangerous. He had a death-wish, that one.

"So to resolve things, Father said 'Well, boys, since so few of you are with me in this just and God-blessed venture, I reckon you had better hold a democratic vote and select a leader who'll do it *your* way.' He knew, of course, that there was no-one else who *could* lead, and so the sheep were called to the fold.

"I have told you really all that I can. Martha and I were sent home a couple of weeks ago, our work done. We waited and waited for news and now, dear God, all this."

"Annie, my dear, you are a brave young woman," pronounced Alex. "I want you to know that as we are friends of your father, so we are of you, and we share your sorrow and distress in full measure. Judging from what I have been able to discover in the last couple of days, the best idea seems to be to try and see Governor Wise in Richmond, secure permission to see your father, and find out what arrangements are being made for his legal

---

*The rebellions, all black-led, that came to mind during this conversation were the "Gabriel Rebellion" of 1800; one in 1819 in Augusta, Georgia; the well-planned Denmark Vesey Rebellion in 1822 in Charleston, South Carolina; and the Nat Turner uprising in Virginia, referred to previously. Although these events were isolated, they were sufficient in fervour and commitment to put the entire American nation in a state of gloomy unease.

defence. Now, Annie, did you tell me where you were staying? I forget."
    "The Willard."
    "I will see you back, then. This is no hour for ladies to be unescorted."

JOHN BROWN'S DAUGHTER ANNIE.
COURTESY OF HARPERS FERRY HISTORICAL ASSOCIATION, HARPERS FERRY

CHAPTER THIRTY

Over the next while, we watched John Brown become larger than the life he was to lose, and over the intervening years, his name has lost none of its magic or mystery. The *Battle Hymn of the Republic* acquired its well-known "other" text, the one about John Brown's Body. And John Greenleaf Whittier added to the repertoire of poetry these apocryphal lines about John Brown's last moments:

John Brown of Ossawatomie,
Spake on his dying day:
"I will not have, to shrive my soul,
A priest in Slavery's pay;
But let some poor slave-mother,
Whom I have striven to free,
With her children, from the gallows-stair,
Put up a prayer for me!"

John Brown of Ossawatomie,
They led him out to die,
When, lo, a poor slave-mother,
With her little child, pressed nigh,
Then the bold, blue eye grew tender,
And the old, harsh face grew mild,
As he stooped between the jeering ranks
And kissed the negro's child!

How one is remembered is what counts for posterity; were it not for the incident at Harpers Ferry, John Brown would have been remembered by only a few as one who had led a notably chaotic and unfruitful existence. Originally from Connecticut, Brown at various times managed a tannery, speculated in land, bred race-horses, did survey work, sold cattle and sheep, farmed, studied for the ministry, and even contemplated opening a winery. This was hardly the background for a career as we generally understand it.

A venture in the woollen business collapsed in 1849, leaving Brown not only destitute but responsible for the grand total of twenty children from two successive marriages. When Annie had told us of her outsize family, Alex had remarked in wonder afterwards, "The man didn't sire those children, he spawned them."

An economic gadfly, Brown lurched from crisis to crisis, and his financial ability is reflected by his astonishing record of being involved in twenty-one business lawsuits in Portage County, Ohio, alone.

i am not an adherent to the idea of predestination. I would not say that

A SCENE INSPIRED BY JOHN GREENLEAF WHITTIER'S POEM,
JOHN BROWN OF OSSAWATOMIE.
COURTESY OF HARPERS FERRY HISTORICAL ASSOCIATION,
HARPERS FERRY, WV

I was necessarily *born* to be in the railway business, and as to my Underground Railroad activities leading to the present situation, absolutely none of it would have happened but for Alex. To me, it was all a matter of random chance. Brown, in contrast, was a fervent believer in predestiny, and I hope this does not sound misanthropic, but I suspect that in reality he ultimately took sanctuary from his own failures by addressing the wrongs done to others. I have said so much in conversation, not making myself too popular in certain company. But now America had her martyr, her monument, her Prometheus, and nothing I can do or say will likely change national sentiment.

I can say this with certainty, though: John Brown selected the abolition of slavery as his cause through compassion rather than being drawn into it through chance meeting, as I had been. The first seeds were planted in him when Brown was not yet twenty years of age. The spectacle of a hotel-keeper abusing a negro lad of about his own age left a thorn in his sensibilities, and when his various business ventures collapsed one by one, he took it as a sign that he was being directed away from the ordinary and mundane into a Christ-like career of helping others.

At the age of fifty-five, Brown settled his family on a farm near North Elba, New York, loaned to him by the opulently-landed Gerrit Smith, and shortly after left for Kansas to begin his career as an active crusader against slavery. Kansas, created as a territory by the Kansas-Nebraska Act of 1854, would, on attaining full statehood, be in a position of accepting or rejecting slavery. To press the issue, there were already two factions at work, the Border Ruffians in favour of slavery and the Jayhawkers against. Five of Brown's sons were members of the Jayhawkers.

John Brown assembled a freelance group of militia called the Liberty Guards, and in revenge for the Border Ruffians' destruction of the town of Lawrence, Brown shot five of their members on the banks of Pottawatomie Creek. Although the deed propelled him into national notoriety, he was never charged nor brought to trial, so chaotic was the state of law enforcement in Kansas. Alex, never at a loss for comparisons between Canada and America, remarked, "Slavery aside, that could never happen here. In Canada, the law is always one jump ahead of the people."

Free thus to roam at will, John Brown spread terror all along the border between Kansas and Missouri, and in the summer of 1856, he clashed with a force of pro-slavery Missourians, losing his son Frederick in the resulting *melée*. The place was Ossawatomie, the name Brown virtually made his own.

The Harpers Ferry raid began its long gestation when some of its leading characters began their ill-starred association with John Brown. John E. Cook, the captor of Colonel Washington, joined him, as did the group's resident thinker, John E. Kagi, and the reckless renegade, Aaron Stevens. Stevens was a particularly wild and woolly sort ("So very American," sniffed Alex) who had fought in the Mexican War and was subsequently jailed for striking an officer. Latterly, he had escaped and joined the Jayhawkers for further adventure.

On the night of December 20-21, 1857, the Liberty Guards struck again, crossing the border from Kansas into Missouri and delivering a rude Christmas present to the three plantations that they devastated by theft of slaves, livestock, and household items. Additionally, Aaron Stevens saw fit to shoot and kill the owner of one of the plantations.

If this were in fact justice, it was certainly executed with great economy to the public purse. Because of its irregularity, however, President Buchanan felt obliged to put a price on Brown's head, but so great was popular applause in the Northern states that nobody was prepared to deliver Brown to the authorities. In fact, those same authorities turned an eye so blind that Brown and Kagi lectured publicly in Cleveland in February, 1858 with no legal repercussion.

Naturally, none of this could go unanswered by pro-slavery sentiment. During the summer immediately past, which is to say 1859, a movement had taken root in the South denouncing "Northern tyrannies" and demanding full states' rights in the territories (of which Kansas was one), including the right to enact their own laws either for or against slavery. Whereas the Mason-Dixon Line had come to contain slavery to the South, the South wished to extend this odious institution westward. And should these demands not be responded to, the American union was in danger of disintegration.

It was no haphazard threat, either. That autumn, John J. Pettus, an avowed disunionist, was elected governor of what Gerrit had called the despised state of Mississippi, to join forces with his like-minded colleagues William Henry Gist of South Carolina and Andrew B. Moore of Alabama.

So our neighbour America was a conflagration waiting to happen. The firewood and kindling were all in place and all that remained was the match. Blizzards of words alone would not strike the spark; the Underground Railroad had supplied a few dull coals, but it would have to be sudden, dramatic action that would light the fire. After all, had it not been the Boston Massacre that was the final propellant of the American people against the Crown in 1775?

The matchbox was opened at John Brown's "quiet convention" in Chatham, an event as much political as military, instituting as it did the "provisional government" to exist in parallel with the elected U.S. Government , its sole mandate the prohibition of slavery. How such an arrangement could ever work continues to lie beyond my comprehension.

Though the bleak chill of both autumn and unease was settling about the land, these were indeed palmy days for journalists. Alex and I collected two valises of news reports filed both during and after John Brown's trial, some fair and accurate, some poorly researched, some too heavily editorialized to be taken seriously. Brown's original mission of freeing the slaves had now blossomed into treason, into a conspiracy to tear the general social fabric to shreds.

Beneath it all, the scribes loved every minute of their craft, for who could resist writing about a character like John Brown? There were few reporters who, on a personal level, did not show some respect for Brown's level of commitment and courage, and there was even a sort of reluctant affection for "Old Brown".

The ailment that had stricken me in Washington, causing me some embarrassment at our meeting with Annie Brown, vanished a day later, to be replaced by the *joie de vivre* that comes in the wake of such misery. In fact, it was I now, rather than Alex, who was taking some initiative, for he, the poor soul, was too worn out with worrying about Brown, spying on the U.S. Government, and tending to me. And there was an additional worry now dawning on both of us: in this time of direst need, where was Gerrit? He had not responded to our telegraphed plea for money. We had heard nothing, seen nothing. It was as if he had fallen off the edge of the earth.

So accustomed was I to Father's accounts of lengthy preparations for trials, delays, adjournments, continuances, and so on, that the announcement of John Brown's trial, to commence on October the 25th, knocked the collective wind from us. At the time, we were trying to make some sort of constructive decision whether to stay in Washington and soak up the news like a couple of drones or to try to gain access to John Brown to at least let him know that we were still with him and hadn't jumped ship to the sanctuary of Canada.

Reports that the Charles Town jail was heavily guarded and Alex's discovery that one needed military authority just for transportation, never mind getting into the place, ended any thought of a visit. There was no time for the bureaucracy of getting clearance; it was a horrid, nightmarish time of complete helplessness as we sheltered impotently in Washington, continuing our total reliance on the newspapers as events unfolded.

John Brown, still bed-ridden from his injuries in the raid, lay on a cot for the duration of his trial. Although he had asked for a postponement on grounds of health, the trial proceeded without delay as Southern America and her collaborators demanded their pound of flesh. Two defence lawyers were assigned to the case, but so deeply felt was Brown's cause that three more attorneys journeyed from the North to function, I believe free of charge, and so he had an entire legal panel working on his behalf.

Part of the defence's strategy, which died a quick death, was to indicate to the court the presence of insanity in Brown's blood-line. His aunt had died insane, and even at the time of the trial, three cousins were confined to an asylum. Were Brown completely "normal", it was argued, he never would have undertaken the raid in the first place. Whether he was actually insane remains a matter of speculation, but suicidal he must have been, for rather than being thankful for his legal advisors' manoeuvre, he waxed most indignant to the court, declaring himself to be wholly responsible for his actions.

As evidence was unveiled to the court, a portrait quickly developed of

THE TRIAL OF JOHN BROWN, AT CHARLESTOWN, VIRGINIA, FOR TREASON AND MURDER.—[SKETCHED BY PORTE CRAYON.]

THE TRIAL OF JOHN BROWN AT CHARLES TOWN, VIRGINIA (NOW WEST
VIRGINIA). BROWN MAY BE SEEN LYING ON A COT TO THE LEFT.
THE DRAWING IS BY PORTE CRAYON, A POPULAR NEWS
ILLUSTRATOR OF THE 1850s.
COURTESY OF HARPERS FERRY HISTORICAL ASSOCIATION,
HARPERS FERRY, WV

a seriously deluded man whose great misjudgment had been of huge numbers of slaves banding about him, of Northern whites racing to his assistance, of Southern whites falling before his massed and righteous hordes. It
was a Romantic, magnificent vision with no substance; Colonel Washington's neighbour, Farmer Allstadt, described to the jury the spiritlessness and
apathy of the negroes he had observed during that incredible night at Harpers Ferry. And there had not exactly been a avalanche of white assistance.

Brown himself, from all accounts, was superb, composed and civil
throughout the trial, though in considerable pain. And a number of those
giving evidence spoke of his fair and gentlemanly behaviour during the raid,
even though his son Watson had died under a flag of truce. The charges
were multiple, consisting of murder, treason, and insurrection. The defending lawyers took the position that, first, Brown had killed only for self-
protection and not in premeditation; that because he had not sworn alle-
giance to the Commonwealth of Virginia, he could not be prosecuted for
treason*; and that, relative to the charge of insurrection, he had merely
abducted slaves and, contrary to the original plan, they took no active role
in the raid with the pikes we had helped to buy.

Judgement came speedily and was rendered on the second of November. John Brown, said all the jury, was guilty on all counts. The judge, His
Honour Richard Parker, asked Brown if he had anything to say before
sentence was pronounced. The embers of John Brown's fire glowed once
again, though briefly, as he addressed the court.

He spoke of what the Bible had taught him, of treating others as he
would want to be treated, of how he would feel to be in bondage himself
until those in bondage were set free. "I believe," he said, "that to have
interfered as I have done, as I have always freely admitted I have done, in
behalf of His despised poor, is no wrong, but right. Now, if it is deemed
necessary that I should forfeit my life for the furtherance of the ends of
justice and mingle my blood further with the blood of my children and with
the blood of millions in this slave country, whose rights are disregarded by
wicked, cruel, and unjust enactments, I say let it be done."

There was a brief silence, and then the dreadful words from the bench:
"John Brown, being that you have been found guilty of the multiple charges
of murder, treason, and attempted insurrection, and that no reasonable
doubt of your guilt exists, this court directs that you will be taken from your
place of imprisonment in the forenoon of Sunday, December the second
next, and that you will be hanged by the neck until pronounced dead. May
God have mercy on your soul."

---

*The Virginia Law of Treason covered the "levying of war against the
State, the giving of comfort to its enemies, and the establishment of any
other government within its bounds, the punishment being death". Alan
Nevins, *The Emergence of Lincoln.*

"May God have mercy on your poor country," said Alex sorrowfully to his old mentor, the poet/editor William Cullen Bryant, who had come from New York and was now with us in the offices of the *Washington Post*.

Hands in pockets, Mr. Bryant stared bleakly out the window. With a sigh, he shook his head, saying, "This country needs all the mercy it can get. It is a grumbling cauldron, a volcano, waiting to boil over in a great shower of God-knows-what. Right or wrong, John Brown is a hero and as of Sunday, December the second, will be a martyr, and as everybody knows, no-one has more power than a martyr. He probably thinks this is the best thing that could have happened."

"We've got to see him," urged Alex.

"Isn't it a bit late in the day for that?" I queried. "What good would it do? From what I understand, the risk is enormous, assuming you could get to him in the first place."

In listening to Mr. Bryant's discourse, all I could think of was my secret hope that Alex would just drop the idea. The thought of a conversation with a condemned man was more than I could absorb.

"It would do a *lot* of good," contradicted Alex. "We couldn't try to save him and he wouldn't want it anyway. But we should let him know that the march of freedom has not been halted in its tracks and that we'll look out for his family...oh, God, poor little Annie. But December the second! James, isn't that kind of irregular? Should there not be more time for an appeal? Is this typical of American justice?"

"If it *is* justice," I said, "it's the quickest I have ever heard of. That prosecutor, what was his name?"

"Hunter. Andrew Hunter," said Mr. Bryant.

"Thanks, Mr. Bryant... Hunter, propelled by the rage of his fellow Virginians. Whatever we may think of his views, on a purely professional level he did a hell of a job. Probably has it rigged somehow so an appeal gets avoided altogether."

"A martyr," repeated Mr. Bryant. "Once the abolitionists are in a position to canonize Brown as their own saint..."

"St. John of Ossawatomie," I interjected.

"He would like that," from Alex. "Sorry, Mr. Bryant. We didn't mean to interrupt."

"It's all right, gentlemen. It *does* have a ring to it, doesn't it? What was I saying...the movement will strengthen and it is conceivable that an entire army of martyrs might spring up, like a phantom regiment, ready to do battle to the death with the infidels of the South."

"Even with Brown's failure to be remembered?"

"Failure does not deter Americans. They just try again in an effort that transcends determination and becomes pig-headedness. Romanticism is writ large in this country, in fact, I think it has yet to reach its full flowering. Oh, yes, urban America is acquiring the trappings of civilization: there is theatre and music, some first-rate painters and writers. But there's also a latent crusading spirit that needs an outlet. Settlement of the West is one, abolition of slavery is another; add the national fondness for guns, well, the picture becomes pretty obvious."

"A fanatic Brown may be, but insane, I think not," responded Alex. "We have talked to the man ourselves and he never said one irrational thing."

"His quasi-Biblical mumblings were a bit hard to follow," I pointed out.

"You have a point there, James," said Alex, "but if the situation were presented to the authorities in light of the public perception of his insanity, it might improve grounds for commutation, if indeed he wanted it."

"Which he doesn't," said Mr. Bryant. "Anything like that would be up to Governor Wise anyway. Brown's own brother Jeremiah has certified in a letter that for at least two years he has considered John insane, at least as far as slavery is concerned, sort of a selective insanity."

Alex was so determined to see Brown that I soon weakened and consented, but we remained firmly moored to Washington, stuck in a quagmire of emergency regulations. Nobody, including its own residents, was allowed in or out of Charles Town without written military permission, and as is typical of any sprawling, monolithic bureaucracy, nobody knew whom to see for advice. The one fact to brighten things was the receipt of some money from Father, now a self-described "armchair abolitionist".

"Alex," I said in one of my rare displays of enterprise in his presence, "we may as well spend the damn' money on the train as on a hotel and see just how far we can go with this. Maybe along the way we can find out who to get permission from. Maybe in Harpers Ferry, hell, I don't know. Nothing to lose at this point anyway."

"You're right, James, we have to be doing something, anything. It reminds me of a year ago last summer, fumbling about in the South. I wonder if young Annie has had any better luck than we have. Disturbing that we haven't heard anything from her. I can't find her anywhere, poor dear. She reminded me of a hunted doe."

"Uh-huh," I grunted, an Americanism I had unconsciously adopted. "And why can't we find Gerrit? Where is the man? You don't suppose he could have just bailed out, do you?"

"Not likely, but don't forget that bank draft with his signature they found among Captain Brown's effects. He is probably just keeping out of sight for a bit."

We decided on the spot to try to see John Brown and caught, with about three minutes to spare, a mid-morning express to Baltimore. As we stowed our luggage, hung up our overcoats, and settled into the prickly plush seats, I was moved to remark, "I need this. It's so nice and ordinary!"

"I'm starting to think, James, there might be something to your affection for trains after all. Trains don't hate each other or play stupid games. You just light a fire in them and they go."

"Well, no, there's more to it than that..."

"Of course, dear friend. But a man-machine relationship is vastly simpler than man-to-man..."

"This is an interesting change of attitude in view of our initial encounter."

"Ah, yes, by the dear old bridge. Seems so long ago now. Well, whether or not animal migration routes get disrupted tends to lose its importance in the face of what we are witnessing, but I still have no intention of abdicating my original values altogether. Nature will be here long after we're gone, unless we ruin it altogether, but in the meantime we have an immediate and urgent situation to be looked after. Lord, it's hot in here. When you consider it's only November, this is a bit overdone."

Alex opened the window two or three inches. "Hey, fella, shut that there winda," drawled a voice from the seat behind us.

"Don't you find it hot in here?"

"Nah. It's cold. Now, shut the damn winda."

This was too much; suddenly I was back in Shelbyville, Kentucky, and I didn't like the sensation. I leaned over the back of our seat and, well, yes, I snarled, "We didn't hear you."

"Ah said, shut the damn winda."

"Jesus Christ, you've got a tongue on you!" I blazed. Alex winced, but said nothing. "This window stays open until you ask in a civilized manner."

"James, the man is not civilized. Don't waste words on him."

"Go soak your head, mister." A foul whiff of stale bourbon stung my nostrils, Murphy's Tavern all over again. Our verbal assailant had a gleaming, lobstery cast to his face and was dressed in a grey uniform of some sort. As he reached forward to take matters into his own hands and shut the damn winda, I noticed a shoulder flash on his tunic: "Independent Grays, Balto., Md." He slammed the window shut and Alex, his face tight with anger, started to get up.

"Hold your horses," I said quickly. "Have you been at Harpers Ferry?"

"Who wants to know?" asked Bourbon-breath.

"We do."

"Who the hell is 'we'?"

"Young man," began Alex, who was no older than the officer, "we are just curious. We are from Canada, on a, um, trade mission to Washington."

"Canada, huh? Gettin' some of our nigras, ain't you?"

"Yes, we are," said Alex with a touch of defiance, "and they are welcome, too."

"Should be here too, but they ain't, unless they're treated like livestock. Whole thing smells."

"You mean slavery?"

"Yeh. Hey, keep yer voice down, y'all hear? Never know who'll hear you. Yeh, this has been strange, all right." He sat down on the arm of my seat, the matter of the winda apparently forgotten. "Yeh, Ah was at Harpers Ferry the day it happened. Missed the action, but Ah don't mind tellin' you

Ah wasn't too sorry to miss fighting old Brown. What a guy. Time someone did somethin' like that. Ah hope there's a good bloody war and even if Ah have to move North for a bit, Ah'd love to take these Southern bastards to the laundry."

"We lied," I said abruptly. "We weren't really on a trade mission. We are from Canada, but we have been working for the abolitionists."

"You don't say! Ah truly admire what you guys are doin', but you watch your butt, stranger, 'fore someone shoots it fulla holes as a kitchen strainer. 'Round here near the Mason-Dixon,* there's no knowin' who you'll run into. Abolitionists, huh? Well, well."

"Since your sympathies evidently lie with the cause, young man, perhaps there is no harm in telling you that we know John Brown..."

"Yeh?"

"...and we are on our way to Charles Town to see him..."

"Yeh? Well, brother, you can forget the train out from Harpers. They won't let anyone board the bugger without permission from the C.O. Ah think it's still Colonel Lee. Dunno for certain. Been down in Warshinton with some sealed papers last few days."

"I guess we walk it, then."

"Forget that, too. They have guys out on roadblocks and all over the woods. Look, Ah'm headed there mahself, so mebbe Ah can try to help you get set up. Can't guarantee results, but we'll give it a crack. And, listen, uh, sorry about the winda. Ah went on a bender from eight last night until eight this mornin' and, well, you know..."

"We can live with it," said Alex pleasantly.

We made the connection at Baltimore with the afternoon local to Martinsburg, and very local it was too, crawling through the rolling hills and past the well-tended farms of Maryland, stopping to set out the mail, passengers, and assorted express at every settlement. Monocacy, of course, attracted special attention because of Conductor Phelps' now-famous telegram, and in any case was a major stop, serving as it did the nearby town of Frederick.

As on any of these trips, the sounds and smells of the railway enveloped us reassuringly, an extraordinary library of rattles, screeches, and jingles, the smells of lamp oil, of the inborn mustiness of plush seats, of the omnipresent wood smoke, even with the window sashes drawn tight against the dank chill of autumn.

Although our knowledge of Harpers Ferry was gleaned strictly from the newspapers and from *Harper's Weekly* (an intriguing coincidence of names), there was an uncanny sense of homecoming as the train rumbled

---

*The Mason-Dixon Line was surveyed 1763-67 to settle a border dispute between the colonies of Pennsylvania and Maryland. In the public mind, it came to symbolize the division between free and slave-owning states.

slowly into the gloom of the covered bridge over the Potomac River. Through the openings in the side we could see the river glimmering placidly in the twilight; and marching past in orderly procession were William Williams' pesky oil lamps.

"This is so strange," remarked Alex. "It looks just as I had imagined it. Look at all those soldiers, though. I would say the U.S. Government means serious business."

"That it do, with a lot of urgin' from the State of Virginia," said our military companion, Lieutenant Sam Chase. "You can count on it."

Off the bridge came the train, trailing wet plumes of steam, the wheel flanges squealing and rasping on the sharp right-hand curve into the station. "Harpers Ferry," called the conductor as though this were the high point in his daily journey, which it probably was. "Harpers Ferry, this way out. Change here for Charles Town and Winchester. Passengers for Charles Town must have a military pass."

"Hell," growled Alex. I felt my eyebrows shoot up. He must have really been feeling the pressure for such an utterance.

"Heh," said Sam Chase, "don't go worryin' just yet. You may have a purple Jesus of a time gettin' through, but lemme see what Ah can do." We descended to the militia-thronged station platform.

"Now, then," said our benefactor, "let's jest see who's guardin' this here now train...oh, shee-it, it's the Virginia boys. Hoped it might be some of ours."

"Ours?"

"The Grays, or at least someone from Warshinton. But these Virginia boys, my, Governor Wise has 'em on the go all the time, day an' night. Wants to keep up the excitement. Thinks he may run for President next year and this is how he gets attention. Well, let's jest try our luck. Captain, sir!' Our Grays officer snapped a salute to another officer, one with three silver bars on the collar of his tunic.

"Yes, Lieutenant?" Rather than "leftenant", he pronounced it "lootenant", an American linguism new to us. At least we were not too far gone to be able to absorb trivia.

"Have two men here," explained Lt. Chase, "wanna go to Charles Town and got no clearance. Couldn't find out in Warshinton who to see. Can you help 'em?"

"What is your purpose, gentlemen?"

"We're not going to try fooling with you, Captain," said Alex quietly in his Voice of Iron. "We wish to see John Brown."

"For what purpose?"

"Friends of the family. We want to assure him that his family will be looked after..."

"Mrs. Brown already has clearance and that's the only visitor he gets."

"When is she expected?"

"End of the month. Let me see my C.O., but Ah don't think Ah can do anything for you. Wait here, please."

In a few moments, he returned with a major, who eyed us glacially and said abruptly, "You are under arrest." This we had not bargained for.

"For what?" spluttered Alex. "On what charge?"

"This community is under martial law and all legal processes are under suspension. No charge is even necessary. Under the circumstances, you are accountable only to me, so no snotty questions, understand? You will be held in confinement until the night express to Baltimore comes through. And, Captain."

"Sir?"

"If these two show up in Harpers Ferry ever again, *shoot them at once.*" The Captain winced and Lt. Chase looked mortified.

"Is there a problem, Captain?" barked the major.

"Er, no, sir."

We listened impotently as the conductor of the connecting train brayed, "All aboward for Charles Town, Berryville, and Winnnnnchester!" That was normal; this was not.

Now that the Winchester train was on its way, huffing around the sharp curve southward toward the Shenandoah River, its guardians surrounded us, the two desperadoes, and marched us away to the baggage room adjoining the station, until recently presided over by the late Hayward Shepherd. Nearby loomed the Wager House Hotel, its windows glowing cosily in the dusk.

I had wearied of hotels, but I can assure you that one would have looked very good at this moment as we tried to seek a modicum of comfort among the grimy mail sacks, boxes of eggs, cases of preserves, and whatever other cargo that was destined for Baltimore on the very train so celebrated in the story of the Harpers Ferry Raid.

Alex and I were kept separated, presumably that we should not conspire to escape, and were under surveillance the entire time, even to the extent of having to relieve ourselves in a bucket under the black eye of a rifle's muzzle. It was my first time in confinement of any kind and even after my journey from Mississippi it was peculiarly unnerving.

We were each given a sandwich, straight from the kitchen at the Wager House Hotel, and then slept sporadically until the train should come, under the command of Conductor Phelps, to take us away on schedule at 1:25 a.m.

GOVERNOR HENRY A. WISE OF VIRGINIA.
COURTESY OF HARPERS FERRY HISTORICAL ASSOCIATION,
HARPERS FERRY, WV

CHAPTER THIRTY-ONE

Alex called it lack of backbone, I called it being realistic. Whatever it was, I still found myself being persuaded to do things his way. I was not, as I wished, on my way home, but back to Richmond for an audience with Governor Henry A. Wise of Virginia. Funds were so low now that we had to resort to telegraphing Father for more money and I was becoming very uncomfortable over it, but to Alex lack of money was but a minor nuisance, a fly buzzing about in the cosmos. He was far more interested in challenging Governor Wise's reputation for intransigence.

We were bidden to wait in an overheated ante-room at the Governor's offices by a male secretary of such slender mien and pale complexion that he reminded us of a parsnip. He had *pince nez* that kept sliding down his nose as he scratched away with a quill pen at some bureaucratic irrelevance under the stolid gaze of past governors of Virginia, a company that included Thomas Jefferson. A conversation, occasionally punctuated with laughter, came from the Governor's office.

Our appointment was for two o'clock, but it was the better part of three by the time our predecessors, two large and florid lobbyists, departed.

"This way, please, gentlemen," invited Parsnip, fluttering towards the door like a friendly moth. "Governor, may I present Mr. Ramsay and Dr. Ross."

"Gentlemen, welcome. What can Ah do for you? No, never mind by the desk, come over by the fire. It's more friendly. Days sure are drawing in early now, aren't they? Sit down, sit down. Sorry about the delay. Ah have only about a quarter of an hour to spend with you, so what can Ah do? Where y'all from?"

"Canada," said Alex, our spokesman by established custom.

"*Canada*, hey? What brings you down to the Old Dominion?"

"We have an interest in the John Brown case and we wanted to discuss it with you."

The Governor's face became pink and a certain madness flickered in his eyes. This was not a good sign. "Well, well, *well*," he said. "Quite a business. *Very* hard to be an American these days. Ah'm not a betting man, but if Ah were, it would be mah inclination to put money, yes, good folding American money, that there's a Northern conspiracy behind all this. And Ah would further bet there's Republican support behind it too. John Brown is just the tip of the iceberg."

"He said he acted on his own," Alex reminded the Governor.

"He's a clever man. We never pretended he'd be an easy adversary..."

"Insanity aside?"

The Governor snorted. "Had Ah believed him insane, if Ah could even entertain a rational doubt of his perfect sanity, Ah would stay his execution, even at this hour. All Virginia should not prevent me. But Ah have no belief, no such doubt."

"But, Governor, supposing he were," I interrupted, "or you professed belief that he were, and he were committed to an asylum, it might save a major blood-letting. If he is hung, then he will be a martyr for the forces you feel threaten you."

The Governor's pink face was turning magenta as his blood pressure rose. "Feel threaten me? *Feel threaten me?* Young man, I know God-damn' *well* they threaten me, they threaten Virginia, they threaten the entire Southern way of life, they threaten ultimately the relationship of the states to the federal government. States are as they are by virtue of their surroundings, local requirements, culture, and personality, which you'll find out *if* Canada ever becomes a country. Why, hell, boy, half of you don't even speak English."

Well, I guess that fixed me, I thought, but I made no comment. Governor Wise sucked in a great breath to fuel his next utterance. "Brown still knows the character of his acts, even in what on the surface appears to be a lunatic adventure. An insane man does not engage in the methodical and extensive preparations *he* did."

The Governor glanced at his watch and, seeing some time left, continued his harangue as though determined to fill the air with words and generally control the situation until Parsnip should announce time up.

"If our fellow so-called Americans in the North choose to be our enemies over the matter of slavery, so be it. They have started already, the likes of those who sent arms to Brown in Kansas...from Canada, heh? Tell me, what do *you* think of this heinous crime perpetrated by *Captain* John Brown?"

With an enterprise rare in such situations, I said quickly, "We don't approve of *any* heinous crimes, Your Excellency. In asking our opinion, you certainly didn't miss a chance to editorialize. His means, the violence, we deplore and wish it hadn't happened. The motives are another matter. We applaud them with everything we have, with everything we are." I glanced sideways at Alex, who was busy rearranging his legs. He said nothing, but his eyes sparkled approval.

The eyes of Governor Wise, by contrast, blazed with such malevolence that he looked like a cornered animal. The magenta was now verging on purple. "What is *your* interest in all this?" he snapped.

Fuelled with derring-do, I retorted, "Frankly, sir, I was beginning to wonder if you'd ever ask. The true situation is that we are, very loosely, please understand, associates of John Brown."

The Governor sprang to his feet, reaching for a little brass bell on his desk. Presumably he intended to summon Parsnip and have us thrown in the calaboose. Alex had been in one already, but it was not in my recommended catalogue of life's experiences. The baggage room at Harpers Ferry had been enough; my mind locked even at the possibility and no words would come out.

Alex, however, was ready. "Governor!" he spoke sharply, almost a bark. "We are not part of any conspiracy. We had only the vaguest idea of what Captain Brown was up to in the first place and simply encountered him in the course of our work. I am a medical doctor and Mr. Ramsay here is a civil engineer. At least that is how we are declared on the public record. We are also abolitionists..."

"God-damn' busybodies, from across the border at that!" erupted the Governor. "What affair is this of yours?"

"It is a human affair. We are admirers of the great American humanitarians...John Quincy Adams...Theodore Weld..."

"Admirers! Hrumpf! And Ah suppose of Loyalist stock to boot."

"Perhaps," I snapped, although my own family had arrived in Canada long after the Revolution. "But nationality doesn't enter into this. As Dr. Ross said, this is a human matter. It's a straight and simple case of right and wrong." It was the most reckless and inflammatory thing anyone could have said, but this horrid man with the mad eyes was bringing out a side of me not generally made public. I expected a verbal holocaust, but Alex cut in before the Governor could clutter the air again.

"These great and good men, your Washingtons and Jeffersons and many others, came to deplore slavery in this republic and I don't think admiring them is necessarily an American prerogative."

The Governor smashed his fist down on the table by his chair, making the display of cast lead soldiers on it jump. "Have you come here to judge mah state, mah *office, mah DECISION*?"

"No, sir, we merely wish to see John Brown..."

"*What*!" screeched the Governor in an apoplectic frenzy. "You jest!"

"...not to save him or in any way compromise your due process of law, but to..."

"Ah should say not!"

"We," added Alex, "or maybe even just I, would be willing to go to Charles Town under military escort..."

"Damn it, Mr. Ross..."

"Doctor."

"You miserable snot-nose! Ah think Ah just said *no*! You people really have gall, not just from north of the Mason-Dixon Line, oh, no, but out of the damned *country*! Tell me, now, how are *Indians* treated in Canada?"

"Not too wonderfully, from what I understand," I said. "But they are neither massacred nor enslaved."

The Governor's cravat was pulsing along with his heart-beat. I hoped we were inducing a coronary seizure; men like this the Earth did not need. He fanned himself for a moment while a few silvery streaks of rain from a burdened sky stroked the windows. "Mah family's motto is *Sapere Aude*," he remarked with an air of cultivated patience, as if forestalling the coronary seizure I so devoutly wished. "Ah am wise enough to understand your object in wanting to go to Charles Town, in fact, Ah *dare* you to go."

The Governor's voice was rising again, there was a feral look to the eyes. "If you attempt it, Ah will have you both shot. It is just such men as you who have urged John Brown to make his crazy attack on our constitutional rights and privileges. You shall not leave Richmond until after Brown's execution. Who has put you up to this, that unspeakable Giddings? He is responsible for all this damned interference from Canada." Joshua Giddings was the United States Consul in Montreal and was using the position to further his own opposition to slavery.

"We've never even met the man."

"If Ah could *bag* old Giddings and Gerrit Smith and all the rest, Ah would hang them all without trial! For that matter, Ah would like to hang a dozen of your leading abolitionists!"

The Governor leapt to his feet, a bubble popping from the corner of his mouth. He gestured wildly. "No, sir! Neither of you shall leave Richmond. You shall go to prison and remain there until next Monday; then you may go north and slander the state which ought to have hanged you!"

"Since you have refused us permission to see Captain Brown," said Alex calmly, seemingly oblivious to the Governor's ravings, "we could both leave Virginia at once and save the state much expense and bother on our account." John Brown no longer figured in our plans. Escape was the priority.

"Did Ah not just tell both of you that you should remain prisoners here until Monday?"

"Yes, Governor, you did."

"Well, you just listen, then..."

"Governor...sir...you certainly did say that. But I am sure the executive of this great state is too *wise* to fear two unarmed men." Alex, that tongue of yours could land us in the calaboose yet!

Governor Wise's fingers tapped the table for a moment, sending the little soldiers into a drunken, wobbling saraband. Then he burst into life again, flailing his forefinger at us as if brandishing an imaginary pistol. "Well, you may go, then, and Ah would advise you to tell your Giddingses, your Greeleys, and your Garrisons, cowards that they are, to lead the next raid on Virginia themselves."

"Governor," I petitioned, "just so there is no misunderstanding by any of the authorities, could you be kind enough to write us some sort of a pass to get us out of the state?"

He gave me a poison-laden look and, without a word, went to his desk, took out an official calling-card, and wrote on the back:

> The bearers are hereby ordered to leave the State of Virginia
> within 24 hours. 3:30 p.m., November 27, 1859.
> Henry A. Wise, Governor.

"The sooner you go, gentlemen," concluded the Governor, "the better for you. Our people are greatly excited and you may regret this visit if you stay another hour."

We took our leave, minus the usual courtesies, passed the Parsnip at his post outside the executive office door, and went out into the bitter November chill, a chill in which we revelled. Anything was better than prison, except, of course, hanging.

"I trust, James, that you feel properly chastised."

"*Chastised*! I'd call it being drenched in *spleen*. Dear God, did you see the eyes?"

"Totally mad. They're all mad. Let's be shut of this place; the air is very bad here. Do you have your R. and P. schedule at the ready?"

"I have, sir," I declared. "Let's see...there's a train out at 6:35, arriving Washington at 10:40. Let us be on it."

Being insolvent, we skipped a stay in Washington. Instead, we endured, and I feel like a traitor saying this, three consecutive train journeys in the scorched heat of the Richmond and Potomac, the Baltimore and Ohio, and the New York and Philadelphia, all the way to the last-named city. We crept in slightly after midnight to throw ourselves on the merciful hospitality of our original contact in Philadelphia, the Reverend Harold Thompson.

"Lawd!" he rhapsodized. "So good to see yu once again! '*Course* yu kin stay heah, Ah wouldn't have it no othah way. No, nevah *mind* payin' for food, a person's got a right to eat."

With Sunday, December the second, looming on Rev. Thompson's kitchen calendar (printed for the African Methodist Episcopal Church by Cliff and Sons, Perth Amboy, New Jersey), we could distance ourselves no further from Virginia. We had to be among those with a feeling for John Brown, and no-one had more than Rev. Thompson.

"Lordy, Ah be real glad to see yu boys right about now. These is sore troubled times, ain't they? Sore troubled...we needs some tea."

Rev. Thompson, other than Gerrit Smith (whereabouts still unknown), had been our first accomplice on the Underground Railroad, and so I had a curious sense of having come full circle but with my perspective drastically altered in the process. From conjecture to reality had been a long and often terrible journey.

Over our tea, I gave Rev. Thompson a synopsis of our encounter with Governor Wise, making the comment, as I recall, that it looked as if Virginia had turned into an absolute monarchy.

"Governor Wise, he be an American Pontius Pilate," pronounced Rev. Thompson. "It's all comin' togethah..."

Alex's eyes, slitted with fatigue, popped open. "Are you suggesting another Messiah, Reverend?"

"Ah am indeed, praise be unto His name."

"You can't be serious."

"Leave it alone, Alex," I said in a low voice.

"Ah *am* serious," persisted Rev. Thompson. "History repeats itself. All de signs is about us. John Brown, he come to save us black folks from bondage and you white folks from de sin of imposing it..."

"*Us* white folks?"

"No, no, not yu boys, Ah means de ones down South."

"But as a clergyman," pursued Alex, "could you encourage the belief of Brown as a Messiah? His life has been a mess, there has been violence, he certainly wasn't chosen at birth."

"Ah certainly could. John Brown is a angel in disguise. Look at de signs."

"But, Reverend, wouldn't this be tampering with church doctrine?"

"The Book of Revelations allows for a second coming," I interjected. "Angels and salvation and such don't have to be confined to the past."

"Is this really my pagan friend, the engineer?" said Alex quizzically.

"You don't have a monopoly on Christianity," I said rudely. "I know a bit too. Please carry on, Reverend." I was at once appalled and fascinated.

"So many similarities wid de Passion, except de day of de...oh, Lordy, Ah can't say it..." Rev. Thompson shook his head; my eyes prickled at the sight of his suffering. "...on a Sunday, not a Friday..."

"A singularly obscene choice of a day for an ex...er, excuse me," fumbled Alex.

"But John Brown, he goan rise, right befoah de very eyes of his tormentors."

Whereas the flight of Jesus' body was a nocturnal mystery, John Brown, according to Rev. Thompson, was destined to go streaking heavenward in broad daylight before a presumably fascinated crowd of several hundred. So convinced was Rev. Thompson of the divinity of John Brown, so heartfelt was his belief, that we did indeed leave it alone. The whole thing was too surreal so late at night anyway, and we would be finding out soon enough if we were to witness a second Passion.

Our nights at Rev. Thompson's humble vicarage, though an improvement over the baggage room at Harpers Ferry or cotton bales on a Mississippi steamer, were a bit of a torment. We had to share a bed, Alex enduring my twitching and kicking and myself trying to ignore an unlovely tendency of Alex's nose to whistle. As a result, we did little sleeping and much talking.

Bizarre though it was, we were so intrigued with Rev. Thompson's hypothesis that we felt compelled to pursue discussion. We wondered if it came from him or from his congregation; he had evaded our challenges and, as we both knew from direct encounter, there was nothing more unyielding than a black person's faith. Alex did not think a second Easter was possible, at least not in this context, while I, the pagan, was in the curious position of thinking that it might, just might, be a potentiality; after all, was our age not called the Romantic? Did our minds and souls not reach out towards the very heavens in those uninhibited and expansive years?

And then, sleep still eluding us, our dialogue degenerated into the inane. Rev. Thompson was not entirely black and we tried to decide whether he was mulatto, which is to say half black, or quadroon, a quarter black.

"He's pretty light, even has freckles," yawned Alex. "Maybe he's an octoroon."

"Or a macaroon."

"James, don't be stupid. I love you like a brother, but just don't be stupid."

"I'm not," I said indignantly. "There is such a thing. It's what you call a black Scot."

"Oh, no. Spare me."

"And you call a black inhabitant of Picardy a Picaroon. Or maybe it's a chap who plays the banjo..."

"Enough, James, that'll do. Go to sleep and give the world some relief."

PROCLAMATION!

IN pursuance of instructions from the Governor of Virginia, notice is hereby given to all whom it may concern,

That, as heretofore, particularly from now until af er Friday next the 2nd of December, STRANGERS found within the County of Jefferson, and Counties adjacent, having no known and proper business here, and who cannot give a satisfactory account of themselves, will be at once arrested.

That on, and for a proper peri before that day, strangers and especially parties, approaching under the pretext of being present at the execution of John Brown, whether by Railroad or otherwise, will be met by the Military and turned back or arrested without regard to the amount of force, that may be required to effect this, and during the said period and especially on the 2nd of December, the citizens of Jefferson and the surrounding country are EMPHATICALLY warned to remain at their homes armed and guard their own property.

Information received from reliable sources, clearly indicates that by so doing they will best consult their own interests.

No WOMEN or CHILDREN will be allowed to come near the place of execution

WM. B. TALLIAFERRO, *Maj. Gen Com. troops*,
S BASSETT FRENCH, *Military Sec'y*.
THOMAS C. GREEN, *Mayor*,
ANDREW HUNTER, *Asst. Pros. Att'y*.
JAMES W. CAMPBELL, *Sheriff*.

November 28th 59

PUBLIC NOTICE OF NOVEMBER 28, 1859.
COURTESY OF ENOCH PRATT FREE LIBRARY, BALTIMORE, MD

JOHN BROWN ON THE WAY TO HIS EXECUTION.
COURTESY OF HARPERS FERRY HISTORICAL ASSOCIATION,
HARPERS FERRY, WV

CHAPTER THIRTY-TWO

Sunday, December the second, 1859, was almost spring-like, a belated Indian summer morning, a suggestion of hope and renewal. "It be an omen," pronounced Rev. Thompson as we walked to his church for the Sunday morning service.

The dread preparations for institutionalized ritual murder then under way in Charles Town weighed heavily on Alex's and my spirits; Rev. Thompson, by contrast, looked positively expectant. And his city of Philadelphia, why, it looked like the Fourth of July, a day of flags, hundreds of flags dipping and rippling in the faint north-westerly breeze.

Rev. Thompson's service, usually scheduled for 10:00, had been delayed until 11:00 this day to coincide with the certain demise and anticipated resurrection of John Brown. His church was called All Souls' and as we went in and took our seats, I made some remark to Alex about it being a "sincere" church.

"Sincere? What do you mean? Aren't all churches sincere?"

"No austere Anglican majesty, no Roman Catholic flamboyance, nothing bleeding..."

"Nothing visual to distract you from God, is that what you're saying? Yes, I see what you mean. Personally, though, I love a lot of the Roman art...look at all these people, will you?"

"They're all black."

"Please evolve, James. I'm talking about the number. Colour I've virtually ceased to notice. If there are even just a few more, the place will burst open like a cracker box."

Shortly, there was only standing room in the poor little church, which at one time had been a stable. There were still stone gutters to carry the by-products of the previous tenants, of whom a faint bouquet yet persisted. Marks of where the stall partitions had been were still on the walls; actually, apart from the removal of stalls and mangers and the like, the only change to the building had been the addition of splintery wood benches that were a menace to one's trousers. Alex already had one of those awful triangular rips in the seat of his and there was no money left to get it mended.

Not by coincidence, the service resembled one from Good Friday, and the general conviction that it was happening all over again was to me exciting, disturbing, and surreal all at once. The readings all had to do with the Garden of Gethsemane, the Last Supper, the Betrayal, and all at a time when in normal years folks begin thinking about Christmas.

Yet there was no direct mention of him who dominated our thoughts. The symbolism was implicit in the Bible readings and in the singing, all of which was *a cappella*, for the parish could afford neither an organ nor a pianoforte. And there was no hymnal either. Everything had been learned by what the historians call oral tradition. But what singing it was! In spirit if not polish, I would match the congregation of All Souls' Church against the finest choirs in Canada West.

In a last-minute planning of the service, Rev. Thompson had invited Alex and me to be guest speakers; Alex was more comfortable than I at the prospect, so he spoke for both of us. We were introduced as "our brothers from Canada" and warmly applauded, a demonstration that could not have occurred in a "higher" church. As Alex went forward to speak, I noted the time, a quarter to twelve, or as they say in the States, a quarter *of* twelve. I tried to envision the scene at Charles Town. Had it happened yet?

Alex was speaking now, an unvarnished description of the attitude toward blacks in Canada, explaining that it was not the paradise promised by certain well-meaning but fanciful Abolitionist literature. "What we *can* offer, though, is a place where you do not toil for a master, as many of you have had to, where you do not have to live in fear of beatings and abuse, of a mis-applied Fugitive Slave Law. You are protected by the law, like anyone else, and if you are a man, you can even vote...my friends, it is over, it is finished."

A distant church bell was tolling, then another and yet another, until the very air of Philadelphia was an inferno of bells.   Alex stepped aside and Rev. Thompson led the congregation in singing *My Lord, What a Mourning:*

You'll hear the trumpet sound
To wake the nations underground,
Looking to my God's right hand,
When the stars begin to fall

My Lord, what a mourning,
When the stars begin to fall....

I turned hot and cold all over, nearly overwhelmed by the singing and the ringing.

At about the time Alex had discovered the triangular rip in his trousers, the final act in the terrible drama at Charles Town was just commencing. John Brown was taken by wagon to his Golgotha, a forty-acre field at the edge of town, from which could be seen the distant Blue Ridge Mountains shedding the last stubborn tendrils of morning mist. Stark and angular against the cobalt sky was the scaffold, the noose swaying obscenely in the gentle breeze. Soldiers surrounded the area, supported with cannon to discourage any attempt at rescue, and Brown was heard to remark, "I am sorry citizens have been kept out." But Governor Wise was taking no chances.

Brown himself led the way up the thirteen steps to the platform, as though eager to be shut of his worldly cares. He had declined the comfort of clergy, for there were so many of the cloth who endorsed slavery. He might have chosen a black minister, but, migawd, that was out of the question.

Nor was any friend permitted at Brown's side. He shook hands with the jailer and the sheriff. His life had been a shambles, but he was meeting death with the elegance of King Charles I at the hands of Cromwell. A white hood was placed over his head and the noose slipped about his neck. "Step on the, er, trap, please, Mr. Brown," instructed the jailer.

"Lead me please, I cannot see." A delay. "Why is this not being got over with?"

"More soldiers are arriving, Mr. Brown, and are taking their places. I am sorry about this, truly sorry. Are you getting tired?"

"No, not tired," came the muffled answer from under the billowing hood. "But don't keep me waiting longer than necessary."

The sun was perceptibly higher by the time the final troops were in position, making a human wall a score deep around the scaffold. Among them was an actor-soldier named John Wilkes Booth. So many soldiers. But right to the final moment, Governor Wise was taking no chances.

The jailer nodded to the sheriff. Some winter birds cawed in the distance; and then the sheriff's hatchet came down upon the rope that secured the trap as Col. Preston of the Virginia Military Institute declaimed, "So perish all such enemies of Virginia! All such enemies of the Union! All foes of the human race!"

Telegrams flashed forth over the wires of the railways and of Western Union to Washington, Baltimore, Philadelphia, New York, Boston, and Richmond:

JOHN BROWN EXECUTED
CHARLES TOWN VIRGINIA
11:41 A.M. SUN. DEC. 2 1859 END MESSAGE

And hardly had the wires into Philadelphia stopped humming than the bells started to ring and all those wonderful Fourth of July Stars and Stripes drooped sorrowfully to half-mast like falling eagles. Most of the North was a vale of tears that Sunday, but not at All Souls' Church, which exploded into hysteria the moment *My Lord, What a Mourning* died away. "Hallelujah! Praise de Lawd!" erupted the congregation.

The thought of a miracle in the nineteenth century had appealed to me earlier, not only as an event laden with Romanticism, but as a foil to the creeping ugliness of industrialization and urbanization. But in witness to this mindless pandemonium, I recanted in about three seconds. "This is horrible!" I shouted to Alex. "It's unbelievable! I want to get out!"

He put a hand on my arm. "No, wait. I don't know what to think, but this is almost certainly the only time we'll ever see anything like it. I'd like to see what comes out of it."

In the twinkling of an eye, John Brown had, for those who cared for humanity, been transformed from a mortal being to a national state of mind. All that Sunday and through the ensuing weeks, there were services and meetings in virtually all the Northern states. America's greatest writers and thinkers gave voice. Henry Wadsworth Longfellow called December the second the day of a new revolution. Henry David Thoreau called John Brown an "angel of light". Ralph Waldo Emerson referred to him as a new saint. To William Cullen Bryant, Brown was a hero and martyr.

The fervour outside All Souls' Church took a good two hours to dissipate and had evaporated entirely by late afternoon, when it was learned that John Brown's body had *not* risen, but was instead to be transported by train to its final rest at North Elba. I was frankly relieved that the supernatural had not taken place, but Rev. Thompson was heartbroken, prepared as he had been for the ultimate.

"De signs was all dere," he lamented. "How'm Ah goan look to mah flock now?"

"Reverend, there's no telling how these things turn out. None of us are soothsayers," I tried to soothe him, pitying this simple, kindly man in his mortification. "I think the biggest miracle of our time is yet to come. Slavery *will* die because of what happened today. It won't take long now, believe me." Now *I* was being a soothsayer.

"The signs are still there, Reverend," reassured Alex. "I just have this terrible feeling that a lot more than just John Brown's blood is going to be spilled before this country is wiped clean. We're all human beings, doing the best we can with what we have, so nobody's going to think badly of you if it didn't turn out exactly as you thought. But be assured of this. Slavery will yet be banished. It has to be."

Late in the afternoon of Monday, December the third, the winter sun was riding low over Philadelphia's suburbs of Bryn Mawr, Upper Darby, and Cynwyd, all good Welsh names. The oasis of warm weather had fled in the night and it was cold indeed on the platforms of Chestnut Street Station. Alex and I were not well-equipped for winter and we shivered in the knife-edged breeze that keened through the eaves of the train shed.

We were by no means alone. Crowded about us were hundreds of Philadelphia citizens, some white, furred, and well-to-do, and the rest, roughly-dressed negroes. Of the white "lower orders", there was little sign.

A whistle blared down the track. Heads turned. The setting sun brushed plumes of steam with copper as the saddest train in the world came rolling in, making all the sounds and smells that trains do: the creaks and clanks, the seared smell of hot brake shoes, all so comfortable and commonplace, yet this evening carrying the instrument of America's destiny in its baggage car. The train squealed to a halt.

"Excuse me...stand clear, please," commanded a member of the station staff, trying to manoeuvre a baggage wagon into position.

"No, suh, not necessary. We'll do it." The long pine box was eased to the baggage car doorway. Eight pairs of black hands reached for it and, through a parting in the crowd, bore it to the baggage storage room to await forwarding to North Elba. There were choked sobs, a few muted "hallelujahs", a few whites crossed themselves, a sprinkling of American flags could be seen.

"Employees Only - No Public Admission", said the sign over the baggage room door. It was ignored. This was the lying-in-state of black America's new saviour, not in the rotunda of the Capitol in Washington, not in a great cathedral, bathed in incense-perfumed candle-light, but in a railway baggage room, surrounded with crates and boxes, trunks, and bags of the United States Mail. Not an honour guard of soldiers with reversed arms or of cherubic choir-boys with bowed heads, but a silently surging crowd of the poor, the recently-liberated, and those who just wanted to help.

"Hello, Dr. Ross. Hello, Young Man. Thank you for being here."

"Annie! Oh, look, it couldn't be any other way. We don't know what to say. Being sorry is far from being enough."

"But you're *here*. That counts for a great deal right now. Let's go down to the station waiting room and sit for a bit. My feet cannot take any more standing. I'm supposed to be looking after Father, but he'll be safe here for a bit by the looks of it."

"You sound so matter-of-fact. Are you all right?"

"No."

"Oh."

"I was just getting to know my father and then they took him from me. I feel, well, numb. I'm just trying to do the job here the best I can. Mother has gone ahead, back to the farm. She's the one who is suffering the most."

The waiting room was chill, drafty, and cheerless, a drab-looking crowd assembling for the evening train up to New Jersey and New York. We sat down on a hard wooden bench, the kind with baroque wrought-iron armrests and legs. The station quaked to the arrival of an inbound train as life went on its uncaring way.

"Are you still with us?" asked Annie quietly.

"Of course we are," reassured Alex. "But we'd certainly like to know about some of our colleagues. We have heard nothing, particularly about Gerrit Smith. We're worried, but we didn't want to risk asking the wrong people."

"You're not going to like this," said Annie. "Everyone connected with the raid, including Mr. Smith and that lot, is facing charges, but instead of standing with Father, they have all covered their tracks. These fellows are fine for spending money and writing inflammatory literature and giving speeches, but when it comes to...oh, God above, what's the use?"

Annie gave a bleating wail and a deluge of tears pattered to the marble floor. Alex cradled her in his arms and rocked her like a bearded Madonna.

I paced about the station, the chill forgotten, such was the heat of my own anger and disillusionment. I remarked a few lines back about the wealthy whites we had seen on the station platform; it was plain that Abolitionists were people of, and I may as well say it, class, who saw more to existence than merely making and spending money. But something had gone seriously amiss, not just the failure of the raid, but the evidently hollow motivations of do-gooders who, once it was time to take some personal risks, had figuratively speaking taken to the woods. And we had liked and respected Gerrit so much.

"Shit!" I snapped savagely in my exasperation, just loudly enough to bring a station officer striding purposefully towards me. I held up my hand in a conciliatory gesture.

"Sir," sniffed the officer, "we don't permit that sort of language here. Rail travellers are ladies and gentlemen."

"Sorry, constable."

"Now, we have enough problems with these hordes of blacks..."

"Do you not like blacks?"

"Not in hordes."

"Well, I'll wager they don't like whites in hordes any better, especially whites with whips and tracker dogs." I turned on my heel and returned to where Alex and Annie were sitting. Annie was still weeping.

"What was that all about, James?" asked Alex.

"I was thinking about that snake-in-the-grass Gerrit. I don't like being fooled. And that officer made a snotty remark about negroes...damn it to hell, Alex, have we been wrong? You got thrown in jail in Columbus, I risked my arse to bring those slaves to Canada, and this lot, Jesus Chr...sorry...the first major operation goes amiss and they disappear."

"I know," sighed Alex. "Doesn't do much for your faith in humanity, does it? Annie, if you feel alone, so do we. And if we're alone together, we're still together." A few moments passed.

"I don't know who else is carrying on," said Alex in his iron voice, "but *I* am."

Oh, no, thought I in desperation. I have to get out of this chamber of horrors they call a country. I was actually drawing breath to call it quits when Alex, bless him, saved me from disgrace with his next utterance. "James, I think I'll go to Kentucky and do some organizing there, maybe work with your friend Mr. Sloane for a bit. Could you go with Annie and help her out?"

"Yes, but my gear is still at the Reverend's. The train leaves in half an hour. I don't have time to go and get it."

"Ladies and gentlemen!" boomed a voice through a megaphone. "Due to mechanical difficulties, the train to New York will be delayed an hour. We are sorry for any inconvenience."

"Get your gear and bring mine too," commanded Alex. "Thank the Reverend for me. Now, go!"

I went.

CHAPTER THIRTY-THREE

John Brown's legacy to our mission in particular and to humanity in general was perhaps summed up most succinctly by the *Republican* of Springfield, Massachusetts: "We can conceive of no event that could so deepen the moral hostility of the people of the Free States to slavery as this execution. This is not because the acts of [John] Brown are generally approved, for they are not. It is because the nature and spirit of the man are seen to be great and noble...His death will be the result of his own folly, to be sure, but that will not prevent his being a martyr to his hatred of oppression, and all who sympathize with him in that sentiment will find their hatred grow stronger."

The flames of hatred towards slavery and the institutions that propagated it were being fanned by ardent hands wielding mighty bellows. Daily there was an outpouring in the newspapers, a ceaseless deluge that often quoted Brown's injunction to his own family to "hate well".

While I felt a great degree of satisfaction at my role to date in the Underground Railroad, I wanted to extend it no further; I had no desire to be drawn into the war that was now inevitable and so I left America at my earliest opportunity, right after John Brown's funeral at North Elba. I had kept company with his daughter Annie all the way up from Philadelphia and I would be a liar, at least in the sense of omission, if I did not admit to some degree of attraction despite her visual plainness. She was one girl to whom one could honestly say, "I like your mind", for someone of her intelligence, sensitivity, and moral strength is rare in today's world. But the time was, to put it mildly, not right, and for all her maturity she was still but a girl.

The mystery of Gerrit's whereabouts continued to plague all of us. It was my supposition that, as owner of the farm at North Elba, he would certainly be present at the funeral, but there was no sign at all. "They say he's in hospital down in Utica," a depleted and careworn Mrs. Brown told me, "but I don't know why. I am sorry, though, because he has been so good to us and has done so much for the Captain."

"I am going home to Canada, Mrs. Brown, and I'll stop off in Utica to see what the situation is. I'll write you and let you know."

"Thank you, Young Man." She smiled wanly, knowing of John Brown's designation for me. "And thank you for being with us. It has meant more than you could ever know. God bless."

I made my call in Utica during a snowfall and it took me no little time of silent trudging through the thickening white to find the hospital, whose designation was "Mohawk Valley Asylum". Asylum? I soon discovered why. I entered its white, cell-like sterility, shaking the thick snowflakes from my coat, and could hear faint moans at regular intervals, punctuated by an occasional cry or scream. I began to wish I hadn't come.

"Yes, sir, may I help you?" asked the nursing sister in the entryway.

"I'd like to see Mr. Gerrit Smith."

"Visiting hours were over at four, sir. I am sorry."

"Well, ah...I'm just passing through...from out of town...on the train..."

"Let me see, then. Just a moment."

"Thank you, Sister."

Dispensation was granted by the doctor in charge. "Who shall I tell him is here?"

"James Ramsay. From Canada." New York was a state with its moral values in order and I felt no need for subterfuge.

Some time passed while I paced the entryway, trying to screen out the distant, dismal howling. I studied the notices on the wall about the joys of Christmas, feeling the cold dankness in my boots; and then the nursing sister returned.

"I'm sorry, Mr. Ramsay, he doesn't want to see anybody. Are you close to him at all?"

"Friends. Haven't seen him for some time. We were, uh, doing some...er, business together."

My delivery awakened something in the sister. She looked me straight in the eye with just the merest flicker and said, "I think I understand. Come in and speak with Dr. Fraser. He can outline Mr. Smith's situation for you."

Dr. Fraser was the saddest-looking man I have ever seen: wet poached-egg eyes, a face that sagged in folds like a bloodhound's, ear lobes that dangled like hot wax from a candle. "This is in confidence, you understand," said Dr. Fraser in a voice so quiet that I had to lean forward, almost with my chin on his desk, to hear him. "Ordinarily we don't discuss matters of this kind outside the immediate family, but we have a certain sympathy for yours and Mr. Smith's business...hardware and dry goods, wasn't it?"

"That's right, Dr. Fraser. Hardware and dry goods."

"We are speaking the same language, then. Say the wrong thing to the wrong person..."

"I know only too well."

The folds of Dr. Fraser's face rearranged themselves in recognition. "*Now* I know who you are! Your name rang bells."

"Really?"

"Mr. Smith speaks of you often, you and your friend the doctor...Milton or something?"

"Alexander Milton Ross."

"Ross, that's it." Dr. Fraser was now audible. "The two of you were, though inadvertently, part of the reason for his condition."

"I beg your pardon?"

"He felt he had not done enough for the Cause."

"Really?"

"He feels an unbearable guilt at being what he calls a back-room thinker rather than a man of concrete action. He thought Harpers Ferry

would be an easy and spectacular victory and then it went all wrong, innocent people died. Mr. Smith was, of course, part of the conspiracy and
became terrified at the prospect of the charges he might face, especially in
view of the papers with his name on them that Brown had left all over the
place. He tried to cover his tracks, but the fear and fatigue from loss of
sleep have put him in a state of nervous collapse. Remember he is getting
on a bit, so try not to judge him harshly."

"I'm not judging at all. Actually, I'm relieved in a way. None of this ever
occurred to either Alex or me. We thought he had gone cowardly on us."

"Affairs," explained Dr. Fraser, "had just gotten out of control. I think
he had been able to rationalize his own lack of physical involvement because of it being the domain of the young, but then..."

"John Brown was almost his own age."

"That too is part of the problem. It all comes down to a morbid sense
of guilt and shame and at the moment he cannot deal with it. I understand
he was a very witty and urbane man when he was himself. I hope we can
return him to that state. If you remember him as he was, it's probably just as
well you're not seeing him now." The bloodhound folds sagged back into
a state of deepest sorrow.

Feeling hollow and dispirited, I went on my way, leaving Gerrit with
his invisible but terrible wounds, wanting nothing more than to be able to
reach out to him and tell him that if not for the courage and enterprise of
him and his associates, there would *be* no Underground Railroad, no abolitionist movement, no raid, no anything. It is the gravest mistake to give
courage only a physical measurement.

There were no more westbound trains from Utica until mid-morning the
following day, and having but two dollars left to my name, I prepared to
spend the night in the station waiting-room. The night agent wanted me to
leave, but took mercy on me when I explained my situation. He let me stay,
provided I kept the stove stoked up, for he would be on duty for freight
traffic all night.

I arrived home late the following evening, depressed, bankrupt, my
clothes worn almost to rags, and with the first abrasive symptoms of a cold
lodged in my throat. Signs of Christmas were out and about in increasing
profusion, but they instilled no feeling of festivity and, God knew, no
thoughts of peace on Earth and goodwill to men. In my deepening illness, I
was dominated by thoughts of John Brown's family, trying to come to terms
with their triple loss and their continuing national notoriety.

I did get a letter, quite a long one, from Annie, and another from Alex:

Louisville, Kentucky
December 14, 1859

My dear old friend,
I am staying for the time being in Louisville, doing some systematic investigations for the next move. I <u>have</u> to do something;

the spectre of John Brown haunts me day and night, a ghostly American Prometheus adjuring me to carry on his work. It is so strange, such a shadowy co-existence with my "real" life. To sacrifice yourself as Brown did for the deliverance of those you have never even met is, I suppose, as close to being divine as is possible.

I am going to continue where you and I left off, starting right here in Kentucky, as from here I can get the greatest number to safety in Canada before the storm begins.

How I miss my homeland! Please think of me at Christmas and do look in on my poor, dear wife from time to time. My fondest regards to your parents.

Alex

It was not for a week or so that I realized how distraught Alex must have been not to cloak his letter in some sort of disguise, and the awful thought nagged at me that he might have been trying to uncover himself for a martyrdom of his own. Months later, I was relieved beyond words to be told that it was a simple matter of fatigue and carelessness.

In Alex's continued absence, Hester and I reached a sort of brotherly-sisterly accord in which I kept her company and cleaned up the soggy mountain of leaves from the garden she had been unable to tend. We behaved very well for the circumstances, although there was one near-lapse a few days after Christmas; she started to weep right in the middle of a conversation, I put my arms around her by way of consolation, and we held each other for fully five minutes. But that was as far as it went. Victorian morals reasserted themselves, although I hardly need to enumerate how difficult it was for both of us. Hester had never had Christmas with her husband and my own lonely, celibate, post-Ruth period continued to loom endlessly. Later, we complimented each other lavishly for being so responsible and mature in such a situation of great temptation and the matter was past.

Hester had to make ends meet by taking in laundry (my mother was one of her leading clients) and as a result she had fallen behind in her routine tasks, the leaves being but one. I took over, for the time being, the picking up and delivery of the laundry, and Hester in turn helped me to bring my newspaper files up to date, a formidable task in view of the diverse opinions unleashed by the raid on Harpers Ferry.

Little of the Canadian press had much that was kind to say about it. George Brown of the redoubtable *Globe* applauded the sentiment but not the means. His rival, the Toronto *Leader*, remarked on the insanity of the raid and warned that the South would stand no more.

Among the general populace, there was a certain sympathy for the Brown family (John's, not George's); a public meeting was convened in

Montreal, attended by nearly a thousand people, but only $66.86 was actually collected. The Legislative Assembly of Canada West did considerably better, collecting about four hundred dollars, but the donation had been cancelled during Brown's trial when the casualties of Ossawatomie were revealed.

Hester, who had traditionally gone to her family in Sophiasburg for Christmas, elected to spend the day with us as honorary daughter of Mr. Justice and Mrs. Ramsay, and on that account was the recipient of a gift from Father by her breakfast plate on Christmas morning: a book by Theodore Dwight Weld called *American Slavery As It Is - The Testimony of a Thousand Witnesses.*

"You won't feel too wonderful when you read it," said Father. "In fact, I suggest you save it until after the holiday season. But I think it will help you to understand what drives Alex."

CHAPTER THIRTY-FOUR

A lengthy illness of my mother in the first months of 1860 gave me the perfect opportunity to lead a "normal" life without squeamishness being my primary reason. As the days and months passed, the whole matter of John Brown had unnerved me more and more. Something I thought I had handled rather well at the time now kept returning to haunt me in the most vivid yet shadowy images, like some peculiar moonlit daguerreotype. It seemed as if America's new and brave civilization, so filled with promise a few years ago, was fast retreating to a condition of medieval barbarity.

Father called the Americans the "new Visigoths", a label to which I reacted with mixed feelings. Levi Coffin, John Pilkington, our Quaker accomplices along the Underground Railroad, the unseen Joshua Giddings, and, when fully functional, Gerrit Smith were not only great Americans but in the pantheon of the finest human beings to be found anywhere. At the other end of the scale were the likes of Major Ramsay, the bounty-hunters, and the apparently half-mad Governor Wise. The question was, who would outnumber whom in the event of the final struggle between good and evil? An Apocalypse right on the doorstep of my own Canada, to which I had developed a fervid attachment in my absence. The developing scenario was anything but reassuring.

Mother's illness was a moderately serious pneumonia from which, I am happy to say, she made a full recovery. But it was a long time of trial for her, a matter of about three months' confinement. Once Father and I had traversed the initial anxiety and knew that all she needed from now on was bed-rest, I went out in search of gainful employment and through some judicious wheedling was once again reinstated to the employ of the Grand

Trunk Railway. I felt like the cat with nine lives, but my other activities had by that time earned me at least minor celebrity status that I think worked in my favour.

The Grand Trunk had been an enormous success and so heavily used that its trackage was now in need of constant upkeep. For that purpose I was offered (and took) the position of Maintenance of Permanent Way Inspector for the Kingston sub-division. It was quite good fun; I was given the use of a conveyance that ran on the tracks, having two wheels on the driver's side and a third on a sort of outrigger opposite. It had a push-pull mechanism to propel it and before long, I was giving my upper body some wonderful development as I trundled up and down the line, rocking back and forth at the propulsion lever.

On a fine spring day, it was idyllic, especially on a down-grade, to roll along on what was essentially my own train, hearing the regular ka-thunk, ka-thunk of the wheels and the familiar and comfortable sounds of nature along the right-of-way. I came to be good friends with the station agents along the subdivision, often sheltering with them from rain-showers, having a cup of tea, having country conversations ("Sap's runnin' real good this year, Jim"), or simply passing the time of day as the telegraph snicked and clattered and, on a chilly day, a fire rustled in a Quebec heater.

Abolitionism in the current context seemed a digression from what I had been born for; the rail life, I reaffirmed, was my true calling and now it would be the turn of others to work on behalf of oppressed humanity. I would serve humanity by way of the ribbons of iron that shimmered and wobbled in summer's heat before me, and I could do it without being beaten, hunted, shot at, or hanged.

Alex, in the meantime, continued relentlessly the work I had now forsaken. I heard from him from time to time, terse, guarded little notes, many of them from a village in Kentucky called Harrodsburg. I wrote to him once or twice, gleaning from him that "business was good", but no more, obviously, could be said.

The summer of 1860 passed, a singularly pleasant one, for Mother was now fully recovered, lifting a shadow from our household. And as bait to keep me from running off on another scheme (not that I was so inclined at this point anyway), Father bought me the ultimate birthday present to play with during my fortnight's holiday in August. I had derived so much exercise from my railcar that I would feel terrible when *not* physically active, and the present in question was a nearly-new rowing skiff, a little beauty that I still have and which is called *Prometheus* as an oblique memorial to John Brown.

On the penultimate day of my holiday, I was rowing up to my mooring place, a tree on the east bank of the Moira River just below the first set of rapids. Leaning casually against the tree, hands in pockets, was the *soigné* figure of Alex, complete with jacket, waistcoat, and necktie. His beard was gone and it its place was a moustache that would have done credit to a desperado.

"Taxi!" he called with a wave. "On second thought, I ought to call you Charon."

"Lord Jesus, it's good to see you!" I blurted, scrambling up the limestone ledge at the river's margin. We fell upon each other like long-lost brothers, which, except for an actual blood connection, I suppose we were.

Alex eyed *Prometheus*. "Nice boat. What are chances of a peaceful river cruise before you call it a day?"

"By all means. Alex, meet my new friend *Prometheus*."

"Aptly named, my friend, and I think I know why." Alex looked stricken for a moment so brief that I would have missed it if not looking straight at him. Then he grinned and said, "Let's answer the call of the deep. This looks like fun."

We drifted lazily on the bubble-specked current, past the shelves of limestone that edged the river, as the rushing sound of the rapids receded.

"Ah, this is pleasant," commented Alex, lounging luxuriously in the stern.

"Start talking, Alex."

"Me? About what?"

"Don't be difficult."

"Me difficult? You malign me."

"Come, now, Alex. It's been the better part of a year."

"Well, I'll tell you. The worst tea in America is in Kentucky. It's so awful that I changed to coffee and now I rather like the stuff, although it needs a lot of sugar."

"Get on with it, Alex."

"Peremptory, aren't we? Oh, very well, James, I shan't try your patience any longer. I suppose the beginning is when I went to Louisville. By the way, you're hearing all of this before Hester. I've been home all morning, but not much was, um, said...what I mean is, there was a lengthy, er, dalliance, and when that was finished, there was another..."

"You don't have to explain it to me. All I can say is it's about time." Thank the Lord, I thought, for Hester's and my good Victorian prudence. I could never have lived with myself had I cuckolded Alex.

"God, what I have been missing," said Alex with more than a touch of reverence. "Anyway, I went to Louisville, but not out of any rational decision. John Brown was a pretty frightening person, but I came to, well, worship the man, thought of him as a deity, and I felt so...left out. I had to carry on with his work however I could and so I went to Kentucky because I felt I could help more people more quickly."

"You mentioned that in a letter."

"So I did. I had forgotten. I figured I could work better if I put myself in a position of trust, so I made it my business to find out who had the biggest plantation in the area. It belonged to, oh, isn't that the oddest thing, I can't even remember, except the name started with a B. I think I have strained my mind beyond functioning.

"I presented myself to a land agent in Louisville, describing myself as a Mr. Hawkins, an emigrant from Canada. Said I didn't like Canada because of all the blacks coming in there who didn't know their place."

"You must have felt just wonderful saying that."

Alex laughed mirthlessly. "I should be in the theatre, except this is more useful. This Mr. B.'s plantation was up for sale, so I trotted down to Harrodsburg with a letter of introduction from the bank. This was quite a big spread, over a hundred acres, and quite a population: eleven slaves and their children, and Mr. and Mrs. B-whatever and *their* three children, and snotty little beggars they were too.

"Mr. B. was, as they say, 'fixin' to move to Taxus' and wanted to take his slaves along. I spent some time acting as if I wanted to buy the place, roaming around and inspecting and all that, meantime giving the sales pitch to the slaves about Canada. There seemed to be some guarded interest, at least enough to give me a bit of optimism.

"In the meantime, Mr. B. had to go to Frankfort, the state capital, to get a copy of the title to his property for my inspection..."

"Frankfort," I interrupted, "is also the Bourbon capital of the entire world."

"I know, and I think it contributes massively to the collective mentality of the state of Kentucky. That reminds me, I have now had my own first experience of belly-bucking, though, thank God, only as an observer."

"Thank God is right," I remarked, "although I think you would have been a more effective opponent than I was."

"I have missed you, James, my friend. Don't make me change my mind. Anyway, just before Mr. B. went to Frankfort, he asked me if I'd like to go 'gunning', and I said yes, although I hate the bloody things, but, well, you know what that sort of situation can lead to, and it did. I was escorted on the 'gunning' excursion by a mulatto slave named Peter, very handsome chap he was, and he had quite a horror story for me. Mr. B. had sold his wife Polly to a hotel owner in Covington..."

"Oh, I remember Covington! Sold the man's wife, did he? What a bastard."

"Well might you say. Peter wept and it was so sad, I wanted so badly to help. I had a few odd dollars in my pocket, gave him my picnic lunch and the gun. I told him where to find your friend Jeremiah Fitzgerald, who would get him to Levi Coffin's house in Cincinnati to wait for me. He was *not* to use the gun except to avoid capture.

"Before Peter started on his way, I asked him specifically who else among the other slaves might want to leave also, bearing in mind the apparent interest that had been expressed, so I wasn't at all prepared for his answer. He said, 'Dr. Ross, dey be bad niggers. Ah wouldn't trust 'em."

"What? And he actually called them *niggers*?"

"He did indeed. Peter was an odd man out on the plantation. The B.

family had very skilfully allied the other slaves against Peter; Mrs. B. told me he was a 'wicked nigger', just wanting to do something in revenge for the sale of Polly. She just couldn't understand that he had any right to sorrow."

"Stupid cow," I said. "I suppose I should be beyond amazement by now, but it strikes me afresh every time."

Alex shrugged. For him it had become an old story. "It was a Wednesday. I told Peter I would go up to Covington, pry Polly loose, and if Peter left before Saturday night, we should converge on Levi's at more or less the same time. Peter became *so* excited; I had to caution him about showing his feelings, or Mrs. B. would suspect something was afoot.

"The whole thing was so lunatic. I look at the bay here, the trees on the shore, that bank of clouds reflected in the water, and the whole thing, this, John Brown, the Underground Railroad, all seem like an out-of-focus nightmare."

"That poetic bank of clouds looks like trouble," I said. "I think we had better head back in."

"I admire prudence in the seafarer. This really is a nice boat, James, very nice indeed. So...Mr. B. came back on Thursday minus his title. There was still a small mortgage outstanding on the property and the title couldn't be released until the mortgage was discharged, which let me neatly off the hook. It gave me the chance to leave without arousing any suspicion, and if Peter left around that time as well, it was just bad luck, wasn't it? I did get one more chance to talk to Peter and his gratitude was really touching; I recall that he kissed my hand as if I were the Pope or something.

"I left on the Friday, ostensibly for Louisville, but in truth for Covington. I found the hotel where Polly worked and it was the most revolting fleabag of a place I have ever seen."

"What?" I asked. "Worse then the calaboose in Columbus?"

"The calaboose did not purport to be a hotel. James, that sky looks really ugly now. Should we pull *Prometheus* up on shore?" We should, we could, and we did.

As we hurried along to Alex's house before the storm should start, along shady streets redolent with that over-ripe and decadent end-of-summer smell, Alex continued his saga: "The hotel-keeper owned Polly, as well as a man with whom Polly, as he put it, should 'take up'. He was a talkative type and for some reason took to me, poured bourbon and branch into me, which I accepted to gain his confidence...almost poisoned myself, oh, and this is where I saw the belly-bucking...looked like walruses mating, just ludicrous. This...uh, person..."

"I think you really want to say 'son-of-a-bitch'."

"James, you know I hate that kind of talk."

"Yes, I do know, which is why it must be all the more horrible to want to say it so badly."

"Very well, then, this...son-of-a-bitch...happy now?...said he had bought Polly for twelve hundred dollars but could sell her in New Orleans for anywhere from sixteen hundred to two thousand. I have been around this for some years now, but I just cannot get used to people having a price tag. I never will."

We were now at Alex's front gate. He hesitated. "Would you like dinner with us?"

"Oh, thanks, Alex, but not tonight. You need time with Hester. I'll talk to you later."

"I was rather hoping you'd say that. Give me a day or so, and then I'll finish my tale. It's a good one."

It was indeed, and in slightly edited form, went thus according to Alex: "Polly brought me my bath water that night and I verified her identity. I told her about the arrangement with Peter and that she must meet me the following night at midnight in front of the post office. It was like what happened with you; I had to tell her what the clock would look like. My word, the things you have to think of!

"It was quite charming - she was so amazed, she thought it was a dream and kept having to be told over and over. She became quite giddy and I had to warn her not to be too 'up' or her unusual behaviour might attract attention.

"I went down to breakfast a bit late the following morning, hoping to be able to talk to Polly again and generally refresh her on her instructions, and as luck would have it, she was assigned to wait on my table. 'Tonight at midnight for sure,'" I whispered.

"'God will help me, massa, Ah'll try,' she whispered back."

"You're really good at the dialect," I complimented.

"It's almost second nature by now," responded Alex. "I made the arrangements with a couple of boat-men across the river in Cincinnati that Levi had recommended, and villainous-looking types they were too. They were like maritime versions of those outlaws you read about these days, but, Lord, James, you should have seen them move a boat.

"So off we went that night in the boat, crossing over to Covington and timing our arrival for midnight. There, according to plan, was Polly on the shore...sounds like a folk-song...right in front of the post office. And just as she was getting into the boat, there was this policeman..."

"Oh, shit," I said apprehensively.

Alex ignored my profanity and continued, "He asked me what my business was, on the water at such an hour. Polly gasped like a whale about to sound and all I could think of was just trying to buy the good constable off, really a bad idea since I was almost bankrupt. I gave him a dollar and mumbled something about it being 'all right'. It was so transparent as to be embarrassing and had the policeman taken exception, God only knows what would have happened to me, but he just touched his cap, said 'Thank you, sir, and a good night to you' and disappeared into the darkness.

"He *had* to have been a sympathizer to walk away from the chance of a bounty. Talk about sheer, random luck. So we had, as the British like to say, a good crossing. We connected with a cab I had waiting on the Ohio side of the river, decanted a block or so from Levi's house, and walked the rest of the way.

"I took Polly on the train to Cleveland the next day and retired to a friend's farm nearby to wait for news of Peter's arrival in Cincinnati. We waited the better part of a fortnight and were becoming pretty worried, and then came a letter from Levi that Peter had made it safely, but that his feet were a mess. I hadn't been able to get him shoes. And then, a couple of days later, a Monday, as I recall, another letter came informing me that box car No. 705 had been hired to convey one box of dry goods and three of hardware to Cleveland. Somehow Levi had had a copy of the key to the lock of the car made and it was in the envelope. The train was to leave Cincinnati the day after I got the letter, so I had to make arrangements in quite a tear.

"I went with my friend Ephraim into Cleveland and just as we were passing the American House Hotel, who should I see but the inn-keeper from Covington! I thought for certain I was going to have a heart attack. Far too young for such a thing, of course, but I wonder how many shocks like that a body can sustain.

"I don't think the man saw me, but just to make sure I wasn't followed, I sent Ephraim to distract him while I went down to the harbour to arrange passage across Lake Erie. Again Lady Luck was in a good mood; I found a Canadian schooner loading for Port Stanley..."

"*Mayflower?*"

"No, *Primrose* was the vessel. The captain was a Freemason, which always oils the way in these matters, and he planned to be on his way the next morning. He was also no stranger to the carriage of hardware and dry goods.

"So that was settled. I rejoined Ephraim down-town and he reported the innkeeper to be in the state of highest dudgeon over Polly's disappearance. He was travelling about, offering five hundred dollars in way of a reward. He was also on the lookout for me.

"To keep some distance between us and him, Ephraim and I spent the rest of the day in the tap-room of a tacky little hotel by the rail-yards, not the sort of place you'd look for Quakers and their associates. The train showed up about ten in the evening, a bit of money changed hands - where does Levi get it all, anyway? - and the yard-master, to whom this must have been routine, had car 705 shunted off to a remote siding where we could unload it without any interference.

"We loaded the cargo onto the *Primrose* just after midnight. There was quite a south-westerly breeze kicking up, just the right direction, and there had been some suspicious people hanging about earlier, so the captain decided not to wait until morning to leave. He did some things with an anchor that I couldn't understand, got the ship out into the harbour, hoisted the sails, and off we went. I have no idea how the man found his way out of that harbour, all those lights around and everything, very confusing, but before long, we were on the bosom of the deep, and some bosom it was, too, all these great liquid hills sweeping down upon us out of the darkness. The seafaring life is not for me, but for gentle cruises in *Prometheus*.

"Well, James, you know how often we lose sight of what we are doing. But when I saw Peter and Polly kneeling together on the wharf at Port Stanley, murmuring about the Promised Land..." Alex looked away and gulped audibly.

"I remember," I said. "It's pretty overwhelming."

"For a certainty," said Alex. "I took the two of them up to London and found them jobs at once in a hotel. You know, even if our country's hospitality is far from perfect, it still is hospitality and is really the only place for these poor people to live in security."

"What are your plans now, Alex?"

"Oh, well, I think it's time to consolidate things a bit, take a couple of months to travel about Canada West and see how our new citizens are getting along. The way things have gone since Harpers Ferry, I think we're going to be in for an exodus that will eclipse anything we have seen so far and I want us to be ready for it."

"Not to sound pessimistic," I said, "but do you think our good, white, so-called Christian fellow Canadians can deal with it? Quite a few haven't managed so well."

"They'll damned well *have* to," said Alex with atypical vehemence. "We may be beyond any choice. In any event, it'll separate the men from the boys where Christianity is concerned. And what our white brothers and sisters can be grateful for is that only the brightest and most determined blacks are likely to make it to Canada anyway, so all we can do is benefit."

Alex rose from the glider on our front veranda, where so many of our great conversations had taken place, patting his watch chain into position. "Well, my friend, home to my own bed and to my dear wife, who is the real reason for the easing of my activities. Why she stuck by me all this time is a mystery which I am not prepared to question. Now I must rest up and be ready for whatever God sees fit to send our way."

Chapter Thirty-Five

During the fall of 1860, I was back at work on the Grand Trunk. Alex, in the meantime, was leading a hand-to-mouth existence practising medicine on an irregular basis, generally deputizing for doctors indisposed or on holiday. When not so engaged, he spent his time visiting newly-arrived blacks in Canada West to see how they were getting on.

To our satisfaction, the negroes were finding more acceptance than before among the general population. Some, however, had become perceived as a threat because of their ambition and industry in contradiction to the popular vision of blacks as being layabouts when slavery did not force them to work. When concern of this was expressed, Alex would simply shrug and say, "Well, it's simple. Some of the poor white trash will just have to work a bit harder. There are always those who feel threatened by excellence."

During this time, I had the pleasure of travelling up to Owen Sound for a brief reunion with Agnes and Precious, who, having been represented as man and wife on so many occasions, had decided to make the partnership real and legitimate. I had a multiple role in their wedding, both to give away the bride and to be best man for the groom. The resulting choreography lent a faintly comic element to the ceremony, but the newlyweds were too happy to be anything but accommodating of the antics of what Precious called his "fair brother".

Back in Belleville, because of the continued upheaval following the year-past Harpers Ferry raid, Alex, Father, and I had a particular interest in the coming U.S. presidential election. To keep informed, we depended, as always, on George Brown's fine *Globe*. Then as now, it was a singularly cosmopolitan newspaper and by all odds the best source of information available to us, aside from the letters Alex was continually receiving from his abolitionist cronies.

We spent many hours clipping out pertinent articles from the *Globe* and organizing them into folders to understand and keep track of what was developing. On one such evening, I remarked, "I've never seen an election that required homework like this. If I were an American and didn't do what we were doing, my vote wouldn't mean a bloody thing."

"Most Americans *won't* be doing what we're doing," said Father. "Emotionally they're just too close to it. We can afford some objectivity, but I can tell you right now I wouldn't vote for Senator Douglas."

"He wouldn't get in anyway," said Alex with total assurance. "The Democrats will be the victims of their own division. One candidate in the North, one in the South, it's lunatic."

"I like the sound of the Republicans' chap Lincoln; it doesn't sound as if he supports slavery," I declared, waving a pair of scissors.

"So do I, James," said Alex. "Put those things down, would you? You're making me nervous."

"The whole thing reeks of revolution," I expounded, clicking the scissors. "You've got the slave issue. You've got urbanization of a rural society happening at an unholy rate of speed. The Southern states are obsessed with their so-called rights..."

"James, about those scissors."

"Oh, sorry. You know, we've felt and said some pretty awful things about the States, at least in the South, but at the same time, there are some wonderful people down there. I'm kind of fond of the place and this whole thing is rather like having a sick friend and it's frightening because it could happen to you."

"I don't think, though," put in Father, "that anything like that on such a scale could happen in Canada. We don't have the mentality for sheer size the Americans have. The slave problem is *big*. This second coming of the Industrial Revolution is *big*. The whole country is *big*. And whatever emerges from this election, whether some sort of civil war or not, will be *big*." The prognosis was not reassuring.

Our evenings of political speculation were livened up by a package from Levi Coffin of newsletters put out by the campaign organization for the Republican candidate from Illinois, Abraham Lincoln. This little publication was called the *Railsplitter* and was, for a presidential candidate, a pretty home-made effort. Its heading bore a mutilated likeness of Lincoln and the motto "An honest man is the noblest work of God", a worthy sentiment that was all but destroyed by the presentation.

Despite the public sobriquet of "Honest Abe", the *Railsplitter* made discouraging reading. Little was written about Lincoln and his political beliefs. The primary emphasis was on a series of tasteless and gratuitous attacks on Senator Douglas, Lincoln's Northern Democratic rival; Senator Douglas, by way of example, was Catholic and had once visited the Pope, an observation whose importance, even in our Orange-dominated part of the world, completely eluded us.

"Listen to this one," said Father. "Anyone presenting a thing like this in court would be instructed to re-write it. Here goes: 'The Democrats are pretty much bankrupted for arguments, but they have one last resource when everything else fails - everlasting "nigger equality". Of course there will be no "nigger equality" where there are no "niggers", and as the Republican Party proposes to save the (new) territories for free white men, while the Democrats leave a way open for their introduction, it is difficult to see how the slang phrase here quoted applies to any other party but themselves.'"

"Even if it was in quotes, I hate the word 'nigger'," I said. "And what the hell did all that say anyway?"

"Bad writing tells you nothing," said Alex. "Do we take it to mean introduction of negroes to the new territories as *slaves*?"

"That's what *I* would assume, at least from this," said Father. "So if that is indeed the Democratic intention and they carry it out, then your work and John Brown's death would have been for nothing. In spite of the *Railsplitter*'s garbled message, if I were voting in the States, it would certainly have to be on the Republican ticket."

So thought the majority of voting Americans. There is a lingering misconception that Lincoln won the election of 1860 because of his opposition to slavery, but as everyone knows, politics are never that simple. The reality was that, although Abraham Lincoln found slavery to be morally repugnant, to try to overthrow what was so long-established would be sheer political folly. The only congruency to found between idealism and political reality was to be on record as opposing the extension of slavery into the new territories in the south-west. And there were other considerations too, such as protection of emerging American industries from foreign competition and the administration of orderly settlement in the west.

So slavery was just a fact of life in the South, an institution that could not be shut down, an institution that would keep succeeding generations of Underground Railroad personnel busy until the end of time. But related to that, what vexed us was the idea of the rights of individual states that ran through the campaign like a malignant *leitmotiv*. The *Railsplitter* was so vague as to the Republican position on states' rights that, just to see what would happen, we wrote for clarification:

> Belleville, Canada West
> September 18, 1860

Dear Mr. Lincoln:
We are writing as observers rather than as participants in the coming election, but since we have been extensively associated with the cause of the Abolitionists, we feel that we have a vested interest in its outcome.
Our question is this: If any slave-owning states were to assert their "rights", such as they are, and break away from the Republic, what would a government headed by yourself propose to do about it? Would you allow secession of the so-called Slave States to happen, casting those poor wretches, the slaves, adrift with even less protection than they have now? Would you be prepared to return the errant state to the Union by armed force? Or is there a way you know of and we do not of settling such a situation peaceably?
We are sure many of your citizens must share these same apprehensions and we would be happy for your response to be made public if you see fit.
Thank you for your consideration in this matter.

Yours & c.

Alan Ramsay, Q.C.
Alexander M. Ross, M.D.
James Ramsay, P. Eng.

The response was neither directly from Mr. Lincoln nor illuminating in the least. It was a letter identical to hundreds of others and read as follows:

Springfield, Illinois
October 12, 1860

Your letter to Mr. Lincoln of September 18 last and by which you seek to obtain his opinion on certain political points, has been received by him. He has received others of a similar character; but he has also received a greater number of exactly the opposite character. The latter class beseech him to write nothing whatever upon any point of political doctrine. They say his positions were well-known when he was nominated and that he must not now embarrass the canvass by undertaking to shift or modify them. He regrets that he cannot oblige all, but you perceive that it is impossible for him to do so.

The letter was signed by Lincoln's secretary, one John G. Nicolay. It told us nothing, of course. But a bundle of Southern papers sent to Alex by U.S. Consul Joshua Giddings in Montreal (the same "unspeakable" Giddings that Governor Wise of Virginia had wanted to "bag") made some interesting reading on how the slave states were reacting to Lincoln's campaign.

The already-familiar *Mercury* of Charleston, South Carolina, described Lincoln as a "border ruffian...a Southern-hater in political opinions."

Our old friend, the *Richmond Examiner*, wrote of him thus: "...an illiterate partisan...possessed only of his inveterate hatred of slavery and his openly avowed predilections of negro equality." At least we were being told something. But the fact of Lincoln's distinguished reputation as a litigation lawyer in Illinois seemed to have had no impact on the *Examiner's* opinion of his literacy. The *Examiner's* editorial writer must have been awash with spleen anyway, writing of the bitterness of Lincoln's prejudices and the insanity of his fanaticism.

"They make him sound like another John Brown," I remarked. "If he is as they say, America is in for some rough times, but, what the hell, she's in them already."

Election Day in the United States was on November the 6th. I had my usual railway duties to perform, it being a Monday, but Alex, with his wonderfully flexible routine, was able to travel to Toronto and spend some time in the offices of the *Globe*, wherein he had connections, to watch the results coming in by telegraph. He maintained his vigil until the polls closed and thereby knew before any of us in Belleville that Lincoln had won the election.

The new President's home town of Springfield, Illinois, was understand-ably jubilant, addressing him immediately, although it would not be correct until Inauguration Day, as "Mr. President." Republicans in Pennsylvania

and New York, the two most significant states in terms of population, celebrated far into the small hours. Bonfires scorched the night all over the
North as the health of the new President was toasted deeply and comprehensively unto oblivion.

And in the South, in Charleston, the home of the vitriolic *Mercury*,
there were celebrations as well. Republican victory had been total. Yet the
burghers of Charleston celebrated with intensity and fervour, celebrating
because all doubts were now dispelled and the battle-lines were drawn. For
the Republicans, the Union came first. Total oppression could be expected
from the North with Lincoln in charge; the South had now, in its own eyes,
complete justification for breaking away and forming its own nation. Exulted the *Mercury*, "The tea has been thrown overboard; the Revolution of
1860 has been initiated."

CHAPTER THIRTY-SIX

The afternoon of January 1, 1861, was, like so many other New Year's
Days of my early life, something of an ordeal. It was Father's custom to
hold what he called his "New Year's Levee" in the manner of a governor-
general, a bit of pretension that had begun with his appointment as a judge
of the Queen's Court. On this day, all sorts of people converged on the
Ramsay residence: friends and colleagues of Father's, neighbours both near
and distant, people we never saw between the turn of one year and the
next. Defence and Crown attorneys, adversaries for 364 days of the year,
stood chatting and reminiscing amiably before the fire, bellowing with
laughter and reeking of cigars and whisky. Distant aunts clucked among
themselves.

Alex and Hester were on hand and great interest was shown in our
Underground Railroad activities. Speculation was rife as to the final outcome of the battle against slavery and on this, there were about equal
proportions of genuine sorrow for what was happening to America and a
certain nasty rejoicing, a supposition of the superiority of our peaceable
kingdom called Canada.

As Father was holding his "levee", so, for his final time in office, was a
weary and ageing President Buchanan in the White House. As if to match
the foulness of the weather in Washington, there was a palpable gloom that
could not be dispelled by the artificial gaiety of the party. Many of the
political community had already left for the South rather than endure festivi-
ties in what was clearly the bastion of Northern oppression. More would be
on their way during the next couple of months that preceded the swearing-
in of the new President, friends torn from friends by what they thought was
their duty.

Even as these colleagues now in opposition were taking their leave, a stand-off had developed in Charleston, South Carolina, between the government of that state and the U.S. forces occupying Fort Sumter out in the middle of the harbour. Over the matter of States' Rights, in particular the right of citizens to own slaves, South Carolina no longer considered itself part of the American union and viewed the presence of United States forces in its midst as an affront. Governor Pickens of South Carolina urged the surrender of Fort Sumter; a desperate proposal was also made that bloodshed could be avoided by the fort's sale to South Carolina. The fort's commanding officer, Major Robert Anderson, declared he would surrender only on orders from his government. The U.S. Government's position: Fort Sumter was not for sale and for the renegade state to acquire it would take an act of war. In short, the United States would not let go without a fight.

In hearing these things, Alex and I shared a feeling of having, in some small way, helped to set a juggernaut in motion. In contrast to the unease at our first meeting with John Brown, we now felt a guilty sense of exhilaration. If the abolitionists working peacefully could not put an end to slavery, an Armageddon might; maybe Rev. Higginson of the Secret Six was right after all. Each day now revolved around the afternoon delivery of the *Globe* as the story unfolded, slowly, very slowly, but definitely surely.

We had daily bets, not only in the family, but at our respective places of work, that war would begin within a week, war that would spread to places Alex and I had seen, to people we had known. In that context, our sense of anticipation retreated; even for the likes of Major Ramsay, a civil war seemed too nightmarishly extreme. And daily we lost our bets as negotiations ground ponderously along, both sides struggling to buy time.

There was a twilight quality about the whole episode. Father, of course, was eloquent on the matter of precedent. And to clutter matters further, there was no properly constituted organization or chain of command on the South Carolina side of the fence. In any event, as of January the 8th, South Carolina was the only state not considering itself part of the American Union. There was not much it could fight a war with anyway and needed time to ready itself.

The Union was now in dire trouble, trouble made worse by the lack of governmental activity in Washington prior to the inauguration of the new President. The *Globe* furnished an almost daily litany of horrors: Mississippi, along with Major Ramsay's plantation, pulled out of the Union on January the 9th; Florida went on the 10th, Alabama on the 11th. Georgia followed on the 19th, prompting Alex to remark, "This is like Queen Victoria taking the throne when Canada, India, and the African colonies were all leaving the Empire."

"Worse, when you think about it," I said. "If that happened, the United Kingdom would still be united. This is like having Scotland, Ireland, and Wales going their own separate ways. This is so bizarre, a revolution in the making, and yet so bound by diplomatic niceties. Everybody knows it's going to happen, so why not just get on with it?"

"The diplomatic niceties are the last remnants of civilization," said Alex, "but you have a point, James. All this is doing is prolonging the overture to an unspeakable drama. It's quite without precedent."

There was still loyalty to the Union to be found here and there in the Deep South, but at the same time there was a growing awareness of a momentum bound in a direction that few fully understood but nevertheless found new and exciting. On the passing of the Ordinance of Secession in Alabama, the port city of Mobile celebrated on such an epic scale of uproar as to make the Fourth of July look paltry by contrast: a one hundred-gun salute, fireworks that reddened the sky for a radius of fifty miles, the majestic thump and blast of brass bands. In the neighbouring and former state of Mississippi, there emerged a song called *The Bonny Blue Flag*, whose popularity was to engulf the entire South in a matter of days.

"Is there no compromise for these people?" said Father in exasperation. "Could the Southern states not be accorded some sort of special status within the Union?"

"That could only mean continuation of slavery, Father, and after what we've been through over it, surely you wouldn't want to be party to such a thing."

"No, I wouldn't. I just wouldn't want to be party to a war either. In law, there are usually ways to sort these things out, but all I can say is thank God *we're* not mixed up in this."

On the morning of January the 21st, the senators representing the Southern states rose in Congress to address their Northern colleagues for what was rightly suspected to be the last time. They wished each other well with regret rather than rancour, like, as Father observed, an amicable divorce on a grand scale. And now without a Southern voice in its midst, the United States Government moved to augment its shrunken domain with the admission of the erstwhile territory of Kansas as a free state, in a sense vindicating John Brown of Ossawatomie.

By February, six states had left the fold. All Abolitionist and Underground Railroad activities had been suspended as too risky, not to mention the disruptions to communications by the individual state mail services in the South.

Life did go on. The trains still ran and I continued my railway work to the sound of my hand-car's wheels and the bitter February wind moaning in the telegraph wires that paralleled the line. Alex was now associated with the hospital in Belleville and was likewise making a steady living, but, like me, with the continual distraction of far-off events. We could not, without thinking, name the mayor of Belleville. But we could have told anyone that Sam Houston had been Governor of Texas and had left his office when his state had voted itself out of the Union on the first of the month.

The border states wavered. They were not as formally dedicated to the idea of one human being owning another. And they did such a volume of business with the North, business which would obviously be disrupted under a different political alignment. Much of what would ultimately happen was contingent on the border state of Virginia, a state with a sterling reputation for leadership (Washington and Jefferson had both been Virginians), a state with Southern attitudes but with a strong attachment, despite the rantings of Governor Wise, to the Union, a state whose shoreline on the Potomac River was in full view of the capital city itself. Resolve stiffened in both the Northern and Southern camps and so compelling did the daily drama become that Father and I almost came to blows over who was to read the afternoon edition of the *Globe* first. To avoid our own bloodshed, we took out separate subscriptions; when hospital duties permitted, Alex brought his own copy and we would editorialize and debate far into the evening, quite often with Mother and Hester on hand, doing lady things like needlework.

"We have been there and we have seen it," I said to Father one blizzard-stricken evening when Alex was working late at the hospital, tending storm-resulting injuries. "Many in the South own slaves, some do not. But what is really at issue here is a way of life, a cultural thing so ingrained as to go far beyond legal and ethical boundaries..."

"Like the caste system in India."

"Exactly. We find it appalling, but try telling that to an Indian," I said.

"Universal acceptance doesn't make a thing right."

"I don't like it any more than you do, Father, you know that. But I think I can understand it. If the caste system or slavery were to be abolished, what for some people is a wonderful way of life would come to an end."

"Could *you* live like that, James?"

"Er...well, I have spent a bit of time as the beneficiary of slavery...shall I say the acceptable thing, or be honest?"

"Be honest."

"I could not in all conscience own slaves, but there is a certain appreciation of being cared for or having your business being done by people trained to perfect obedience. And I think we all like to dominate, whether it's pets...well, you *love* being in command of the courtroom...and a lot of people, I daresay, feel a certain boldness in the company of people they feel to be inferior to themselves. For whites, it's bloody pleasant down there, even if it is dead wrong. In fact, I would wager their way of life gives Southerners a longer life-span." I did not like the direction of our dialogue and I could sense myself drifting into a trap. It is not easy having a judge for a father.

"Very well, James, let us consider the lot of the black man if the status quo were maintained. As long as there were slaves, you and Alex would be working on the Underground Railroad, your work would never be finished, there would probably always be the Fugitive Slave Law. It would either have to be that way or all free citizens, and then there's the problem of attitudes regardless of the outcome. Let's talk about the Northern attitude towards blacks."

"Eh?"

"I want your opinion."

"Ah, well," I said, feeling as if treading into quicksand, "it's pretty much like right here in Canada. Where there are blacks, they tend to be isolated. Where there are none is where white people tend to be most liberal. Love the blacks as long as they're not on the front doorstep. Most of them, down deep, are convinced the blacks are not equal to them."

"And you?"

"My actions speak for themselves."

"You dodged my question."

I felt rising panic. "I despise slavery."

"You still haven't answered my question."

"Well, there is no point pretending negroes are not different."

"I'm not letting this go, son. I want to get some feeling about sentiment towards black people in North America generally. You see, I don't know any. I have to rely on you. How would you feel if the Simpsons moved out from next door and a negro family moved in?"

"I wouldn't scream and moan about property values, like some of the people in St. Catharines and Chatham."

"I didn't ask what you would say or not say. I asked how you would *feel*." Father leaned forward, his eyes boring unsettlingly into mine, eyebrows arched like black toothbrushes.

"It wouldn't bother me, in fact, I think I'd welcome it."

"To demonstrate how liberal you were?"

I almost wanted to weep, were it not unmanly. "Father! You know me better than that! Don't you think I haven't thought of this right from the start? Don't you think I haven't talked about it with Alex and Gerrit and whoever else?"

"Do you feel superior to blacks?"

This was terrible; I was not one hundred percent certain and I hated myself for it. "Those who came with me from Mississippi, well, a few were an exasperation, but many were equal to us..."

"Us?"

"Yes! Us!" I almost screamed. "The wonderful bloody white race, the great yardstick against which all other beings are measured! I might say I would have taken any of those people over that crew of white trash that lives just north of the station, you know, the ones in that shack with the chickens running in and out."

"Could you marry a black?"

"Would you want me to?"

"Don't answer a question with another one."

It was nothing more harmful than Father keeping his mind sharp between trials, but it was absolutely the worst line of questioning he could have taken.

"At one point, I actually wanted to. Father, let me tell you something...only Alex and Hester know this...on the trip from Mississippi, there was this girl Ruth..." I told the entire story, re-awakening the stubborn grief that had not diminished in the two and a half years since, omitting nothing, a great bubble coming and going in my throat. I related my sad conclusion concerning children of a mixed marriage, feeling an emotional equivalent to a burst appendix.

I had never seen Father like this; he was silent and ashen of face. "James, my son, I am so very sorry. Why have you kept this all to yourself?"

"I told Alex because he is familiar with black people and I told Hester, well, she's my own age and she missed Alex and I missed Ruth and it was sort of a mutual confession. I just didn't know if you and Mother would have understood..."

"Too old is what you're saying?" said Father with a sad smile.

"Well, uh, I just didn't want to shock you needlessly. I thought it would go away after a while. I was wrong."

"James, believe me, if you loved Ruth as much as you say and she made you happy, your mother and I would have welcomed her into the family. But, yes, about the children, I can see your reservations. Relative to how society would probably react, you did the right and honourable thing, but how painful it must have been for you. I wish we could have shared it."

"You did just now. Excuse me, I think I'll go for a walk."

"On a night like this?"

"It's no worse than what's going on inside me." I hugged Father, put on my coat, and went out into the storm.

CHAPTER THIRTY-SEVEN

Not since the Roman Catholic Church's Great Schism of 1036 had anything like it happened; America now had two presidents. At a convention in Montgomery, Alabama, the breakaway Southern states adopted a provisional constitution on February the 8th, 1861, and ratified it on the 22nd. Heading the new government was Jefferson Davis, a Mississippian of impeccable military background. In the event of a conflict, he would have preferred service in the field. But it was Jefferson Davis the convention wanted and it was Jefferson Davis the convention was to have.

Starting on a collision course with Mr. Davis was the legitimate President-elect of the United States, Abraham Lincoln, on his way to take up office in Washington. He left Springfield on the night of February the 11th for a meandering train journey to Washington. Its progress we followed in the *Globe* and its character quite endeared the new President to us. The journey was so informal and unpretentious that at Indianapolis station, the

President-elect stood in line for his dinner, the better, as he said, to mingle and chat with his fellow Americans.

This roundabout journey was to culminate in a truly alarming drama at Baltimore. Detective Allan Pinkerton, later the founder of the famous security firm, got wind of a plan to murder Lincoln while his coach was being shunted from one railroad to another. The operation made the coach exceptionally vulnerable, for it had to be dragged by horse along trackage laid on city streets and could not be isolated from the public. To allay any disaster, the Presidential coach was sent through its switching operation in Baltimore minus its distinguished passenger, who went in disguise aboard a regularly-scheduled train. The murder plot came to nothing and just how serious or real it was nobody knows to this day, but chances could not be taken. Even so, because of a less-than-conquering hero debut in Washington, the unfortunate Lincoln found himself exposed to considerable public ridicule, even before officially assuming office.

Under the cloud thus generated, Lincoln had but nine days to finish preparations for his inauguration. Even at this time, even with Jefferson Davis as President of the new so-called Confederate States, there were flickers of hope that the Union might not fall apart after all.

Major Robert Anderson still endured his exhausting isolation at Fort Sumter. Although separation was all but a *fait accompli* and a matter of regret for any Yankee, it could still be achieved peacefully. But there were persistent rumours that reinforcements had been sent by Washington, reinforcements whose appearance would be perceived as an act of war by the Confederate States. Because of disrupted communications, the rumours could not be verified, so as a precaution, Anderson had his forces on a twenty-four hour alert in case Fort Sumter was being set up for an attack by trigger-happy hotheads on the mainland. If it came to that, Northern forces would have to shoot their way in past Southern-held Fort Moultrie to bring assistance and a war would be on, whether anyone wanted it or not.

South Carolina's Governor Pickens aimed to have Fort Sumter in Southern hands before Lincoln's inauguration and put unrelenting pressure on the government of the Confederate States of America in Montgomery. Although Pickens was hardly the soul of patience, he was rewarded rather more quickly than is usual in governmental functionings. On February 12th, the Confederate Government pledged to resolve the matter of United States Government property within its realm, entailing any and all real estate from post offices to naval dockyards. As of the 15th, these were to come under possession of the Confederacy by negotiation, or failing that, by force. With Fort Sumter at the centre of public attention, it had to be made clear that if a war started there, it was at the behest of the Confederate government rather than local politicians itching for a fight.

As apprehension deepened daily in Charleston, there was apprehension as well in Washington, not only from the possibility of war within American borders, but from fresh rumours of a plot to kill Abraham Lincoln on Inauguration Day, March the 4th. Whether the plot was someone's individual initiative or rose from fears of a mob running amok was never established, but many breathed more easily once the day was over.

As if in mockery of the ceremonies in Washington, on that same day the new flag of the Confederate States of America was hoisted for the first time over the capitol building in Montgomery.

The outgoing American President, James Buchanan, departed his office commenting that he had done his best and that it was a pretty good best. He had, as he said, "acted as a breakwater between North and South, both surging with all their forces against me." After all that he had endured during those difficult years, he was thankful and relieved to return to his home in Lancaster, Pennsylvania, and leave the cares of public office to Mr. Lincoln.

The Inauguration, as things turned out, went without mishap.   The sun emerged in glorious fullness during the inaugural address; the people, clutching, as they say, at straws, viewed the sunshine as an omen of better things. After all, the border slave states were still in the Union, the Stars and Stripes still flew over Fort Sumter. Yes, slim as it was, there was still hope.

As Lincoln put on his glasses, someone in the crowd shouted, "Take off them spectacles. We wanna see yer eyes!" A spectator fell out of a tree with a crash of rending branches. But these were the only exceptions to an otherwise grand occasion.

The speech itself received mixed reviews. "Hand of iron, velvet glove," was the verdict of Alex's friend, Senator Charles Sumner. The *New York Herald* wrote, "The most extreme Southern men regard it as meaning war, while the more conservative men of the border states view it as conciliatory." Richmond, Virginia, was reported to take it as no less than a declaration of war, wrote the *Herald's* correspondent in the city that held so many bitter memories for me and Alex.

Northern Republicans were ecstatic, Northern Democrats apprehensive. In Montgomery, the Confederate capital, Thomas Cobb wrote that the speech "will not affect one man here...it matters not what it contains." Senator Wigfall of Texas, who had remained in Washington for the Inauguration, was moved to send a telegram to his home state, saying "INAUGURAL MEANS WAR STOP BE VIGILANT END OF MESSAGE".

The Charleston *Mercury* had the last word: "If ignorance could add anything to folly, or insolence to brutality, the President of the Northern States of America in this address achieved it. A more lamentable display of feeble inability to grasp the circumstances of this momentous emergency could scarcely have been exhibited. The United States has become a mobocratic empire and the Union of States is now dissolved." I still have my copy of that issue of the *Mercury*, dated March the 5th. Alex had one too, but I think he used it to wrap fish.

The new President was now fully installed in office, trying to digest the unpleasant news from Fort Sumter that Major Anderson and his garrison of eighty men were short on food, they were exhausted, they had held out long enough, they were in desperate need of reinforcements no matter what. Deciding enough was enough, the President clarified his own position, that the nature of his office demanded that he take an active stand against disintegration of the American Union as promised in his inaugural address, and that his stand would be made at Fort Sumter. If the Confederates wanted to fight, they would have to shoot first.

In point of fact, shots had been fired already, though not in hostility, as gun crews on both sides in Charleston had been maintaining and honing their dread skills. The Northern Federals and Southern Confederates, because war had not yet been declared, regarded each other as professional colleagues and fellow Americans in spite of all, and there were eloquent and neighbourly apologies whenever one side put the other in any danger.

A Union shot went awry, landing near Charleston's business district and eliciting a visit by Southern officers under a flag of truce to ask Major Anderson if he were trying to start a war. Expressions of regret and a small ration of the Major's dwindling stock of brandy put the embarrassment to rest. A few days later, the fort was struck by a wild Confederate shot and within minutes a Confederate officer was on his way to express penance. The whole strange business went on, day after day, being taken less and less seriously. The thought of Americans actually coming to blows with each other was just too improbable.

Alex, Father, and I thought the same. What had at first been alarming had degenerated in our minds to the status of an operatic farce. But the frustration of our Underground Railroad work being halted was almost unbearable, made even more so by our Canadian negroes still having friends and relatives isolated in the Confederacy. We had no way of knowing what those still in bondage might be thinking or feeling, and our only clue was an unsigned article in the January, 1861 issue of the *Atlantic Monthly* by a resident of Charleston that read in part, "Our slaves have heard of Lincoln - that he is a black man or a black Republican or a black something - that he is to become ruler of this country on the 4th of March - that he is a friend of theirs and would help them." For the nigras to have a Messiah would be likely just another of those danged things to rob decent folk of a good night's sleep.

Instructions from President Davis in Montgomery indicated that unnecessary bombardment of Fort Sumter was to be avoided, but if the Federal forces were determined to stay put, the fort was, as the military orders read, to be "reduced... as your judgement decides to be most practicable." And the garrison did indeed stay, the situation being brought to a head shortly after midnight on April 12 by the failure of negotiations and the last departure from the fort of Confederate emissaries.

A low, drizzle-laden overcast glowed evilly in the orange light of the bonfires and torches now dotting the shoreline of Charleston harbour. Faint sounds of barked orders came across the still, inky waters as Confederate soldiers went to their posts. Sundry clankings and raspings betold of great cannon being manoeuvred into position. There was a pungent smell of impending rain. At half past four, there was a flash, followed by a concussive thump, from Fort Johnson. Something like a great red firefly arched over Fort Sumter, bursting into an umbrella of flaming streamers and making the harbour as bright as day.

Somewhat over twelve hours later, I was at Belleville's substantial limestone station, having just completed inspection of some renewed sleepers to the west of the town. As at Charleston, there had been some rain, but it had blown eastward towards Kingston and now it was a beautiful spring afternoon, our first real day of spring. A warm breeze sent the clouds tumbling in the sky, their shadows pursuing each other over the fields and woodlots of Canada West.

I parked my track inspection car in its shed and went into the station to pass the time with the afternoon agent, Fred Parsons. "Hey, Jimmy," he said. I hated being called Jimmy, but I liked Fred too much to complain.

"Hey, Fred."

"You heard?"

"Heard what?"

"War. Good old U.S. of A. went over the edge this mornin', eh?"

"Lord Jesus Christ! How did you hear?"

"Telegraph. It's been jabberin' away all afternoon. Made train orders lots of fun."

"Is No. 6 on time? I've got to see the *Globe*."

"A tad off, I think. He was seven or eight minutes late into Trenton. Be here soon."

I went outside. God, war! And in good part over what Alex and I had fought in our own way for the past six years.

A steamy blast sounded down by the bridge where we had first met and the train came flailing giddily into the station, actually skidding to a halt with a hot, metallic smell.

"Easy, there, hogger," called Fred. "You'll give that thing flat wheels."

"Just get this crap off my train, friend. Gotta get going."

Off came the "crap": a dozen passengers, some soiled sacks of Royal Mail, several parcels, something in a great long tube, and the precious bundle of *Globes*. I pinched one and took it into the station out of the breeze. "WAR IN AMERICA", blared the headline. The lead story told of the uncouth rousing of Charlestonians from their beds by the sudden racket, of how they were yet watching the battle from windows, rooftops, and church bell-towers, for the fight would go into the small hours of the next morning. I tried to imagine such a thing happening in Belleville and it was quite beyond me.

I read about half the paper and then, judging that I was close enough to quitting time, set off at a trot to the hospital to find Alex, who was treating a small boy with a sprained knee. I read the article aloud while Alex worked wordlessly but for the interruption, "There you go, my lad. It'll hurt and be stiff for a day or two."

"Do I gotta go to school, Dr. Ross?"

"Oh, I think you should stay off it for tomorrow, " said Alex, a smile in his voice. "I'll write you a note...carry on, James."

I finished the story. Alex looked out the window, rubbing his re-grown beard. "That it should come to this...James, I want nothing less than to be back in it in whatever way I can. Our work must begin anew. This time it must be completed."

CHAPTER THIRTY-EIGHT

Now that the so-called War Between the States was in full cry and any Underground Railroad work was out of the question, Alex redirected his undertaking to help enslaved blacks by offering his services to the Union, the vehicle that in victory would put slavery in America to rest. Each evening after he finished his work at the hospital, he would write letters to various agencies of the U.S.Government, sometimes at our kitchen table. As often as not, he would casually include me in his offer.

"For heaven's sake, Alex," I protested. "If you want to do this, fine. I just feel as if I've been through enough hell over slavery. Others are looking after it now and I just want to get my career in order and make a life for myself. It's only by the grace of the Almighty that I got back in with the Grand Trunk. It's what I am trained to do. I can't throw it all away by quitting *again*!"

"Nobody is asking you to quit, old friend. This is simply a constructive way to use your vacation time."

"Oh, yes, plan my life, why don't you?"

Alex beamed benignly. "I am."

Some times Alex received replies, sometimes not. He had, for a time, a lively correspondence with Joshua Giddings in Montreal, who was directing Alex's name among the nabobs of Washington. For a spell, nothing developed, but towards the end of that fateful year, when the cold night stars were coming out early and *Prometheus* had been laid up for the season, Alex came crashing through our back gate as I was splitting some firewood. He was waving a letter.

"James!" he bellowed. "My prayers have been answered! You couldn't get away for a week or so, could you?"

I shook my head. "No, Alex. I used up all my vacation time in the summer."

"Miserable hedonist." Alex still had a knack for making me feel defensive.

"Well," I spluttered. "Well, er...nothing was happening and I didn't feel like waiting around. I wanted to make that trip in the boat to Picton..."

"Indulging yourself at the expense of enslaved humanity, hmmm?"

"You always know how to make a body feel good, don't you? Now, tell me, what's in the letter?"

"Oh, yes, the letter. Better still, I'll let you read it. It's from Senator Sumner. What a splendid chap. Look, oh, look, and be amazed."

UNITED STATES SENATE

Washington, D.C.
November 15, 1861

Dear Dr. Ross:
It was good to hear from you again, if indirectly. We understand from Consul-General Giddings that you have expressed a desire, though not a citizen of this country, of continuing to assist us in our cause against slavery.
The President has directed me to express his appreciation of your offer and to enquire if you may come to Washington to discuss the matter with him personally.

"Alex, the *President*! Damn the luck, I want to go too."

"Such is the price of your gross self-indulgence, although I know you would have been welcome too. Now read the rest of it."

Because of the way the conduct of the War has evolved, it seems as if you could do valuable work on our behalf from within your border.
We await your earliest possible response.

With all good wishes,

Charles Sumner
Senator for the State of Massachusetts

"I am so elated, I am completely unstrung!" exulted Alex. "James, I am a little nervous about this. The President himself...is there no chance you could come with me?"

"None at all, I'm afraid, but I'll lay aside my holiday time for 1862 so I can work with you again. That letter certainly got me steamed up, and working up here, well, I wonder what they have in mind."

I saw Alex off on the train for Washington a fortnight later, comforted only by the fact that it was *almost* 1862. It was so frustrating that this was not happening five weeks later. But I could not take time off without being let go from my job again and, despite my renewed feeling of mission, I was just not prepared to do that. Like Colonel, I had to rent my space in the world.

So I must therefore turn over the account of Alex's visit to Washington to Alex himself, who, his Falstaffian proportions preserved by Hester's homecoming dinner, offered this report:

"James, meet Surgeon Officer Alexander Milton Ross, United States Army Sanitation Commission. I'm even entitled to wear Union blue with a lieutenant's silver collar bar."

"Alex, you're the only person I know who collects armies. First Nicaragua, now the Union Army..."

"The Grand Army of the Republic, to use the full title. Even for a non-American, it makes the blood tingle. I have not yet taken tea with the Queen, but I have been to the White House for luncheon and was received with the utmost cordiality."

"What was President Lincoln like?" My question must have sounded like something from the lips of a stage-door johnny, but I had to know.

"Well," said Alex, "at first I wasn't too optimistic. He looked a wreck, poor man, you know, from all the strain and stress. I think it must have done something to his facial nerves. His left eye didn't open all the way and it gave him a curiously dissipated look. But he still has a great sense of humour. Just before lunch, he said to no-one in particular, 'The North against the South is like a cello against a violin.' I asked him what he meant and he replied, 'A cello takes longer to burn.'"

"Ouch," I said.

"I know," said Alex. "Funny but not-so-funny. Now, don't be duly impressed with this luncheon business. I was added on to a bevy of senators and congressmen and the like. But I was placed on the hot-seat almost immediately by Mr. Lincoln, who introduced me as 'a red-hot abolitionist from Canada'. One of my fellow guests turned to me and said rather disparagingly, 'Our problems would be over if all these here negroes would emigrate to Canada, as you-all seem so fond of 'em.' And the President said, 'It would be all the better for the negroes, that's for certain.'

"Well, this individual had really got my back up, one of those dreadful border Northerners who don't own slaves but dislike the blacks anyway and blame them for what has happened, as if they had wanted to be in America to start with. Ridiculous.

"I may have overdone it a bit, but I said, yes, it would be all the better for the negroes, for under our flag, the blackest negro was entitled to and freely accorded every right and privilege enjoyed by native Canadians..."

"And what is a native Canadian?" I interrupted. "Not my good Scots parents, certainly."

"Don't be technical, James. This was all on the spur of the moment and I'm sure the intent was understood. It is an interesting point, though, for another time.

"I went on to say that we made no distinction in respect to the colour of a man's skin. I anticipated that the man might say something snide about our being under a monarchy, and I covered that possibility by saying that under our government, every man and woman, whether black, white, or brown, has equal rights before our laws."

"Except that I cannot vote or hold public office," said Hester demurely from behind her knitting.

Alex's eyebrows shot up in astonishment. "Well, uh," he blustered, "nobody took issue with me on that one. But, you know, my dear, you have a very good point. As soon as the slavery business is finished, I shall take up the cause of women's suffrage.

"To carry on, now, when I had finished my remarks, not a soul was eating lunch. They all stared at me as if I had just uttered a string of obscenities. I thought, well, Alex, my boy, here you are at President Lincoln's table and throwing everything away with all sorts of imprudent remarks. These people cared nothing for the slaves, only about keeping the Union together.

"There was a tense silence, and then the President said in a bantering sort of way, if I wasn't careful, I might bring on a war with Canada. He said they had a big enough job on hand as it was."

Alex took a swallow of tea. "Someone then inquired why so many British and Canadians seemed so unfriendly to Americans from the Northern states when their cause was on the side of justice. I asked him how it could be expected any other way when the cause was presented variously as the abolition of slavery or reunion of the states. Anything said by an Englishman or a Canadian, whether in sympathy or not, is noted with surprise, while the most outrageous utterance and acts in their own country pass virtually without comment."

"That must have stung," I commented.

"I didn't give it time to," said Alex. "I said, 'Besides that, you cannot expect the sympathy of the Christian world in your behalf, while you display such an utter disregard for the rights and liberties of your own citizens, as I witnessed in this city yesterday'."

"What was that?" said Hester and I in unison.

"That's what the President said, and in exactly the same way. He was quite taken aback. I told him about seeing a U.S. marshal at the railway station, taking a coloured man back to *Virginia*, for the love of God, under provision of the Fugitive Slave Law."

"What?" I squawked in astonishment, dropping my teaspoon. "You mean, even with the slave states out of the Union, it's still valid and in effect?"

"It's still valid and in effect, believe it or not. I pursued the matter and was told by the marshal that the man had escaped to Wilmington, Delaware, and was being returned to his 'massa', who technically was no longer a U.S. citizen. I said I thought the Fugitive Slave Law would have been voided by the outbreak of war, but the officer's reply was that, as far as he knew, it was still on the books and was to be enforced. The President looked bitter and said, 'Isn't it lamentable what slips through the cracks in times like these? We'll have to put a stop to it.'

"After lunch, the President drew me aside. He is enormously tall, by the way, and I had to tilt my head back to look him in the eye. He told me that Senator Sumner had sent for me at his request. Said they needed a confidential person in Canada to look after the rebel emissaries here..."

"Here? Confederates?" I was both alarmed and amazed.

"Yes, here. Confederates. There is considerable sympathy towards them by the English ruling classes, partly because of the South being their main source of cotton and partly because they think of the South as a bastion of aristocracy. I think a lot of them would change their minds if they saw what it was really like. That aside, what the Confederates are doing is using British soil, in the form of Canada, as a base for border raids into the North and as part of a clandestine courier route for mail and diplomatic correspondence, since their own coastline is now blockaded by Union forces.

"The President asked if I would monitor their activities and report any schemes that I saw afoot. He commissioned me as an officer on the spot so I wouldn't be shot as a spy or something. The Confederate agents are centred in Montreal, so I shall go there for a while. Mr. Lincoln said all correspondence was to be sent directly to him through Consul Giddings, addressed to Major...well, I cannot tell you the code name. It's that secret."

"You're enjoying this, aren't you, Alex?" I said. Hester looked, not apprehensive, but merely resigned.

"To be honest, I am," admitted Alex. "It's exciting and it's worthwhile, although it is possible nothing may happen in the long run. But we shall see.

"Mr. Lincoln asked me to sleep on it and come to the White House at nine o'clock the next morning with my decision. He's an amazing man, the President. He has an aura of dreadful sadness about him, 'a man of sorrows and acquainted with grief', and yet there are some wonderful asides to his conversation. I guess that's how he stays sane.

"He said to me, 'Dr. Ross, do you know how the White House became white?' I said no, I didn't, and he said 'It used to be stone, but when your people burned it in 1814, it was so badly scorched it had to be painted. I'm glad our relationship is so much improved'.

"I went to the White House the next morning to say yes, and that alone was worth so much to the President. Obviously not too many of his colleagues thinks as he does; they'd like to restore the Union, but would be happy to leave slavery alone. He shook my hand until I thought my wrist would come apart, saying, 'Thank you, thank you, I am so glad of it'."

Alex sighed and said, "He's sitting in such a viper's nest...this man Seward, the Secretary of State, leads a group now that wants to write off the South entirely and annex Canada instead. There's even a song about it." Alex cleared his throat and sang to an approximate version of the tune of

Yankee Doodle,
>   Secession he would first put down,
>   wholly and forever,
>   And afterwards from Britain's crown
>   He Canada would sever.

"Great God," I breathed, feeling the colour drain from my face.

"It is an unspeakable prospect, isn't it? Like that Manifest Destiny idea..."

"It is, but there is worse," I said.

"What's that?"

"Your singing. And at the tea-table..."

"It *is* a vile little ditty, isn't it? It does not deserve impeccable musicianship. As for at the tea-table, please forgive my rudeness. I haven't done that since I was eight years old and got thrashed for it.

"You remember how nervous and awe-stricken I felt about meeting the President. Well, by this time, I felt so at home with him that I may have been a bit intemperate. I said 'Mr. President, if only *one* of the objects of your government was the liberation from bondage of the poor slaves from the South, I would feel justified in accepting any position where I could best serve you. But when I see so much tenderness for that vile institution and for the interests of the slave-holders, I almost doubt whether your efforts to crush the rebellion will meet with the favour of heaven.'

"I imagine those weren't words the President wanted to hear, but he was very gallant about it anyway. He said he sincerely wished that all men were free and especially wished for the abolition of all slavery in the country. He still considered the South as part of the Union, on temporary leave of absence, as it were. But the dreadful reality, he said, was that his private wishes and feelings must yield to the necessities of his position."

"Aren't politics wonderful," I said sourly.

"For a certainty," said Alex, helping himself to a scone. "But among its spider-webs there is hope. Mr. Lincoln said to me, 'My first duty is to maintain the integrity of the Union. With that object in view, I shall endeavour to save it, whether with or without slavery. I hope that does not disillusion you, for I too am a devout anti-slavery man. Let me tell you a story that may help you understand. Have you a few moments?'"

"And did you?"

"For the President of the United States? Oh, I think I did. He told me of having been on record in the Illinois State Legislature as being opposed to slavery back in 1839, so he had been at it for a few years. If the destruction of the institution of slavery should be one of the results of this conflict, which the slave-holders had forced on the Republic, he should rejoice as heartily as I. He asked in the meantime that I help his government circumvent the machinations of the rebel agents in Canada. There was no doubt they would use our country as a communications link with Europe, and also with their friends in New York. Probably they would make Canada a base, to annoy Americans along the border. The President's closing was, 'Keep us well posted of what they say and do.'

"We discussed some of the mechanical details of my mission - pardon me, James, *our* mission - and then he, the President of the United States, offered to walk back to my hotel with me! Said it was no trouble, it was right on the way to the Capitol, where he had a conference at noon. So there I was, strolling along the street with Abraham Lincoln! The President reminded me to report weekly and then went on his way. I watched him going down the street and of course all the passers-by recognized him and said good morning as if to the mayor of a small town in Indiana or Ohio.

"What a hellish responsibility! Twenty million Americans depending on him for the salvation of their republic, four million slaves looking to him for their freedom. I'm definitely going to need you, James, possibly at short notice. I'm off tomorrow at noon for Montreal, so I will bid you *au revoir* now. Even though this is a new game for me, even if it isn't the Underground Railroad this time, it feels good to be involved again. I have a feeling this is going to be very interesting."

CHAPTER THIRTY-NINE

The day after Alex left for Montreal, Hester, with a great air of intrigue, brought me a sealed note:

December 2, 1861

Dear James,
It occurred to me after I took leave of you yesterday afternoon that if I needed your help in a hurry and there was not sufficient time for you to arrange a holiday, I am enclosing a medical certificate, signed by myself, which you may use relative to your employer should the necessity arise. All you need to do is fill in the date to render it valid.
Should you have any qualms about this "arrangement", just remember how sick you are of the white man's exploitation of and cruelty to his dark brethren. The symptoms I have laid out on the certificate are concomitant to such a condition.

Yours aye,
A.M.R.

Just like the old days! It was written on stationery from the Belleville Hospital, from which Alex had abruptly sundered himself. I hoped nobody from the Grand Trunk would investigate too carefully when my own time came.

Nearly a year rolled by before it did, although my promotion to Assistant Road Superintendent of the Kingston Subdivision in March, 1862, was gratifying enough and a further elevation to Road Superintendent in October of the same year was positively exciting.

I spent my summer holidays, not on the water in *Prometheus*, but in Montreal with Alex. Although nothing dramatic happened, there was still a feeling of anticipation, as Alex had done much to penetrate the Confederate *milieu* in that city. He had not only accumulated an astonishing dossier on a wide assortment of Confederate agents and functionaries, who moved about quite freely in the belief that Canadians, being fundamentally British, were their friends. But he was actually on social terms with some of them and I had to admit to being impressed at his audacity.

"Don't be," said Alex cheerfully. "I found some of these individuals on my second night in town, right in this very tavern. Let us go in. I'd like to see if you can figure out how it was done."

"You in a tavern, Alex?"

"Me in a tavern and drinking, yet, you know, to blend in. Horrible. I'm up to sixteen glasses of water a day to flush it all out, but with you along, I can skip the drinking for tonight."

With my limited powers of observation, at least with people, I dislike being in a situation of having to figure things out. I would have made a very poor detective.

"Alex, I'm just going to end up looking foolish," I protested. "Why don't you save yourself the time and me the embarrassment and just tell me how it was done?"

But Alex was without mercy. "Just bear with it. The same thing that tipped me off may not happen tonight, but just watch and listen."

I thought I could detect some Southern speech from adjacent tables, but the place was so full of the usual hubbub of English and French that I could not be sure. We ordered dinner and since I had developed a belated fancy for ale, I ordered a bottle to go with my meal. When the waiter returned, he had my ale, a glass of water for Alex, and two pastel-green drinks for another table. He continued on his rounds as Alex stared expressionlessly at some men playing darts. I poured some ale, took a sip, and suddenly choked.

"I could have told you it was bad for you, but you wouldn't have listened," said Alex mildly. "Swallow it wrong, or was it a bad brand?"

"Molson's," I wheezed. "Only the best. Those green drinks...they were mint juleps, weren't they?"

"Good lad. That didn't take long, did it? Look at those people over there, just so arrogantly casual, operating practically in the open. Want to meet one?"

"A Confederate?"

"The genuine article, my son, a Rebel, an undoubted lover of the institution of slavery. That one over there...Philip!"

The Confederate in question turned, smiled, waved in recognition, crossed the floor to our table. "Philip," offered Alex, "I'd like to introduce my good friend James Ramsay." And to me, "Philip is from Georgia and is in the clothing business."

"Really?" I said rather coldly, recoiling from the alien sound of Philip's broad Southern accent right in my own country.

"Yes, sir, Ah am indeed in clothing. The business, that is, ha, ha! Fact, Ah am a supplier to our boys in grey - they're in grey 'cuzza me, ha, ha! - strugglin' for the very existence of our new country. Clothin', boots, we got 'em all. Lissen, Ah can't talk to yew at the moment, bein' we're discussin' a shipment in from Nassau, but, hey, lissen, we'll see y'all again real soon an' get acquainted an' hoist a julep or two."

"I'll look forward to it," I said uncertainly, the quiet desperation of my time alone in the South returning to life and engulfing me like a bad dream.

Alex leaned forward and said in a low voice, "He works for Louis Wigfall, who used to be senior Senator for Texas under President Buchanan. Savoury individual. Now he makes millions out of the War. I am going to bide my time, James, but when it comes, I am going to mess up Mr. Wigfall's operation so badly he'll want to skin me alive and hang me up to dry."

Alex never did mix up Mr. Wigfall to any great degree, at least not directly. But what he was to achieve in the overall picture far eclipsed what he had in mind relative to the Senator's ill-gotten business.

To a point, getting information out of the Rebels was astonishingly easy. They were friendly, they were arrogant, they were cock-sure, and they loved talking about their various exploits. But that was as far as it went; the talk was all of past exploits, but not of the ones to come. Those were the ones that most interested us.

So all that had been gained from my holiday was a sighting of the enemy. I went back to work, was promoted to Road Superintendent, and as befitted my new position, most of my work was done in an office, variously at Kingston or in a corner of Belleville station. With winter coming, it was a great physical improvement on being out on the line. The responsibility was far greater than before, but so then was the money.

With the responsibility came the decisions; one November morning, the weather was threatening and I was trying to decide whether to call out the snow crews. I watched the leaden sky from my office window, the one in Belleville, and as I did so, there was a knock at the door.

"Enter," I said imperiously. It was Eccles, the morning station agent.

"Enter, 'e says. Like bloody Buckin'ham Palace, eh? Look, I've got it off the wire there's snow in Port Hope, real bad and comin' this way."

"Very well," I said. "Thank you. I'll put the snow crew on stand-by."

"Very well," I was mimicked. Where did they get some of these people, anyway? Standards were slipping.

"Another thing," said Eccles. "'Ere's a wire to you personal, eh? Came in right after Port Hope." He hung over me as I read the flimsy.

MONTREAL, C.E.
NOVEMBER 22 '62 9:09 A.M.
GERTRUDE CRITICALLY ILL STOP
LAST RITES THIS MORNING STOP
PLEASE COME WINDSOR STATION MONTREAL SOONEST
END MESSAGE.
/S/ ALEX

"Bad noose?" asked Eccles cautiously.

"My sister. Oh, God, she's dying...oh, Gertrude..."

"Very sorry, Mr. Ramsay. Should I get Mr. McGregor to cover for you?"

"Please do. Thank you. I'm going to try to get the 10:57." I sniffed wetly and as soon as the agent had stepped out, I broke into a grin of anticipation. Poor, dear Gertrude...so unexpected!

I ran home, stuffed some belongings into a bag, withdrew my emergency fund from a jam jar under my bed, kissed Mother good-bye, and charged back to the station. The snow was in full blow now, drifting about the wheels of the baggage wagons parked on the platform and whitening the station windows. McGregor had reported rather sullenly to relieve me and the snow crews were already at work, clearing switch points and generally having good, clean fun in the snow.

The 10:57 was more like the 11:26, still not bad in view of the violence of the storm. The train hove into view in a fog of steam and blowing snow, the great oil headlight glowing in a yellow orb atop the engine. Aboard I went with a casual wave of my pass and spent much of the trip contemplating my own embarrassment at my treatment of Eccles. True, he was a bit objectionable, but give a man some authority and he will lord it over anyone. I was not immune, I realized, no better than those Southern grandees brooding in their plantations to await the inevitable.

I had been (secretly) elated by the telegram, but this new and awful revelation about myself depressed me. And as if depression weren't bad enough, the stove in my coach failed just before the stop at Prescott and now I was both despondent and freezing. While my fellow passengers sought accommodation in the other coaches, I took to the locomotive cab, the warmest place on the train, for the remainder of my journey.

I swung myself down as the train wheezed wearily to a halt against the buffers of Windsor Station, Montreal, retrieved my bag, and set out for the booking hall. Just inside the door was Alex, looking every inch the Federal agent, coat collar up, hat pulled low.

"James, thank the Lord! I was wondering just when your train would get here. Come with me quickly, I'll explain on the way." We engaged a cab, or as they say in Montreal, a "hippomobile", and set off for destinations unknown.

"I have evidence," said Alex portentously, "*strong* evidence, of a regular Confederate postal system routed through Montreal, but so far I haven't been able to nail anyone to rights with it. I have been so bloody frustrated, so totally ineffective...I was going to take the 9:00 westbound train to Windsor tomorrow morning to see if I could find out anything about Rebel courier traffic around Detroit. I was starting to think the people here were actually nothing but decoys.

"I have a regular cab driver, Jean Brassard, fine chap, too...he has an agreement with my hotel and is there on call when not on the road. I went out this morning, oh, just after eight, to make arrangements with Jean about getting me to the station tonight. He said he was sorry, he was already busy, standing in for his brother, who is also a cab driver and is home ill. Jean is a really chatty fellow and told me he was looking after a regular customer of his brother's, a lady who takes a cab from La Prairie to Champlain, New York, just by the border. She does this, Jean said, like clockwork every fortnight."

"A cab!" I explained. "That is a pretty expensive way to travel. What's wrong with the train?"

"That's what I thought. It didn't make sense. I think anyone going that way must be trying to dodge being checked at the border. You and I, dear friend, are going to Champlain to have a look."

Our "hippomobile" set us down at Central Station, from which we took the Champlain and St. Lawrence Railroad to Rouse's Point at the northern end of Lake Champlain. From there, we would take a cab to our destination.

The snow by now had abated almost to nothing, so Jean would be running pretty well to schedule. "If he leaves La Prairie, say, at 8:00 tonight," calculated Alex, "he should be in Champlain anywhere between eleven and one. We'll take up watch at ten."

"Just how big is this Champlain?"

"Not much to it. I've been there before. The lady gets dropped right at the hotel, so we'll get a front room and spy away."

There was no opportunity for dinner and I was quite disgruntled when we disembarked at Rouse's Point to be checked exhaustively by soldiers in Union blue. Despite Alex's credentials from the United States War Department, we were not spared; they rummaged through our luggage, made us turn out our pockets, checked the linings of our coats. After about half an hour of this, we were let out through a barrier that had been erected around the station grounds.

"You couldn't get away with much from these fellows," I remarked as we boarded our cab for the short run to Champlain.

"Of course not. But if you crossed the border on foot or by cab and paid the driver enough, you could give anyone the slip over obscure back roads, as I suspect our quarry has been doing. I would wager a lot of Montreal cab drivers are in danger of becoming rich. This war is probably the best thing that ever happened to them."

"Cads."

"Yes, but rich cads."

Between my starvation and the spastic lurchings of the cab, I was nearly swooning with nausea by the time we reached Champlain and paid off the driver. We checked in at the hotel, got our desired front room, and went down to the dining room for a late dinner. While it was under preparation and while we tore into some dinner rolls to keep from expiring, Alex, in his usual gregarious way, engaged the landlord in conversation. "Well, landlord, you're to be complimented on your rolls."

"Why, thank you, sir. My wife bakes them."

"Excellent. Just the thing for hungry travellers...pass me another one, would you, James, there's a good fellow. Have much business this time of year, or is summer busiest for you?"

"Summer mainly, sir, but we do have quite a few hunters in the fall. The two of you were a surprise. We only had one guest actually booked in for tonight."

"Another hungry traveller, perhaps," said Alex. "We had better save him some rolls."

"It's a she, actually, a Mrs. Williams. She's a regular here, every couple of weeks or so."

"That's unusual. For a woman."

"She works for the, let me see, forget the name, now. One of those outfits to do with religious literature. Does a route between Boston and Toronto. Should be coming in soon. Here's your dinner now. Enjoy it."

We dined, trying to look ordinary, and were just on the brink of dessert when sounds of an arriving carriage came from without. Alex craned his neck to see out the dining room window. The horse stood steaming in the frosty night, a figure alit from the cab, and escorted by the driver, carrying her luggage, she started for the hotel's front door.

"Jean's coming in. I had better disappear," babbled Alex urgently, leaping from the table. "Try to talk to the woman, James, and see if she does or says anything that gives her away as a Confederate."

"Don't worry. I'll be a proper Southern-lover."

"I am sure you will. I'm off to our room. If anyone asks, I was taken sick." Alex barely made it up the stairs before Jean and Mrs. Williams came into the entry-way.

"Hello, Mrs. Williams, how are you tonight?" I could hear the landlord say.

"Tired, but healthy, praise the Lord. And hungry."

"We have some excellent shepherd's pie tonight. I'll take your bag up, if you'd like to go ahead into the dining room."

In she came and I tried not to gape in astonishment. I had expected Mrs. Williams to be the usual plain and dismal agent of uplift, but such was certainly not the case. I was surprised to learn later that she was forty-five years of age, an age that I, until I turned forty-five myself, considered Definitely Matronly.

Matronly Mrs. Williams was not, by a long chalk. She was tall, elegant, rosy of complexion, with impeccably arranged jet-black hair, and proportioned according to a man's fondest dreams. I felt stirrings of more than ordinary interest and it took considerable effort to address myself to the cottage pudding that was the evening's dessert.

Mrs. Williams took a table nearby while Jean went out to the kitchen. To my discomfiture, she kept glancing in my direction as I glanced in hers, our eyes making contact each time. My cottage pudding steadily diminished, as did the size of my bites. This was so damnably awkward; my mandate was to extract evidence, if it were there, and my heart's desire was to get to know Mrs. Williams as fully as possible. So dazzled was I that the title of Mrs., which generally suggests non-availability, did not register on me. She was simply the most beautiful woman I had ever seen and I had to meet her.

I felt a twinge of panic. What was I to do once my dinner was finished? I thought of approaching her with "Don't I know you from somewhere?" but it was too old and tired an artifice to merit consideration.

The pudding was gone now. I had to do something. I had to do something for the abolition of slavery, something for the preservation of the Union, something to assuage my curiosity about this unspeakably lovely woman. Oh, what the hell, I thought, you don't get anything done without a try. I arose and walked over to her table.

"Good evening, madam."

"Well...good evening," said Mrs. Williams, looking me up and down in frank appraisal.

"My friend," I explained, "wasn't feeling well and had to retire early. I'd like some company, if it wouldn't be an imposition. I hate being alone, even for a few minutes."

"I hate being alone too and I spend much of my time thus," said Mrs. Williams wistfully. "Is your friend a lady or a gentleman?"

"A gentleman. A business associate."

"Good. I would not wish to be party to any sort of infidelity." She smiled, dare I say it, seductively. I wondered about the unseen Mr. Williams.

"Please sit down," she invited. "I take it you have had dinner. Ah, here is mine. Thank you, landlord. Perhaps the young gentleman would like some tea?"

"The young gentleman would very much."

"One pot of tea, then, for the young gentleman, please, landlord."

"Yes, madam, right away."

"Now," asked Mrs. Williams, "what is the young gentleman's name?"

"James Ramsay, madam. And what is the young lady's name?"

"You flatter me, sir, but I enjoy it. I am Lucinda Williams, of Boston."

We shook hands like two business-men. She had a scent about her that was fast bringing out the animal in me and I had to remind myself that I was not playing games.

"And where are *you* from, Mr. Ramsay?"

"Oh, a place you've probably never heard of. Belleville, in Canada West."

"Oh," said Mrs. Williams brightly. "I know Belleville quite well." Jesus, Mary, and Joseph; Confederates right in my own home town! "I'm with the North American Bible Society and do quite a lot of travelling, distributing pamphlets and other literature."

"Sound like interesting work. Do you enjoy the travelling?"

"It is not my position to enjoy or not enjoy. The Lord has ordained that I should do this and I am certainly not disposed to question His wisdom. He has stood between me and total despair since my husband passed away a year and a half ago." Mrs. Williams pressed the back of her hand to her forehead in a tragic gesture.

My heart leapt. "I'm so very sorry," I sympathized.

"He was much older than I, over twenty years my senior, but a good man. He looked after me well."

I groped wildly about for something intelligent to say. "Do you find all your travelling to, er, take your mind off your, ah, situation?"

"Not really. If anything, the travelling engulfs me in it, all those hours and days on trains" (on trains when you took a cab? Aha! A clue!) "and in hotel beds, alone..." Her voice trailed off.

"I'm sorry," I apologized, not feeling in the least sorry. "That was a thoughtless thing for me to say."

"No, it wasn't. There was no way you could have known. You are very kind to be so...concerned."

Madam, if only you knew how...concerned. "Well," I said earnestly, "I hope your situation may change some day. If I may say so, I think you're a very attractive lady."

She reached out and squeezed my hand. "What a dear young man you are! If you're lying, just don't tell me. Leave an old woman with some illusions..."

"Old woman! Mrs. Williams, do yourself justice!"

"Would that I were younger or you older, Mr. Ramsay. Forgive me, I'm not usually this bold...tell me, what do you think of our silly little war?"

"Silly. I fail to see why some of the states cannot be allowed to continue the option of slave ownership and why slavery must be confined from the states entering the Union. After all, the manpower is needed, especially in the cotton states, and if any slaves are ill-treated, and I believe only a minority are, just think of all the white factory hands that are dealt with just as badly. Not that it makes slavery *right*, you understand, but it seems a singular hypocrisy to cry foul if a man is dark but to ignore a similar situation if he is white."

Oh, I was doing well! But I felt cheated at the same time. I could sense being on the brink of something exciting with Mrs. Williams and then being held at arm's length with all this war talk. Perhaps she was one of those women who could play a man like a marionette on strings.

"It's as though," I plunged onward, "there are too many people tripping over too many other people to try and show yet too many other people how tolerant they are. Besides, you can't tell me the black man is advanced as we are. After all, what great civilization flourishes on the African continent?"

"Nothing since Egypt and that's ancient history."

"Mrs. Williams, I hope I didn't offend your Yankee sentiments. Perhaps I spoke too freely. If I did, I apologize."

"Though I am Yankee to the core, I agree completely with what you have said," reassured Mrs. Williams. "This is indeed a war of doubtful justification. It is better that the Southern states secede and be done with it. It is far better that way than liberating thousands of ignorant slaves who will then come north and work for starvation wages, throwing our own people out of their jobs. I feel like a traitor saying it, but I hope we lose this war, and quickly, so no more lives are needlessly thrown away."

The landlord took away the dishes and began turning down the lamps. The clock on the wall said 10:34. "I think," I said, "the landlord wants to close things down for the night. I guess that's the end of our conversation for now. I'll look forward to more in the morning." I was so close, so very close to unlocking Mrs. Williams' secrets, both as a Confederate agent and a woman. Time, how I needed time. And then...

"We have only just become acquainted, Mr. Ramsay. It seems a pity to end it so soon. If it wouldn't offend *your* sentiments, perhaps you would like to visit with me in my room. I know it is not a ladylike suggestion, but we're new friends in a strange place and there's a war on, so perhaps posterity will forgive us. Shall we?"

"Let's. I just want to pass a look on my friend and see how he's feeling."

"How miserable, being sick so far from home. Is there anything I can do?"

"I'll let you know. Excuse me for just a moment." I poked my head into our room. The lamp was out. "Alex?"

"Have you found out anything?" whispered Alex hollowly.

"She's openly sympathetic to the South, that much I know, which may or may not mean anything. She also said how much she travelled on trains, and that sounded pretty funny if she came in a cab."

"Definitely funny. The smell of rat hangs heavily in the air."

"She invited me to her room."

"She *what?*"

"She invited me to her room. I have to go now."

"James," said the voice in the darkness.

"Yes?"

"I know that I can count on you to do whatever it takes in our noble cause."

"I could hear that grin, Alex, even if I couldn't see it."

"Be careful, James."

When I knocked at Mrs. Williams' door, she asked me to wait a moment. I waited and then at her bidding went in to find her seated in an armchair wearing a robe. She waved me to another chair, explaining, "I was so tired of those travelling clothes. I'm trying to hang the wrinkles out of them."

"That's fine, Mrs. Williams. I don't mind."

"Yes," she mused in an abrupt change of subject. "Our poor young country is in such a predicament. It may surprise you that there are many in the so-called Northern states who think as I do. It is such a tragedy that the authorities in Washington have seen fit to pursue this folly. I, by the way, voted for Senator Douglas."

"I would likely have too, if I were an American," I lied. We conversed for forty minutes or so, I being careful to agree with all Mrs. Williams' social and political opinions, many of which were not especially well-informed. I was even able to recall some of the scriptures invoked by slave-owners to justify themselves, impressing Mrs. Williams to no end.

"Secession of the South is the only solution," she pronounced. "Let us devoutly hope that it all ends quickly, that lives on both sides will be spared. Mr. Ramsay, would you pray with me?"

I was startled, but I acquiesced, and we knelt together by the bed. I, truth to tell, paid little attention to what was being said, distracted as I was by her scent. That is to say, I paid little heed until I realized she had begun to weep. Oh, dear Lord, what to do now? Say soothing things? Put my arm around her shoulders? I elected the latter and she put her hand over mine. It was ludicrous, making what were not so much gestures of comfort as amorous overtures in an attitude of prayer. My head was swimming in confusion.

"I'm sorry," sniffed Mrs. Williams. "I have family in the war."

I bet you have, madam. "Oh," I said wisely, "then this weighs most heavily on you. I wish there were something I could do to reassure you."

"There is. Please lie down with me for a while. You're such a kind young man and, well, I just need someone to hold me."

I thought my ribcage must be rattling with the hammering of my heart. I took off my shoes and the first thing Mrs. Williams said as we lay down was "Heavens, Mr. Ramsay, is that your heart? Bless me, so it is."

"It, ah, does that sometimes. Forgive me, Mrs. Williams, I feel most impertinent, but, well, to tell the truth, I find you to be a most attractive woman, so much so that it's almost frightening. I know I had no business to say that..."

"Why not? I feel so complimented."

"Well, after your loss and your worries about the war..."

"Let us put that aside. The attraction you voice is by no means one-sided. If you'll pardon one more reference to my late husband, he was more of a father to me than a real lover. I lost my own father when I was sixteen and married Mr. Williams a year later for security as much as anything. He always looked after me as though I were a child, correcting me, gently, mind you, when I went astray. But it was not a normal husband-and-wife situation. I had in Mr. Williams a second father, not a lover, and before I am too old for it, I need a lover. I need *you*, Mr. Ramsay."

In a flash of melancholy, I thought of Ruth. To her, there was a gentle quality of beseeching; with Mrs. Williams, the attitude was one of demand. Mrs. Williams! Not for one moment did I address her as Lucinda or think of her as anything else, and here I was on the brink of one of the most volcanic experiences of my entire life.

"Come to me, Mr. Ramsay," came a distant whispered summons. I obeyed the call. Through the portals of paradise I rode, trumpets playing, banners flying; o, man the hunter found his quarry, which was once again praying. The cultural anomaly of it all drove me to a frenzy.

"The Lord is my shepherd...thy rod and thy staff, they comfort me...until the end of my days..."

"Dear heaven!" we gasped when it was all over.

"My angel, you are my angel," whispered Mrs. Williams, nibbling my ear.

"As you are mine," I said truthfully, now hoping fervently that we had been wrong about her being a Confederate agent. But even if she were, I would not turn her in, but would hold her as my own prisoner, immobilizing her political activities by keeping her in our own love nest, bound in chains when I went off to work on the Grand Trunk each day. Oh, the secret life of James Ramsay! On return from my day's labours, I would unchain her and ravish her in punishment of her sympathy to slavery. I would be supporting humanity's cause in my own way, I would have my job on the railway, *and* I would be having fun. It would be a truly glorious and perfect life's plan, even if conceived in dementia.

But now the most mundane of practicalities intruded. The tea taken with Mrs. Williams had worked its way through my system and now sought release. I sheepishly excused myself.

"Don't be long, Mr. Ramsay," purred the voice in the darkness. "I shall need you again shortly."

The oil lamp, which we had turned down somewhere along the way, had flickered out, and I had to grope about in the darkness to find my clothes. I got all mixed up in a chair with something draped over it, something frilly, a petticoat or something, and I realized in a flash that there was something peculiar about the garment. There was a strange articulation to it as if something were sewn up in it.

I got some clothes on and tiptoed out into the hallway. I looked into our room; Alex was lying on his back, mouth wide open, whiffling gently.

"Alex."

"Eh? Who's that?" said Alex loudly.

"Ssh. It's me, James. Are you awake?"

Alex's head detached itself from the bedclothes. "I am now. What is it?"

"She has something sewn up in her petticoats."

"Are you certain?"

"I could feel it. Found it accidentally in the dark when I was looking for my clothes."

"What was it like? What did it feel like?"

In light of the past hour, I had to concentrate for a moment. "James?"

"Uh, yes. It was kind of lumpy. There was no opportunity for extensive research, but it felt like envelopes and things."

"Has this woman a first name?"

"Lucinda."

"Are you spending the night with her?"

"Yes."

"Well, get back to it. See what else you can find out. I'll wire the border people at Rouse's Point first thing in the morning. And, James."

"Yes?"

"Sterling work, my boy. Shows what lengths Canadian men are prepared to go to for a great cause. I'll recommend you for the Victoria Cross or whatever the U.S. Government gives for extreme gallantry."

"*Au revoir*, Alex."

I attended to my errand of mercy and returned to the warm, inviting, and ample bosom of Mrs. Williams. Who had whose way again with whom was academic; it was so fast and furious as to border on mutual rape before we subsided into oblivion.

In the brittle winter dawn, the deed was done a third time, although I was now feeling somewhat depleted. But there was something perversely thrilling about making love to a woman whose days of freedom were probably numbered.

At breakfast time, Mrs. Williams and I went to the dining room separately in the interests of propriety. I went first, to find Alex reading a newspaper at a window table and nibbling on a meticulously buttered slice of bread with marmalade.

"James, you old devil. How are you?"

"I'll never walk again."

"Where is Mrs. W.?"

"On her way down. Appearances, you know."

"Lord, I hope she doesn't take off out a back window or something. I have already telegraphed the border station at Rouse's Point. The agent should be here at any moment."

"I don't think she can possibly suspect. Look, Alex, she's a wonderful woman. If she's guilty, maybe I could keep her, you know, save the U.S. Government money, keep her in Belleville under house arrest..."

Alex choked on his coffee (his boycott of American tea being virtually permanent). "James, you cannot be serious."

"But I am."

"You astonish me. This is a serious, serious thing we're involved with, not your own playground of the flesh."

I stiffened and hissed, "Who found the damned petticoat, anyway?"

"You did, but what you have suggested just is not appropriate."

"But as a reward..."

"Receiving a person as a reward, virtually *owning* that person?"

"Not owning, just taking responsibility."

"James, if we are right about the petticoat, we will being doing something absolutely spectacular. Don't compromise it with all manner of Romantic nonsense."

Very well, I thought. I shall testify on her behalf, I shall write to her in prison, and take her for myself on her release. I was trying to speculate how long a prison term a lady might draw for what we thought she had done when Mrs. Williams swept elegantly into the dining room, perfectly preened and groomed, and primly sat down at another table with not a glance in my direction. She looked so beautiful, so innocent of her coming apprehension, and I felt like a Judas, hoping again that we were wrong. Of course, if we *were*, she still would not have been too pleased with me for trying to turn her in.

I was trying to concoct some kind of explanation when there was a frantic thudding of hooves from without and a carriage slithered to a halt before the hotel steps. Alex, calmly but quickly, went to the front door and returned with the border agent, to whom I gave a subtle nod in Mrs. Williams' direction. I hated to do it, although for sheer panache I have never been able to match it.

"Mrs. Williams!" said the agent.

She looked up, startled. "Yes? What is it?"

"You are under arrest on suspicion of Confederate activities..."

Mrs. Williams leapt up, started for the front door, was intercepted by Alex, spun around, and raced to the kitchen door for a messy rendezvous with the landlord's wife, who was coming through with a bowl of oatmeal. It splattered in a great, sticky geyser all over the wall.

"Mercy!" exclaimed the landlord's wife.

"Damn!" cursed Mrs. Williams.

"You'll have to come with me, madam," instructed the agent. "Settle down, now..."

She tried to push her way past him and was pounced on by Alex and me simultaneously, oh, the beauty, the scent, now hot with agitation. She looked into my face with venom, she knew, she spat straight into the face that had loved her but an hour before. I was devastated.

"That's enough, now, madam," said the agent, his civility strained beyond endurance. "Handcuffs for you if you're going to be that way. We're going for a ride. Which one of you is Mr. Ross?"

"I am Dr. Ross."

"I beg your pardon, Dr. Ross. I need you to come too."

"And this gentleman is Mr. Ramsay, my colleague." Alex showed his U.S. Army identification.

"I guess I should call you 'lootenant'," said the agent. "I'm Federal Agent Deane."

"Pleased to meet you, agent. We'll need a couple of minutes to settle our bill and pack. Landlord, our apologies for all the drama."

"That's all right, Dr. Ross, it wasn't your idea. Mrs. Williams, you have a bill too."

"I'll pay it," I said hastily, trying to salvage a shred of my previous status, to redeem myself enough that I could be Mrs. Williams' prison keeper.

"Oh, thank you so very much!" snarled Mrs. Williams, her lovely face twisted into a sneer. "I am innocent of whatever you say. There will be an accounting for this."

"Oh, sure, sure, Mrs. Williams," said Agent Deane.

At Rouse's Point, we went directly to the agent's house. Mrs. Deane met us at the door. "George!" she exclaimed. "What is all this?"

"A delicate matter, my dear, that requires your assistance. Mrs. Williams here is a suspected Confederate agent and we're not equipped to deal with ladies at the office. Never occurred to anyone that this would happen. Would you take her up to our room and have her remove her petticoat?"

"Well...very well, George."

The three of us stood guard outside the bedroom in case of violence, but there was none, just some angry voices and rustling of garments. And then Mrs. Deane's hand reached forth with the petticoat. We took it downstairs and laid it on the dining room table. Oh, the scent! I vowed to save part of the petticoat as my own Shroud of Turin. First Ruth, now Mrs. Williams. My love life was surely doomed to tragedy.

Agent Deane, with the expertise of much practice, slit the petticoat open, exclaiming, "Aha! You were right. Here's something...something else...another...and another." He pulled out an assortment of envelopes and packets. "...another...and another...good God, how long do you suppose this has been going on? Another, another...the woman is a regular travelling post office...forty-six and counting...another...fifty-five now...should charge her for bypassing the U.S. Mail...sixty-seven...and another...is there no limit?...seventy-five...more...another... gentlemen, we have here eighty-two pieces of evidence. That should put the lady away for a while, unless" - his voice rose meaningfully - "unless she'd like to tell us everything and we'd make some kind of arrangement."

I drew breath to suggest some kind of arrangement and was jabbed in the ribs by Alex. "I'd die in prison first!" cried Mrs. Williams from upstairs.

"A fanatic, huh?" appraised Agent Deane. "All right, madam, it's your choice. Gentlemen, I'm going to take Mrs. Williams over to the holding cell at the office. What's this?" Alex handed him his confidential orders from President Lincoln. "The Chief himself! Well, I'll be damned. All right, the stuff is yours, then. I'll need you to sign a release form, so if you would be kind enough to make a list of what is here, that'll be all and you can do what you need to. I'll do a formal interrogation and be back in an hour or so with the form. One other thing."

"Yes?"

"Your orders will be verified by telegraph from Washington, so don't leave town before I get back. Some of our boys are first-rate squirrel-hunters."

"Don't worry, we won't, Agent. We're on your side."

"I have no doubt. Regulations. Aren't they wonderful? What a business. Months of boredom and now this. The boys at the office'll love it."

Mrs. Williams was removed, fixing me with one last homicidal look. And then we went to work on the dining room table, sorting and cataloguing the various items of mail and copying the addresses thereon. I had never seen Alex so excited. He was like a child on Christmas morning, chattering away: "Not much there...kind of innocuous...James, look at this one, the British War Minister..."

"Don't open it, Alex. We'd better leave it for the President."

"Of course. You're right. Here's another. Oh, this looks like a good one. Have a look." I was just gazing off into space. Alex looked up sharply; my mind had wandered completely. "You weren't joking about Mrs. Williams, were you?"

"Well, no. Did you think I was?"

"It was such an improbable adventure that I couldn't be sure. You did what you had to, and if it weren't for what you did, we would have none of this."

"I feel like a pig."

"One night and you think you love her. Had you been less honourable, you could have disappeared with her into the night."

"I never even thought of that..."

"Which is why you are an honourable man. I am sorry you were dragged into this. I guess the boundaries between duty and passion and love get pretty blurred at times. Had you shown any mercy to this woman, you would have been betraying Ruth...I know that was a cruel thing to say, but think about it...not to mention Precious and Jerge and Joe and all the rest. You built up an enviable catalogue of righteousness, and I mean that in the truest sense. Why throw it all away for one night of passion?"

"You don't understand..."

"Perhaps not. Maybe we need to discuss it further, but I must ask you to save it until we are done with this. There isn't much time. You know, what you could do is go over to the railway station, show the agent my orders, and telegraph the President about this. Tell the agent it's urgent and stand by for an immediate reply. Here is some money, although they'll probably send it free or charge the government."

The agent's eyes widened as he read the message Alex had written:

MR. A. LINCOLN
THE WHITE HOUSE
WASHINGTON, D.C.

CONFEDERATE AGENT APPREHENDED CHAMPLAIN N.Y. STOP
82 PIECES MAIL SEIZED STOP
ACKNOWLEDGE ASSISTANCE OF JAMES RAMSAY IN OPERATION
STOP PLEASE ADVISE NEXT ACTION IMMEDIATELY END MESSAGE

/S/ A.M. ROSS

"So you're one of the fellows did this, hey? Congratulations. Come on into the office and you can watch me send it. Oh, wait'll I tell the wife."

He sent the wire and then we awaited the response, drinking muddy coffee from a tin pot on the stove. Some time passed. I handed up orders to a northbound freight for something to do, to take my mind off my personal tragedy, and to keep the station agent by his apparatus. He nodded affirmatively at me as I went back into the stuffy, overheated office.

The agent wrote furiously in response to Mr. Morse's ingenious pattern of clicks and beeps:

THE WHITE HOUSE
WASHINGTON, D.C.
NOVEMBER 23 '62
10:14 A.M.
DR. A.M. ROSS
c/o CHAMPLAIN AND ST. LAWRENCE AGENT
ROUSE'S POINT, N.Y.

WELL DONE STOP COME IMMEDIATELY AND BRING THE MAIL
STOP ARRIVAL TIME NO CONSEQUENCE END MESSAGE

/S/ A. LINCOLN

"Lincoln!" exclaimed the agent. "You fellows sure deal in high places, don't you? There you go."

"When is the next southbound train?" I asked.

"12:10 noon. You'll need to get a move on if you want to catch it."

"We'll be on it."

I hurried back to Agent Deane's house with the telegram. Alex was still having the time of his life, sorting, organizing, collating, listing. I gave him the Presidential message, urging, "Alex, the next train out is in less than two hours. We've got to pack all this. What do we put it in? What do we do, abandon our clothes here?"

Mrs. Deane laughed. "Bless you, no, Mr. Ramsay. I'll lend you a portmanteau. And George has a spare pair of handcuffs. Maybe one of you should be shackled to the portmanteau. I'll get it out of the store-room and then the two of you should have a sandwich before you're off to Washington. To see President Lincoln."

PRESIDENT ABRAHAM LINCOLN.
COURTESY OF HARPERS FERRY HISTORICAL ASSOCIATION.

CHAPTER FORTY

The trip to Washington was a misery, tempered only by the President's office having covered our train fare. Although it was only a few minutes after noon when our train chuffed out of Rouse's Point, all the theatrics at the hotel seemed a week ago. My head ached right into my jaw, the depression over my fleeting *amour* deepened. These hopeless loves of mine might have served as a model for Richard Wagner in far-off Germany, working as he was at that very time on his heart-wrenching epic *Tristan and Isolde*.

Though *en route* to an audience with the President of the United States, all I could think of was Mrs. Williams. I wanted to hold her, I wanted forgiveness, I wanted to negotiate a presidential pardon from Mr. Lincoln. It was all Romantic foolishness, I knew; after all, were we not living in what has become known as the Romantic Age? But in the glorious dreams endemic to Romanticism, I had imagined something more chivalrous than this, a slimy betrayal. In my despair, I had completely lost all thought of the four million or so still in slavery.

Once on the train, I sank into a stupour, both from exhaustion, for the night had imposed unusual physical demands, and as a means of emotional escape. No sooner was I asleep, it seemed, than I was roused out for a change of trains at Boston, Springfield, or New York, stumbling through gates and across tracks, unable to focus, my head feeling as if about to fall off. It was like the aftermath of an epic drinking spree.

There was a cab waiting for us in the black night at Washington station. As it clip-clopped its way through the deserted streets of the capital, Alex nudged me, saying, "Look alive, friend. We may not be going to tea with the Queen, but a midnight rendezvous with the President of the United States has its own merits. This'll be something to tell our grandchildren..."

"Should we live that long," I interrupted.

"Don't be a pessimist. You're *still* feeling badly, aren't you?"

"Yes. I'm scarred for life."

"Well, you are not, although I know you're not joking. This has been awful for you and it'll take some time to get over it. Look, there's the White House now. Try to forget Mrs. Williams and savour these moments. It was she who was the betrayer, not you."

The cab paused at the gate while the sentry inspected Alex's letter of commission. " Go ahead, sir!" said the sentry, a young Marine, snapping to attention. Alex gave him a half-wave, half-salute, just as Queen Victoria does when passing by a crowd.

The cab rumbled up to a side entrance under an overhanging portico and we alit, myself tethered to Agent Deane's portmanteau, which had alternated in our custody during the trip. A black porter ushered us in.

"Good evening, Dr. Ross, Mr. Ramsay," greeted the porter. "The President is asleep, but left instructions to be awakened. Ah'll show you to his office and then wake him up. He'll be just a few minutes."

We went upstairs to Mr. Lincoln's office, at the moment a clutter of military maps. They and sundry other documents were on the desk, on the floor, in an armchair. The place looked more like professors' studies I had seen at the University of Glasgow than how I had imagined the office of the Chief Executive of the United States.

"Wait heah, please," said the porter. "One moah thing."

"Yes?"

"The President has tole me what you have done for mah people and Ah want to thank you from the bottom of mah heart." He was gone before we could properly respond, but those few simple words were all we needed to hear.

Alex unlocked me from the portmanteau and I stood, rubbing my wrist and glancing at the maps. I love maps and wanted a closer look, but Alex cautioned me, "Better not, James, these might be classified or something. Look at all those paintings! That one over there looks familiar. I think it's John Bright..."

The door opened and in came President Lincoln, all six-foot-four of him. His craggy, careworn face broke into a smile of welcome as he extended his hand.

"Our apologies for the lateness of the hour, Mr. President," said Alex with a slight bow. "May I present my friend and invaluable colleague, Mr. James Ramsay."

"I'm delighted to meet you," said the President in a surprisingly light tenor voice. "And please don't worry about the time. You may rouse me up whenever you please. I have slept with one eye open since I came to Washington and never closed both, except when an office-seeker was looking for me.

"Dr. Ross, I appreciated your letter about the Emancipation Proclamation.* I am glad you are pleased with it, but there is work before us yet. We must make that proclamation effective by victories over our enemies...it's a paper bullet after all and of no account unless we can sustain it."

"Surely God must be aiding the Union cause," said Alex.

"Well, I certainly hope so!" said Mr. Lincoln. "But the suffering and misery that attend this conflict are killing me by inches. I wish it were all

---

*The Emancipation Proclamation had been passed into law on September 22, 1862, by the 13th Amendment to the United States Constitution. It outlawed the ownership of slaves within the boundaries of the U.S.A., but, as Lincoln commented, it would be ineffective until the slave states were returned to the Union.

over, but that is my problem, not yours. Now, before we get to work, would you like some coffee or a sandwich or some fruit? Or all three? We can offer just about anything you could want. The food here is the best part of the job. Some days, it's the only good part."

"I would like a cup of tea, if I could," said I.

"*American* tea?" said Alex in astonishment.

The President laughed. "If it's tea you want, it's tea you shall have. Our cook is Irish and knows all about scalding the pot. And we have a war prize in the form of a Virginia ham, which, whatever you may have thought of Governor Wise, is the best ham in the world. A sandwich?"

"Yes, please, Mr. President," we chorused. "Thank you."

"And an apple for myself." The President rang for the porter. "Now, let's see what you have brought."

I opened the portmanteau and started handing Mr. Lincoln the various documents and pieces of mail. He looked at the names and addresses, murmuring to himself between bites of his apple. "Great Lord above! Here's a letter to Franklin Pierce.[1] He lives...let's see...in New Hampshire. What could the Confederates possibly want with him? Oh, no, here's another to Caleb Cushing. He used to be Attorney-General."

The President sighed deeply. "I will have copies made of these letters and then we'll send the originals to the parties concerned in official enve-lopes. That way, *they* will know that *we* know... now, these letters to private individuals, I won't bother with them myself, but those other ones look official. I guess I'll go through them now. This will take some time, but I need you, so don't go to sleep just yet. If you would like to look at those maps, you're welcome to. Just don't disarrange them."

Some time later, Mr. Lincoln broke the silence with "Have a look at this one and let me know what you think of it."

OFFICE OF THE SECRETARY OF STATE

Richmond, Virginia, C.S.A.[2]
November 18, 1862

Office of the Ambassador to France

Dear Sir:
This is to inform you that preparations are being made to invade the Eastern Frontier of the United States in the vicinity of Calais, Maine. It is our opinion that an attack in so unexpected a

---

[1]Franklin Pierce had been President of the United States from 1853-57.
[2]The Confederate Government had relocated from Montgomery, Ala-bama, in June, 1861.

quarter would dishearten the Northern people and encourage the Democrats to oppose continuation of the war.

The proposed base of operation will be the British colony of New Brunswick. We recommend in the interests of discretion to supply this force by sea and since we are currently short of the necessary vessels, you are instructed, with the utmost discretion, to arrange for the charter of two vessels, preferably steam-driven, of no more than 200 tons' burden.

Please respond at your earliest opportunity.

R.M.T. Hunter

"I had heard rumblings in Montreal about such a possibility," said Alex tensely, "but there wasn't enough to go on. Now, by God, there is. But why is this letter coming *into* the States? The idea of this whole courier business is to get around the coastal blockade on the Confederacy."

"Oh, it's a carbon," said the President. He turned the letter over. "Here we are," he said. "It says 'original forwarded to Paris 22/12/62' and there's some illiterate Confederate scrawl in way of a signature."

"Pretty amateurish security," I remarked.

"Well," said Mr. Lincoln, "we can't let ourselves be outwitted by a band of amateurs, can we? I wish you would go up to New Brunswick and see what the Rebels are up to." It took us a moment to comprehend what had just been said, as casually as asking us to go to the post office for stamps.

"The information in these despatches is of great importance," continued the President. "There are two in code, so they'll have to go to the proper people, but one way or another, we'll get at their contents. I have to say you two have done yourselves proud. Mr. Ramsay, would you consider being commissioned officially as Dr. Ross's assistant? It only seems right if you do all these things for us."

"Could there be any doubt?"

"Excellent! I will have the documents made up first thing in the morning. Then I'll be able to *order* you to New Brunswick! The government's treat, of course, including unlimited tea."

Alex arose, myself following his cue. I thought I would faint from sheer weariness. "Well, Mr. President, I hope our revelations have eased things for you somewhat. If there's nothing else for the moment, Mr. Ramsay and I are in desperate need of some rest, so I think we had better find a hotel..."

"At this hour? I won't hear of it. This is a big house with plenty of rooms. Let me find you one."

Abraham Lincoln was not one to let servants do everything for him. He took us to a guest room, lit the gas for us, and said, "Have a good sleep, now, you shall not be disturbed. There is a commode right across the hall. Good night, now."

"Good night, Mr. President."

We settled into bed, but despite our fatigue, sleep came reluctantly as our minds raced under the momentum of the past two days.

"James?"

"Eh?"

"Isn't he incredible?"

"Amazing," I said. "All the cares he has, and yet he makes sure we have something to eat and a place to stay."

"I'm thinking, if the Almighty ever raised up an individual for a special task, it has to be Abraham Lincoln," said Alex reverently. "He's almost like a parent to his country. He won't sleep as long as this damnable war is on."

A quiet knock awoke us to a sun-flooded room. Alex's pocket watch, parked on a bedside table, said 11:05. Another knock. "Yes?" I yawned.

The door opened; not a housekeeper or a porter, but again the President of the United States.

"Eleven o'clock!" I exclaimed in mortification. "You must think we are bone lazy, Mr. President. What an abuse of your hospitality!"

"You had a long day yesterday, so please do not worry. When you are ready, I'll pilot you down to breakfast."

Breakfast, because of the hour of the morning, was more in the fashion of an early lunch. Mrs. Lincoln and their son Tad were at the table along with the President. Mrs. Lincoln, to put it gently, was rather abstracted for reasons that were to emerge a short time later. And young Tad, well, there was all manner of energy and intelligence to the boy, but it was hampered by a seeming lack of direction and a speech defect brought about by a cleft palate.

Tad asked questions non-stop and dragged it out of me that we had apprehended a "bad lady" who had all sorts of secret material sewn up in her petticoat. Tad giggled at the mention of such an intimate garment. His thin ten-year-old eyebrows rose in an alarmingly man-to-man look. "How did you find 'em?"

To my horror, I felt a scarlet rush to my face. Alex looked away and the President, who knew none of the private details but was nobody's fool, looked at the ceiling. The silence thickened.

"Uh..."

Mrs. Lincoln came to my rescue. "Son, I think this is something nobody is meant to know," she said firmly. "Nobody except Father and the government."

"I wanna know!""wailed the child. I was becoming annoyed, but of course I couldn't tell the President's son to mind his own business.

"Mother is right," said the President firmly. "The fewer people who know, the better. It's too easy with these things to get excited and tell someone by accident."

"I wanna know!" came the strident bellow.

"Tad, *I* can't know," explained Mrs. Lincoln. "I can tell Mr. Ramsay is dying to tell us everything, but he can't. We'll just have to be ignorant together." Just as well, I thought, before I get revealed as a master of debauchery.

"Taddie, I'll tell you all about it when the war finishes, which reminds me indirectly, Mr. Ramsay, I understand you're with the Grand Trunk."

"That's right, Mr. President." I gulped, wondering if that were indeed still the case.

"Before I started this, ah, job, I was an attorney for the Chicago, Alton, and St. Louis. We railroad men should stick together, shouldn't we? Maybe," the President remarked wistfully, "I could invite you to Illinois when this damnable war is over and I can get back to the railroad. Maybe I could invite you out for a visit and we can do some serious train-riding together."

"And I would certainly want to reciprocate and have you up to Canada for a ride on the Grand Trunk. There are a lot of people up there who would be very glad to see you."

"I'd enjoy that on both counts," said the President.

"What happened to our trip to the West Coast, Father?" asked Mrs. Lincoln plaintively.

"Still on, Mother, still on. Just as soon as I can take a holiday. Maybe there'll be a trans-continental railroad by then..."

"I wanna..."

"Of course, Taddie. Whither we go, you go."

A young man, evidently a secretary, came into the dining room. "Good morning, Mr. President. Mrs. Lincoln. Master Tad."

"Hello, Johnny," greeted the President. "I'd like you to meet a couple of visitors from Canada, Mr. Ramsay and Dr. Ross. Gentlemen, this is John Hay." We shook hands.

Continued Mr. Lincoln, "These fellows apprehended a Confederate agent carrying eighty-two pieces of mail, half of them classified..."

John Hay let out a warbling whistle. Mrs. Lincoln's eyes narrowed in disapproval. "Excuse me," blushed young Hay.

The President laughed. "Well may you whistle, Johnny. Events are moving with the speed of the four-legged chicken." A moment of silence.

"Sir?"

"Well, now."

Mrs. Lincoln sighed. Tad looked at his father expectantly.

"Well, yes," said Mr. Lincoln. "There was this farmer in Illinois, riding along a country road on his horse. He found himself in a race with a four-legged chicken and no matter how fast the farmer rode, the chicken could stay ahead of him. The chicken took off up the lane to a farm and the farmer followed. Asked his neighbour about this creature and the neighbour explained, 'I bred the thing so's you could get four drumsticks out of it. But I don't know how they'll taste because I can't catch him!'"

Mrs. Lincoln sighed again. Alex, John Hay, and I laughed, more at the style of delivery than the content. And Tad screamed with delight, banging on his plate with his cutlery.

"Son, son," said Mrs. Lincoln urgently. "Calm down right this minute. I do not need another of those dreadful headaches."

"Ooh. Thorry, Mum."

"Now, Mr. President," said John Hay, struggling with a lingering grin, "some memoranda just came in from the War Department for your signature. And I guess Secretary Stanton will be interested in those eighty-two whatever they were."

"Right you are, Johnny. Let's go and deal with those right now. Dr. Ross, could you come up to my office when you have finished your pancakes? Are they all right?"

"More than all right, Mr. President. We should come here to have breakfast more often."

Mr. Lincoln, understandably in high spirits, laughed again. "You're welcome any time. I'll tell cook what you said, she'll be most pleased. And , Mr. Ramsay, we'll ride the cars together one of these days. Thank you again for everything. You have done perhaps more than the soldier, more than the American. You have no direct interest in this conflict, but what a sense of justice! God bless." My eyes prickled as we shook hands.

The President and his secretary went up to the executive office, Alex following a few minutes later. Tad went tearing off to play, leaving me alone with the First Lady. I am not at ease with new people and it was made no easier by Mrs. Lincoln's elevated position. But it was Mrs. Lincoln who initiated conversation, the most bizarre I have ever had.

The Lincolns some time before had suffered the worst tragedy a parent can know, the loss of a child. Their middle son, Willy (their eldest, Bob, was at university) had been struck down by some virus or another, but what made Mrs. Lincoln's account most singular was her declaration that she kept in touch with Willy via a medium named Mrs. Laurie. Out of social cowardice, I agreed that having a medium was very special and not to be doubted.

She smiled tentatively and tremulously. "I wish others believed as you do. I don't think Father does, although he pretends, but I think he is humouring me. Mr. Hay, whom you met a few minutes ago, is an arrogant young puppy whom I would be more than happy to see fired. He acts as though I were crazy and I cannot discuss these things with him at all."

"That must be so difficult."

"Indeed. I had so looked forward to being First Lady, but what a horror..." Mrs. Lincoln's lamentations continued: the White House had been a mess when the Lincolns moved in, Mrs. Lincoln was criticized for the money she had spent on renovations, another reference to the late Willy, the fact of her having family "on the other side", which was to say Confederates in the border state of Kentucky, a family divided by the War Between the States.

I tried to cheer her up. "It cannot be long now, not with the information we have found."

John Hay poked his head through the dining room door. "Excuse me, Madam. Mr. Ramsay, could you come up to my office to sign the articles for your commission?"

"On my way." I bade Mrs. Lincoln a good day and excused myself.

As we trod silently along the carpeted hallway, John said in a low voice, "How did you find her?"

"Well...I suppose sad and confused would describe her."

"You're a charitable man, Mr. Ramsay. I'm not disposed to telling tales out of school, as it were, but since little Willy died, she has descended from difficult to impossible. She was unusually mild this morning. Usually we call her the Hellcat. I had visions of you being verbally roasted to death, although I guess that is usually reserved for me or"...he opened his office door... "my cohort and partner in crime, John Nicolay."

A young man of about Hay's age, but with a spade-shaped beard, arose from a cluttered desk for introductions. "I remember your name," I said. "I think it was on some campaign literature we sent away for."

"I remember your name too, from Canada West, was it not?" said Nicolay with a slight Germanic cast to his speech.

"John remembers everything for both of us," said Hay. "It's like having a pet who can think. Now, where are those things...here we go."

I signed the articles and then waited for a courier to take them over to the War Office on 17th Street for processing. By afternoon, I was a lieutenant in the United States Army Corps of Engineers. I thought I would be equal in rank to Alex, until my discovery that he had been promoted to first lieutenant. And it had been I who had taken such risks!

Between that and the President's last words to me, my tattered sense of purpose was renewed. My job and my private life would just have to wait a bit. Now was the time to follow direct orders from Abraham Lincoln and go forth to battle the Confederates, those dastardly supporters of slavery, right on our own Canadian soil in New Brunswick.

CHAPTER FORTY-ONE

In bland disregard for the probable consequences, I sent a telegram to the Grand Trunk, advising that "due to family circumstances", I would be detained from work indefinitely. I indulged in a modest bit of self-congratulation until it dawned on me that my employers would likely be asking some bothersome questions about the family I suddenly had in Washington. "The Family of Man," said Alex grandly as we entrained for Boston, *en route* for our steamer connection to Saint John, New Brunswick.

My professional unease was put aside, however, as we boarded the ship, the *City of Portland.* On settling in, I made the obligatory inspection of the vessel and paid a visit to the engine room to sniff the heady vapours of hot oil and bearing grease and watch the engineers prepare for departure.

The *City of Portland* was heavily booked for this sailing and our one disappointment, which was to turn into a major operating obstacle, was our inability to get a cabin together on such short notice. Mine I was to share with a rather drab fellow, a Mr. Peters, whose evident anticipation of sea-sickness bordered on determination. In Alex's cabin, the other berth had been put aside for occupancy at Portland, Maine, about ten hours' steaming up the coast. We requested a change from the purser, but it was already written in The Book and changing The Book was just not heard of.

The call at Portland was scheduled for 7:30 that evening, the voyage to resume an hour later for overnight passage to Eastport, Maine, and then the final lap to Saint John. The strain of the previous few days had caught up with Alex, who spent much of the day sleeping in his cabin. I, for some reason and in spite of spending a chaotic night aboard four different trains, felt restless, or as our black friends would say, "up". I prowled the decks in the late November sunshine, supervising the ship's passage out past Cape Ann, where a couple of fishing schooners lay gently rolling, their attending dories harvesting the sea. As they faded astern, course was altered to port (or the left, if you are unfamiliar with boat language) on a straight line for Cape Elizabeth, Maine.

Alex surfaced from his slumbers in late afternoon as Cape Elizabeth hove into view ahead, jutting far out into the ocean. "What a sleep!" he exclaimed. "Just what the doctor ordered, ha, ha. *You* seem very chipper, James. Pick up anything? Hear any bits of gossip?"

"I, er, have just been wandering around, absorbing the atmosphere...the engine room..."

"You and your machines. You're incorrigible. You're supposed to be *spying.* And I expect you have had no water..."

"Forgive me, brother doctor first *loo*tenant, for I have sinned. But the few people I have heard or talked to have been all real, basic, and unalterable down-east Yankees."

"And how do you tell?"

"They don't say 'huh' or 'yeah'. When they mean yes, it sounds something like 'aye-uh'."

"Is that right? Well, I suppose anyone who says 'aye-uh' isn't too likely to be a Confederate, although after Mrs. Williams, you really can't tell. Oh, I'm sorry, James, I didn't mean to remind you. Somewhere out there is a Mrs. Williams, a pure-of-heart Mrs. Williams waiting for you. An older woman would be the best thing for you."

A gong sounded faintly before the subject of a woman for me could evolve. "First sitting for dinner," surmised Alex. "Let's eat before the Portland passengers get aboard."

Shortly after dinner, the *City of Portland* was tied up in her namesake port, loading her additional passengers, the first of the Christmas season's mail and parcels, "store-bought" items for the coastal villages, and some wooden cases that excited our interest until we discovered them to contain spare parts for a tugboat's engine.

In the inky winter night the *City of Portland* resumed her trip, thumping and steaming out of Portland on a due easterly course. I went to my cabin to read, but, not caring for the company of the green-faced Mr. Peters, I retreated to a small reading room just below the wheel-house. Alex was to meet me there anyway in mid-evening. After waiting the better part of an hour for him, I became puzzled and then worried. Was he ill? Had he, God forbid, fallen overboard and perished in the frigid Atlantic? After another few minutes, I could bear it no longer and went below to Alex's cabin on the main deck, third one aft of the paddle box on the port side. I knocked at the door. "Yes?" said a voice that was plainly Alex and yet somehow not Alex.

"Alex, are you coming up to the reading room?"

"Oh, I, ah, changed my mind. Felt tired, thought I'd bunk down."

"Are you all right?"

"Just tired." Tired after sleeping so much of the day? Seasickness would have been more convincing, as the ship was now starting to move about in a very unpleasant manner.

"Oh, all right," I said. "I'll see you in the morning."

The familiar and unwelcome feeling of Monumental Discomfort was full upon me. I trod back up to the reading room, forgot about my book, and sat there thinking. Something in Alex's voice niggled at me, so distant, no usage of my name. And with the excuse of fatigue, the whole conversation was just enough out of focus to arouse suspicion regarding Alex's cabin-mate who had boarded at Portland.

I went below to his cabin again. I could hear voices but could distinguish no words. And since it was by no means late, there were sufficient passengers and the occasional crew about that I could not eavesdrop. I decided to try again and see what would happen. I knocked.

"What is it?" came a peremptory voice.

"Alex?"

"He's asleep and Ah'm about to be." The voices had suddenly ceased; the Southern twang was now unmistakable, so reminiscent of Major Ramsay that I turned cold, and certainly not the speech of one from a border state. I could not deal with this on my own and went to the purser's office for advice.

The purser had just finished organizing the manifests for passengers and cargo shipped at Portland, he was tired, and none too pleased to be disturbed. I started by asking where Alex's cabin mate was from.

"Who wants to know and why? I don't usually give out that kind of information." I showed him my articles of commission.

"Wu-all," said the purser, "that there makes a whole big pile of differ-ence. Let's see, Cabin 5. Dr. Alexander Ross, Washington, D.C....and...Lester Harding, Wilmington, Delaware. Booked to Eastport. That answer your question?"

"I think it does. I spoke to him through the door" - I reported the gist of the conversation - "and he sounded to be from a lot further south than Delaware. Does that suggest anything to you?"

"Aye-uh, it sure do," said the purser emphatically. "We have standing orders to watch out for Confederate agents. Got a notice just yesterday over the telegraph about suspected border activity. This is where the Old Man comes into the picture."

The Old Man, otherwise Captain Pike, voiced what I had been think-ing. "If this here now Harding is a Confederate, he may have your friend somehow held as a hostage. We have to get into that cabin...tell you what, I'll get the chief engineer to check all cabin radiators, tell the passengers there's an air lock or something. I'll stand by in the passageway...I'll be armed, the law entitles me, but the only thing I ever shot was a squirrel when I was eleven. I cried buckets and haven't done it since. Reassuring, ain't it?"

"Oh, wonderful," I said to the purser as the captain went to get his gun and change into his uniform.

"Aye-uh, guns on our boat. That's real funny."

"Funny?"

"Funny, as in 'pee-cool-yar'."

"Oh, that it is. I ought to be used to peculiar now, but it seems to have endless variations."

"Aye-uh, it sure do that, don't it?"

I kept my distance as cabins 1 and 3 had their heating checked and their occupants seemed appreciative of personal attention by such high-ranking officers.

Then came cabin 5. There was no response. The chief engineer knelt down to see if any light showed beneath the door. He shook his head, stood up, and quietly tried the door. It was locked. He and the captain came forward to confer with me.

"We'll go into the cabin as a last resort," said the captain. "I want to do a quick search of all public areas before we go in, just in case your friend is out and about. What does he look like?"

"Not tall, rather, ah, round, has reddish hair and a beard."

"Shouldn't be hard to spot, then." All off-duty crew were turned out for a search and my apprehension of looking foolish began to outweigh my concern for Alex.

Their initial efforts revealed nothing; an examination of the freight area on the main deck forward, engine and boiler spaces, storage lockers, and fuel bunkers likewise drew a blank. That only left one choice. As the purser went for a pass key, my senses reached out, as they had in previous situations, grasping for normality, embracing the muffled ka-thunk, ka-thunk of the engine, the faint swoosh of the passing sea, the thudding of the pad-dle-wheels, the creak of woodwork.

"Here's the key, Captain."

"Thanks, George." Captain Pike nodded to the chief engineer, who knocked at the door again as I withdrew to a sort of alcove just forward by the engine room. The chief knocked three times. Still no answer.

"We have to check the radiator in there. Sorry, but we have to come in. The captain is with me and has a key."

I could hear, but not see, the cabin door opening. "What is it now?" snapped a voice.

"As I just said, we are trying to locate a problem in the steam heating. I'm sorry to disturb you, but I have to come in for a look."

"Awl right, but Ah'm not tew happy about this. Make it quick."

It was Alex who made it quick, verbally anyway. "He's a Confederate! Arrest him!"

Unable to resist any longer, I stepped out of my place of shelter for a full view, just in time to see the captain taking aim with a gleaming derrin-ger. Tousled, curious heads were popping out of some of the cabin doors to see what the commotion was all about. A woman screamed.

The captain never did get off his shot. I could not see directly through the door, but was told later that Harding also drew his weapon and had it to Alex's head. "Nobody move, now, or this man's head will be in little biddy pieces," said Harding. "Give me yer gun, Captain, right now, *right now*! This boat is now under my command and is to be considered a temporary unit of the Confederate Navy. Yew will land me, Captain, on Campobello Island..."

"Can't. No wharf there."

"Well, *row* me ashore, then. Jesus Christ. Yew an' me an' this good doctor are all goin' up to the bridge. An' the rest of yew, yew seen nothin'." The man's Southern dialect was thickening with evey passing second. "Now, git along there."

Out he came, preceded by an Alex resplendent in long white under-wear, looking like one of those awful white ceramic bullfrogs. A gun was wedged under his left ear; his face was superbly expressionless but for a slight flicker of his left eyelid as he passed me by. The sight of that wink, buttressed by the barrel of the derringer, is something I will remember until the end of time.

Harding, Alex, and the captain disappeared up the forward companion-way, out of sight to the right, and again I must depend on someone else's description of what ensued. Lester Harding was wearing a full-length flannel nightshirt, not a terribly convincing garb for a Confederate agent, and it proved more than figuratively to be his downfall. The wind was off-shore, but sufficiently strong to have raised quite a swell; additionally, it had backed somewhat to the west, putting the sea on the *City of Portland*'s port quarter, or in land terms, catching her on her left rear corner. Any vessel in these circumstances will take on a nasty sort of corkscrewing motion that is hard to predict; the ship took a sudden lurch to starboard and Harding tripped on his nightshirt, dropping the captain's gun. In the confusion, Alex tumbled down the companionway and the captain retrieved his gun, getting off a shot at Harding as he scrabbled his way to the promenade deck. I came on the scene a second or two later. Alex was just getting to his feet at the foot of the gunsmoke-filled companionway.

"Musta hit the son-of-a-bitch," remarked a crew member. "That there's blood."

"Aye-uh, Ezra, that be blood, all right. Let's go find that damn' fool Rebel and throw 'im in the drink." There was a general stampede right up to the promenade deck, out into the bitter wind, for which nobody was dressed, least of all Alex. But in the excitement, personal comfort was hardly a consideration.

Wind hummed mournfully in the guy wires supporting the twin funnels. There was a dry hiss of escaping steam from up above. The engine's so-called walking beam stood stationary against the starry sky. "What the hell!" I exclaimed, "Why are we stopped? Has that nut got to the wheel-house and taken command?"

"Dunno where he is," said someone. "Whoa, I think he's up there somewhere."

Two shots snapped in the roaring wind, two tiny flashes pricking the darkness on the hurricane, or uppermost, deck. Cautiously, Alex, two crew members, and I crept up a ladder. Wherever Harding was, he wasn't in the wheelhouse; it looked as if the captain, once again in possession of his gun, had him cornered elsewhere.

As our eyes adjusted to the dark, we could see Harding up an inspection ladder leading to the gallows structure that formed the fulcrum of the walking beam. A torrent of sparks flew from the starboard funnel like stormy orange fireflies. "Shit, the skipper's got 'im treed like an old possum," said Ezra.

A series of shots crackled from atop the walking beam, during which I stumbled and sat down jarringly on the deck. The last couple of shots were echoed by the sound of falling glass from a window in the chart-room just aft of the wheelhouse. As I tried to clear my head and pick myself up, I could hear the captain shouting, "Tell the engine room 'full ahead'. Fast!"

"Aye, Captain, right away."

The night-shirted Harding, doubtless frozen by now to his miserable Confederate marrow, blasted off in the captain's direction again, and then concentrated more on the chart-room, taking advantage of the clear field of fire afforded by the wide side-by-side placement of the funnels.

The next shot went wild and tore off over the dark Atlantic as the walking beam ponderously rose, the unfortunate Harding perched upon it. Back and forth, up and down, Harding clinging to it as if riding an enormous industrial rocking horse.

"Drop the gun and we'll get you down," bellowed the captain, but Harding never heard him. Frozen fingers unable to grip any longer, he slid gradually backwards along the beam and then fell with a thin, high, white scream straight down three decks through the housing for the connecting rod. Before the horrified eyes of the engine room staff, he was crushed to a pulp by the great flailing crank on the paddle-wheel shaft.

Captain Pike, Alex, and the two crewmen raced below. I tried to race too, but somehow could not find my feet and kept fumbling and stumbling. It was both puzzling and maddening and made only a little sense when I gained the promenade deck, heard a voice say, "Good God, man, you've been hit," and collapsed senseless.

CHAPTER FORTY-TWO

I remained comatose as the *City of Portland* knifed and rolled her way through a choppy sea, past the islands of Monhegan, Matinicus, and Vinalhaven, Isle au Haut and Swan's Island, the loom of the lights of Bar Harbour off to port. All this I missed as a smear of pink over the horizon to seaward gradually spread, brightening the sky as the *City of Portland* ploughed through the narrows between the mainland and Campobello Island. Then into Deer Island Passage, a sharp turn to port, and there was Eastport, a dusting of fresh snow gleaming in the strengthening sunlight. As the *City of Portland* swung slowly towards the wharf, the clang of a gong pierced my fuddled senses, heralding the order to "stop engine" to the engineer.

"James, old friend, can you get up?" said a distant voice.

"Eh? Oh, bloody shit, what the hell happened?"

"You don't know?"

"Oh...uh...did someone say I got shot?"

"Someone did. You nearly became Canada's first casualty of the Civil War, at least that I know of. Glad it didn't turn out that way."

"Funny, it didn't hurt. I just felt kind of odd, like when you try to get up after you've been sick."

I closed my eyes and tried to marshal my thoughts. "Why would anyone want to shoot a nice chap like me?" I said plaintively. I must have sounded like a child.

"I think it was a stray bullet. It went straight through your shoulder."

"Well, I'll be God-damned. I remember falling on the deck, but, I, well, isn't that strange. There was no sensation of being shot. I'll be God-damned."

"You already said that, James. I would say rather that you have been blessed. We just tied up at Eastport and we're going ashore here instead of Saint John. I want to get you to a hospital. Then I must see the local U.S. marshal. James, we did it again. We got the fellow. As soon as I get my business done, I'll tell you the whole story. It's another good one."

Assisted by Alex and Captain Pike, I wobbled down the gangplank to a waiting carriage and was born away to the local hospital, so tiny as to look like a private residence. My dressings were changed and it was remarked that I had a "clean" wound and that Alex, even with limited resources, had done a first-class job of patching me up. I was welcome to stay but could leave as soon as I felt strong enough.

Alex came by at lunch-time with a telegram to show me:

WAR DEPARTMENT
SECRETARY'S OFFICE
WASHINGTON, D.C.
NOVEMBER 26 '62
11:32 A.M.

DR. A.M. ROSS/MR. J. RAMSAY
C/O INTERNATIONAL S.S. CO. AGENCY
EASTPORT, ME.

WELL DONE ALL HANDS STOP U.S.S. SKOWHEGAN DISPATCHED
EX PORTLAND WITH DETACHMENT OF MARINES STOP NEW BRUNS-
WICK AUTHORITIES ALERTED END MESSAGE

/S/ STANTON

"Dear God, it never rains but it pours," remarked Alex, sitting down in the armchair by my bed. "I diddle away a year getting very little done, and then all of a sudden we get Mrs. Williams and this Harding character in the space of less than a week. It's as though we shook a tree and Confederate agents came falling down like apples."

"Or rotten fruit. You're too generous, Alex. *You* got this chap. I just got in the way."

"No, my friend, if you hadn't divined that something was wrong, if you hadn't acted, I would be over there on Campobello Island with a gun up my left nostril. God and I became closer than ever last night."

I borrowed Alex's prime compliment. "Splendid chap, isn't He?"

Alex closed his eyes and sighed what I had come to think of as his "James" sigh. "Well, you cannot be hurting too much to be your usual flippant self. Can you listen to my tale courteously and attentively?"

"Shoot. Oh, I didn't mean to say that..."

"Of course. This man Harding set himself up for suspicion almost immediately when he boarded at Portland. I introduced myself and he said,

'I'm glad you are not a Yankee. Too many of them around here'. At the time, he certainly didn't sound like a deep Southerner. Said he was from Delaware and they don't call themselves Yankees there."

"What did he expect in New England, Spaniards or something?"

"Well, I laughed, said something sarcastic about too many French in France. Knowing me to be from Canada, he tried to get me to say there were too many French there too. We've all got to live together, so I didn't take his bait.

"He stepped out to go to the commode and I had a look in his bag, which hadn't even a lock. Talk about fumbling amateurism. I wish you could have been there. Maps, maps, and more maps of the border area, places like Eastport and Calais, which they call 'Callous' here, oh, and I just love the way they say 'aye-uh'."

"Aye-uh."

"There were markings on the maps," continued Alex, "that clearly indicated some sort of military operation, and the U.S. Marshal here, fellow called Matthew French, has them in custody. Mr. Harding was mighty quick in the commode, I can tell you. I thought *I* was quick, but he found me just putting the maps away, out came the gun, and the rest you pretty well know. I think he must have been setting me up.

"This Mr. Harding was quite the chatty gentleman. He said, 'We have had all we could do to keep the Yanks away from our homes, but they will soon know how it feels to have the war carried into their own territory. I tell you - Ah tell yew, rather - yew will hear something exciting.' His Southern speech - he was from Georgia - was twanging away full blast.

"It was just like in that letter to the Confederate Secretary of State. I was told that crews of picked men were already in position in Saint John and St. Andrews-by-the-Sea and that there was a store of supplies on Grand Manan Island. He was also expecting, I regret to say, the assistance of thirty Canadians..."

"Bastards. Probably mercenaries."

"Likely, but that's beside the point. He nattered away freely with me in his captivity, boasting so openly that I was able to give a tremendous amount of information to the authorities..."

"He fell from the walking beam," I interrupted. "Tell me what happened."

Alex blanched. "I hope never again to see anything so appalling. I ran down to the engine room...the engineer had passed out cold at the sudden demise of his, ah, vertical visitor and someone else had stopped the engine, but the smell of blood and excrement told me all I needed to know. The remains actually disintegrated and had to be put ashore in spare mail bags. Much as we loathe what the Confederates stand for, no man ever deserved that."

"Is there any point in carrying on to Saint John now?" I asked.

"Not likely. Without further instructions for the moment, I assume we should return to our post in Montreal."

"*Our* post? Alex, I had better get home while I have any hope of a career. And I don't think I'd be much use to you in my present state. It didn't hurt then, but it surely does now. Ow, ow, ow..."

"We have had different versions of this conversation before. But I have to yield a point now that you have been hurt. You really have done so much, James, perhaps it really is time for me to let you alone so that you can get on with your life. For myself, I feel that I must continue until this dreadful war is over and all the slaves are free. Then there will be the matter of settling them into society generally and that will take, well, likely several generations.

"But you do have your life to live and, God, James, your commitment has made my sacred mission so much easier, helping me to be in two places at once and that sort of thing. In fact," grinned Alex, "some of this has been rather fun, hasn't it?"

"If spending entire months in unremitting terror, being caught helplessly in the eddies of history, and being twice frustrated in love can be called fun, the last seven years have been amusing beyond compare," I said sarcastically. "But, you know, Alex, we did make a formidable team, didn't we?"

"I regret your use of the past tense, but, by Heaven, we did. I wish I could give you a big, brotherly hug without hurting you."

I slept the sleep of the just that night in the hospital, once more at government expense. Likely it was my last chance. Alex, long since thoroughly addicted to action on behalf of the slaves, fretted and fidgeted at the lack of a concrete assignment and was therefore a bit haggard at midmorning the next day as we boarded the westbound *City of Portland* for Portland to entrain for Montreal and then home.

The gunboat *Skowhegan* was berthed at the same wharf, having delivered her marines during the night, and her company manned the rails to cheer us as we boarded our steamer. We tipped our hats as the man-o'-war's colours were dipped in our honour. I still get goosebumps at the memory.

We spent the day collaborating on a detailed report on our operation to President Lincoln; the following morning, we took the train to Montreal and I carried on alone to Belleville, arriving as a snowy grey dawn began to break over the surrounding farmlands. Wrestling with a wagon-load of miscellanea from the train was Station Agent Eccles, doing temporary duty on the night shift.

I thought I should make amends for my cavalier treatment of him just before I had left. "Eccles, how are you? Nice to see you," I said jovially.

"Nice to see you too, Mr. Ramsay. How was poor Gertrude's funeral? What a tragedy. My goodness. And so *complicated*...Washington... Maine...Portland..."

I froze. "How did you know about Washington?"

"Hard not to. We know how to read telegrams. Been all over the God-damn' papers too. The *Intelligencer* had a big story. You and your friend are heroes again, but I don't think you have a job any more. I have a wire from Mr. Collins in the office, says 'e wants to see you first thing you're back." Mr. Collins was the division superintendent in Toronto.

Some homecoming! Oh, well, let us face it, I had created this situation and just had to live with it. Perhaps my notoriety would pave the way to other employment. My injury, although not terribly obvious unless I was moving around, might gain me sympathy. And I was still a lieutenant in the U.S. Army Corps of Engineers. But what was I to do? Railways were my heart's desire and were what I was trained for.

Hollow of eye and painful of shoulder, I took a morning train to Toronto, quite literally with hat in hand, to answer the summons of Mr. Collins. I knocked at his office door. "Enter," said he.

"Good morning, sir," I said, trying not to sound servile or take the initiative with apologies or justifications.

"Sit." This was not starting off well. Mr. Collins, spectacles halfway down his nose, studied a sheaf of engineering drawings. He did not ask me if I wanted to see them. A great Seth Thomas clock ticked the minutes away. I sat until I could stand it no longer.

"Mr. Collins."

"Mister Ramsay." He looked up, removing his spectacles with a gesture. "Your employment with this company was terminated as of yesterday."

It was no surprise, but still the word popped out: "Why?"

"Why? Why? you ask. Must I spell it out for you? I speak of your shabby little subterfuge with your friend Dr. Ross. The two of you took up more space in the *Globe* day before yesterday than the Queen, Oliver Mowat, John A. Macdonald, Georges-Etienne Cartier, and Abe Lincoln com*bined,* Mr. Ramsay, com*bined.* Sister Gertrude, eh? Terminated, Ramsay. Saw to it myself. *Terminated!* What have you to say for yourself?"

"I'll clean out my desk directly I get back to Belleville. I'm sorry..."

"Oh, *sorry,* are we? Sorry doesn't even begin to tell the tale."

Oh, God! A lawsuit for breach of contract!

"I saw to your termination yesterday. Personally. And *now,* Mr. Ramsay, *now...*"

I closed my eyes to prepare for my doom.

"Now I am personally going to see to your reinstatement to employment with the Grand Trunk."

My eyes popped open. "I beg your pardon?"

"Belleville would hang the lot of us if you were let go permanently. I was instructed to fire you, but nobody said I couldn't hire you back. We're really proud of you, James. Stay for a cup of tea, tell me your story, and then take the train home. It might be good if you could get back to work tomorrow. I am sorry that we couldn't pay you for the time off..."

CHAPTER FORTY-THREE

The White House

Washington, D.C.
February 9, 1863

Dear Mr. Ramsay,

I tender you the warmest thanks for your part in the effective
and valuable services recently rendered me. Please accept my
best wishes for your prosperity and happiness and my regrets for
your injury in the line of duty.

A. Lincoln

I treasure this little note from President Lincoln, written in his own hand
on his own time, even with the terrible burden under which he was working. The ink has faded now to a yellowish brown, but it is still perfectly
legible. Another letter I have in my collection is this:

Department of State

Washington, D.C.
June 4, 1863

Dear Mr. Ramsay:
I take this occasion to renew my thanks for your solicitous
attention to the interests of this Government. Your zeal merits
the highest praise.

Yours very respectfully,
William H. Seward

Secretary Seward's letter has been saved more as a curiosity; my solicitous attention was not to the interests of any government but to the freeing
of the slaves. And of course, I had not the same warmth of feeling as I had
towards the President.

Alex received similar letters as of the same dates, as well as mail from
such diverse persons as Senator Sumner, William Lloyd Garrison, John
Greenleaf Whittier (with ten lines of poetry!), William Cullen Bryant, his
hero General Garibaldi, and from France, Victor Hugo, the distinguished
author of *Les Miserables*. Perhaps the letters that meant the most to us,

though, were from Gerrit Smith, now recovered from his nervous and emotional collapse.

I was fully back into the "railroading" business, this time to stay. Alex continued his work in Montreal, now directed more towards informing the Canadian public about progress toward the abolition of slavery, bearing in mind, of course, that the War Between the States was still being fought and would be so for another two grinding, fiery, bloody years. The mind still reels from the tragedy of it.

Alex had a leading role in the formation and daily functionings of the Society for the Abolition of Human Slavery and was principal speaker at a meeting in Montreal in October, 1863. It was not only Alex at his best, but a singularly eloquent summation of our values, attitudes, and perspectives that had evolved toward slavery and toward the black race generally. I sought and received Alex's permission to quote his speech in an appendix at the end of this story, though without his realization of the extent to which his words would be made public.

At last I had a normal, regular life. My associates with the Grand Trunk stopped declaring how remarkable it was that I showed up for work so faithfully. And finally, the fortunes of my chequered love-life were resolved, not while enduring the terrors of the Underground Railroad or in the bedchamber of a Confederate agent, but right over our back fence.

During our long-ago conversation about white-black relations, Father had made reference to our next-door neighbours, the Simpsons. Mrs. Simpson, six years my senior, had been widowed in the fall of 1862 and left with two small daughters to look after. We had been friends for years in that she was rather like a big sister to me. Even with the time I spent next door helping her after Mr. Simpson's death in a mill accident, it never crossed my mind that anything could develop.

She was wonderful company and so easy to talk to that it was not long before rambling confessions about Ruth and Mrs. Williams spilled out. Eva, that is Mrs. Simpson, was very touched by what I called the Book of Ruth. As for the tale of Mrs. Williams, told pretty much as related previously, Eva declared it to be one of the most astonishing stories she had ever heard and listened to it with much gulping and blushing. She forgave me my liaisons, we entered into one of our own, and were married on December 19, 1864. Mother was so happy that I am sure I had a fleeting glimpse of a sixth chin. In one momentous afternoon, I became both a husband and a father and, as the story-books like to say, we have lived happily ever after.

The accursed rebellion of the Slave States finally ended the following March, a half-million lives later, and the battered but proud American nation set about binding her wounds. Had there been no war, slavery might still exist today, and while the loss of life and destruction of property attendant to war are to be lamented, those who grieve for their dead, I hope, can take some comfort in the thought of the millions whose lives will now be bearable.

A matter of weeks after the War Between the States came to its conclusion, I happened to be at Belleville station, exchanging pleasantries with the driver of a westbound freight train, for it was one of those leisure-inducing early days of spring and the urge to work was at its nadir. The date was April 16, 1865.

Eccles, now working the daytime shift, came racing out of the station, waving a telegraph flimsy, looking absolutely stricken. I went cold, thinking perhaps there had been a pile-up down the line or an engine off a bridge.

"Look at this," said Eccles. The telegram had only two words:

LINCOLN SHOT END MESSAGE

"Shot? Why? Was he killed?"

"Dunno," said Eccles. "This is all it said. Thought you'd want to know, bein' you met 'im and all."

"You *did*?" said the freight engine driver in awe.

"Yes...once."

I wandered the station platform in an agony of dread until the afternoon train from Toronto came in with the mail, parcels, and the usual bound bundles of George Brown's excellent *Globe*. I filched a copy right from the baggage car and my worst fears were confirmed. Mr. Lincoln's innocent trip to the theatre the previous night and his death at the hands of the unemployed actor John Wilkes Booth have been too thoroughly documented elsewhere to need any further elaboration by me. But I must report my feelings at that moment: my knees went all weak and palsied, I felt light-headed, and having the Crucifixion come as a surprise could not have been more terrible.

Alex was back in town and I would have to tell him. Telling Eccles I would be back presently, I took the newspaper and set out for Alex's house almost at a run, striding along in the spring sunshine, the birds chirping among the still-naked branches, nature going on her oblivious way as she always does at the best and worst of times.

How I dreaded telling Alex! I knew how he regarded Mr. Lincoln as one akin to Our Lord. I knew also how Good Friday was an annual crisis for Alex, how he would weep as though for a lost friend on that day; what his reaction to this catastrophe might be I could guess only too well.

I let myself in at his front gate. Hester answered the door; I could smell muffins baking. "They'll be ready in ten minutes if you can stay. But, James, ah, shouldn't you be at work? James, is something wrong?"

I passed her the newspaper, anything I might have said choked off.

"Oh, dear God in heaven," murmured Hester. She read a few lines, adding, "Oh, poor Alex. This is going to hurt him as much as anything could in this life."

"I know," I said. "Let us get this over with."

Alex was in a sun-room at the back of the house that served as a laboratory, bustling with his long-neglected collection of bird specimens. It was in chaos and Alex hated chaos. "James, my boy!" he greeted me. "This is an unexpected pleasure indeed! Wait until you see...let me show you...uh, what's wrong? What is it?"

I passed him the paper. He read it in silence. The stove made faint rustling sounds, the branch of a rose bush slapped the window sill in the spring wind. As he read, Alex grew paler and paler, slid to the floor, threw the tool he had been using into a corner, and burst into heart-rending sobs. He dropped his glasses and kicked them aside, for nothing mattered any more.

Hester and I knelt by him, wanting to cry too, for we loved him and pitied his agony, but we had to try to be strong. I rubbed his back as I had Colonel's once when he was feeling poorly.

On recovering himself, Alex made some silly apology about being unmanly. "Alex, this is hardly the time for imperial bravery," I said in reproof. "Our Mr. Lincoln was a saviour of no small proportion. Truth to tell, I wanted to cry too, but I had a chance to ease myself through the worst of the shock on my way here."

During the next few days, Alex, Hester, Mother, Father, Eva, and I stayed together as much as we could, huddled like cattle in a storm, almost a family dealing with a death within. We followed the newspaper accounts of Abraham Lincoln's funeral, of the last sad journey back to his final rest in Illinois, the land of the fabulous four-legged chicken. And not long later were the accounts of the trial, conviction, and hanging of the tragic villain John Wilkes Booth.

I mourned the journey with Mr. Lincoln on the Chicago, Alton, and St. Louis that now would never be, Alex wrote a stirring elegy to the fallen President for the *Intelligencer*. And then life returned to normal and somehow has stayed thus ever since.

This properly finishes the story of our doings on the Underground Railroad and its numerous and unpredictable byways. I have preserved it on paper so that the memory will not fade, even after we, the actors in the drama, are long since gone.

It is 1877 now. I live with my family in Toronto and have risen to the rank of Chief Civil Engineer of the Grand Trunk Railway; I stoutly resist the temptation to say "Enter" whenever anyone knocks at my office door. I have the use of a private coach for inspection tours and other railway business and my one secret indulgence is to murmur, "Mine, all mine", as the track unreels astern under a canopy of engine smoke.

Alex continues to astonish. He too lives in Toronto, with Hester, two little daughters, and their young son Norman Garibaldi Ross. We still see each other with gratifying regularity. With some gentle prodding from our children, our conversation lapses into stories and reminiscences; Alex has committed his to a book already and, truth to tell, I found it rather a disappointment, the facts told totally objectively and far too modestly.

I have done the boasting about Alex that he would never do himself. He has no idea yet of what I have done and will not until my own account is published. And then the public, as it deserves, will have a full and accurate perception of a great Canadian humanitarian, character, and, I daresay, hero.

As well as his memoirs, Alex has no fewer than five other books under his imprint, scholarly studies of birds, trees, and flowers of North America. His writings on the flora and fauna of the Southern states have earned particular praise. Under preparation is a book on fresh-water fish, and since Alex prefers to live as close to his subjects as possible, fish by the tankful glide silently about the Ross household, driving Hester to distraction.

His honours have been numerous and include honorary knighthoods from the kings of Russia, Greece, Italy, and Portugal for both his scientific and humanitarian achievements. I hope that before long, Queen Victoria may similarly honour him so that he may be correctly and appropriately addressed as Sir Alexander Milton Ross.

In the meantime, he continues to be just plain Alex and will have, though unwittingly, the last word. He and Hester were over to dinner earlier in the evening on which I am finishing my story, and he had this to say: "I travelled on one of your fine trains from Montreal last Tuesday. I still deplore the amount of smoke and grime those machines of yours spout all over the place" (even after twenty-two years of close friendship, they were still Mine), "but I am always amazed how quickly they can get you from A to B in such comfort. I came on the overnight express and tried one of your new sleeping cars, and most pleasant it was, too. I admire your policy of having negro sleeping car attendants. Did you have anything to do with that?"

"Not directly. That's a different department."

"Still to be applauded, but for the love of God don't let them stop there. Let us not relegate blacks to servile positions for the rest of human history. They should drive the trains, build the bridges...I'd like to see them all over North America, having the same chance at literacy, at education, at the pursuit of happiness."

"A great many people still have to change their thinking," I said. "There's a young black fellow in the States, a mechanical engineer named Elijah McCoy. They say he is a flat-out genius, but prejudice is as strong as ever. He cannot get any sort of good job in the States and I'd like to see if we couldn't bring him up here. We need good minds and whether they are in a black or white head is immaterial to me and should be to anyone else with a brain."

"People," pronounced Alex, "*will* eventually come to their senses simply because they must as part of a maturing process. That's how one deals with change. But for myself, I'd like it to happen much more quickly than it is, in a great blaze of trumpets..."

"It's going to be one long rehearsal for the trumpets at the rate we are going," I sighed.

"I fear you are right," said Alex. "Remember the time we were at dinner with Gerrit in New Orleans and he made all those dire predictions? They have pretty well come true...it was like having zoo animals let out of their cages, as far as much of white society was concerned. Not everyone is created equal, whether white or black, but what can and should be equal is opportunity. And if there is a God, and of that there can be no doubt, equality of opportunity will happen. It may not be in our lifetime, it may not be in a generation, or perhaps even a century. But it will happen as surely as the sun rises tomorrow. And then our trumpets will be ready for their concert, their angelic concert."

END OF TRACK

TEXT OF AN ADDRESS BY ALEXANDER MILTON ROSS
TO THE SOCIETY FOR THE ABOLITION OF HUMAN SLAVERY -
Montreal, October, 1863

Ladies and gentlemen: My views upon the subject of slavery are by many considered ultra; but I have been eye-witness to the cruelty, injustice, and barbarity of that vile and atrocious institution, and know whereof I speak. In October, 1859, while on a visit to Richmond, Virginia, I was forcibly reminded of the truth of the saying 'The wicked fleeth where no man pursueth'. We found the population of that city in a condition of great excitement, a feeling of dread and insecurity which extended to every part of the state.

You will naturally ask the cause of this excitement, this feeling of insecurity and dread. The people of Virginia were at that time living under the protection of a government intensely pro-slavery; they were in the enjoyment of all their State rights. The cause of this unease in the minds of slave-holders was caused by the sudden darting of a ray of light from Harpers Ferry - a ray of light that penetrated the pending gloom over the darkened minds of four *million* enslaved human beings.

John Brown had stricken a blow on the confines of slavery, the echoes of which resounded on every plantation, and entered the humble cabin of the poor slave as well as the mansion of the haughty and proud slave-owner, and roused the long-deferred hope in the bosom of millions of poor, down-trodden, and long-suffering slaves that the hour of their deliverance from a cruel tyranny was at hand. And prayers ascended from a thousand rude cabins to the Almighty Father for freedom, justice, and liberty. Is it a matter of surprise that a feeling of dread was felt in the mansion of the proud and haughty master, when a million earnest prayers were going up to the throne of God Himself?

It is not unusual to hear the tales of cruelty and oppression towards this unfortunate people spoken of as fiction; and that interesting work of Mrs. Stowe [Alex was referring to *Uncle Tom's Cabin*] has been declared by slave-holders and their Northern sympathizers as entirely imaginary and unworthy of belief.

Ladies and gentleman, I have read that and other kindred works on slavery. Let me assure you that I have witnessed scenes of cruelty and barbarity towards the inoffensive people of the Slave States *far exceeding* anything described in these books.

Slavery is demoralizing in its tendencies to the white as well as the black, to the master as well as the slave. Where it exists, it brutalizes and renders the white domineering, brutal, and despotic. The black race is kept in a condition of the grossest ignorance and the circulation of knowledge is guarded with a jealous eye, with a view to prevent the slave from gaining information. The discussion of subjects to reach the darkened but alert mind of the coloured people is sternly prohibited.

For fifty years past, the Government of the United States has been under the control of Southern men and they have persistently endeavoured to extend their domineering tyranny over the entire North; and until within the past twenty-five years, there were few prominent men in the North with sufficient moral courage to face the proud and overbearing dictation of the slave lords in the Senate and Congress. The venerable John Quincy Adams and that noble veteran and apostle of freedom, the late Joshua Giddings, took a firm and decided stand twenty-five years ago for freedom, and bravely asserted that all men, black or white, had the 'inalienable right to life, liberty, and the pursuit of happiness'.

And for so many years, these two noble men withstood a united Senate and House of Congress, and the cowardly and assassinlike threats and abuse of Southern slave-drivers. The lamp lighted by Garrison, Adams, and Giddings, however, continued to burn with increasing brilliance year after year, and in many of the free states, societies were formed to promote the abolition of slavery by the dissemination of information throughout the north, describing the actual condition of the down-trodden slaves and to awaken an interest in their behalf.

The leaders of this movement had to withstand the most vindictive persecution at the hands of Southern men and their Northern sympathizers. Prominent on the roll of men who have rendered their names immortal in the advocacy of the rights of Man may be mentioned the names, not only of Adams and Giddings, but William Lloyd Garrison, Wendell Phillips, Horace Greeley, Charles Sumner, and our particular and special friend, Gerrit Smith. And many other noble men *and* women have likewise laboured with great zeal and sacrifice to bring about the abolition of human slavery in the United States.

The slave-holders used every influence in their power to prevent discussions upon the subject of slavery, and when they failed to meet the arguments of anti-slavery men, they responded with acts of cowardly brutality to stifle discussion with the bowie-knife, the pistol, and the bludgeon.

The late Mr. Giddings, when a member of Congress and addressing the House upon the rights of Man, was threatened with instant death if he uttered another word on the subject. But the brave old statesman knew the cowardly character of slaveholders and continued his address in defiance of this dastardly menace. And more recently, Senator Sumner, a personal acquaintance of ours, was attacked while seated at his desk in the Senate chamber and nearly assassinated by a Southern member of Congress, while another Southerner stood over the proposed victim with a cocked pistol to prevent the bystanders from rendering aid while his Southern *confrére*, with murderous intent, brutally assaulted an unarmed man. This outrage upon Mr. Sumner was committed because his arguments proving the 'Barbarism of Slavery' were unanswerable.

In this manner, the South has endeavoured to control the nation and perpetuate the blighting curse of slavery. And when the slave-holders found they could no longer browbeat and force the liberty-loving people of the

North into acquiescence with their barbarous designs, they rebelled and are now endeavouring to establish a government with slavery for its chief corner-stone.

An eminent English statesman has asserted that the North is fighting for empire and the South for independence. This is a fallacy; the great struggle now being waged in the United States, is a continuance of the contest between freedom and slavery that began thirty-five years ago in Congress. And, thank God, the indications are that slavery will go down beneath the blows of the free men of the North.

It is the custom in both this country and in Britain to find fault with the President of the United States because he has not done more towards liberating the slaves and especially because he failed to declare the freedom of every slave in the Union when the Emancipation Proclamation was issued. I believe Mr. Lincoln has done all he could do constitutionally towards Emancipation and has kept pace with the public opinion of the country. He may appear slow and over-cautious at times, but he has done what he has after grave deliberation and much thought and anxiety.

In issuing his Emancipation proclamation, he acted in his capacity as Commander-in-Chief of the United States Army; he had no power to interfere with the local institutions of a state like Kentucky, not in actual rebellion.

I find from public documents that over one million slaves have been liberated in the last two years alone, and the good work goes bravely on. President Lincoln, in my estimation, merits the approbation and prayers of every Christian for his efforts to crush slavery; and that God will help and sustain them should be the earnest prayer of every true lover of freedom.

Soon all will be free and more may come to our country. Some of us know black people, some do not. They are different in many ways, let us not be naïve, and history has made them more so. But let us prepare the way for any that come to Canada that they may live among us as Canadians, free and equal. It will not be easy. It will require patience and understanding without patronization and condescension. But we will do it - and why? Because we must. It is our destiny.

BIBLIOGRAPHY

In the writing of a historical novel, a great deal of homework is essential before the actual writing begins. And then there is the seemingly endless stream of incoming information once the process is under way. In the preparation of *Hunter of Dreams,* I consulted the following volumes, good books all, and am mentioning them here as they make fascinating reading for anyone interested in abolition and the Civil War era. As well, they are due the respect for the tremendous help they have been.

Beattie, Jessie L. *Black Moses: The Real Uncle Tom*
Toronto, Ryerson Press, 1957
Blockson, Charles L. *The Underground Railroad*
New York, Prentice-Hall, 1987
Breyfogle, William. *Make Free: The Story of the Underground Railroad* New York, J.B. Lippincott Co., 1958
Catton, Bruce. *The Coming Fury* Garden City, N.Y., Doubleday and Co., 1961
Coffin, Levi. *Reminiscences* New York, Arno Press, 1968
Currie, A.W. *The Grand Trunk Railway of Canada*
Toronto, University of Toronto Press, 1971
Drew, Benjamin. *Narratives of Fugitive Slaves in Canada*
Cleveland, John P. Jewitt, 1856
(facsimile edition by Coles Books, 1972)
Everitt, Susanne. *The Slaves* New York, G.P. Putnam's Sons, 1978
Frederickson, George M. *The Arrogance of Race*
Middletown, Conn., Wesleyan University Press
Haynes, Robert V. (ed.) *Blacks in White America Before 1865 - Issues and Interpretations* New York, David McKay Co., 1972
Jones, Robert H. *Disrupted Decades: The Civil War and Reconstruction Years* New York, Charles Scribner's Sons, 1973
Mellon, James (ed.) *Bullwhip Days: The Slaves Remember*
New York, Weidenfeld and Nicholson, 1988
McKitrick, Eric L. (ed.) *Slavery Defended: The Views of the Old South* Englewood Cliffs, N.J., Prentice-Hall, 1965
Mika, Nick and Helma. *Railways of Canada*
Toronto, McGraw-Hill Ryerson, 1972
Modelski, Andrew M. *Railroad Maps of America - The First Hundred Years* New York, Bonanza Books, 1987
Morgan, Henry James (ed.) *The Canadian Men and Women of the Time: A Handbook of Canadian Biography*
Toronto, William Briggs, 1898
Nevins, Allan. *The Emergence of Lincoln: Prologue to Civil War*
New York, Charles Scribner's Sons, 1950

BIBLIOGRAPHY Continued...

Owens, Leslie Howard. *This Species of Property: Slave Life and Culture in the Old South* New York, Oxford University Press, 1976

Ross, Alexander Milton. *Memoirs of a Reformer* Toronto, Hunter and Ross Co., 1875

Ross, Alexander Milton. *Recollections and Experiences of an Abolitionist* Toronto, Rowsell and Hutchison, 1875

Siebert, William H. *Underground Railroad, from Slavery to Freedom* London, MacMillan, 1898

Smedley, R.C. *History of the Underground Railroad* New York, Arno Press, 1969

Still, William. *The Underground Railroad* Philadelphia, Porter and Coates, 1872

Stowe, Harriet Beecher. *Uncle Tom's Cabin: A Tale of Life Among the Lowly* New York, Grosset and Dunlap

Thomas, John L. (ed.) *Slavery Attacked: The Abolitionist Crusade* Englewood Cliffs, N.J., Prentice-Hall, 1965

Vidal, Gore. *Lincoln* New York, Ballantine Books, 1988

ISBN 155369311-6

9 781553 693116